TOM CONNOLLY

THE
SPIDER
TRUCES

Myriad Editions

First published in 2010 by
Myriad Editions
59 Lansdowne Place
Brighton BN3 1FL

www.MyriadEditions.com

1 3 5 7 9 10 8 6 4 2

A CIP catalogue record for this book is available from the
British Library.

ISBN: 978-0-9562515-2-7

Printed on FSC-accredited paper by
Antony Rowe Limited, Chippenham, UK

In memory of Mark Bullock,
who would have been a great writer.

1

It was Great-aunt Mafi who told him that spider blood is blue. When that revelation made him feel queasy, she said that spider blood is blue the way the sea is blue when the sun shines. He liked that.

"That's nice," Ellis said. "That doesn't give me the willies."

And Mafi told him that when a spider dies its blood flows out of its body into the seas and rivers and lakes and that's how the earth gets its water, but this only happens if a spider is allowed to die naturally, of old age.

Ellis's dad told him he was more likely to be killed by a champagne cork than by a poisonous spider, but this didn't have the desired effect.

"That's no good! That's just another thing for me to worry about! Champagne corks as well as spiders! You have to tell me something nicer, not something badder!"

His sister helped out too, reading from the encyclopaedia that spiders don't get caught in their own webs because they have oil on their legs, so Ellis took to rubbing oil over his body in secret, every morning. At primary school he was known as Mr Sheen, due to the shiny appearance of his arms and face, and at home the diminishing stocks of cooking oil in the larder baffled Ellis's dad as much as the discovery that soap could no longer form a lather on Ellis's skin.

But of all the many discoveries Ellis O'Rourke made during the truces, his favourite was the first, that spiders give us the seas and rivers and lakes as their dying gift. He still thinks of the sea that way.

And it was Great-aunt Mafi who said to him, "Any day you see the sea is a good day." This she said on the day she told

1

him how his mum had died.

He sees the sea every day now. And he waits with a patience a young man should not yet possess.

Even here where it can be so bleak, the sea is often blood-blue, the sort of blue Ellis can fall into. From his rented house, he looks at the water. He loses focus and the water floods in; the image of blue fills his head and for a time that could be moments or hours he is nowhere. Free of thought. He barely exists. It is bliss. Like the mid-air moment of diving in.

The beach is a shingle peninsula. It heads to a point on the south-east corner. Ellis's house faces due south across the Channel. It is the last building before the lighthouse and after that there's the Point. Three hundred yards out to sea, on a sandbank, is the wreck of the *Bessie Swan*, a trawler that ran aground in June 1940, returning from Dunkirk with fifty men who waded to shore through waist-high water. You can't wade out to the *Bessie Swan* nowadays. The Channel currents have gouged out ravines in the silt that are deep and treacherous.

On his first night on the beach, in the pub close by the lifeboat station, the old men had looked on without mercy as the young seasonal fishermen challenged Ellis to swim to the *Bessie Swan* and back. They marched him across the shingle, led by a callous and bloated-looking man in a black woolly hat, called Towzer Temple.

"You swim towards the steeple on the Marsh. The currents take you to the *Bessie Swan*."

"If you swim straight for her, you'll be in France tomorrow."

"In a body bag ..."

"Do it now and by closing time you'll be back in the pub, a legend."

"We've all done it," said Towzer.

"It's tradition."

At the water's edge, Ellis stared into the blackness and somewhere amongst the fishermen's drunken voices, in which there was humour that Ellis was deaf to, he heard himself say, "But I'm only renting here ..."

These limp words returned the men indoors, where the evening seemed impoverished and Ellis felt out of place. He began to wonder if they had been telling the truth, that they had all swum the ravines at one time or another, and they really did know best when they said he would be the greater for doing it.

The unfamiliar ceiling above his unfamiliar bed spun a little that first night and every single sound on the beach was new. As he waited patiently for sleep, Ellis noticed the glow of a cigarette at the open window and behind it the face of Towzer Temple, reddened by a map of fissured blood vessels. The fisherman leant easily against the sill, his elbows annexing a portion of the cabin-like bedroom, and as a wide grin disfigured his looks still further, he said, "It'll bug you. You didn't do it because you're scared. And it's going to bug you and bug you. Goodnight, Mr Only Renting. Sweet dreams."

Money spiders populate the shingle and leave their egg sacs on the shore. Fishing boats line the beach and there's a lifeboat station beyond them. Ellis likes to go shrimping north of the lifeboat, in shallow tides which scuttle in and out across the wide mud flats of the bay. He made a frame up last year, four foot by two. He wades out against the incoming tide, sweeping his net, and the frame makes a noise like distant music on a small box radio as it cuts through the water. He catches plenty, but could probably catch more if he knew more about it and didn't get distracted by the far-away music.

Near the lifeboat station, the strip lights of the workers' café pulse cold blue through the windows. Ellis usually goes there three or four times a week. People greet him but still don't know his name.

At dusk, when the sky is angry, he heads out along the beach to the army ranges, then inland across the Backs where the shingle is carpeted with moss, and gorse surrounds the scattered lakes. A line of wooden posts betrays the route of a disused railway and beneath his feet he hears the thud of a sleeper encrusted in the ground like a dead bird. He imagines that he's in Montana or the Australian outback or some other place he's never been. He walks until his leg muscles burn. When darkness comes, a line of silver remains on the horizon and silhouettes the container ships, which turn to black. The winds rise up off the waves and tear across the peninsula and Ellis digs his feet into the shingle and allows the furious, thrilling gusts to pound against him like the souls of every man lost at sea. Furious souls or ecstatic souls, he is not sure which. Sometimes, he waits for hours. Patient. Devoted.

There is a line from a song his father once whispered to him and it plays in Ellis's head as he returns across the flatlands to his unlit home. *We must not go astray in this loneliness.*

He moved here on Good Friday, 1989. A mist settled over the Point for a fortnight and the fog signal on the lighthouse boomed across the bay. He opened every door and window in the house and gave the spiders a few hours to move on without being harmed. The rooms gave up their mustiness to the salt air and Ellis felt the same excitement he had felt when he was a child.

So this is where that feeling has been hiding, he thought to himself.

At first he kept up his job, assisting a photographer called Milek, driving two hours to London. Then he worked a little less. Then he asked for a couple of months off.

"To clear my head, Milek."

And that was a nearly a year ago.

This is another of those slow-motion mornings, Ellis tells himself. He wonders what time it is. He doesn't wear a watch. Any that have been given to him over the years are gathering dust and he couldn't tell you where. He thinks it through. He went out shrimping first thing and then he came back and the metal box was here on the dining table and then he's been daydreaming. So it is probably late morning. He's not idle and he's not simple. It's just a blissfully slow start to the day and he doesn't use a watch. But, yes, he was shrimping first thing, he remembers clearly.

He can always tell if his sister has visited, and even though they are no longer good friends he likes the sensation of knowing she has been in. It means that Chrissie either saw her brother out on the flats and decided to leave him be or forgot to look for his silhouette in the silver bay. Either way, he likes the thought of her leaving him be or forgetting to look.

It is Chrissie who has left the metal box on the dining table. The box was once black but the paintwork is faded now and speckled by a slow rust. Ellis leans closer and looks down on the rust until it looks to him like a landscape photographed from a plane.

He's in no hurry to open the box. He knows the contents exactly – he watched it being filled – and there's nothing there of great significance. But for Ellis, having the box is almost like having his father back in the room and to feel his father nearby is the reason he moved here. Chrissie's world doesn't work that way. Dead means dead, and the inconsequential objects inside the metal box are the sorts of things that cannot combine to mean much to her. She wishes they could and that's why it's taken her a year to give Ellis the box. That's why she has occasionally intimated that she might have lost it, an idea that gives Ellis butterflies because, although there is nothing particular in the box, all the pieces of nothing in particular belonged to Denny O'Rourke, and Denny

O'Rourke was his dad.

If you rest your head against the metal box as if it is a pillow, and you close your eyes, and if your name is Ellis O'Rourke, then the crunching of shingle underfoot on the beach outside could be the sound of a spider perched on your shoulder eating a packet of crisps.

He opens his eyes and sees a woman walking. She puts down her bag, unfolds a stool and begins to sketch. A sparrowhawk hovers above the bushes where starlings and rabbits hide. Ellis listens to the wind piping around the lighthouse and watches as the woman with the sketch pad takes off her jacket. She is older than Ellis. Maybe twenty years older. He wants her to get into conversation with him, accept a cup of tea and sleep with him. He wants her to leave later that afternoon and there to be no talking. Only mute understanding. He would never tell anyone about her and would be able to get on with his life without the need for intimacy cropping up again for some weeks. He knows this is all wrong, but such thoughts are risk-free and a habit he's fallen into.

The phone rings, startling Ellis. It's Jed, his best friend.

"I have to tell you what I dreamt last night," Ellis says immediately.

"I'm fine, thanks for asking," Jed replies.

"Bear in mind," Ellis says, "that I was two years old when man landed on the moon."

"What?"

"And that I am not a particularly complicated person."

"You are joking."

"So how is it that last night I dreamt I was in the living room of the house in Orpington where I was born and my dad is there and my mum, but I can't see her face, and we're all gathered round the TV even though I'm pretty sure they didn't have one, and my sister is just a pair of legs standing on the window sill holding the aerial up into the sky—"

"Wait! You're getting detailed and weird. Let me get comfortable."

Ellis waits as Jed lights a cigarette.

"I recognise some of the people in the room. There's a few of the guys you and me knew on the building sites, and my Great-aunt Mafi is there pouring gin for everyone. Neat gin. The only historical inaccuracy is that it's not Buzz Aldrin on the lunar surface with Neil Armstrong but Simon Le Bon. And the whole dream is in black and white, not just the TV screen. I look and see that to the left of me on the sofa is a young, unshaven, dark-haired man sitting with his girlfriend. And I realise as I look at this bloke that it's that actor guy from *Man About the House* and *Robin's Nest*—"

"Richard O'Sullivan."

"Thank you. And I watch him in his studenty donkey jacket, smoking his cigarette and turning excitedly to his girlfriend, and I realise, My God! He doesn't know he's about to become the star of *Man About the House* and to be associated for ever with the greatest thing that ever ever happened on telly when we were kids, namely *George and Mildred*. He will be a part of that, and I know it and he doesn't. Look at him! He's just an aspiring actor watching the 1969 moon landing with his girlfriend and I know what's going to happen to him in life and he doesn't! I know he'll never do Shakespeare or really crack that big screen role and that he will in fact be a sort of good-looking, understated Sid James. And do you know what it made me think?"

"I pride myself on not knowing what or how you think."

"What else is there to dream? Being with my mum until I was four years old? How my dad was when she had gone? All the things that are somewhere in my head because I was actually there even though I was far too young to know it? It could crucify you! All this stuff locked away inside your head ready to appear in your sleep, it could bring your life to a standstill."

There's a long silence until Jed drags on his cigarette and says, "Your life is at a standstill."

They go quiet. Jed is the one person who isn't freaked out by Ellis going silent on the phone for minutes at a time. In fact, he considers such pauses a respite. Ellis lies back on the floor and wedges the telephone against his ear.

"You know why it's at a standstill?"

"I've one or two ideas. What's your version?"

"When I'm alone I dream of being with someone and when I'm with someone I wish I was anywhere else."

"Ah, well, I'm glad you've brought that up because I have some answers for you," Jed says kindly. "It's because you are what we, in the outside world, technically term 'an arsehole'. Private. Evasive. You're a daydreamer and you keep all your best thoughts to yourself. People like me and the women you occasionally sleep with get the fag ends of your thoughts. If you didn't make me feel so good about myself just by being you, there'd be nothing in this friendship for me. I am also willing to bet good money that when you are busy fucking the wrong people and wishing you were somewhere else, that somewhere else is wherever Tammy might be these days."

"Out of bounds."

"Why? What do you care if we talk about her?"

"I just don't want to ... except to say I was more committed to her than she was to me, before you slag me off."

"Oh yeah, that's right. I remember the evening you went away to America without telling her you were going. I remember that night thinking how 'committed' to her you were. Yeah, I reckon your decision not to even call her and say goodbye before fucking off to Iowa could easily have been misinterpreted as a proposal of marriage."

This is why Jed is Ellis's best friend.

"Fuck off."

"Up yours."

They each place the receiver down, gently.

Jed is right. When Ellis lies awake at night – in bed, or on the grass, or on the beach – he imagines that Tammy is lying beside him. He whispers sounds to her which are not quite words but are perfect for an imaginary love affair. He didn't call her before he went away because it might have mattered to her that he was going but it might not and he didn't want to risk finding out. And now two years have passed and he has left it too long.

He can't understand why he feels so lost today. Or why he feels as if time is short when he has the whole of his adult life before him. He opens the metal box and it releases the smell of cherrywood fires in the cottage he grew up in. He sifts through a pile of photographs taken in the fifties and sixties of elderly relations he never knew, moves to one side a prayer card from his mum's funeral in 1971, and picks up a passport-sized document which he remembers his dad showing him years ago. Denny's name is written in ink on the faded cover and beneath it are the words: *Continuous Certificate of Discharge Ministry of War Transport /Merchant Navy.* Inside are five entries which map Denny O'Rourke's career in the merchant navy, beginning in 1943, age sixteen, aboard the SS *Papanui* and ending in 1946 when his eyesight fell below acceptable standards for service. There's a loose page inside, a temporary shore pass for Colombo Port, dated 15 November 1946.

My dad was twenty then, Ellis thinks. Two years younger than me.

He half closes his eyes and imagines being propelled across the sea, hugging the curvature of the earth, and arriving at Colombo Port. He sits there a while, in the heat, his image of the place indistinct and blinded by the sun. A wave breaks and he finds himself back home, listening to the shingle being dragged by its fingertips into the sea. It is a sound softened by its journey across the beach to Ellis's house and it reminds him of the breeze that swept through the walnut trees on the morning his dad died. Joseph Reardon the farmer, who had been praying for Denny O'Rourke, told Ellis that the back door of the church flew open and a wind swept in at the exact time of Denny's passing. Ellis doesn't know what he thinks about that sort of thing but he does know that in the days and weeks that followed he and Chrissie received many letters and they sat shoulder to shoulder, knee to knee, silently passing them back and forth until their bodies came to rest against each other and he felt a surge of love for his sister which found no expression and would inevitably dissolve as the day wore on. Jed, whom Ellis had never seen hold a pen, wrote a letter; *Ellis, your dad was one of life's good blokes. Not all of us can say that. Be happy. Jed*. Ellis showed Jed's letter to Chrissie and she handed an envelope to him in return.

"Make sense of this," she said. "Got it yesterday."

It was a card from Dino, a Maltese guy Chrissie slept with on and off for six months when she was doing a journalism course in London. Dino had written: *Dearest Spaghetti and Ellis, my condolences at your sad loss. Love Dino*. And try as they might, Ellis and Chrissie could not begin to recall what cryptic, spaghetti-related episode or in-joke had occurred between them back then that Dino had clearly never forgotten.

"Did you ever tell him about the pasta spider webs?" Ellis asked.

"No. We just fucked."

"You must have done. There's no other possible explanation."

"I didn't. I tend not to chat about you and your weirdness when I'm having sex. Maybe he was just writing a shopping list at the same time as the card and got confused."

"Write back to him," Ellis said, "and tell him we were touched by his writing to us after dad had pasta-way."

They laughed until their stomachs hurt. Then they sat awhile in silence and thought their own thoughts and felt the taste of grief on their tongues and discovered that in the space of only a few days the taste had grown familiar and now it felt second-hand. Ellis shut his eyes and watched his father emerge from the bike shed at the cottage, carrying a bucket full of water. Denny swung the bucket round in wide circles above his head but none of the water fell out.

"I thought he was a magician when he did that," Ellis said. "Did you know how he did it or did you think he was a magician too?"

"You're doing that thing again," Chrissie said.

"What thing?"

"That thing of having a conversation in your head and then bringing me in on it late. You've always done it. You're so useless, Ellis. If you were the last man left on earth, you wouldn't notice it for weeks."

She kissed him and left him to the freefall of random memories in his head.

Another wave breaks. Ellis drops the Colombo Port shore pass back into the box and notices the dark scratched wood of a once familiar picture frame, in which is held a photograph of a lighthouse and a fishing boat run aground. He carries it outside and looks across the water to that same lighthouse and wreck. He watches the fishermen arrive at the huts in their battered trucks. Towzer Temple leans heavily against his boat and coughs himself awake. He takes a banana from his coat pocket and eats it. He delves into the same pocket and pulls out an old crisp packet, which he seems surprised to have found. He makes a chute out of the packet and pours the crisps into his mouth, pulling a sour face as he tastes them. Lazily, he kicks the side of his boat, betraying their stale marriage, and pulls a bottle from the other coat pocket, and starts to drink.

A few hundred yards away, the tide snakes around the wreck of the *Bessie Swan*. Ellis watches it curiously, as if he's arranged to meet someone there but can't remember who.

Perhaps, he tells himself, if I swam out there ...

But he knows he will not do it.

If I walked out of the house and across the beach without stopping and dived in and swam there and back and ran straight home and dried myself in front of the fire, I'd have done something extraordinary. I'd have pushed myself. Kick-started my system. If I did it once, I could do it again the next day, and again, and I'd do it every day, it would become second nature and I'd be a different person, the sort of person who did that every day. My life would have changed.

But he's not able to change it. He's too busy. Too busy playing tunes on his shrimping net, watching his neighbour's washing loop the loop in the wind, seeking out pebbles with perfect holes, lying beneath the lighthouse and watching it sway. Too busy photographing clouds when the colour of crimson bleeds into them at dusk. Too busy waiting. Too busy keeping watch.

He takes from the metal box something unfamiliar. It looks like a blue plastic cigarette, and when he picks it up the plastic unravels and Ellis sees that it is the long, thin wrapper of a packet of dried spaghetti, the sort Denny used to buy when Ellis was a child and pasta was as long as your arm. As long as your dad's arm.

2

They made spider webs out of pasta in the drought of 1976, a calm time, before the need for boundaries or truces. Denny O'Rourke would lay a single piece of cooked spaghetti in a circle on an empty dinner plate. On a good day, Ellis manoeuvred it into the hexagonal shapes of the *Uloborus* as his dad's deep, treacly voice encouraged him.

"There's no building ever built as intricate and brilliant as a spider's web ..."

That dry summer, Great-aunt Mafi came with them on holiday. On a village green in Dorset they ate ice cream in the shade of a tree. The grass was brown and there were cracks in the earth the size of snakes. They stayed on the water's edge on the estuary at Exmouth, in a bungalow made from two railway carriages. Three wooden steps led to a sandy beach with a palm tree. Ellis has a photograph of Mafi and Chrissie posing under the palm tree, holding fruit in their hair and laughing.

Denny drove them to Budleigh Salterton to see *Jaws*. He had taken them to see it earlier that summer but the queues were too long and they watched *Earthquake* on the second screen instead. The poster for *Earthquake* promised Rumble-O-Rama special effects that would make their seats shake, but the rumble never materialised.

"If I live to be a hundred and fifty years old, I'll never see a worse actor than Charlton Heston," Denny O'Rourke said on the way home. Then he laughed to himself, wound the window down and lit a cigarette.

"Could you?" Ellis asked, more than an hour later, when his dad kissed him goodnight.

"Could I what?"

"Live to be a hundred and fifty years old."

"I'll give it my best shot."

There were no problems with spiders in Exmouth. Ellis didn't think about them. He was too concerned about the sharks. On the last evening of the holiday, when Ellis finished saying his goodbyes to the sailboats on the beach and the lights of the Penzance train across the bay, he found Chrissie,

Mafi and his dad waiting for him inside. He shook with fear, because they wore the same expectant faces they had worn five years earlier, moments before they told him he would never see his mother again.

"What's happening?" he asked.

"Sit down," his dad said.

Denny made a joke of squashing his children as he sat on the sofa between them.

"Take a look at this," he said.

He showed them a colour photograph of an old tile-hung cottage with a large cherry tree and a weeping willow in the front garden.

"Who lives here?" Chrissie asked.

"An old man and his wife," said her dad.

"It's pretty," Ellis said.

"Yes," Denny said, "it's very pretty but it's pretty worn out too. It needs a lot of time spent on it to make it good again. But it's quite big and there's a lovely garden and an orchard and lots of space." Then Denny added softly, "Space to play in."

Chrissie flung her arms round her father and they tumbled back on the sofa.

"What?" Ellis asked. "What's going on?"

Denny pulled his son to him and whispered in his ear.

"Would you like to move out of Orpington and live in a beautiful village surrounded by farmland, in this house?"

Ellis whispered back, "Yes. Please." And in an act that left his father speechless, Ellis crossed the room and hid behind his Great-aunt Mafi, burying his head against her back, because his happiness was more than he could bear.

Denny O'Rourke parked his Rover 110 at the top of Hubbards Hill and took photographs. His daughter and son stood beside him, taking in the view. The Kentish Weald opened out in front of them, wide and majestic, a ruffled quilt of fields watched over by majestic oak and trustworthy beech, their trunks dark in the low autumn sun.

The lane in front of him descended into the Weald, crossing a new main road built into the seam of the valley. By the bridge, a toll cottage with two chimneys watched begrudgingly over the fast new traffic beneath it. Beyond a church tower, amongst woodland and half hidden by the undulant fields, were the village rooftops. The village was surrounded on all sides by fields and farm buildings. Two giant silos rose side by side above the tree line. Beyond them, ripples of countryside overlapped in shades of green and brown and yellow towards the Crowborough Beacon and beyond that was the faint outline of the South Downs on the horizon.

Ellis looked into the expanse and pictured Great-aunt Mafi threading her way along an invisible network of lanes from the coast.

"She's out there, somewhere," he said. "I am looking at where she is but I can't see her."

Denny smiled. "Ready?" he asked, ushering Chrissie and Ellis back to the car.

"Yes!" said Chrissie. "Very, very ready!"

"Ready for what?" Ellis asked.

His dad shrugged and smiled happily. "Everything," he said, "everything."

When the car drew to a halt again, they were in a narrow lane. To the left of them was a short row of council houses in the shade of a beech tree. Denny leant forward in his seat and sunlight flooded into the back of the car. Ellis put his hand up to shade his eyes and saw, to his right, emerging from the glare, a garden with a weeping willow, a tall cherry tree, and beyond them the cottage in the photograph. Their new home. A home without the ghost.

The cottage had welcoming eyes and a low fringe of Kent

peg tiles. The leaves that had settled around the walls were oak and cherry and cobnut. At the bottom of the garden they were willow and Ellis threw a pile of them above his head into a small, short-lived cloud. If laughter had a colour in October 1976, it was pale yellow, the colour of weeping willow leaves in mid-air.

"Look, Mafi!" Ellis said, pointing up into the willow tree. "Look at those two big branches. They look like Felix the Cat running fast!"

Mafi looked up.

"See it?" he urged her.

"Yes, I think so."

Ellis stared happily at his discovery and Mafi looked happily at him.

"We never ever get to see a tree from the top down, do we?" Ellis said.

"We don't. You're right."

"What I would have for my ninth birthday if I could is to be able to fly."

"Me too, for my seventy-ninth!"

"Why can't we fly?"

"It's technical, I think. No wings and all that."

"There must be a good, you know, there must be a ... why we can't, a ..."

Ellis looked skywards and scrunched up his face, the way he did when he couldn't think of a word.

"A reason why?"

"Yes! There must be a reason why we're not allowed to fly. Something we're not supposed to see."

She held her hand out to him.

"Let's go for a walk and get our bearings," she said.

From the high point of the village green they watched people come and go. Ellis introduced himself to the rolling hills distributed equally to the north, south, east and west of the village.

16

"Is this our bearings?" he asked his great-aunt.

Mafi kissed Ellis on the head. He had no idea why.

At the lower end of the village, the old forge was a petrol station that had room for one car at a time. Opposite it, by the bus stop, was Ivan's greengrocers with tiered counter displays covered in rolls of plastic grass. Whilst Mafi set up her account, Ellis ran his fingers through the grass and wondered how plastic was grown. He would feel that grass beneath his hand hundreds of times in the next decade. He would wave to William Rutton the butcher just as many times and Carrie Combe would wink at him from her window in the middle of the village as many times again. Carrie had a hairdressers in her front room. There was space for two blow-dryers, and every other Thursday morning Mafi occupied one of them immediately after collecting her pension. Carrie was round and busty and pretty and was the first person in the village to have an Afro. She had a beauty spot above her lip and it was this that Ellis would stare at when she cut his hair. Sometimes, after a haircut, he would go to the bench on the village green and wonder why Carrie Combe's beauty spot was called that of all things. Often, when he didn't notice it growing dark, traces of crimson would paint themselves into the evening sky, and by the time he got home the sky above Ide Hill would be emblazoned with blood-coloured clouds. He pictured himself searching for a seam in the crimson sunset and when he found it he unpicked the stitches and peered through to the other side, and his mum was waiting for him there.

It was before they moved to the village, during the strange times in Orpington when Ellis was four years old, that Mafi began to visit frequently, to babysit the children and wake Ellis each morning with the words, "Let me see those beautiful big blue eyes."

The first time she visited, she sat on the edge of Ellis's bed reading *The Water Babies*. Over her shoulder, in the corridor beyond the bedroom door, a policewoman and a man in a suit walked past. The man in the suit supported Denny O'Rourke by the arm and the policewoman held Denny's hand. When Ellis saw that his dad was crying he looked away to a green-ink illustration of a water-baby kissing the hand of Mrs Bedonebyasyoudid. He never wanted to see his dad cry again, and nor would he have to, not for a very long time.

Mafi was born in 1899 on the day of the relief of Mafeking. She was the youngest daughter of Henry King of Ilford and he christened his daughter May Ada Florence Enid. For nearly eighty years, M. A. F. E. King had been known as Mafi, pronounced Maffy.

She had no big toes. They were amputated long before Ellis was born. Whenever he thinks of Mafi he starts with this fact, as if he is telling someone who never knew her.

"The first thing I should say is that Mafi had no big toes. The next thing I want you to know about her is that she lived on the south Kent coast where she was landlady of the Gate Inn. She taught me how to play cribbage when I was seven and she took me for walks along the Military Canal."

Her big toes were amputated because of her circulation but it didn't do the trick. She left the pub and went to her best friend's house on the hill, looking across the Channel to France. She was told she would die within a year. That was twenty years before the holiday in Exmouth. Now her best friend had died and Mafi was moving on, with the slow, stiff walk she had, and a handkerchief up her sleeve to wipe away her tears when she laughed. Moving on to live with her nephew and his two children in a creaky old cottage in the Kentish Weald where she had her own bedsit and kitchen in one corner of the downstairs. Chrissie named it "MafiKingdom".

"If you try to move me to a new school I'll tell everyone

you're on LED," Chrissie warned, even though the subject
of school hadn't been mentioned.

"LSD," Denny corrected her, politely.

"I'm thirteen and I have my friends! This is 1976, not
1876, children have rights."

"I've no intention of moving you from your school."

"Oh. Thanks."

Denny O'Rourke turned to his son. "Nor you."

Ellis shrugged. He had no strong opinion on the subject.
His school in Orpington was acceptable because there
was swimming once a week and his enormous capacity
for daydreaming was tolerated. His teacher had a habit of
reminding him he wasn't particularly good at anything,
a view that Chrissie reinforced from time to time, but he
didn't seem to get in trouble for being ungifted so he didn't
care. More important, there was the deal which he and his
dad had struck. When Ellis reached the age of thirteen, they
had agreed, he would be allowed to cycle from the cottage
to Hildenborough station and catch the train to Orpington
each day. Alone. This was the sort of freedom and adventure
Ellis dreamed of. He would go to the Wimpy bar with his
friends after school and they would look on in admiration as
he headed off to the train station for his epic journey home.
Alone. A girlfriend would soon result, surely, and she'd have
a mum who would smell the way a mum smells and she'd
stroke the fringe up off Ellis's forehead, as a matter of habit,
from time to time.

Life was getting good again at nearly nine, Ellis thought,
but at thirteen it was going to be simply fantastic.

Denny gave his son a Brazilian football kit on his ninth
birthday. Ellis tore off his clothes and put it on and ran down
the corridor to show Mafi. As he did so, he dropped the tin
mouse Chrissie had given him. The mouse was grey with red
plastic wheels, a shiny black tail and painted-on whiskers,

and it was small enough to bury in the grip of your hand. It was still lying on the floor when Chrissie got back from school. That night, she slumped down heavily on Ellis's bed and grimaced at him.

"Goodnight, Smelly-Ellie. Happy birthday," she said abruptly.

"Night-night ..." he ventured, unsure of her tone.

"I threw your tin mouse somewhere you'll never find it and if you tell Dad I'll just deny it and insist that you're making the whole thing up and who do you think he's going to believe?"

"Me?"

"No, stupid. Me. Because I'm thirteen and you're only nine and five hours."

"Where did you put it?"

"I didn't put it anywhere. I threw it away and you'll never find it, so forget it."

"Why did you take my tin mouse back?"

"I didn't take it back, you left it on the floor and I heard you tell Mafi it was a boring present."

"I didn't mean it. Can I have it back please?"

"Too late. You should learn to be more grateful."

Chrissie went to her room, and as Ellis listened to the floorboards creak beneath her feet his eyes strayed to the attic hatch above his bed. Not for the first time, he thought he saw the hatch door open and spiders emerge. He buried himself under the bedclothes and called out, "I'm not scared of you but you ought to be scared of me. Look at the size of me."

"Stop hiding and we'll see the size of you," they replied.

Ellis couldn't think of a response to that. He listened to his own thudding heart and reminded himself what his Great-aunt Mafi had told him. Before houses existed, spiders in England lived in caves. Nowadays, old houses are the same as caves from a spider's point of view.

And the problem, Ellis thought to himself, is that the

house my dad has moved us into is a really, really old house. But I've got to remember they're only here because they think it's a cave. It's nothing personal.

"I'm going to let you off," he called out. "But don't think I'll be so lenient next time."

He made himself an air hole and slept beneath the sheets.

When they lit the first fire of winter, the flames reflected in a glass-fronted cabinet which held trinkets, glasses, and china that Denny O'Rourke's father had collected from all over the world.

"Now it's home ..." Denny purred.

An oil tank was installed at the back of the cottage and a new boiler in the walk-in cupboard in the kitchen. When the boiler men drove away, Mafi wedged the driveway gate open.

"I think it's more friendly to leave that gate open seeing as we've just moved in," she told Denny.

He shovelled a heap of left-over coal into potato sacks, which Ellis held open. They hosed the coal shed down and, it being Ellis's bath time anyway, his dad soaked him through until Ellis nearly laughed himself sick. Mafi and Chrissie whitewashed the walls and the coal shed became the bike shed and the place for stacking up anything to be burnt. Sunday evenings was the time for bonfires and a charred pile established itself in the far corner of the orchard, next to the compost heap. A path to it was worn in the grass. Mafi kept her distance as glow-worms and grass snakes and toads lived around the compost and she welcomed them as readily as Ellis welcomed spiders.

Chrissie would stray from the bonfire and look through the back hedge to the working men's club. It was an old wooden pavilion, patched with corrugated iron. There was a skittles alley out the back which had a tin roof but was open at the sides. From a vantage point beneath the hedge, where they lay on their bellies, Chrissie and Ellis watched the skittles matches and other less clear transactions between the men, in which money and goods and whispers were exchanged. Saturday and Sunday evenings, when women were allowed, were occasionally rowdy and Ellis heard noises which he could not account for and his sister declined to explain.

She often spent time alone there, hidden within the gnarled old hedge, hugging her knees to her chin, watching the inanimate wooden building. When she caught herself thinking of the change that had entered their lives with their mother's leaving, she would scold herself and some force would rear up in her, a defiance in a girl with no previous inclination to defy, an instinct to push blindly towards wherever the new boundaries might be. The tools with which she pushed were not unique to her. Cigarettes and attitude. Harmless boys and dangerous girlfriends. Things that did not truly interest her but appeared to be what she ought to show interest in, because the previous things were those of a girl's life and she couldn't pretend to herself that she was a girl any more.

With Ellis she was sometimes censorious and other times tender as she responded unsurely to the instinct to protect him and the temptation to stifle him and preserve the adoring little brother that suited her well.

She liked to make a mug of tea for her dad when he returned from work and then leave him alone. Denny drank his tea at the kitchen table, sitting in his shirt and braces, with his suit jacket hanging on the kitchen door. Sometimes he would stare into space, his top lip resting on the rim of the mug. Other times, he drew sketches of the renovations he had in mind and wrote lists, in unintelligibly small handwriting, of jobs to do on the cottage.

Ellis would follow his dad upstairs and sit on the bed whilst Denny changed into his "messy clothes". More often than not, Ellis would examine the framed photograph on Denny O'Rourke's bedside table. It had always been there, in the old house too. It was a black and white image of a lighthouse on a shingle shoreline. In the foreground was a length of railing from a ship's deck and between the railing and the shore, surrounded by a choppy sea, was a sandbank upon which a fishing boat had run aground.

"What was the name of your ship?"

"You know. You've asked me a million times."

"Don't exaggerate. The *Hororata*. And you drank a lot of rum all the time."

"Only the once."

"How old were you, again?"

Denny stamped his feet into his work boots and beamed his son a smile. "Seventeen, when I drank the rum."

"Seventeen is only four more than Chrissie," Ellis said.

Denny's face altered a little, the way it did before he changed the direction of a conversation.

"The great thing about having no carpets in this house yet, Ellis, is that I can wear my boots indoors and not get told off." He grinned and headed out of the room.

"Who's going to tell you off?" Ellis asked.

Denny faltered but kept on walking. Ellis followed him down to the utility room where antique ledge and brace doors were stacked up on Denny's workbench, ready for planing. Ellis watched his dad measure up the doorframes in the hallway and repeat the measurements under his breath, "74 by 38, 74 by 38, 74 by 38 ..."

"34, 78, 44, 68, 78, 34 ..." Ellis whispered.

"You little sod!" Denny said, and chased Ellis into the orchard where he tickled him purple and left him for dead in the old goose bath.

Returning inside, Denny noticed that damp stains had appeared on the hallway ceiling.

"Bugger!" he muttered. He rolled up his sleeves and sat

on the bottom stair to think. Ellis joined him, breathless from laughing. He stroked the hairs on his dad's arm, his fingers dwarfed by the contours of muscles and veins.

"Change of plan, dear boy," Denny said. "I'm going to need your help. We're going into the attic."

There were three attics in the cottage. The one immediately above the top of the stairs was the least interesting, in Ellis's opinion. The water tank was in it but the rafters were bare so nothing was stored up there. The second attic was known as "the hatch" and Ellis was the only one small enough to do anything useful inside it. Entry to it was through a hatch in a cupboard used to store suitcases. Inside the hatch, the roof was vast and slanting but claustrophobically low. Even Ellis could only fit in on his hands and knees. Denny directed his son across the rafters until he was kneeling directly above the hallway ceiling, but Ellis found no sign of dripping water.

"You sure?" his dad asked.

"Yup!" Ellis confirmed proudly.

He sat next to his dad in the suitcase cupboard whilst Denny deliberated what to do. It was like being in a tent together, where everything was gentle and close-up, especially the faint growling noises Denny made when he was thinking long and hard.

The following Saturday, Denny removed the Kent peg tiles from the dilapidated garage in which Mafi kept her Morris Minor and used them to replace the damaged ones on the roof of the cottage.

"But there weren't any leaks in the hatch attic," Ellis protested, from the bottom of the ladder.

He got no reply. His dad was preoccupied. Chrissie had been gone for a few hours and he didn't know where. When she showed up for lunch, Denny was subdued and attempted to find out where she'd been without asking her directly, a process that amused Mafi.

"You'll always be very careful, won't you?" he said to Chrissie, out of nowhere. "When we're not all together. Don't do anything silly or unusual, will you?"

His voice was grave but not unkind. He said it as if the thought was a new one but Chrissie had heard it from him often in the last five years. She smiled at him reassuringly.

"No sweat, Dad."

"I'm allowed to do silly things though, aren't I, because I'm only nine?" Ellis asked.

"We can do silly things when we're all together, at home, safe and sound," his dad answered.

"But I still don't get why you are putting tiles up there when there wasn't any drips," Ellis said, faithful to his own unique train of thought.

"I know, Ellis, but somewhere that roof is damaged and hopefully this'll do the trick."

"But what if it doesn't?"

"I'll have to sell you to the slave trade to raise money to employ a roofer."

Chrissie laughed, whilst Ellis weighed up whether or not he liked the sound of this.

"I wouldn't mind being a slave if it was in some interesting country."

"You're my slave," Denny reminded him.

"Then you ought to pay me!"

"You don't pay slaves, you spaz," Chrissie said.

"Charmingly put," Mafi said. "What have you been up to, Chrissie? I haven't seen you all morning."

"I've cured the common cold, cut a hit LP, written to Idi Amin about his diet and concocted a formula to rid the world of Communism which I'll unveil after lunch."

"Chrissie?" Denny said.

"Yes, Daddio?"

"Remember late 1973?"

"Not particularly. Why?"

"That was the last time you gave a straight answer to a question."

Chrissie opened her mouth to rattle off a response but couldn't come up with anything. Her dad smiled, victorious, and she buried her head in his chest with a stupid smile. Mafi reached for her handkerchief. Her watery eyes spoke only of how she loved being part of this nonsense.

"In 1973 I was six," said Ellis, counting his fingers. "But now I'm nine."

Chrissie stared at him bug-eyed. "Reeeeally, Ellis? Do keep us informed!"

His children were still wrestling on the front lawn as Denny O'Rourke surveyed the roof from the foot of the driveway. Their screaming and laughter filled the air. He smiled to himself and leant back against the gatepost and as he did so he felt the breath of a woman on his neck.

"You must be the widower."

Denny turned. The middle-aged woman standing far too close to him was handsome, a rural version of elegant, with shining eyes that swallowed him whole. Her voice was throaty and coarse and she stared into him as she spoke.

"Yes. Very nice indeed. I see what they mean."

An impulse Denny had not hosted for half a decade was upon him. He introduced himself and learned that she was Bridget and she ran the village shop that formed a triangle at the foot of the green with the post office and the pub.

"Come in and set up your account. If the shop's empty, just come straight upstairs."

She pressed her hands against her rib cage and filled her lungs, in a gesture of her appreciation of this crisp winter's day that left Denny helpless but to imagine the strong, full, impressive physique beneath her clothing. For a moment, as Bridget watched the children, Denny let himself fall deep into her body.

"Yes. Very nice ..." she repeated, and left.

Denny found his son and daughter staring at him. Ellis burst into laughter that made his face vibrate. Chrissie stared angrily at him and said, "NO!"

Denny shook his head dismissively and smiled, swatting away her fears and his own lust. He kicked the wedge from beneath the driveway gate and let it swing shut behind him as he returned to work. Ellis followed him inside.

The third attic in the cottage was above Ellis's bedroom, the door to it directly over his pillows, and it was where family heirlooms, Christmas decorations and dressing-up rags and costumes were stored. Ellis found his bed pushed aside and the ladders propped against the open attic door.

He called out, "Can I come up?"

"If you're careful."

The attic was long and narrow and low enough to force Denny on to his hands and knees. There was a bare light bulb hanging from the rafters, which blinded Ellis as he climbed in. He found his dad peering over the end wall. It was a strange wall, Ellis noticed, in that it didn't reach the roof.

"What's the other side of this wall?" Ellis whispered.

"I think this must be the join in the roof where they extended the cottage. The bit we're in was added two hundred years ago but the other side of this wall is what was the original little house."

Denny leant further over the wall and strained. "I think ... that what I'm looking at, Ellis, is the slope of the original roof. It used to be on the outside of the cottage. It's four hundred years old, Ellis. Think of that."

"Older than Mafi."

"Yes ..."

"Has it got tiles on?" Ellis asked.

"They'd have taken them off and used them on the new roof. It's just the timbers."

"Oh."

"I'll tell you, Ellis," Denny said, "there's a helluva lot of roof on this old cottage. I hope there're no nasty surprises."

Ellis liked his dad saying things like "helluva" because he didn't use words like that very often.

"It's a really big house," Ellis agreed. "Lots of nooks and crannies."

Denny smiled to himself. There was something he liked about his nine-year-old son saying things like "nooks and crannies".

"So, what room is under that old roof?" Ellis asked.

"My bedroom," Denny said.

"Oh, yeah. Can I look?"

Denny lifted his son up to see over the wall. The bulb threw enough light to see the faint outline of the old, sloping roof. As Ellis's eyes adjusted, a skeleton of rafters and beams materialised in front of him. The timbers disappeared into a well of blackness. He wondered what could be down there. It was the darkest, most unreachable place he could imagine a house to have. A place not originally intended to exist, brought about by change. If there are places one never goes, places that one would never ever have reason to find oneself in, if such places exist, then this well was one of them.

3

In his dreams, Ellis walked through the cottage and found secret doorways to hidden rooms and stairways. For a few moments, upon waking, he'd believe they were real.

Behind Denny's bed, set into a low wall beneath the slope of the old roof, there was a wooden door, three feet high, covered in syrupy black paint. And although it was just like the doors in his dreams, Ellis was scared of it. He saw it as a mouth that could eat him alive.

Pholcus phalangioides lived amongst the ceiling beams in the downstairs of the cottage. Back then, Ellis knew them simply as daddy-long-legs. He wasn't too bothered by them as they showed no tendency to descend into his air space. Two *Nuctenea umbratica* took up residence over the front door. When winter came they ceased replenishing their webs but, by then, Ellis had taken to using the kitchen door instead.

The downstairs toilet had no door, just a temporary curtain destined to remain there for many years. Hanging from a nail in the wall was a paint-splattered cassette player with a tape of Strauss's *Four Last Songs* in it. A drawn curtain and the sound of Strauss meant that the toilet was in use. This room was heavily inhabited by various orb-web spiders. Most of them were too small to see but their webs were in the angles of the doorframe, window and pipework. Ellis couldn't go in there.

The garden shed was also a complete no-go area. It was jammed full with spiders and webs. The first, and only, time Ellis stepped inside it, he fainted. Mafi found him lying half in and half out of the shed and he was rushed to hospital, for fear of meningitis.

It angered Ellis that the shed was held by the spiders because it meant he couldn't get his hands on all the things inside it, his outdoor toys and Denny's tools, without asking either Mafi, Chrissie or his dad to go in there for him. He believed that the shed was where all the bad and deformed spiders lived. It was the home of the lawless. The spiders there were freakishly large and jet black in colour; they sat around playing Russian roulette. They ate each other without a care and were weighed down by weird growths. The shed was the wild west of the spider world. Ellis couldn't even walk past it. He had to run at full speed and as he did so he'd shout bitterly, "You are leper spiders, so rubbish they won't even let you live in the cottage. Everyone hates you! I'm not scared of you!"

At night, he heard sounds of movement which had no explanation. Asking about the creaks and groans in the cottage caused his dad to tense up or change the subject, the same way as asking about his mum, and in the absence of an explanation Ellis suspected that the noises were spiders turning in their sleep. The creaks grew noisier in the second winter as a freezing cold January was met by an unusually mild February. April showers arrived a month early and set in for three weeks, by the end of which the hallway ceiling was turning brown again with water marks. Denny O'Rourke cursed the stains and Ellis knew not to bother him.

Ellis went to his sister's room but the door was locked.

"Let me in."

"No thanks," Chrissie said, from the other side of the door.

"Please."

"Give me one good reason."

"Dad's got us a puppy!"

Ellis listened to a crashing sound as Chrissie fell off her chair, thundered across the room, grappled with the lock and flung the door open.

"Where?" she said breathlessly.

Ellis stepped into her room and threw himself down on the bed.

"Let's do something," he said, lazily.

She glared at him. "Have we got a puppy?"

"No. I'm bored. Do you wanna do something together?"

Chrissie skulked back to her desk.

"Yeah. I'd like to play with our puppy, you horrible little pile of dogshit. Go and bother Dad."

"He's fixing the roof. It's falling down, apparently."

"Fascinating," she said, and returned to her work.

"Why are you always in your room doing homework nowadays?" he asked.

30

"They're called O levels and they're the devil's work," she replied. "But they'll be over in June and then I'll never work again."

"Until your A levels."

"Not for me, buster."

"Dad won't like that."

"He'll get over it. You can be his golden boy."

"You know I'm rubbish at school. I'm having an allotment."

"That's not a job, Ellis. That's a hobby, like chess or riding or peeking at my friends through the curtain when they're taking a pee."

"I don't!"

"Never said you did, derr-brain. Is lunch ready? Is that why you're up here?"

"No. I wanted to ask Dad something but he's busy, so I came to ask you instead."

"Do I want you to go to boarding school in China? Yes please." She beamed him a psychotic smile.

"Have spiders got eyes? Can they see us?"

Chrissie slumped and pulled a face. "That's worth failing an O level for? What sort of a question is that, Ellie-belly?"

And as he started to protest at being called that, she jumped off her chair and tickled him until he begged for mercy and agreed to be her slave for the rest of the day.

The spare room at the top of the stairs was bare and sun-filled. It sucked in warm rays of light even in winter, as if awaiting the arrival of someone wise. The vast cherry tree laid its fingertips on the window sill. Denny decided this room should be Mafi's bedroom and her bedsit downstairs a proper living room.

"We don't need a spare bedroom because we don't have any visitors," Chrissie muttered, as she and Ellis helped Denny carry Mafi's bed into the room. Chrissie slipped and the bed fell against the wall, tearing a hole in the wallpaper. Behind the tear was a black-painted beam. It was set back into the wall and the wallpaper had been pasted over it, shoddily, leaving a gap between the two. As Denny peeled the wallpaper away, Ellis watched the beam emerge. It was colossal. Near the corner of the room, it disappeared behind plasterwork into the centre of the cottage.

"How could anyone slap wallpaper over a beam like this?" Denny sighed. "We'll sort this out next weekend. Can't leave it like this."

"Then Mafi will have a lovely beam in her bedroom and we can paint it shiny black and hang stuff on it."

"That's right," Denny said. "These things matter."

But they didn't matter to Mafi. She decided that the best place for her wardrobe was against that wall. It would cover the beam anyway and there was more pressing work for Denny to do on the cottage. When she made decisions they tended to be final, owing not so much to a profound strength of opinion on her part as to her preference for keeping debate on trivial issues brief. Chrissie pinned a paper horseshoe to the beam for good luck and then the beam disappeared behind the wardrobe, to remain out of sight for as long as Mafi lived.

At six o'clock every morning, Mafi took a cup of tea back to bed and watched the cherry tree. She called it her special time, when she felt lucky to be alive, and she called the years since she left the pub her "borrowed life", the life after hers was meant to have finished. Ellis encouraged her stories of being landlady at the Gate Inn. His favourites were of Mr Prag getting stuck inside the grandfather clock, the piglets falling into the beer cellar, and the war: of Nissen huts going up along the canal, doodlebugs and Mafi refusing evacuation to Hampshire. She taught him and Chrissie how to clean a glass properly and how to shuffle a pack.

In spring, the garden looked dewy and luscious from Mafi's bedroom window. Ellis studied her face. She was lost in thought and had barely noticed him come in. From beneath them, in the dining room, came the sound of Denny's electric shaver. Ellis wondered what part of her life Mafi was revisiting. She had never married. Chrissie claimed she had been engaged to a man in the war and he died of TB. Ellis didn't know if this was true. He liked Mafi as she was, old and unmarried and inclined towards throaty laughter.

"Ellis, old thing," she said, "I'm afraid to say that cherry tree is not well."

The woodsmen came on the same day Ellis found spotted jelly bubbles in the pond on Eggpie Lane. They said the tree had to come down. Before they returned, Ellis visited the pond four more times. The black spots grew into semicircles and by late March the jelly had fallen apart and a sprawl of wriggling tadpoles appeared. When he took his dad to see them they found a mass of froth on the water's surface.

"They've disappeared," Ellis said.

"They do," his dad replied.

In April, Mafi showed Ellis how to tap a bird's nest and set off the calls of baby blackbirds inside. Sometimes, the young poked their heads out and Ellis caught a glimpse of their open beaks clamouring for food. By the time the woodsmen came, the nests in the garden were empty and the shrubs nearby filled with birdsong. Cats prowled beneath the bushes. Chrissie tried to adopt them and Mafi shooed them away.

Denny O'Rourke took photos of the cherry tree and Mafi unravelled the roses from its trunk and laid them out across the lawn.

"We'll plant a new one," Denny said.

"How long will it take?" Ellis asked.

"When you're as old as Mafi, the new tree will be half the size of that one," Chrissie said.

Ellis sighed. That was far too slow.

"You plant trees for the next generations," Denny explained.

Chrissie joined her hands together and chanted "Aaaaa-men." Ellis copied her. Their dad marched them away in a head lock, one under each arm.

"I've a pair of idiots for children," he told the woodsmen.

Ellis watched from Mafi's bedroom window. The woodsman with a thick orange beard dangled from a rope within touching distance. A chainsaw hung from his waist and a cigarette was wedged behind his ear. Ellis felt Mafi's breathing on his neck as they watched. After lunch, a young apprentice woodsman turned up on foot and was bullied by the two men for being late. They barked orders at him all afternoon. Later, the apprentice was caught sharing his cigarettes and hip flask with Chrissie. The bearded man dragged him away and struck him.

After nightfall, from his pillow, Ellis heard shouting and doors slamming. Chrissie ran past Ellis's bedroom to her own and his dad thundered after her. Later, Ellis found Chrissie lying under her blanket, still dressed. She had been crying and now she was staring at nothing and twisting the ends of her long hair round her fingers.

"What happened?" Ellis whispered.

She pulled him close. "Dad caught me crawling back through the hedge," she whispered.

"Where had you been?"

"Drinking beer in the skittle alley with that lad."

"The man with the drink in his pocket?"

"It's called a hip flask."

She held Ellis's face in her hands. Her eyes twinkled.

"Ellis ..."

"What?"

"I saw a man and a woman doing it, in the toilets. I saw

them actually doing it."

Ellis stared at her wide-eyed and she saw the need for clarification. "Having sex, Ellis. They made these ridiculous noises. Don't mention it to Dad or Mafi or anyone."

Ellis nodded his head earnestly. He didn't know what she was talking about. But, feeling that he should respond to what she clearly considered momentous news, he said with equal seriousness: "Another interesting thing is that the man with the chainsaw never smokes the cigarette behind his ear. It just stays there all day."

The Formula 1 racetrack in the hallway was renowned on the F1 circuit for its challenging combination of breakneck quarry tiling and slow rug. Because the ceiling beams were lushly decorated with berried holly from Dibden Lane, the pre-Christmas Grand Prix was coming from the jungle, somewhere in South America – Ellis's commentary didn't specify where. Or it was, until the appearance of a house spider straddling the chicane caused a cancellation. The spider was huge and made Ellis's stomach churn and his feet tingle, as if he were standing on a cliff edge.

"Right!" he hissed. "That's it! I want a meeting with the most highest-up of spiders. It's not fair!"

There was no reply and the sound of his own voice embarrassed him. He wondered if Ivy had heard him. She was the only other person in the cottage. Ivy, who was unfeasibly old in Ellis's opinion, lived on the lane and babysat for Denny O'Rourke on the rare occasions when Mafi couldn't do it. She was reading the local paper in the kitchen. Ellis had shut her in there so that he could commentate on his F1 race without feeling self-conscious. Ivy did not remove spiders. She had made that clear from the start.

Ellis grabbed his toy cars and made a run for the kitchen, leaping over the spider and slamming the door behind him.

"Impersonating a stampede, Ellis?" Ivy muttered, without

looking up.

"When are Dad and Mafi getting back?" Ellis asked.

"Don't know," she murmured.

Ellis walked on the spot to relieve himself of the last shivers of repulsion.

"Do you need to go to the toilet, Ellis?"

"No, thanks. Do you?"

"Don't be cheeky." She put down the paper and lit a cigarette.

"Don't suppose you want to come outside and play in the garden?"

She shook her head.

"Are they my dad's cigarettes?"

"No, they're mine, thank you for checking."

"Wasn't checking. He wouldn't mind." Ellis put his boots on. "You're not like a real babysitter."

"Aren't I? How's that?"

"Not out. Well, you don't seem to like being with children very much and you're not very chatty and you don't like playing."

"If I wasn't here they wouldn't be out buying you Christmas presents and you'd get nothing."

Ellis thought this through. She had a point. He stamped his boots on and threw on his coat. He felt braver with boots on.

"You don't like doing stuff with me," he concluded. "That's what I'm getting at. I like you but you're not much fun."

On the bookshelves in the dining room Ellis found a large hardback volume of *Jane's Fighting Ships*. An idea had come to him as he was putting on his boots. He hadn't decided on the idea exactly, nor advanced it once it had appeared in his head. He simply realised that he was going to do this certain thing and that it was better for him not to stop and think about it.

From halfway up the stairs, he leant out between the stairwell beams and dropped the book on to the floor below. Then he went outside to play and the voices of accusation and denial began in his head.

Mafi used a damp cloth to remove the carcass of the spider from the book cover. When she kissed Ellis goodnight, she whispered, "If you want to live and thrive, let a spider run alive."

Ellis woke with itchy nipples. This was happening more and more. He knelt up on the bed and resolved to speak to Mafi about his harsh polyester pyjamas, the purple ones with gold trim. He yawned and stretched, and as he thought of breakfast Chrissie glided past and, without breaking stride, pointed under Ellis's bed in horror.

"Jesus, Ellis! Under your bed! Three huge tarantulas!"

She screamed, a cheesy horror-movie scream, and ran downstairs.

When his dad found him, half an hour later, Ellis was marching on the spot on his mattress. Denny stepped forward to hold his son but Ellis became hysterical.

"They'll kill you, Dad! They'll bite you and kill you!"

Denny rocked him and soothed him with whispers. "You've got to do something about this," Denny said.

"About what?"

Chrissie appeared at the doorway, holding a volume of her encyclopaedia. "I'm sorry, Ellis," she said.

Denny pointed an accusing finger at her. "We'll talk about this later." He looked his son in the eye. "Come on, Ellis, you've got to get over this."

Chrissie found the page she was looking for and read from it with mock seriousness. "The tarantula lives in a burrow and darts out to catch passing prey. It can inflict a painful bite if molested but, despite the legends surrounding it, it is not a dangerous spider."

"I don't care if they're dangerous, they freak me out!"

"Only trying to help." Chrissie slammed the book shut, put it under her arm and swung one-handed on the doorframe. "It also says the only place in the world you could live and be sure not to see a single spider at all is Antarctica."

Ellis tapped his dad on the arm. "Can we move to Antarctica?"

"It's very cold, Ellis. Me and your sister wouldn't fancy it at all and it would probably kill Mafi instantly."

"Please."

"Too cold."

Ellis crossed his arms defiantly. "Well, I'm not staying here with them."

"We could send Ellis to Antarctica on his own," Chrissie offered. "I'd chip in if it were a matter of the fare."

"Chrissie, shut up!" Denny snapped.

Ellis began to shiver. Tears streamed down his face.

"They keep appearing out of nowhere and scaring me. I call out that I'm coming in and give them time to get out first but they don't. It's not fair. It's our house and we were here first."

"Well, that's not strictly true, I'd imagine, Ellis," his dad said. "You don't mind the glow-worms and things like that though, do you? Up at the bonfire?"

"No, they're amazing," Ellis said.

"Well ..." Denny sighed, "just try to think of spiders the same way. You've really got to snap out of this." He lifted Ellis off the bed.

"Don't put my feet down!" Ellis cried.

"Come on, Ellis! This isn't like you."

"It is like me! It's exactly like me. We have to move house!"

"Well, we're not moving! So get dressed and come down for breakfast."

Chrissie followed her dad to the kitchen.

38

"Nice one, Dad. What a hero!"

"Help me get the breakfast, Chrissie. We're all late."

"Dad, look, I don't particularly like spiders either but I don't talk to them and demand meetings with their elders. Ellis does. So telling him to snap out of it really doesn't cut the mustard. You're going to have to be more creative."

"I'm not creative."

"Then get creative!"

And because Chrissie sounded like her mother, her challenge stuck with Denny, though at first he had no idea how to rise to it. When an idea did come to him, he bought a book about spiders, did some research and took notes in his unreadable handwriting. But when he thought about putting the idea to Ellis, when he imagined saying it out loud, he felt foolish and hoped instead that in time Ellis would forget his fear.

One evening soon after, when Denny went to Ellis's bedroom to say goodnight, he found the room empty. A glow of light outside drew Denny to the window, where he saw the children's tent erected, unsteadily, on the side lawn.

Denny stopped a few yards short of the tent and peered in. Ellis was reading a *Whizzer and Chips* annual by the light of a kerosene lamp. He had blankets above and beneath him. Denny crawled in on his hands and knees and lay on his stomach, beside his son.

"Evening."

Ellis smiled.

"Having fun?"

Ellis nodded and returned to his reading.

Denny watched him for a while and then he left the tent and circled it, moving the pegs further out and pushing them firmly into the ground. Ellis watched the canvas tauten around him then listened to Denny go back inside the cottage. There were two large house spiders in opposite corners of Ellis's bedroom, down by the skirting board. Denny cupped them in his hands, one at a time, and ushered them out of the bedroom window.

"They're gone," he called out.

"Don't care," the glowing tent called back. "Never going inside again. Never ever."

Denny wrapped up warm and took a chair outside where he guarded the tent from a distance, without Ellis knowing. At nine o'clock Mafi joined him for a cigarette and together they watched Ellis's shadow put the book aside and turn off the lamp. Later, Denny scooped his sleeping son up and laid him in his bed.

Mafi had poured Denny a glass of whisky.

"You've got to be pretty unhappy about spiders to take yourself outside to sleep, all alone, at his age," she said.

"Yes ..." Denny said. He was distant. "I did think of one thing, but ..."

"But what?" Mafi asked.

"I really don't know if it will help him."

"Don't know until you've tried. What is it?"

Denny shook his head. "It feels a bit silly."

"Try me," Mafi said.

Denny remained tentative. "What I thought of is an 'agreement'. It sounds ludicrous, but a sort of agreement between us and ..." He laughed at himself. "An agreement between us and them. Based on a little science and a little mopping up of stray spiders on your and my part."

"Sounds good."

Denny blushed and hid his face in his hands.

"What are you worried about?" Mafi asked.

"I'm too embarrassed to put it to him, so I don't know what to do."

"Embarrass yourself," Mafi said.

"I'll pay you 50p to empty this shed."

Gary Bird opened the shed door and peered inside.

"Easy," Gary said. "Show me the 50p first though."

"I'll give it to you up front. You're my best friend. I trust you."

Gary looked at Ellis suspiciously and then at the shed again. "What do you mean exactly, empty?"

"Take the mower and the cans and everything else out and put it on the path. Just leave the shelves and the shed."

"Obviously. I can't take the shed out of the shed."

"I'll wait inside."

"Am I going to get bollocked?" Gary asked.

"There's no one here," Ellis assured him.

Gary weighed this up. Fifty pence was worth a bollocking, even though Ellis was now proceeding to pay him in 2p pieces, which were going to be annoyingly bulky in his pocket.

When Gary had finished, he found Ellis upstairs.

"Done it."

"Was there much activity?"

"What do you mean?"

"Nothing. Is it completely empty?"

"Yes, except for the shed. The shed's still in the shed. Why do you want it empty?"

"I'm going to paint it."

"So, why didn't you empty it yourself?"

"I'm saving my energy for the painting. See you later."

"I'll help you paint."

"No, I'd better do it on my own. You go to Bridget's and start spending that money."

Gary Bird knew when he was being got rid of. He waved goodbye to Ellis, walked down the rutted driveway, as if returning to his house across the lane, and then double-backed up the alleyway alongside the cottage and watched from there. Ellis appeared from Mafi's garage with a cardboard box full of newspaper. He dropped a yellow can of cigarette-lighter fuel into the cardboard box, set fire to the newspaper and threw the box into the shed. At this point,

Gary ran, as fast as the twenty-five coins in his front pocket allowed him.

The simplest ideas are sometimes the best. But sometimes they're just the simplest.

"What do you mean you just found it on fire?" Denny stood with the contents of his shed at his feet and a smoking black scar, where the shed had been, nearby.

"Someone must have, you know ..." Ellis said, shrugging his shoulders.

"So, what we have here is a vandal who burns down people's sheds but he likes to empty them first so as not to damage the contents."

"Or a she ..." Ellis said, "it could be a woman."

Ellis smiled, satisfied that he had distanced Gary from the crime scene by raising the spectre of a female arsonist. He was blissfully unaware that Gary was not in the frame and that there was one suspect and one suspect only. Denny smiled and discovered that he could not feel angry about this. Ellis motioned towards the cottage, a little unnerved by the peaceful expression on his dad's face, and said, "Well, I've got a busy day so I'll be in my room if you want me."

Denny and Mafi watched Ellis wander inside.

"Denny," the old lady said. "Might I suggest you embarrass yourself with that truce idea before Ellis burns down the cottage."

Ellis was confused. Any ten year old would be. He'd been told to sit up for Sunday lunch but there was no food on the table.

"Is lunch ready?" he asked tentatively.

"In a moment or two," Mafi said.

Denny laid a sheet of paper down in front of him, shifted in his seat and cleared his throat.

"Right then ..." he murmured, laughing nervously under his breath and blushing. "Ellis, I've been in discussions with the spiders, on your behalf."

This didn't shock Ellis. He had, after all, been talking to them for over a year.

"They're as upset as you that you don't get along."

"Did they say that?"

Denny nodded. "They've proposed an agreement and I think it's a sensible one. Do you want to hear it?"

Ellis nodded.

"During the winter, when you tend to spend more time indoors, they've agreed to mostly withdraw from the cottage and leave you alone. What they said was that because there aren't many insects about in winter anyway to be caught in their webs ..."

Ellis swallowed sickly at the thought

"... they will pretty well stop spinning their webs in the cottage in winter, and if any did accidentally appear then, during the winter, it's permitted for us to take them down."

"Where are they going to live?"

"They will be allowed run of the downstairs toilet, which you never use anyway. But, mostly, they've agreed to hibernate outdoors, in the soil or under the leaves."

"Ace!" Ellis said.

His dad continued, "But, Ellis, this is a two-way street. One of the conditions is that you will learn about them. I'll teach you; we all will. You learn what an incredible species they are, just like humans. This is important. I've bought a book we can learn from."

"I cannot look at pictures of them!"

"OK, but you'll have to listen. This is a condition of the agreement, Ellis."

Denny looked down at his notes and read from them, his voice more formal than he had wanted it to be.

"Spiders are incredible creatures, Ellis, and everyone concerned wants you to understand that. For instance, the hunting spiders that have agreed to spend the winter in the garden, they have a thing called glycerol in them and it's an antifreeze, like we put in the car radiator. It's so clever, they have antifreeze in their bodies and in their eggs too, so that's how they can survive the winter out there. Some of the others will build themselves nice warm sleeping bags with their own silk."

"That's clever," Ellis conceded.

"Very clever," agreed Mafi.

Denny continued, "I have told the spiders how nervous you are of them. As I said, they were very sorry to hear it."

"They really said that?"

"They did," Chrissie said.

"Part of the agreement, though, is that you think about all the dangers they face and all the creatures they are frightened of. As you learn about this, I'm sure that the last thing you will want to be is another one of the animals harming them every day, don't you think?"

Ellis didn't respond. He didn't want to give any ground without being sure what he was agreeing to.

"Did you know that spiders stroke each other, Ellis?" Mafi asked encouragingly.

"They eat each other too," he responded.

Denny intervened. "Well, that's true, yes, but not often. Not most of them. It's a complicated business, but ... where was I?" He returned to his notes. "Yes, that's it ... I'm sure you don't want to join the long list of things that harm spiders, do you, Ellis? Starlings and robins like to eat spiders, so do the blue tits we encourage with the monkey-nut strings. Frogs and toads eat thousands of spiders. Spiders are under attack from all these things all the time, Ellis, and they have to live somewhere."

Ellis's face lit up. "We could dig a pond in the garden and have frogs and toads in it, loads of them."

"No fear!" Mafi said.

"That would just drive the spiders into the house,"

Chrissie said.

"Then have the frogs in the house."

"Mafi hates frogs," Chrissie countered.

"Even if Mafi loved frogs, we're not having them inside our house," Denny said.

"But Dad," Ellis said.

"Yes, Ellis?"

"Wait a minute." Ellis didn't know what he wanted to say, but he didn't want to lose the initiative here. "Oh, yeah, what about putting toy frogs all around the house, like scarecrows, to scare the spiders back to the garden?"

Chrissie shook her head. "Ellis! Spiders don't see frogs and think, 'Oh shit! A frog.' They sense them by smell and sound. A toy frog isn't a frog to a spider."

Ellis turned to his dad. "Is it OK to say shit?"

"No, it isn't. You're getting confused, Ellis. There's no point having frogs inside the house to scare off spiders that have only flocked inside because they're scared of the real frogs you've put in the garden pond. Especially when we have a better solution here in front of us."

"I don't think spiders 'flock', Dad," Chrissie said. "Sheep flock. I can't believe spiders and sheep share the same word for group-movement."

Ellis was confused now. He had no clear image in his head of this truce thing so it wasn't real to him.

Denny leant across the table, closer to his son.

"Ellis, this agreement isn't foolproof. By that I mean that there are bound to be moments when you come into contact with spiders. When that happens, you come to one of us and you accept that it was just an accident, that they weren't intentionally trying to make you nervous. You just stay calm and in time you'll be fine with them. On the occasions when you accidentally kill a spider without even being aware you've done it – which happens a lot, by the way – they have agreed to accept that this is an innocent accident and not to retaliate."

"They'd better not," Ellis said.

His dad looked him in the eye. "It's a generous, helpful offer on their part. Can I go back to them with your agreement?"

Ellis thought about it, looking as serious and thoughtful as he could. Then he nodded, gravely.

"Good." Denny put his notes into his breast pocket and pushed his glasses up the bridge of his nose.

Ellis felt exhausted and very grown up. He climbed on to his dad's lap. They hugged and rocked back and forth.

"There's nothing for you to be worried about," Denny whispered, in a way that sent a rich, warm chocolatey feeling through Ellis's heart.

"OK," Ellis whispered back.

"Can I tell you one more thing?"

"My brain's full."

"One more."

"All right, then."

"See those beams?" He pointed to the ceiling beams.

"Yeah."

"If it weren't for them, you know our house would fall down?"

"Yeah."

"Well, guess who it is that protects those beams from the woodworm that would eat the beams up, given half a chance?"

"Spiders?"

"You said it."

4

Ellis and Chrissie sat by the open fire and watched their father gardening in the last vestiges of daylight. Shin-deep in willow leaves that refused to dissolve into the earth, Denny stopped to rest. Steam rose from his head. Momentarily, his broad shoulders slumped and he appeared defeated. Then, catching sight of his children, he slung the rake over his shoulder, stood to attention and saluted them. He smiled and his flushed cheeks rose to transform his face.

His limbs were long and lithe and he laboured relentlessly. He warned himself against becoming obsessive or joyless in renovating the cottage. It remained an act of love. What he did he did well, with care and to the best of his abilities, but he did not confer or seek advice, as if he and his family were living on an island, beyond reach, or as if he wanted them to be.

When Denny worked on the cottage Ellis was beside him, watching, learning, hoping to be asked to help in any way. And even though on this island there was no one to show off to, Ellis bragged nevertheless to imaginary observers of his life. He bragged not about the fact that he was his dad's right-hand man or that he knew how to mix lime mortar and straighten old floorboard pins and plant bare-root hedging without creating air pockets. He bragged about having a dad whom the spiders respected enough to do business with.

The cottage walls had contours that appeared tidal, but they were dry and the rooms warmed quickly when the fires were lit. The contours hinted at the huge old timbers within the walls. Sections of these brutal beams were exposed here and there and one vertical post stood proudly, two feet thick, in the middle of the dining room. Chrissie snaked gold tinsel around it at Christmas. The brick-floored dining room was a room that prolonged winter. Ellis preferred the living room, where he would sit at dusk and watch the silhouettes of furniture and familiar objects take on a new appearance in the low light as he waited for the sky above Ide Hill to fill with crimson, which it would from time to time, especially in autumn.

The evenings grew longer by a few precious minutes each day and Ellis became impatient for spring. The snowdrops stayed late on the front lawn, exchanging glances with the violets as they departed.

Before it all, Denny O'Rourke would pick the first violets of the year and give them to his wife in a posy tied so delicately it defied the apparent brute strength of his hands. How she had loved violets.

Denny stock-fenced the garden boundaries and hid the fencing within new hedge lines of hornbeam, hazel and spindleberry. At the back of the orchard, he erected a tall panel fence to push the working men's club out of reach and out of sight. But, to Ellis, the goings-on there became more exotic for being spied on through a knothole.

Ellis watched his dad from the side lawn as the hills around the village turned to silhouette. He noticed that the old latch-gate in the fence beneath the conifers had been replaced by a fixed wooden panel. The discarded gate was propped against the trees, out of sight. It was mossy and rotten but Ellis had always liked it and considered it a veiled doorway to the world outside. The garden was enclosed now. There were no nooks and crannies left in the boundary, no loose timbers in rotten fencing, no gaps in the hedges, no hidden gates leading to the village green. The only way out was the driveway gate, in full view of the house, and that was shut.

He peered in through Mafi's kitchen window. There was a plate of meat cuttings on the table. His taste buds stirred in the knowledge that she would put that meat through the hand-cranked mincer and mix in some hard-boiled eggs and mustard, to make sandwich fillings. He walked along the cottage wall to Mafi's living room, to knock on the window and ask for a sandwich. But he stopped and watched instead as she smoked a cigarette. She ran the palm of her non-smoking hand back and forth across the velveteen tablecloth. A deck of cards was laid out in front of her. She studied them and occasionally moved the cards. He watched the smoke rise in an ivory-white column from the ashtray to the light bulb overhead. The bulb sent back a rim of bright light which caught Mafi in a halo and revealed the shape of her bare head through her thinning white hair. Ellis thought of skulls, skeletons and X-rays from school books, and in a moment of lucidity he grasped the idea that Mafi was an animal with body parts and a shell to protect them and that her shell was growing old and would, one day, break down. He imagined her old naked body and he squirmed. His appetite was gone.

Denny called out to him from beneath the willow tree.

"Look, dear boy!"

"What?" Ellis wandered down to him.

"Watch." Denny held his thumb across the hose and created a spray of water which revealed a dewy sheet of spider webs in the wire squares of fencing.

Ellis grimaced. "I'll show you something then," he said, opening the front gate and stepping on to the lane. Denny followed him to a dense, low beech hedge which lined the track into Treasure Island Woods. Ellis crouched down and peered at the hedge with one eye closed.

"Look from here," he told his dad.

Denny lowered himself to Ellis's height where the low, pink dusk light unveiled strands of silk bunting, which fluttered horizontally in the breeze.

"You can only see them first thing and last thing, when

the sun's low," Ellis said authoritatively.

"Well done," his dad whispered.

"I'm not saying I like them."

"Of course ..."

"Do you want to see Treasure Island?" Ellis asked.

"It's getting dark," his dad said.

"Don't be scared," Ellis said encouragingly.

Denny O'Rourke smiled to himself.

"What?" Ellis asked.

"Nothing."

They followed Ellis's own footprints into the woods until the footprints disappeared into a stream. They trudged through the stream, and laughed when their wellingtons were breached and their feet squelched. The stream joined another rivulet and twisted beneath steep banks of mossy clay until it reached a pool. Four streams ran out from the far side of the pool. Two headed into the fields and two ran through the woods either side of the track to Reardon's farm. A small mossy hillock sat in the middle of the pool with a cluster of rotten tree stumps to sit on. This was Treasure Island and to Ellis and Gary Bird it was a place of infinite adventure.

Denny sat there and Ellis explained the names he and Gary had given the four streams: the Medway, the Rother, the Panama and the Mississippi.

"Some rivers feel as wide as the ocean," Denny said. "I would love to see the Mississippi."

They went on to the wooden gate at the far end of the wood. The sensation of his son leading him by the hand and the cold water swilling around his boots sent ripples of happiness through Denny O'Rourke.

"This is as far as I go," Ellis said.

Opposite the five-bar gate, across a narrow lane, was the entrance to Reardon's farm. Ellis sat there often to look for activity in the yards or to watch Reardon in the fields. The farmer was rugged-looking and strong, despite some sort of injury to his left leg, for which he used a stick. His face was expressive and his cheeks were lean and bronzed. His hair was wavy and thick and silver grey. He remained defiantly handsome in the face of old age. His was the face of a man who has done many interesting things, Ellis had decided. He felt drawn to him and scared of him at the same time.

The yard lights of the dairy lit up the moisture in the dusk air. Ellis longed to be under those lights doing whatever work it was that went on there. It was dark when he and his dad got home. Their faces were flushed and their heads full of the images that only woodland in twilight can conjure up.

In the Wimpy Bar in Orpington high street, Ellis saw Chrissie kissing a boy. The boy's hand crept up his sister's skirt. What the hell for, Ellis couldn't fathom. He wondered if his dad had done this with his mum and concluded that it was highly unlikely.

Ellis found out that the boy was called Vincent and that he was in the final year, a year above Chrissie. He was the first boy she ever brought home. Denny was welcoming but formal. Mafi overfed him. Ellis watched Vincent as if he were a lab rat, which in some ways he was.

"Have you had sex with Vincent?" he asked his sister, having made the trip up to her bedroom especially to use this word he didn't comprehend.

"No." She was reading the spider book.

"Are you going to?"

"Yes. Definitely. Someone has to be first and I've decided he's got the gig."

"What if he doesn't want to?" Ellis asked.

She laughed disdainfully. "He's a boy."

"So am I."

"He's a boy of seventeen. Boys of seventeen want to. You're eleven and a half. I don't know what boys of your age want to do."

"When?"

"When what?"

"When are you and Vincent going to have sex?"

"At eight twenty-three on Tuesday week."

"Really?"

"I don't know when! When you're not around."

She pushed Ellis to the ground and knelt on his chest. This made him laugh, automatically. She held the spider book open above him.

"Don't show me pictures!" he screamed.

"This'll make you hurl, spider-boy!"

"No pictures!"

"I'm not going to show you any fucking pictures. I'm here to educate you."

He loved her to swear.

"Get this, freak-boy ... 'Throughout the whole of their development, spiders may fall victim to other predators. From the egg stage to adulthood they may be eaten by insects, other arachnids (including spiders), birds, mammals, reptiles, amphibians and fish. Perhaps the only thing worse than being eaten alive is being eaten alive slowly. Some parasitic wasps lay their eggs in spiders' egg sacs or on the spiders themselves. The larvae hatch and either eat the eggs, or feed on the living spider as it moves around.'"

She slammed the book shut triumphantly. "Feel sick?"

Ellis shook his head. "Uh-uh. We've got to get loads of wasps next summer."

Chrissie climbed off Ellis's chest and stood over him.

"Ellis, I don't think you're getting your head round this truce thing at all."

Gary Bird's arms and legs were twice the thickness of Ellis's. The two of them spent most of their time on Gary's dad's allotment at Long Barn. Gary told Ellis that when his dad was a teenager he ate a frog, for a dare. Ellis wasn't sure if this was true but he liked the way Mr Bird lit his cigarettes, leaning down towards his lighter and throwing his head back as he took the first puff.

That's how I'm going to do it too, Ellis told himself.

Gary played for the village juniors football team. He talked Ellis into going along. The changing rooms at the recreation ground were in an unloved wooden pavilion. It wore thick layers of peeling green paint and Ellis found it strangely enchanting.

"Like *Hector's House* on TV," he whispered, to no one other than himself.

The two toilets were in wooden sheds, symmetrically set one each side of the pavilion, up a small set of steps. Inside the gents shed was a large oil drum, which Ellis had to stand on tiptoe to be able to pee into, whilst swatting away the flies and holding his breath.

Soon after he was brought on as a substitute, Ellis lay down on the pitch and rested his head on the turf. From there, as he had begun to suspect, the pavilion looked just like a miniature Swiss weather-house, seen through colossal blades of grass. He waited patiently for a man and woman to glide out of their respective toilets and forecast sun or rain, but before they could, out of nowhere, Mr Souter, the manager, was kneeling beside him with a bucket and sponge.

"Are you all right, son?"

"Yes, thanks," Ellis said, bewildered. "I'm fine."

He wasn't called on again.

When they weren't at the allotment, Ellis and Gary played football on the side lawn or cricket on the driveway, using the green metal grass box from the mower as stumps, or they played in the oak tree, which bordered the bottom corner of the garden. It was one of the oldest trees in Britain. A man from a magazine once came to photograph it. The roots were exposed above the ground and Ellis could squeeze between them on his belly and climb up the inside of the hollow trunk to the first or second boughs, which were huge and cast shadows over the footpath to the village green. The boughs were split open and hollow, like canoes, and Ellis lay on his back inside them and enjoyed being invisible. He looked at the branches above him and patches of sky in between and then he rested his head against the bough and his eyes looked across the landscape of fissured bark canyons and mountains, and his heartbeat thumped in his ear like approaching foot soldiers.

Chrissie was too big to crawl inside the tree but strong enough to climb it. From the front door of the cottage, Ellis watched her sit in the high bough on the evening that Vincent split up with her, which was a week after he slept with her.

"When you cry," he whispered, "your face goes red and the freckles round your eyes come out and you look like my baby sister not my big sister."

And when you lie curled up on your bed crying, he thought to himself, I want to rub your tummy and accidentally touch your boobs with my thumb, just to find out what they feel like.

An invitation from Chrissie in early August led Denny and Ellis to visit the reservoir at Bough Beach for the first time. The still water turned purple in the early evening and Ellis lost himself in thoughts of vast oceans and far-away places and a girl of no vivid description holding his hand.

"It must be so good to go places," he sighed.

Denny's stomach turned. "Don't go disappearing on me." He tried to say it lightly.

"Don't go disappearing on *me*," Ellis countered.

They crossed a meadow towards the nature reserve. Chrissie was waiting for them in the office. She introduced her dad to James, the assistant warden. She was nervous, and as a result she was polite, which Ellis found hilarious. They walked up the lane to the Frog and Bucket, where Chrissie and James had met three weeks earlier, watching a band called the Messerschmitts.

When Denny asked James how old he was, Chrissie tensed up.

"Twenty-three," James replied confidently. "Six years older than Chrissie."

Ellis stared open-mouthed at the scandalous age difference and waited for the shit to hit the fan.

"My maths could have coped with that one," Denny O'Rourke responded, with the hint of a smile.

"My dad is capable of twenty-three minus seventeen, you know," Ellis said assertively.

"Right," said James.

"So am I, in fact," Ellis added.

Chrissie fled to the bar.

Denny offered her daughter's new boyfriend a cigarette and lit it for him. "Seventeen is very young," he purred. "Do not get her up the duff."

James didn't flinch. Denny settled back in his seat and put an arm round Ellis, who felt confident he knew what "up the duff" must mean and decided it would be more grown up not to seek confirmation.

The house spider waiting for him in the bath when they got home was the biggest yet. Something inside Ellis buckled and, as the shivers of repulsion shot up his body from the soles of his feet, he became angry. He lunged for the taps and sent two jets of water plunging into the bath. He turned his back and counted to one hundred, then turned the taps off. When the water had run away, he glanced to check the bath was empty and saw a waterlogged spider-carcass lying a few inches from the plughole.

From the living room window, Ellis picked out the shapes of the cattle in Scabharbour Meadow in the balmy half-dark. The accusing stares of the drowned spider's family weighed heavily on him.

"Ellis! You haven't bathed!" Mafi turned him round to face her. "Upstairs now and get in that bath."

"I bathed!"

"You're filthy!"

Denny followed Ellis up to his bedroom.

"Where is it, dear boy?" he asked.

"In the bath. I killed it. They're going to get their own back on me."

From the bathroom, his dad called out, "Ellis, you didn't kill it. Come and look."

"I don't want to look. And I did kill it."

"How can I show that you didn't kill it, if you won't look?"

Ellis hadn't killed it and in the pages of the spider book Denny found out why. "'Spiders in the bath are usually male house spiders that have fallen in while searching for females. By closing their book lungs and tracheae, they can survive in water for half an hour or more. Even spiders that appear quite dead can suddenly get up and walk when they dry out and open up their breathing systems again.'" He jabbed the page with his finger.

"You're making that up," Ellis said.

"I'm not!"

"You must be."

"I'm not!"

"Is there a picture?" Ellis asked.

"No, I promise."

Ellis read it for himself. Denny wasn't making it up. Whilst Ellis bathed, Denny sat on the toilet seat and read more to him.

"Oh my Lord, Ellis!"

"What?"

"There's a spider here they talk about and it's absolutely covered in hairs and it spits a poisonous juice on to its prey and eats them."

"Don't, Dad!"

"And, ugh! Sometimes it injects its prey with venom first to paralyse them and then eats them. When it isn't killing other creatures it kills its own."

"Don't!"

"Imagine that, Ellis, a hairy, killing, cannibalistic monster with eight eyes."

Ellis scrunched his face up. "I feel sick."

Denny growled. "Guess how big it is?"

Ellis shook his head. "Don't want to."

"The body of this savage, savage beast is ... a quarter of an inch long."

"Oh," said Ellis. "That's tiny."

"Isn't it just?"

Ellis thought on. "Really small ..." he murmured, holding his thumb and finger a quarter of an inch apart and examining the gap.

Denny put the spider book down. "Imagine how we look to a creature that tiny. Our horrible smelly flesh, our body sounding like an old boiler."

Ellis didn't intend to, but he found himself picturing Ted Heath sitting in a cellar eating chips and smoking cigarettes and drinking Tizer and burping and farting and scratching himself.

"Ellis ..."

"Yes, Dad?"

"Do you know what 'infinite' means?"

"Sort of, not really though. I get the gist."

Ellis climbed out of the bath. Denny knelt and wrapped the towel around him and held him.

"Infinity means never-ending," Denny told him, "as big as for ever. This world is infinite and we are a tiny part of it. From space, you, Ellis O'Rourke, don't even register as a speck, but down here you and your sister are the biggest thing in the world to me. You are infinite to me: there is no part of my world that you don't touch. And yet, in the infinity of space, you and I are invisible. That's what makes the world so amazing. Do you see?"

Ellis didn't see, but it reiterated two things to him. First, that a quarter-inch-long spider really shouldn't be worth getting into a tizz over and, second, that he loved his dad more than anything in the world. More than Mafi and Chrissie put together. So he looked at his dad and said, "Yeah, I see," and dished out one of his wide-eyed smiles, the sort that makes adults feel useful.

That summer, Ellis took to standing on the compost heap until he was bitten by midges and horseflies, so that Mafi would rub cream on to his bites. When the holidays arrived, he usually chose a walk to the Rumpumps as his first excursion of the day. He tended to go alone because the Rumpumps, though it was about many things, was mainly about the train track and Ellis liked to look at trains alone and not have talking, the same way he prefers to go to the cinema alone nowadays and not discuss the film afterwards.

He had to cross the bull field on Elsa's farm to reach the Rumpumps and if the bull was on the near side of the two beech trees he didn't dare go in and the trip was aborted. He struck various deals with the gods on his approach to the field. "I promise not to think about Virginia Wade's knickers for a week if the bull can not be on the near side today ..." And, more often than not, the gods would go along with it.

In the next meadow, a cattle tunnel passed beneath the railway embankment. In the shadow of the embankment, a small stone bridge crossed a stream. This bridge, the stream, the cattle tunnel, the railway line and the surrounding copse was known by all the children in the village as the Rumpumps. Ellis didn't know why then and he doesn't now.

The harbour train between Folkestone and London

passed every fifteen minutes. The tracks chimed and vibrated and Ellis stood in the cattle tunnel to listen to the carriages pass overhead before scrambling up the embankment on to the tracks to watch the train recede.

When he took his dad to see the Rumpumps for the first time, he assured him that he never went near the line. They hung by their knees from the iron railing on the stone bridge, with the sun glistening on the upside-down stream.

"Your face is going red," Ellis said.

"Yours is purple."

Crack willow swayed in the warm August breeze and the sound of flowing water filled Ellis's head. His dad's hair was nearly in the stream and his glasses hung precariously off the bridge of his nose.

"Give in?" Ellis asked.

"Not on your nelly," said his dad.

Ellis reached for the water but his fingertips fell a few inches short.

"Dad?"

"Yup."

"Why do you go all quiet on Sunday evenings sometimes?"

"The weekends go too fast for my liking." Denny let his arms hang down too, plunging his hands and forearms into the cool water.

"Dad?"

"Uh-huh."

"Why don't you marry your secretary?"

"Her husband wouldn't like it."

"Oh," Ellis said. "I didn't know she was married."

"I didn't know you wanted me to get married."

"I don't. Don't know why I said it. I'd hate it if you got married."

"Then I promise I won't."

"You know the photograph beside your bed, of the

lighthouse and the shipwreck?"

"Yes, dear boy."

"The water in that photograph, from all those years ago, that water could be in this stream right now. It could be the same water, couldn't it?"

His dad thought about it. "In a roundabout way, yes."

"Don't you think that's amazing?" Ellis exclaimed.

"Yes, you're right, Ellis. It is rather amazing."

"In the time it took you to grow up and leave the merchant navy and meet Mum and have Chrissie and me, in all that time ..." Ellis stretched out his arms, "for all those years, the water in the photo was slooooowly coming and going in all the seas and rivers and today it ended up here. That is absolutely amazing!"

Denny's upside-down smile looked like a grimace. He felt the blood rush in his head.

"But ..." Ellis went on, "why don't you have a photograph of Mum next to your bed instead?"

Denny took his glasses off and threw water on to his face. He splashed his son and challenged him again to give up. Ellis refused.

"Then you win."

Denny heaved himself up on to the bridge. The railway lines began to chime and Ellis leapt instinctively to his feet and moved towards the tracks. Then, remembering he had a visitor, he smiled innocently at Denny and sat down again before the train roared past.

They dragged their feet through long field grass. Ellis's flares threshed against the stalks. From her bedroom window, Mafi saw in their walking a reluctance to return home, and it made them look like brothers, not father and son. They helped each other over the fence and on to the lane as a tractor passed. Denny waved to the driver.

"Who was that?" Ellis asked.

"Reardon," his dad replied.

"Reardon the farmer?"

"No, Reardon the ballet dancer who drives to the theatre on a tractor."

Ellis laughed so much he squirmed and Denny chased him home, calling him a fool.

Ellis went straight to his room and because he felt so happy he knew it would be safe to go to his shoebox, to see his mum. Inside the box were war-torn ping pong balls, Plasticraft paperweights, used Instamatic flashbulbs and Top Trump cards held together by elastic bands. From beneath these objects he took a matchbox. He slid it open and took from it a solitary slide, which he held up to the window. He held one eyelid closed and moved his open eye up close to the photograph. This slight head movement took him into an Ektachrome world, where he stands as a four year old in the back garden in Orpington. He is wearing wellington boots that reach his shorts and a mac and a thick mustard-coloured sweater. The garden is wintry and a little overgrown. The shadows of the trees are long. The grass is tingling with dew. Standing at the garden gate is Ellis's mother. She is holding her hand out to Ellis and saying something to him. She has a smile on her face. She looks happy and her expression is the embodiment of what Ellis perceives, to this day, to be beauty.

The next thing she will do is place her hand in Ellis's hand and lead him out of the garden. Whenever he returns to this scene she is waiting for him, offering to take him by the hand.

He knew from Chrissie that she had called him "Ellie". Sometimes, when he dreamed about her, it was of her voice calling "Ellie-boy ... Ellie-boy ..." But it was only her voice. He could never see her for all the sunlight glaring into his eyes. Chrissie remembered her vividly but not her death. She knew that her mum was going on holiday and then that she was very ill and that they couldn't visit her. Not even their dad could go. Then she died. Once, she asked if their mum had died of cancer and her dad nodded and said yes. Another time, when Ellis was alone with Mafi, the old lady said she had "died of adventure".

5

No matter how he worded the conversation, Denny O'Rourke felt as if he was asking his children for permission to stay out late.

"Guess where I'm calling from?"

"Where?" Ellis asked.

"Longspring Farm."

"You're so lucky! What are you doing there?"

"I'm going to stay and have supper with Mr Reardon and some of his friends, if Mafi doesn't mind holding the fort. Do you want to put her on?"

"Are you going to milk a cow or anything?"

"I hope not."

"I won a goldfish," Ellis said, in what was to him a seamless line of conversation. "I'm calling it Yootha. Can I keep it? And before you say no can I just say that do you realise I was born in 1967 and now it's 1979 and this is the first time I've ever won anything, so think about that before you say no."

The answer was yes. His dad reminded him that Chrissie had had one in Orpington.

"We've still got the fish tank, Ellis."

"Where?"

"I think I might have put it in that little cupboard in my

bedroom. We'll dig it out tomorrow."

But Ellis couldn't wait until then. He pulled his dad's bed away and yanked open the small black door. He saw the fish tank immediately. It was beyond reach and shrouded in cobwebs. He recoiled and went to the bedroom window. Felix the Cat was still running through the willow tree, getting nowhere.

If I am brave enough to get that fish tank, then my mum is in heaven, Ellis told himself.

If I'm not, she's in hell.

He crouched down to the same height as the miniature door and readied himself to step, crab-like, into the tiny cupboard. What he had to do was clear in his head. He had converted the challenge, which scared him, into a picture, which did not. He would pull the tank out into the bedroom in one swift movement. Then he'd ask Mafi to dust the cobwebs off whilst he stripped and washed.

He made his move and got a hand on the fish tank before losing his balance. Instinctively, he came up off his haunches to prevent himself from falling backwards, raised his arms to hold on to the low cupboard ceiling and discovered there was no ceiling. Curious, he extended his arm fully but still felt nothing. He looked up. High above him was the faintest hint of light and in it he thought he could make out two walls converging towards each other and, on top of them, the skeletal frame of a roof. Looking down again, he saw a switch in the gloom, the sort houses had when electricity was a new invention. He flicked it and was instantly blinded by a light bulb a few inches from his face. He looked down, and as his eyes recovered his mind made a connection between the bare bulb that had blinded him and the bare bulb that hung in the attic above his bedroom. He realised that the cupboard he was crouched in now was the bottom of the dark, bottomless well he had peered down into from the attic, the well that he had once decided went deep into the earth, possibly to Australia. Now the well was lit and he stood and looked into it, and instead of seeing the cave of magic he had once dreamt of finding through this small black door, he saw a maze of timbers draped in cobwebs which seemed to groan beneath the weight of house spiders. He detected movement by the doorframe and, despite the warnings in his head not to look, his eyes fell upon a community of *Scytodes*. He had encountered them before, on page 74 of the book. Each spider was swamped by clusters of small white growths. Ellis began to shake. His breathing became rapid and sucked the triangular cobwebs towards his face. He shut his eyes and brushed the webs away, activating silken tripwires which, his mind decided, was the scuttling towards him of a million spiders. He let out a succession of long, piercing screams until a wall of noise spewed from his mouth.

Mafi found Ellis's legs floodlit by the bare bulb and framed by the cupboard door. Unable to talk him out, she crawled inside and dragged him out. She pushed him on to Denny's bed and wrapped the sheets around his shaking body until he was curled up on his side. She held him there and he screamed until exhausted. Barely strong enough to breathe, he wiped the tears from his face and smiled bravely.

"I'm fine," he whispered.

"You're not yourself," Mafi said, stroking his hair.

This was one of those adult sayings which Ellis didn't understand.

"I am, actually ..." he corrected her, politely, then passed out.

He woke in his own bed. Denny was asleep in a chair close by. The world was perfectly quiet, the night over but the sun not yet up. Ellis's eyes came to rest, inevitably, on the attic door above him. A house spider squeezed its thick, black legs through the gap and took up position, upside down, on the ceiling overhead. The longer Ellis looked at it the less he could be sure it was there. His back tingled with sweat, his head swam in the anaesthetic of semi-consciousness and he fell back to sleep.

He woke again when his dad drew back the curtains and daylight broke into the room. The attic door and the ceiling were clear, for now at least. Ellis arched his head back on the pillow and looked at the wall separating his bedroom from his dad's. In his mind's eye, he saw through the wall and into the spider well.

"Don't worry, dear boy. I've cleaned up in there."

"If you've killed them, all the others will take revenge," Ellis said reproachfully.

Denny O'Rourke placed a finger on his son's lips.

"There's been no killing," he whispered. "Just a little dust up. They were warned; they had time to move out first. It was all quite amicable."

Ellis looked at his dad doubtfully. He'd never suspect him of lying. But he thought he was being naive.

The truce that had held firm for over a year was over. All around him, Ellis knew, there was an exodus taking place from the spider well. A colony of *Tegenaria* had taken the hatch attic. Ellis would now live in fear of rain, because it was rainfall that sent him into the hatch attic to move buckets to catch the drips. The dining room fireplace, the boiler cupboard and the pantry, all previously protected areas, were now spider zones. Worst of all, the spider hub had relocated from the well to the attic above Ellis's bedroom.

Ellis now had to raise the subject of their selling the cottage and moving on. He suspected his dad would take a few days to come round to the idea.

Things were a mess. A brief ceasefire was ruined when three spiders appeared in the corridor between Ellis's bedroom and

Chrissie's. Ellis complained bitterly but the elders insisted that those particular spiders were members of a small, unaccredited, anti-truce movement.

"How is that fair?" Ellis moaned. "You can use that excuse to get away with anything. There's only one of me! If I do something wrong, I can't blame someone else!"

The spiders took offence.

One thing we are not, Master O'Rourke, is liars.

Early in the New Year, Ellis inadvertently stepped on one of four spiders that had formed a scouting party to investigate the plausibility of moving into the landing cupboard, where toilet paper and cleaning materials were stored. Ellis argued that he hadn't seen the spider in time to avoid it.

"Seeing as you lot seem to know what I'm thinking before I do, you'll know that I'm telling the truth!"

He offered them the complete run of Mafi's garage in return for leaving the cottage. They reminded him that they had been in Mafi's garage since he burnt down the shed. If spiders could laugh, they'd have laughed at him now.

He knew that if he were to ask his dad to sweep through the cottage and clean out the spiders, not bothering to preserve them in the process, his dad would do it for him. But even as a twelve year old, Ellis sensed that a conquest of this nature would be a defeat; that to drive the spiders out would be to put out of reach the possibility of there ever being peace in his head. And sometimes, when he imagined life without the spiders, after a successful war, he got a sense of incurable emptiness.

In the spring the cobwebs became as sinister to Ellis as the spiders themselves. They were everywhere, at all times. In the grassland, in the meadows, in the woodlands surrounding the village, in the moss banks of Treasure Island, in the boggy fields around the Rumpumps. They were beside the streams and ponds and lakes. In all these places, which Ellis considered his playgrounds, they were there. He had seen them glistening in the dew and he had seen them caught in the low evening sunlight. He had seen them fluttering in the breeze. He'd seen them even if they weren't there, because he'd read about them in the book.

Chrissie was trying to be a more serious human being. She had taken to reading the papers and watching the news.

"Is it so you hope James will think you're interesting and not dump you?" Ellis asked.

James dug his elbow into Ellis's ribs. Ellis had planted himself in between Chrissie and James on the sofa, uninvited.

"No, death-breath, it's because I'm thinking of doing a journalism course."

She glanced at Denny to see if he had heard her. He was scribbling in his notebook. Chrissie had been waiting all evening for a good moment to talk to her dad. Now, she felt her lips tremble before she spoke.

"Dad?"

"Yeah?"

"Dad, please don't throw an eppie, but I was thinking I might not go away to college next month. I might do a journalism course in London instead, and stay living at home another year. You know, commute with you."

Denny O'Rourke took a sip of his tea and hid his elation in the drinking of it. Without looking up from his note-making, he said in a firm yet whispered voice, "Very sensible, my dear girl ... good idea."

Chrissie and James glanced at each other blissfully. She snuggled up against Ellis and draped an arm round him. She was often lazy and affectionate with her brother after she and James had been making love.

At the point when the newsreader said it, no one was watching the TV. Chrissie and James were looking at each other and the prospect of another year's lovemaking. Denny appeared to be reading his list but was in fact thinking joyfully of another year with his family remaining no further undone. And Ellis was using his vantage point, and the pretence of sleep, to cast an eye over the curves of his sister's maturing body. Beneath this inactivity, almost but not quite unheard, unfolded the story of two Brazilian children killed in their sleep by a *Phoneutria fera*, one of South America's deadliest wandering spiders. The spider had crawled into their bed during the day. In the footage, a mother was screaming and tearing at her hair.

"The South American wandering spider occasionally," the newsreader explained, with the pained expression he adopted for any human interest story, "turns up on our own doorstep in Europe, having hitched a ride in a consignment of bananas and surviving as long as it remains in well heated buildings."

An exceptional calm enveloped the room. The calm that is aware of an approaching storm.

"Here we go ..." Chrissie muttered.

Ellis marched out.

"That's a bloody stupid thing to say on national television," Denny O'Rourke muttered bitterly.

They found Ellis in the boiler cupboard, grappling with the thermostat.

"The heating's off," his dad assured him.

Chrissie shut the fridge door.

"Leave that open!" Ellis shouted. "We've to get the temperature down in this house." He climbed up on to the kitchen table and scoured the floor for any activity.

"I'm never getting into bed again. I want a hammock, hanging from the ceiling."

"The hammock would still be attached to the floor, Ellis, via the walls," Chrissie explained. "You can't levitate in mid-air." She saw no point in giving him false hope.

"I assure you there aren't any of those spiders here, Ellis," his dad said.

"You don't know that. It was on the news. They could be here! In the bananas! It does happen! And they eat you alive, you can see them doing it as they eat you."

Denny took Ellis in his arms and held him tight. He knew that now was not the time for science or common sense.

"Ellis, I promise you, I will not let anything bad happen to you. Do you think you are going to throw up?"

"Can't tell yet."

They wandered into the orchard, holding hands, and walked in silent, meandering shapes beneath the apple trees whilst Ellis's shivering waned. The light came on in Chrissie's bedroom. Ellis watched her draw the curtains and he wondered what it felt like to be a boy in Chrissie's room, when Chrissie wasn't your sister.

I never get spider shivers when I think about girls, Ellis thought to himself. Maybe that's the thing, maybe if I was allowed to have some sex I'd not be afraid of spiders any more.

He looked at his dad.

No, he'll never buy that.

Ellis didn't mention the Brazilian spiders again but for some weeks he wouldn't allow himself to be alone in the house. One June evening, he found his dad kneeling at the dresser in his bedroom. Denny was holding a pair of silk stockings. He laid them across his wrists and studied them. He held them to his cheek. And then the floorboards creaked beneath Ellis's feet and Denny turned with a flash of anger, which disappeared when he saw his son.

"Are they Mum's?" Ellis asked.

"Yes." Denny placed the stockings back inside the bottom drawer. "I wanted to show you them for a reason," he said, thinking on his feet. "Something amazing and very beautiful ..."

He walked out of the room to the bookcase on the landing.

"But you didn't show them to me," Ellis said, confused.

Ellis stared into the drawer. Next to the stockings was Denny's blue canvas-bound diary from his time in the merchant navy. As a three or four year old, Ellis had pestered his dad to read stories from the diary. At some point after his mother died, it occurred now to Ellis, the diary had disappeared. There was a bundle of airmail letters wedged between the pages of the diary. The letters had been written by his mum, to his dad. Ellis had caught sight of them from time to time when he was younger and had often fantasised of being allowed to search through them for mention of his own name.

Denny returned, holding the spider book. "Have you heard of denier?" he asked, pushing the drawer shut with his foot.

"What?" Ellis muttered, watching the stockings, the diary and his mother's letters disappear from view.

"The denier of a silk stocking is how they measure how fine it is," Denny said, locking the drawer and putting the key in his pocket. "Listen to this ..."

He began to read from the spider book: "'The denier of a thread is the weight in grams of a nine-kilometre length. Human hair averages about fifty denier. Silkworm silk is about one denier, meaning that a nine-kilometre length weighs just one gram. But the dragline silk of the garden spider is 0.07 denier. A strand of silk long enough to encircle the earth – about twenty-five thousand miles – would weigh twelve ounces. Yet spider silk is the strongest of all natural fibres.'"

Ellis offered no reaction.

"I think that's pretty incredible, Ellis, don't you?"

"S'pose so ..."

And although he did think it was amazing that a strand of silk that long could weigh so little, he didn't want to encourage the spider book any more. It didn't really help. He didn't need convincing that they were interesting creatures. He knew he shouldn't kill them and it was rare he ever did so knowingly. But knowing more and more about them was not helping. He was still repulsed by them, occasionally to the point of being physically ill. He wanted to fill his mind with other things. That, it seemed to Ellis, was the direction he should take.

"What happens at the top of them?" Ellis asked.

"At the top of what?"

"At the top of the legs. Where do the stockings stop?"

"They just stop. They're just held up by ... another bit of clothing," Denny offered.

Ellis persisted. "But what's there, what is actually there?"

"Well, just underwear really, Ellis. Basically, they attach to the underwear with buttons."

"No, Dad." Ellis smiled patiently. "I mean what is actually there? The lady ... at the top of the stockings, what would you find there ... on the lady?"

Denny thought how best to answer. How far to answer. He went again to the landing bookcase and returned with a volume of the encyclopaedia.

"Not another book! Why can't you just tell me?"

"Hold your horses ..." Denny searched the index and, when he found the page, he looked at his son decisively. "You mean, what does a woman's body look like?"

"I suppose so."

"Here."

Ellis looked. On the page in front of him were two black and white photographs and some very small print. One photograph had five naked men standing in a line.

They looked ridiculous, especially the two with beards, who also had hairy chests. The other photograph was of five naked women. The youngest woman was in fact a girl, probably Ellis's age. The oldest was very old. But the three in between were great, Ellis thought, staring at their breasts and at the patch of hair where their stockings would end.

I take it back, he told himself, this encyclopaedia is great. My dad is brilliant. This is the book we should be looking at. This book, not the spider book!

He made a mental note of the page number. Two hundred and fifty-two. The naked women were already making him feel a little different. All in all, different felt good.

Denny O'Rourke took a cigarette from the packet in his breast pocket and lit it with practised ease.

"Do you drive an automatic so it's easy to smoke?" Ellis asked.

Denny smiled. Only his son asked him questions like that. "No."

It was the last day of the summer term. Denny told Ellis to empty his desk and make sure he brought all his possessions home for the holiday.

"Don't leave anything behind," he emphasised.

Ellis wasn't listening. He was thinking about the startling discovery he'd made, whilst watching the previous evening's news, that the Olympic games were to be held in Moscow. He couldn't understand how the Olympics could take place in such a dangerous country full of bad people.

"Won't they try to kill everyone who goes there?"

"I mean everything, Ellis. All your art stuff and everything."

"Won't they though?"

"Ellis! Are you listening to me?"

"Yes! I said yes about five hours ago. Won't the Russians

try and kill everyone at the Olympics?"

"It's not quite like that."

Ellis floated into class. Nothing could better the end of the school year. Two months of summer in the village beckoned and, after it, the deal he and his dad had struck would finally come of age, meaning that the next time he came to school he would do so independently, cycling to Hildenborough station on his own and taking the train to Orpington and arriving at school under his own steam. By then, he'd be two months from turning thirteen. He'd be grown up and free. On the way home each day, he'd freewheel down Philpotts Lane with his hands outstretched and his head thrown back and his eyes showered by sunlight breaking through the trees, the way people cycled in films.

Ellis and two of his friends had decided that they would try alcohol for the first time. When they met in the park under the appointed tree at the start of lunch break, Ellis and Andre Heart immediately suspected that their commitment to alcoholic experimentation did not match Justin Dearly's. For, whilst they came bearing two cans each of Top Deck shandy and ten B&H between them, Justin arrived armed with a Benylin bottle into which he had mixed cognac, Scotch, port and vodka from his dad's drinks cabinet. Although the cocktail was given a comforting aftertaste by the residue cough mixture, one sip was more than enough for Ellis and Andre, who returned to supping their shandy with manful intent.

In the slow, forward-shuffling line that entered the school hall that afternoon, Ellis and Andre Heart became aware that Justin Dearly could no longer support his own bodyweight. The obese and unpopular Reverend Mr Fullah wheezed his way through an opening prayer and then the headmaster motioned for his pupils and staff to sit. As Justin Dearly lowered himself unsteadily towards the moving target that seemed to be his chair, he took the chewing gum from his mouth and placed it carefully on the seat in front of him, moments before Roddy Stockton placed his backside on it. As the headmaster spoke, Justin leant forward in his seat and whispered repeatedly into Roddy Stockton's ear, "It was me, it was me, it was me ..."

Irritation got the better of Roddy. "What was you?" he hissed.

"It was me."

"What was?"

"If you ask yourself later 'Who did that?', it was me."

"Prick!"

Speeches dragged on and the need to rid himself of the shandy in his bladder was almost more than Ellis could bear. Just as he dared to hope that the service was ending, Mr Fullah hauled himself back up to the microphone.

Ellis cursed Fullah and thought to himself, I don't believe in fat vicars, not when there's people starving in the world.

"It is with great sadness," Fullah said, "that I must inform you all of the unexpected death of one of the most long-serving figures in our school. Mr Marshall, who has been caretaker here for thirty-five years, died suddenly the night before last after a massive stroke."

The hall fell into polite silence.

"Mr Marshall will be buried on Friday," the chaplain added gravely.

"GOOD! THE MISERABLE OLD BASTARD!"

It was Justin's voice that had reverberated across the hall, bearing a telltale slur. The standing masses turned and found Ellis O'Rourke bent double holding his crotch and Andre Heart urinating into Dylan Foster's packed-lunch box. In between them, Justin Dearly slumped back on to his chair. Two members of staff wove their way towards the culprits. Then, as six hundred boys and girls sat down, Justin Dearly stood up. And moments after he stood up, he threw up, on Roddy Stockton. And as he was dragged away he smiled at Roddy Stockton and said, "That was me too."

"Sit down, Ellis," Mr Teague said.

He was a good headmaster. Everyone thought so, including Ellis. He limped a little and carried a large bundle of keys in his front trouser pocket and the net result was that you knew when he was approaching from quite a way off. When Ellis had been reported to him for singing "Friggin' in the riggin'" at the top of his voice whilst walking to class, Mr Teague had quickly recognised that Ellis had no idea what the words meant and dealt with him kindly. That was two years ago and Ellis still didn't know what the words meant.

Mr Teague pulled up a chair next to Ellis.

"Are you going to expel me?" Ellis asked.

Mr Teague shook his head ruefully. "Quite the opposite," he said. He delivered a mild warning on the perils of alcohol, then patted Ellis's shoulder and told him to enjoy his summer holiday.

"Do I have to do lines?"

"No, you don't. You just have to have a good summer."

"Oh. Ace! See you in September, sir. I'll be coming by train, on my own. How great is that!" Ellis beamed, smelling freedom.

And then, without a shadow of a doubt, Ellis saw the headmaster's bottom lip tremble, as if he was going to cry.

"I want you to take care of yourself, young man," Mr Teague said, and ushered Ellis out hurriedly.

Ellis wandered off to find Andre Heart, confused by the leniency shown him and trying to figure out what would be the opposite of being expelled.

6

Unlike most boys of his age, when Ellis decided to blank his dad completely, he could actually carry it off. Indefinitely. And this is what he did when Denny O'Rourke told him that he was going to a new school.

"But you can still cycle to school, Ellis, like we agreed," Denny offered. "From time to time, when the weather's nice, I mean. You can cycle to your heart's content when the conditions are safe, but not in winter."

"That's not the point! And it doesn't matter if it's raining or snowing, I'm going to cycle on my own every day, every single day! I will never want a lift from you. You promised me I could catch the train alone to school in Orpington when I was thirteen. You promised and you're a liar. I am never going to talk to you again because there's no point because you're a liar."

Denny expected Mafi to understand.

"When I made that agreement with him, I meant it. But it's come round too fast. He's too young. He's not ready."

"You mean you're not," she said.

Chrissie was indignant on Ellis's behalf and looked for an opportunity to make her point. She found it in the pages of the spider book.

"This is interesting," she announced over dinner. "Baby spiders go ballooning! It's on page one hundred and fifty-four." She looked her dad in the eye. "It's how they leave home."

"Don't read at the table," Denny muttered.

She ignored him and read aloud: "'Dispersal of many spiderlings involves simply wandering off, or finding the nearest unoccupied space which will support a web. However, for moving quickly to a completely new area, spiderlings go

76

by air. This aerial dispersal – known as "ballooning" – is most effectively carried out when warm days follow a cold spell and air currents are rising. The spider moves to a relatively high point, points the abdomen skywards, and lets out strands of silk from the spinners. Success comes when they are carried upwards.'"

Denny snatched the book away. "I've read that bit too." He read aloud. "'The down side to ballooning,'" he repeated the words with emphasis, "the *down side* ... is being eaten alive by swallows, caught in the webs of other spiders, frozen several thousand metres up, drowned in the sea or lakes or landing in other unfavourable environments.'"

"Wow," said Mafi, missing the point, "isn't that amazing and wonderful, Ellis?"

"No!" Denny snapped. "It's dangerous, that's the point. Lots of these spiders die when they leave the nest."

"What nest, Dad?" Chrissie taunted him. "We weren't talking about birds ..."

"Oh, belt up for once, Chrissie!"

The venom in Denny's voice was foreign and excessive.

"That book suits you when it suits you, doesn't it?" Chrissie said.

Denny gritted his teeth. His face reddened. "I'm just trying to protect you both and all you've got is smart-alec comments," he muttered.

"Protect us from what? Look at us! We're so bloody safe it aches. We don't do anything or go anywhere!"

"That's exactly what—" Denny stopped himself.

He stared at the tablecloth. Then he marched across the room and rammed the spider book into the waste bin and walked out.

Ellis placed the book under a stack of Chrissie's LPs, to flatten it out. He woke next morning curled up under the bed sheet and drenched in sweat. He could feel the weight of thousands of tiny spiders on top of the sheet. Determined not to break his vow of silence by calling out for his dad, he lay motionless until Mafi found his small, coiled shape in the bottom corner of the bed and realised that he had visitors. She climbed in under the sheet and lay alongside him.

"They've gone," she whispered.

Together they looked through the cotton sheet at the bedroom window framing squares of sunlight. Ellis cuddled against his great-aunt and fell asleep for a few more minutes. When he woke, the sheet was away from them and it was a beautiful summer's day. He smiled at Mafi and whispered, "Thanks."

But to his father, he remained mute, until Reardon's arrival, ten days later.

"I was thinking," Reardon said, "he might like to spend time on the farm. Maybe it'll help him forget his worries."

I don't have worries! Ellis protested. He was spying from the top of the stairs.

"What about spiders on the farm?" Mafi asked.

"I'm confident he'll be distracted by bigger creatures," Reardon replied, his face lit by a compassionate smile. "He must come! It'll do him the world of good. We'll work him to the bone, of course! That's what this is about, child labour!"

The vitality in Reardon that Denny O'Rourke admired was precisely what scared Ellis. Nevertheless, he wanted to go to the farm. He wanted it so much he was willing to say so.

When he stepped on to the track that led to Longspring Farm for the first time, Ellis felt that a new life was beginning.

He passed the head herdsman's house at the entrance gate and walked through an avenue of lime trees. White-painted cast-iron railings ran at a slant between the track and the farmhouse. Dried orange lichen peppered the Wealden brickwork and moss clung to the peg tiles. The farmhouse was old and perfectly square, with a large lawn to one side which ran down to a pond, and an oast roundel and cooling barn to the other side, where the sweet smell of honeysuckle laced the afternoon.

Ellis glimpsed movement behind the hay barn and headed up there, having no better idea of where he was meant to go. Tractor wrecks waited obediently in the stone pens of the old cowshed. Next to it, the machinery and piping of the modern milking shed hummed and clanked. Ellis waited a while in the foldyard, hoping to be seen. The plinths and crumbling walls of an old granary jutted out from a manure heap, like bones from a burial mound. A dragonfly darted back and forth above crusts of manure. Beyond it, in the pasture, there were dozens of butterflies, mostly Common Blue. The remnants of last year's hay lay low in the barn. A pitchfork stabbed into a bale had a child's T-shirt draped over it. Ellis breathed in the musty smell of dried cow dung. He shut his eyes. A breeze drifted towards his ear and curled itself into a weightless seashell bearing sounds of cattle in the yards and tractors in the fields. He stood in rapture. When he opened his eyes dizzy speckles of light danced in front of him and dissipated to reveal blue sky above. This was heaven and he knew, he knew with twelve-year old certainty, that he wanted to be here for ever.

"Poof."

Ellis looked round. A boy emerged from behind a large steel milk tank. The boy was similar in age to Ellis. Similar, too, in height, build and hair colour. He had wellington boots on and jeans but no shirt. He was skinny but muscular. His hands were grubby and most of his fingers had plasters on them. His arms and face and neck were tanned but his torso was pale in the sun. He made sure Ellis was watching and lifted open the lid of the tank. He ladled out a small pool of milk and nodded to himself expertly. He checked the dials on the side of the tank, furrowed his brow knowingly, and wandered off.

"Come on," he said, with a swagger.

Ellis ran a few paces to get alongside the boy.

"You're not really a poof," the boy said.

"I know I'm not," Ellis replied firmly.

They sat in the hay barn on the low bank of bales.

"When the hay is in and stacked up the sides," the boy said, "we'll cross the girder, all the way across the barn." The boy sized Ellis up. "You'll be strong enough, no problem."

Ellis gazed upwards. A steel girder ran across the width of the barn in the apex of the roof, fifty feet above them.

"You'll be fine," the boy repeated.

Ellis was not convinced.

"If not," the boy muttered, "well ..." and he slapped one hand flat on the ground and made a squelching sound.

The boy stretched his legs out and took a small rusty tin from his front pocket. Inside were loose tobacco and some papers. Ellis looked out across the fields, framed by the walls of the yawning hay barn, but he kept one eye on the boy to see how he was making the cigarette. The boy rolled it expertly, put it between his lips and handed Ellis the tin.

"I don't know how to," Ellis said.

The boy took the cigarette from his mouth and handed it to Ellis. Ellis placed it between his lips and watched, openly this time, as the boy rolled another. They rested back on the bales and Ellis copied the boy's nonchalant exhalation of smoke.

The fields nearest to them were flat and gave way to layers of hillside, which stacked up towards Ide Hill. There were cottages dotted amongst these rolling fields and, in the distance, a dilapidated barn at Reardon's boundary. Ellis felt dizzy and his mouth was dry but he liked the look of the cigarette between his fingers.

"Tim," the boy said.

Ellis copied the boy's detached tone. "Ellis."

A bull raised its head above the half-door of the oast roundel. The boys watched it as they smoked. Ellis wanted to ask Tim if the bull had a name, but he couldn't decide if this would be a mistake. It wasn't a pet, after all. Then again, if it did have a name, Ellis ought to know it.

"Let's go," Tim said, and headed purposefully out of the barn. Ellis took off his T-shirt and hung it on the same pitchfork as Tim's, then ran to catch him up.

"Never ever leave a gate open," Tim said, without breaking stride. "Reardon will kill you."

"I never do," Ellis boasted. "Has the bull got a name?"

"Yeah," Tim said earnestly. "He's called Bob."

I knew it would have, Ellis congratulated himself.

"And all the cows are called Daisy, you prat," Tim added. "Of course the bull hasn't got a name."

They reached a large bell that hung from a piece of rope on a gate. Tim took the bell and led Ellis up to a plateau of rich pasture where Jersey cattle grazed above a ribbon of small hills not visible from the farmyard. Tim rang the bell, the boys waited their arms and the docile herd wandered obediently down to the farm.

Reardon was in the yard with Michael Finsey, his herdsman. The men saw the herd into the milking shed. Tim led Ellis through a metal door into a narrow, raised concrete alleyway where a wall of metal bars separated them from the cattle.

"You don't want to get squashed between these ugly fuckers!" Tim shouted, above the roar of the milking machines. "That's why we have to stand here."

Reardon and Michael Finsey pushed and punched the cattle into their bays and attached the pumps, using their shoulders to prise the cows apart. When he wasn't using it to prod the beasts, Reardon wedged his stick into his wellies to free up both hands.

Later, the farmer walked the herd with the boys. The heifers grazed the fields furthest from the farm and the dairy herd were kept on the pasture nearest to the milking sheds.

"A beast cannot graze if its feet and teeth are no good. If they seem bony, check the feet and teeth. If they hang back when you herd them in, check their udders for a thing called mastitis because they can get sore from the milking. A healthy cow has a straight back and a large udder."

Then he was gone, marching back towards the farmhouse as if prolonged exposure to children would bring him out in a rash.

I will never leave my dad, Ellis told himself, as he watched Reardon go. If my dad was left all alone, he'd become like that. I will never leave his side.

The boys put their T-shirts on and sat again in the hay barn. Ellis looked proudly at the grazes on his arms and the grime on his hands. His skin smelled of cattle. They drank fresh milk and ate bread and jam. The black cherry jam was cold from Reardon's fridge and it was sweet and spread thick on crusty white bread. Food had never tasted so good to Ellis in his life.

Tim Wickham's parents lived in a former tied cottage on the northern edge of Reardon's land. The steep slopes of the garden were covered in black knapweed and wild dog roses tumbled to a fast-flowing brook. The grass was lush and long, especially in the shade of the apple trees, where a hammock was slung. The ground about the brook was never dry, not even in summer. The only flat piece of garden was alongside the lane where an unkempt medlar tree stooped towards croquet hoops lost in the grass.

Mr Wickham was a teacher and he always wore the same brown wool blazer and light green shirt, whatever the season. He was always nice but rarely laughed. Tim's mum was gregarious and loving. She deliberately embarrassed her son by kissing him on the lips in front of Ellis. Tim called her "mad" when she did this and they both laughed about it. Ellis watched in awe.

Ellis liked Mrs Wickham a great deal but thought it strange that she never offered him anything to eat or drink. There were no biscuits or cake or bread or fruit for them when they got in from the farm. Ellis would have noticed this anyway, but was all the more aware of it because since going to the farm he had been perpetually hungry. At least, it was either working on the farm or staring inertly at the naked women in the *Encyclopaedia Britannica*. One of these was giving him an appetite.

In the long grass by the brook, the boys talked about girls. The little that Tim had glimpsed was of his mum. She sometimes walked around the house in just a bath towel, he said, and every now and then he had got a peep when she was rewrapping it round her body.

"That's so good," Ellis sighed.

"Have you seen your sister doing it ever, with whatsisname?" Tim asked.

"Not actually doing it, I don't think. But messing around. No, I don't think I have."

"I reckon you'd know," Tim said.

They closed their eyes. Ellis felt the blades of grass pushing against his skin and wondered exactly what he hadn't seen Chrissie and James doing. He pictured Mrs Wickham taking him upstairs and explaining to him that the way young boys find out about women is for their new best friend's mum to get into bed with them and show them. He imagined Mrs Wickham taking off her clothes and climbing into her bed and telling Ellis to climb in beside her for a cuddle. Ellis fell asleep with his head pressed against her skin and her fingers drawing lines over his clothed body. When he woke, the grass was cold in shadow. He was alone. He went into the kitchen. Mrs Wickham was cooking supper. Her husband was drinking a glass of water at the kitchen table and reading the post. The cottage was dark inside. None of the glorious sunshine of that first summer at Reardon's seemed to make it through the windows.

"Tim's taking a bath before supper," Mrs Wickham said.

"I fell asleep," Ellis muttered, disorientated and embarrassed.

Mrs Wickham ruffled his hair, took his hand and led him into the sitting room. She sat Ellis down on an old sofa with a pattern of faded ivory flowers against pale green. The sofa cushions were deep and swallowed him up.

"You make yourself at home."

She planted a kiss on his forehead and shut the door behind her. Ellis looked at the room. There was no TV and there were no books. The ornate moulding in the centre of the ceiling had been painted carelessly. The room was dark and hollow. He wondered if they ever used it. The black slate fire surround looked as if it belonged to a room twice the size of the house. On the chimney breast there were brown photographs of faded people. From beyond the closed door came the sound of the Wickhams' dinner time. Cutlery scraping on plates and Mrs Wickham's laugh. Ellis slung his legs over the arm of the sofa, cuddled the cushions and fell asleep again. When he woke the next morning he was in his own bed and his stomach was churning with hunger. Mafi was sitting by his side.

"How did I get home?" he whimpered.

"Mr Wickham drove you home and carried you up to bed and you never stirred for a minute," she whispered.

He smiled and turned on to his side, clasping Mafi's hand.

"I've never known a boy sleep like you, Ellis O'Rourke."

Chrissie's bike was leaning against the front of the cottage.

She sat on the front step drinking a cup of coffee. Ellis poked his head out of the window above her. He knew from her sunglasses, bikini top and skirt that she was going to see James at the reservoir.

"If you're trying to get a look at my tits from up there you're a sad, pathetic bastard," she said, without turning.

"What tits?"

"Cheeky boy!" she muttered, pretending to care.

Ellis ran downstairs and joined her on the step.

"More coffee, pesky rat!" She held her mug out to him.

"Yes, your grace." He came back with her mug filled and with a glass of milk for himself. "I've seen better tits than yours anyway," he mentioned, casually

"I'm happy for you, earthling." She soaked up the sun.

"Are you going to see James?"

"*Sí.*"

"Are you going to be a journalist?" he asked, following his own, weaving train of thought.

"I'm going to train to be one, from September."

"So you're not leaving home, you're going to be a commuter?"

"I'm not leaving home."

"Are you absolutely sure Dad doesn't mind? I think he was looking forward to it just being me and him and Mafi living here."

"Nice try, piss-face," she said, delivering an effortless slap to the back of his head. "He's over the moon about it 'cos I'm his favourite child."

"You're his favourite daughter."

She gave Ellis a lift to Longspring Farm on her bike. He had, after all, brought her coffee. Gary Bird was waiting for him at the gate where Treasure Island Woods ended and the farm track began.

"Where have you been?" Gary asked accusingly.

"Don't know," Ellis mumbled.

"I've been waiting for you at Treasure Island every day!" Gary yelled and marched off.

"What was that about?" Chrissie asked.

"Dunno."

"Ellis! You can't just ditch friends like that. You go and say sorry!"

Ellis watched his sister cycle away. He thought of doubling back through the woods to find Gary and apologise. He could ask Reardon if Gary could come with him to the farm and then, from tomorrow, they'd go together and both be friends with Tim. He hesitated, torn between turning left into the woods or right to the farm. He squinted against the sunlight and headed up the farm track, ignoring the bad feeling in his stomach and aware that for some reason he didn't want to share with Gary Bird the new world beyond the lime trees. Everything was coming together on that blazing hot morning. The naked bodies of women lined up for him on a page at home, the smells of cattle and diesel drifting under his nose at the farm, the sight of a rolled cigarette between his fingers, the dark red of his own blood scabbing painlessly on hairline cuts across his forearm and making him feel so very grown up, the feeling of straw prickling his back, the bikini tops his sister would be wearing for the next couple of months, the satisfaction of herding cattle into the yard and the sensation of belonging at Longspring Farm.

Then, Ellis felt a new sensation. Rather, he felt a series of them in quick succession. First, a stinging sense of rock-hard impact across his face. Then a howling noise pouring through his ears, joined by the illusion of ice-cold fluid trickling into his throat. Then a scorching numbness across one eye socket. Finally, a piercing pain at the bridge of his nose and the sound of cartilage squelching as he instinctively and blindly pushed his nose back into place.

He lay with his head in the dust and shit, listening to

the storm in his ears abate, feeling his heartbeat roar out of control. He saw the world through liquid eyes but he wasn't crying. He knelt up and rubbed his face. There was blood and snot streaked across the back of his hand. He blinked his eyes to clear them of fluid and saw Gary Bird walking away down the farm track, a large piece of wood in his hand. He climbed over the gate and disappeared into Treasure Island Woods.

Ellis hid all day, knowing that when his dad saw him he'd not let him out alone again. At the hospital they told Denny that if Ellis had been brought in earlier they'd have been able to do a better job of fixing his nose. The doctor asked Ellis his name and what day of the week it was.

"He doesn't necessarily know that at the best of times," Chrissie said.

Ellis refused to reveal who had hit him.

"I can't remember a thing about it!" he insisted.

Denny banned Ellis from the farm. Then, after rehearsing his lines with Ellis in a phone call, Tim appeared at the cottage with his father.

"It was me, Mr O'Rourke ... me and Ellis were mucking around and I belted him with a plank of wood accidentally. He wouldn't let me tell 'cos he thought I'd be in trouble."

Denny looked to Tim's father, who shrugged.

"We weren't fighting. It was just messing about and I overdid it a bit ..."

"You did a bit, didn't you?" Denny said. "Why don't you go up and see Ellis in his room?"

Tim ran upstairs.

"I'd like to believe it," Denny said.

"Then do," Robert Wickham replied.

Having shut his bedroom door, Ellis opened the encyclopaedia at page 252 and laid the five naked women down on the bed.

"Fucking lovely," Tim said, admiringly.

Ellis took a piece of paper from the desk in the corner of

his room and laid it over the page. He had cut a square out of it so that the girl and the oldest woman were hidden, leaving only the three women in the centre visible.

"That's better," Tim muttered.

"Yes," Ellis said, expertly.

Ellis put Chrissie's Led Zep 3 album on, glanced in the mirror to admire his facial injuries and leant out of the window. Mafi disappeared round the corner of the cottage, working her way along the flowerbeds with a weeding fork. The boys shared a cigarette and looked out across the village at their known universe.

"Page 252 ..." Tim reflected, dragging lazily.

"Page 252 ..." Ellis confirmed.

7

Bright green grasshoppers appeared in the meadow on Philpotts Lane where Ellis went when he wanted to be alone. He could lay himself and his bike down there and disappear from view. The edge of the meadow was flanked by durmast oak and when he saw the green acorns he knew that it was time to start at his new school.

Ellis knew kids who liked school and kids who didn't. He and Tim were kids who didn't. Their cycle ride home was rushed and breathless. It took them twenty minutes to change out of their uniform and meet at the farm.

Only an encounter with Chloe Purcell on Oak Lane was worth delaying for. Chloe Purcell had been at Ellis's school in Orpington until she was eleven, when her parents put her into the convent school. The bus dropped her in the old high street from where she walked two miles home along Oak Lane, in the deep blue of her convent sweater. She had short, straight black hair and a small brown birthmark beneath her left eye. She was quiet and plain and unextraordinary but in the first weeks of that school year Ellis saw that she was the most beautiful girl in the world and decided he loved her. He felt excited and terrified whenever he saw her up ahead on the lane.

On the day that Ellis and Tim had discovered they would be at the same school they were so ecstatic they invented a dance of celebration, which they called "The Goose" because when they performed it in the farmyard the geese got agitated and attacked them. They celebrated because they loved being together, but when Ellis saw Chloe Purcell on Oak Lane he always wished, just for these few minutes, that Tim wasn't with him.

However early in the morning Ellis and Tim set out to pick autumn mushrooms, there was always a light coming from the kitchen at Longspring Farm. They found parasol mushrooms on the path leading into Eight Acre Wood. They picked eight large stems and wrapped them in a piece of cloth. The temperature dropped as they walked into a dip in the fields. Emerging from it, they saw the farmhouse caressed by a slow-drifting, head-high mist.

"Ghosts ..." Ellis muttered.

He watched the ghosts drag themselves across the farm buildings. He sucked the cold air in and it tasted of dewy pasture. Reardon emerged from the milking shed, crossed the farmyard and headed into the flat fields where his Highland herd were. Today, he would move them on to the high pasture and bring the heifers down alongside the bullpens for mating.

It was best to avoid Reardon first thing. He was notoriously grumpy until noon, even on a good day. It took that long for the night to leave him. It was at night that the pain in his shattered leg returned, darting into his spine and filling his head with worries and the memory of two women who had loved him but whom he hadn't wanted to marry. He slept under the same heavy bedding he had known as a child, in a single bed tucked into the corner of a cavernous, sloping bedroom. He had been on the farm for forty years and every single night of them he had felt that he was struggling against gravity, crushed under the weight of bedding and solitude. He didn't know that he could change that. He didn't know how acceptable it would be to reserve for his own life some of the enthusiasm he showed for other people's. It would not be selfish. It would not be immodest. It would not be vain or too earthly. It would not offend God. But this kind, inspirational man did not know that. He knew how to farm. He knew how to tell a story in a delightful way. He knew how to inspire other people into action. He knew how to talk gregariously with people and never allow the conversation to centre on himself. He knew that to read the poems of John Clare and look at the paintings of Constable, Piper and the Wyeths brought him profound pleasure and helped to form his faithful image of what heaven might be. But he didn't know that to buy a double bed and to level the floor around it and to purchase lightweight bedding would be to transform the nature of his nights' sleep. He didn't know that it might change the dreams that plagued him and the moods that were their legacy.

This morning, he appeared weary. Ellis felt a short, painless stab of affection for him and decided to leave some mushrooms for his breakfast. The kitchen was warm. A half-drunk mug of tea stood lonely on the table. Ellis washed the mug up and put it on top of the Rayburn next to the teapot. He unfolded the cloth rag and took out four of the mushrooms. He washed them and dragged the skin off with a blunt knife. He sliced them and left them on the bread board next to the hotplate.

The sun struggled to burn through. When its first beams

perforated the sky, the mist departed, looking over its shoulder at Ellis with a vow to return.

Ellis shrugged nonchalantly. "It doesn't bother me if you do."

Denny's secretary found him sitting with his back to his desk, gazing out at the pedestrians on Jermyn Street. He heard the teacup rattle and said, without turning, "Do you know what I had for breakfast this morning?"

She replied, of course, that she didn't.

"I had fresh wild mushrooms on buttery toast. They were picked for me by my son and cooked for me by my daughter. Can you imagine a more marvellous breakfast for a man to have?"

And she thought to herself, Yes, I can. One shared with your wife. But she smiled kindly at his back and said, "There couldn't be one."

And then she left him and returned to her desk in the entrance hall, moved, because Mr O'Rourke never spoke like that. He was genial but private. He was kind to his staff but they felt they didn't know him. He could name their children but rarely spoke of his own, fearing that to admit how much he loved them would be to risk losing them too.

On Sunday evenings, Denny would sit with Mafi in her living room. They smoked and talked about the children, the village, the state of things. Occasionally, perhaps two or three times a year, when she was feeling bullish, Mafi would tell her nephew to find himself a girlfriend and he would ignore her. From time to time, in the silences they were happy to share, Denny had said, "I'm so glad you're here with us, Mafi." She respected him more than any man she'd known. And she loved him dearly.

"All of this is a bonus," she would tell her friends in the village. "A life I hardly deserve."

Ellis would join Denny and Mafi and tell them what was going on at Longspring. It was the only subject he talked about and Denny loved to listen.

"Did you know that you get paid more money for the milk in winter than in summer?"

"No ..."

"Well, you do, so that's why they had the calves last month so that there's tons of milk now."

"That's good ..."

"And do you know why we didn't let any of the herd into the east fields in July?"

"No, I don't ..."

"Because we were letting the grass grow for hay and if the cows had been in there they'd have eaten the grass."

"I see ..."

"You can't put them in and just ask them not to graze."

"No, I suppose you can't."

"Guess why there's some ploughed fields at Longspring even though we do milk?"

"Fodder?"

"How did you know that?"

"Just a guess ... what are you and Reardon growing for fodder?"

"And Tim and Michael Finsey," Ellis reminded him. "Turnips and maize for silage. Do you know what silage is?"

"I do, yes."

"Mafi?"

"I do, too."

"Oh. Do you have to be born on a farm to run one or can you save up and buy one?" Ellis asked.

"You'd need to go to agricultural college before you do anything," Denny said. "You could go to Wye or Hadlow. They're nearby."

"When could I go?"

"After your A levels."

"Not after my O levels?"

"They'll expect good A levels."

Ellis slumped and sighed. "Even with all the work I'm doing on the farm?"

"Yes," his dad confirmed, "even with."

"You might want to try other things out, or see the world first, before you decide," Mafi said.

Her words hung in the room without finding a comfortable place to sit. Denny O'Rourke stood up. "I've things to do," he said, and left, with an expression which resembled a smile without amounting to one.

"In next to no time you'll be a teenager," Mafi said, as if shocked by the fact.

"I'm in love with Chloe Purcell," Ellis responded.

"And I bet she's in love with you, too."

"No way," Ellis fired back. "Fat chance. Girls don't go for me."

"Well," Mafi sympathised, "you're only young."

"But so are they," Ellis said helplessly.

They brought the dairy herd in at the beginning of November. A sea of breathing Jersey brown flooded the yard and a steam cloud levitated above it. The willow lines were pollarded and Tim and Ellis saw a fox jump from a hiding place inside the rotten middle of one of the trunks. They bundled up the branches and watched Terry Jay split them into three-sided stakes for hedge laying. Terry showed the boys how to set the stakes out an elbow-arm's length apart through the hedge line. He pleached the hedges through the winter. The game crops were well out of sight of the farm and Tim and Ellis ran amok there amongst the kale and root artichoke, scaring straggling pheasant into flight and throwing stones at them once they were airborne.

The calves were released from their weaning pens into

pasture to be fattened as steers. Bullfinches gathered on the phone lines without ever venturing too near to the farm. The boys were allowed into the milking shed for the first time and given the job of hosing down the udders prior to milking. Afterwards, Michael Finsey ordered the boys to wait for him in the yard where three heifers stood in pens. The pens had staggered brick walls on each side, which Tim and Ellis climbed like steps until they were standing on the back wall above the heifers. Michael and Reardon pulled a hired mating bull into the yard using poles hooked to the ring in the bull's nose. Climbing the staggered walls of the pen, they hauled the bull up on to the first heifer's back.

"You lucky lady, you lucky little thing!" Michael Finsey cackled.

Steam poured from the bull's nose as it arched its huge bulk and pumped in and out of the beast beneath it. The expression on the heifer's face turned from alarm to indifference.

"She looks bored stiff!" Michael shouted. "Better get used to that look, boys!" He roared with laughter.

Ellis was open-mouthed. As the bull was manoeuvred from one heifer to the next, pints of semen poured from its gross member on to the yard.

"Oh my giddy aunt," Tim muttered, incredulous.

The bull rammed itself into the second heifer.

"Foreplay's over!" Michael cried out. "We'll bypass the clit seeing as they charge by the hour!"

Tim and Ellis shrugged at each other inquisitively. Whatever a clit might be, it seemed they were bypassing it. Michael's lungs collapsed into nicotine-coated laughter. Within ten minutes, Reardon was returning the bull to the oast barn with all three heifers seen to. Michael, Tim and Ellis skated back and forth across the semen-coated yard floor until Tim was physically sick from laughing and he and Ellis decided they should call it a day.

"Sick and semen stew!" Michael Finsey yelled out, as the two boys disappeared across the fields. "The rats will feast tonight!"

A graphic account of the bull's sexual performance, which Tim Wickham included in his creative writing project the following Wednesday, and its faithful reproduction of Michael Finsey's vernacular, placed Tim in a two-hour detention on the afternoon of Ellis's birthday. Ellis cycled home alone and, seeing the blue of Chloe Purcell's school uniform up ahead, moved down a couple of gears to buy himself some thinking time. He attempted to compose something fascinating to say but arrived alongside her tongue-tied as ever.

"Hello," he ventured.

"You alone today?" she asked.

"Yup."

"Want to come home for some tea?" she said casually.

They had to remove their shoes at the front door, which was a new one on Ellis. Chloe's mum remembered Ellis from the school in Orpington. Ellis didn't remember Mrs Purcell. He had expected her to be serious and religious and not much fun because she had sent her daughter to a convent school, but she wasn't like that at all. Maybe, he told himself, he had this convent thing all wrong.

"Is it like St Trinian's actually?" he asked.

"Is what like St Trinian's?" Mrs Purcell asked back.

He looked at Chloe. "Your school."

Chloe smiled. That, Ellis came to discover, was how she laughed, by allowing a delicate smile to trespass on to her face. To Ellis, it was a fireworks display.

Things like smiling and laughing are all relative to what someone's like the rest of the time, he told himself years later, after finally witnessing Chloe's silent, compact sexual ecstasy.

"I blooming well hope it's not like St Trinian's!" Mrs Purcell said.

Ellis really liked her. She was a proper mum. It would be great if he and Chloe got married.

"Mafi says 'blooming' a lot too," he said. "She's my great-aunt and she lives with us."

They drank tea round the kitchen table. Ellis said what a nice house they had and asked where Chloe's two younger sisters were. They were at ballet. It immediately worried Ellis that Chloe might consider it an embarrassment being married to a farmer. Their children were hardly going to want to be picked up from ballet in a muddy truck.

Chloe and her mother watched the ebb and flow of thoughts and expressions criss-cross Ellis's face.

"What if you don't like farm smells?" Ellis said, unaware he was thinking aloud.

"What if I do?" Chloe replied.

"Do what?" he asked, bemused.

"I love farm smells," Chloe announced.

"Why do you ask, Ellis?" Mrs Purcell asked.

Ellis carefully steered his lips away from telling Mrs Purcell he loved her daughter, even though a part of his brain was threatening to blurt the words out.

"I work on a farm and I'm going to be a farmer."

"You're lucky," Chloe told him.

"Yeah ..." He adored her.

"What sort of thing do you get up to there?" Mrs Purcell asked.

"All sorts, bringing the cows in for milking mainly, throwing out bales into the fields from the flat-bed, mending fences ..." Ellis chose randomly.

"Sounds very exciting," Mrs Purcell said.

"It's brilliant," Ellis beamed, and encouraged by the blissfulness of being in Chloe Purcell's kitchen on his birthday, he forgot to disengage his mouth from the free-fall of pictures in his mind.

"We just recently rented a bull to make the heifers pregnant and its thing was the length of a broom handle, but thicker, much thicker. And once it started to, you know ..."

They shook their heads in unison.

"... once it started to ... once the spunk started pouring out, it didn't stop. It just went from heifer to heifer gushing out this stuff."

Mrs Purcell's mouth had dropped open.

"Poor cows," she muttered.

Chloe sat back and flashed Ellis an adoring smile and replayed in her head the sound of the words "gushing spunk" being said in front of her mother. Ellis interpreted her smile as a signal to continue.

"When Reardon had gone we went skating on the concrete in the farmyard 'cos it was so slippy with all the stuff."

Mrs Purcell slid the biscuit tin firmly towards Ellis. "Shall we talk about something else now?"

Chloe stepped in. "Let's talk about the barn dance. Would you like to come to it with us?" she asked.

"Yes, please," Ellis said immediately.

And in the living room, filled by the fragrance of Lent lilies in a vase, Ellis felt the foreign softness of a deep carpet beneath his every step as Mrs Purcell played the piano and Chloe taught him how to dance for a barn dance. Ellis said nothing. Now that Chloe was taking hold of his hand, now that she was putting her hands on his shoulders to position him, now that he was so close to her that he could smell the fragrance of her sweater, now that all these things had happened, he could not speak. He was a mute in paradise. The afternoon became a succession of smiles and nods and piano notes and his voice failed him.

It was dark outside when they stopped so Mrs Purcell told Ellis she would drive him home.

"We can put your bike in the back."

Ellis looked at her as if she were daft. "Put a bike in a car?"

"It's no trouble."

"No thank you, Mrs Purcell. I cycle home, always."

"Isn't it a bit dark?"

He shook his head. "It's just winter," he explained, unnecessarily. "I hate cars. I like bikes and trains, and that's all."

"What about planes?" Chloe asked.

"I haven't been on one," Ellis said. "We could go on one," he added, then felt like a fool for doing so.

"As long as you're sure you'll be OK," Chloe's mum said.

"More than OK." Ellis beamed. "From the top of Hubbards Hill you can see lights all the way to the Crowborough Beacon. I bomb down there like a bullet."

That wasn't exactly what Mrs Purcell wanted to hear but Ellis was already putting on his shoes and coat. He wanted to get out of the house as quickly as possible because he felt like an idiot for saying that he and Chloe could go on a plane together and he realised that an invitation to a barn dance was not a declaration of love. Maybe she went to barn dances every week and each time with a different boy, or maybe he'd get there and find he was one of six or seven boys she'd invited.

I don't like this, he thought to himself as he opened the front door. I don't know where I stand or what I think and I don't like it one bit.

He wanted to be at the farm right now, doing physical jobs and saying nothing. That's what I really like, he told himself. Not girls.

As he bent over to tuck his trousers into his socks, his coat swung forward and engulfed his head comically. His heart sank.

I look like a tool, he cursed.

Chloe pulled the coat gently off his face, and as she did so she whispered in his ear.

"I'd love to go on a plane with you, Ellis O'Rourke."

And in that moment, Ellis's birthday flipped back over on to its stomach. Girls were the best thing he'd ever discovered, even better than the farm, better than Tim, better than anything he could think of. If we got married at sixteen, he told himself, we could move into Mrs Purcell's house. We'd meet on Oak Lane after school and walk home arm in arm and in the morning I'd come down to breakfast and everyone else in her family would know we'd been in bed together all night.

"Is your dad grumpy in the mornings?" Ellis asked.

Chloe looked at him curiously. "No, he's nice." She smiled her disarming smile.

"Thank goodness for that," Ellis said, somewhat seriously.

Eleven days later, Chloe's father opened his front door to a polite-looking young man.

"You must be Ellis."

"Hello, Mr Purcell."

Mrs Purcell appeared. "Hello, Ellis."

"Hello, Mrs Purcell. I'm sorry I said spunk last time."

When they took their places for each new dance, Chloe pressed her little finger into the soft flesh at the base of Ellis's thumb as a signal for him to start. He spent each dance writing conversations in his head but when the music stopped the words had gone. The more he tried to think of something, the further he got from saying anything. They stopped for a cup of tea and sat on metal-framed chairs with canvas seats, on the perimeter of the dance floor.

You only get these chairs in church halls, Ellis thought to himself, and he opened his mouth to share this observation with his future wife before deciding that it wasn't interesting enough.

"Well, what do you want to do now, go outside for a walk or have another dance?" Chloe asked, threading her arm through his.

Ellis wanted to go for a walk, with her arm threaded through his. He wanted it very much. But, paralysed by guessing what she wanted to do, he managed only to mumble, "I don't mind. Dance, if you like."

And she danced heavily, the light stolen from her face by the indifference of this boy who had declined her offer to step outside. And he, he avoided catching her eye because he felt suddenly so ugly and idiotic for his inability to speak to her. She went to the bathroom before they left and stared accusingly in the mirror at her plainness. He walked her home and asked himself why someone as beautiful as her would have asked him out in the first place.

When I get home I'll look at my map of the world, he told himself, and tomorrow morning I'll go back to the farm and I'll forget all about tonight. I'm not cut out for this.

They said goodbye outside her house. He got on his bike and she watched him disappear.

Neither Tim nor Ellis was sure what the goat-lady did apart from minding Reardon's small herd of British Tappenburgs.

"It can't be a full-time job," Ellis said.

"Search me," Tim agreed.

She lived alone in a shabby cottage, tied to the farm, and seemed to know nobody. The cottage was low and dark and in summer it disappeared beneath creeping ivy. It backed on to the Great Field where Reardon grew wheat and barley as feed. Alongside the cottage was a deep-furrowed track linking the Great Field to the lane. On the other side of the track was a ruined cart shed which Tim and Ellis called the sun barn because there was so much roof and cladding missing that the sun shone in there like being outside.

The goat-lady was about fifty, had short straight hair and wore excessive rouge on her cheeks. They presumed she cut her own hair, as it was bowl-shaped. At all times of the day, she wore a bright pink dinner-lady's overall.

She had never spoken to the boys or acknowledged them until one summer's afternoon when she put out two glasses of lemonade on the garden seat and disappeared inside. Tim and Ellis climbed down from the rafters of the sun barn and sat for a while in her garden, which was wild and overgrown, enchanting and unnerving. They were discussing whether or not to go to the front door to thank her for the drink when she appeared again, carrying a cardboard box. She thumped the box down on the grass in front of them.

"I expect you'd like a look at these," she said and disappeared inside, never to speak to them again.

The boys looked at each other curiously, then delved into the box. Lying inside, at the top of the pile, was a woman wearing a black bra and sucking her fingers. She was staring at Ellis and Tim. Her skin was very pale and her body was round and soft to look at. Her breasts were extremely large. Ellis looked between her legs but she didn't look like the women in the encyclopaedia. For a start, her legs were spread impressively wide apart and her feet were sticking up in the air. She had forgotten to take off her high-heeled shoes but had remembered to take off her underpants. He stared at where the hair should be but there wasn't any there. He didn't quite understand what he was looking at in its place. Beneath that magazine were others, all similar. Ellis's heart thudded and his penis seemed to be bursting at the seams. He felt thirsty and confused and wonderful and ill.

"Oh my sweet Jesus!" Tim muttered, holding a page up to Ellis. "Look!"

Ellis looked. There were half a dozen pictures on the page and the woman in them wasn't alone. There was a naked man with her and they were doing "it". Ellis stared and stared until Tim whispered, "What if she's watching us? Let's skedaddle."

Ellis had to reach inside his trousers and adjust himself before he could stand up, for fear his penis would snap. The boys hurried away across the fields, stopping inside Eight Acre Wood to pee, only to discover that they couldn't.

After that, for many months, whenever they played at the sun barn there was lemonade and the box of magazines. The boys spent as long as they wanted poring over the pictures but they never took a magazine away and they still didn't know what they were meant to do with the erections that stirred as soon as they saw the pink of the goat-lady's coat. Their tastes differed. Ellis liked it to be just two people, not of the same sex, and for the couple to start with their clothes on and for there to be some sense of a story unfolding as they undressed and he liked the man and woman to look as if they really cared for each other. He also found it helpful if one person was white and the other black because then he could unravel exactly which body part belonged to whom. Tim preferred orgies.

"Maybe ... maybe she'll do something."

"Like what?"

"I don't know. Tell us what to do."

"Or show us."

They both feigned retching.

"Maybe there's someone in the village who would let us do it with them for five pounds." There was a hint of desperation in Ellis's voice.

"There are prostitutes in Sevenoaks, apparently," Tim said.

"I don't want to go with a prostitute!" Ellis was horrified. "I meant, just someone nice who would be happy to help out, for a little cash."

"I can't think of anyone. Shall we get the gun?"

Ellis shrugged and nodded. Shooting something seemed a decent alternative to losing their virginity.

"But let's keep thinking," Tim said, "let's bear it in mind and maybe we'll think of someone who might help out."

"We'll write a list and just keep adding to it when we think of someone. My dad writes lists for everything. We'll put down the name of every woman we know or know through someone else and then we'll look at it and see if there's anyone we think we can approach."

"Except teachers. We won't put our teachers on the list. The thought of sleeping with Mrs Stanton makes me want to puke."

"I should think her husband feels the same way."

Considering how adept Tim was at picking locks, it was a skill he abused less than many thirteen years olds would. Mr Wickham's air pistol, kept in a locked cabinet in the kitchen, was easy pickings. The gun was wrapped in a duster and placed inside a blue Mappin & Webb cutlery box.

They returned to the sun barn where Ellis stood on a crossbeam and balanced himself, ignoring the thirty-foot drop to the ground. Tim had lined up bottles and cans on the beam at the opposite end of the barn. He climbed up and pressed the pistol into Ellis's hand and sat on the beam, swinging his legs back and forth as he rolled himself a ciggie. Ellis shut his eyes. The sun bore down on his eyelids. In the heat, he felt his senses refine and heighten. He was as aware of the bright green leaves of hornbeam in Eight Acre Wood as he was of the first target bottle as he was of the Crowborough Beacon on the horizon as he was of the lone house on Bayley's Hill as he was of the erect pink nipples inside the glossy pages inside the goat-lady's house. Nothing was any nearer or further away than anything else. Everything was perfectly vivid.

He had a tendency to take too long over his aim and to squeeze the trigger late, after a shake had settled into his forearm. But today, handling the pistol so soon after having an erection, a combination that had not occurred before, he felt overwhelmed by clarity. He fired immediately and blasted the bottle away. Without taking his eye off the next target he took a pellet from his pocket, reloaded, fired and hit it dead centre. He stared at the next bottle as he reloaded, raised his arm and fired. Tim laughed under his breath as the bottle cracked and fell. This was not like Ellis.

The throaty ticking of a tractor grew in volume as it descended the lane. It came into view at the track to the sun barn. It was one of Sedgewick's tractors, from Dale Farm. It towed a large wooden trailer and sitting in it, legs splayed out and arms draped over the side, was Des Payne, sixteen years old, shaven-headed, built like a brick wall, with hands like coppice stumps and a skull so square a nut and bolt would not have looked out of place through his neck. Des's eyes were shut, his face screwed up against the sunshine, his thick arms straining against his T-shirt, his massive thighs tight against the stonewashed drainpipe jeans that were his trademark.

Ellis trained the pistol on Des's head. He did so without thought or reason, knowing only that the trailer would soon disappear behind the hedge and this moment would be lost for ever. This unique opportunity to be bold would have passed him by. He locked his elbow and squeezed the trigger, shooting Des Payne in the back of the head. Des's bear-like body sprang up on to its knees, clutching its skull. As the trailer disappeared, Des's wild, darting eyes found Ellis, his outstretched arm steady and his pistol aimed still at the eyes that now fixed on him a glare of immeasurable menace.

The trailer took Des away. He made no attempt to stop it or to jump off. He simply wiped away the nick of blood on his shaven head and lay back in the sun, knowing that in doing nothing he was beginning the worst of all punishments for a boy of imagination like Ellis O'Rourke.

Ellis lowered the gun and listened to the tractor fade. He sat down next to his friend and let his legs hang limply from the rafters. His body began to shake with fear and he wanted to whimper with regret, even though what he had done also made perfect sense to him, in a way he would not be able to explain.

Tim stared at the lane where the trailer had been.

"Interesting ..." he muttered.

Five torturous days later, when Des came looking for him, Ellis resolved to look him in the eye whatever happened, to apologise but not to be pathetic. As Des's stale breath hit his face, what struck Ellis as particularly strange was that he didn't dislike Des Payne in any way. He was frightening to look at but he'd never done anything bad to Ellis, or anyone else for all Ellis knew. It was going to be tricky to justify his decision to shoot him in the head.

"I know that shooting you seems confrontational ..."

Ellis trailed off into silence, distracted by the realisation that his fear had brought him to the brink of uncontrollable laughter.

"I don't think everything we do in this world has an explanation and I think that the woman I marry will need to agree on that," he heard himself say.

Des chewed on an old piece of gum.

His breath bears no trace of mintiness, whispered the dangerous little voice inside Ellis's head.

Please don't say that out loud, Ellis implored himself.

Des breathed in and his massive chest expanded as if to cast a shadow.

"Sorry," Ellis said. It was unclear whether he was apologising for telling Des about his marriage plans or for the shooting.

Des took hold of Ellis beneath his armpits, lifted him off the ground and threw him on to the grass bank in front of

Cyril Bates's house. Cyril Bates was elderly and obese. His ankles were permanently swollen and he never wore socks. He moved around on a Zimmer frame and was usually to be seen in his leather farrier's apron, hobbling between the workshop and the forge to the side of his house, where he rearranged the tools and left-over materials of a business that had folded some years previously. He always appeared busy at a glance but if you observed him for any length of time, as Ellis often had, you soon understood that he was merely moving objects from one place to another and then back again. But in passing, all one would see was a busy man with blackened hands, wearing a leather apron, hard at work. And that was how Cyril Bates wished to be seen.

Looking at Cyril's upside-down house, Ellis cursed his luck that, for the first time he could remember, the old man was not in his workshop, from where he would have been able to keep an eye on these proceedings and bring them to a halt before Ellis was killed.

Des knelt on Ellis's shoulders, pinning him painfully to the ground. He leant over and smiled menacingly.

"You're a very silly little boy."

He took the gum from his mouth and shoved it firmly up Ellis's left nostril, further up than gum should probably go. Then, as Ellis braced himself for worse, Des was gone, meandering up the road to the village shop as if nothing much had happened.

Ellis rested his cheek against the lush, long grass. The smells of spring entered his unblocked nostril. It was over. It had hardly hurt at all and he hadn't cried.

This is so much more interesting than a normal day, Ellis thought, and sighed with the happiness of having not been kicked to death.

He pictured his map of the world. Travelling across the world must feel this good, he told himself. Getting into trouble and travelling must feel equally fantastic.

Then he saw Chloe Purcell on the pavement, approaching him. Today, on this beautiful spring day, she looked supremely good, so good that he almost forgot to ask her what she was doing in the village.

"Visiting someone," she answered.

"Who?"

"A friend." She smiled innocently enough for Ellis not to notice the lack of innocence.

"How did you get here?"

"The bus. You've got something up your nose."

"Yes."

"What is it?"

"Peppermint or spearmint, I'm not sure."

"Are you looking up my skirt, Ellis?"

"Yes," he said, blissfully, continuing to stare at the place where Chloe's thighs disappeared into the shadows of her pleats.

She wandered off, unimpressed. Ellis shut his eyes and burnt the image of her into his brain. Some time later he heard the grass beside him move and felt a body lie alongside him. He fantasised for a moment that it was Chloe Purcell's body and it felt wonderful to imagine. He knew who it was though, without looking. Chrissie extracted the gum from his nostril and threw it away.

"I was saving that for later," he complained.

She pinched him and called him a fool. He cuddled up next to her and it occurred to him that since discovering the farm and pornography and shooting people in the head and the touch of Chloe Purcell's hand on his arm, he had ceased worrying about the spiders.

8

During the second spider truce it was unthinkable the truces could ever end again. It was not a formal truce like the first. It had evolved as Ellis's fears became diluted. It was better than a truce, it was the new status quo and in it Ellis was free to enjoy the two mainstays of his life, renovating the cottage with his dad and being at Longspring with Tim. And there were other delights making the first of his teenage years a happy one. His romantic life was perfectly balanced by the combination of poring over the goat-lady's pornography and adoring Chloe Purcell from his moving bicycle. These days, he didn't even slow down when passing her on Oak Lane. In fact, he gained a little speed. The last thing he wanted was to disturb his gradual deification of her by trying to speak to her again. Occasionally, not often, Tim would change down a gear and say something amusing or pleasant to Chloe but Ellis cycled on, casting her a smile that he was fairly confident could be described as enigmatic, a smile that hinted at the fathoms and fathoms of personality he possessed deep inside and which he would, one day when he had found his voice, astound her with. For now, he was content – more than content, he felt actively satisfied – by merely thinking about her. Never did his "reading" of pornographic magazines and his daydreaming about Chloe take place at the same time or overlap or get confused in any way. Debi Diamond, Pandora Peaks and Little Oral Annie occupied a different universe from that which angelic Chloe Purcell called home.

In the autumn, the bulb-planting season brought two small firsts into Ellis's life; he drank tea and he heard his father use the f-word. A local nurseryman had placed an advert in Bridget's window, offering a surplus load of bulbs at a greatly reduced price if bought by the thousand. Gripped by a vision of the orchard carpeted by wave upon wave of narcissus, cyclamen, snowdrops, anemones and bluebells, Denny O'Rourke bought four thousand, and after planting one hundred of them he settled back on his haunches and muttered, "What a fucking ridiculous idea." Ellis sniggered. Denny looked at his son, who had planted thirty or forty bulbs himself, and said, "Down tools, Ellis. Life's too short."

Ellis sat opposite his dad at the kitchen table. Denny shut his eyes with satisfaction as he sipped his tea.

"You should get Michael Finsey's kid brother to plant all these bulbs. He's backward and works like a demon. Pay him to do it."

Denny blew on his tea. "That's a good idea, Ellis. A really good idea. Unless you want to do it. Seems a shame to pay someone else when you could have the money."

"No. No way. I don't ever want to be paid by you for anything. That's official. Anyway, I don't want to plant another bulb in my entire life. It's the most boring thing I have ever done, not including school of course."

"Of course. Guy Finsey is a good idea."

Ellis leant across and peered into Denny's mug.

"Can I try a taste?"

Denny shrugged and smiled and slid his mug across the table. Ellis took a sip and impersonated his father's closed eyes and contented sigh, as if it was impossible to drink tea without them.

"Yeah, I think I like it."

Denny took his son to the stove, opened the fire box and placed more logs on the flames, and showed Ellis how to make a pot of tea, using tea leaves.

"How much sugar do you have?" Ellis asked.

"One."

"Think I'm gonna need two."

"How strong do you want it?"

"Exactly the same as yours."

"Nice and strong, then."

They sat together and drank their tea. Over Denny's shoulder, Ellis saw Mafi in the garden. She inspected the boxes of unplanted bulbs and wiped the laughter from her eyes with a handkerchief.

"Mafi's laughing at you," Ellis said.

"She called me an idiot when I turned up with those bulbs."

Ellis's face creased into a smile at the thought. He had never known his dad to abandon a job before.

"Four thousand is quite a lot," Ellis said.

"Do something for me," Denny said, taking a bulb from his pocket and placing it solemnly in Ellis's palm. "Go and put that on Mafi's pillow."

Ellis wriggled and laughed. "Really?"

"Really. Then we'll go and speak to Mrs Finsey."

It was in the darkness just before dawn, when there was colour in the winter sky and flames in the stove and his father moving softly around the kitchen, that tea tasted best to Ellis O'Rourke. It was a communion wine, warm, dark and sugary, drunk by himself and his living God. After it, the arrival of words and daylight stole something precious from the day.

On Christmas morning, Ellis took tea in to Mafi and placed it beside her bed and she hugged him the same as if he was still a little boy. He carried the tray into Denny's room where he and Chrissie presented their dad with a stocking. It was the first Christmas they had insisted they were too old for stockings and instead reversed tradition by filling one for their dad. They climbed into Denny's bed and drank tea, three in a row, filling the bed with laughter and body-heat, and jostled Denny as he opened his stocking.

"A pair of socks, why thank you ... and a pair of

Superman underpants, fitting ... what's this ..." He read the cover of a pre-recorded cassette. "Felicity Lott, Strauss, how wonderful. Thank you."

Then he delved again, and pulled out a volume of *Colemanballs* and a bar of Woods of Windsor soap and a box of milk chocolate footballs and then a small cardboard box, which he scrutinised but didn't understand.

"What on earth is this?"

"It's a packet of condoms," Chrissie said, "in case you get lucky this Christmas."

"Pop 'em in your bedside drawer," Ellis said.

Denny bowed his head. "Idiots ..." he muttered, and his shoulders heaved a little with laughter. He turned the stocking upside down and out rolled a satsuma. He placed it on the bedside table, next to the photograph of the lighthouse on the shingle beach and the fishing boat run aground. Chrissie cuddled up next to him, resting her head on his shoulder, and Denny flashed his eyes at Ellis.

"More tea please, dear boy, if you're spoiling me."

In the kitchen, warmed by a fire lit that Christmas morning by the son for his father, Ellis stood over the brewing pot and felt the elation of giving.

Reardon taught the boys to shoot rabbits that winter. William Rutton showed them how to paunch and skin them. He crunched the rabbits' testicles under his butcher's knife, to make the boys laugh, and shouted, "There go the Harrises!"

Mafi made rabbit pie which was tough to eat.

"Just bring me the younger ones in future, my darlings," she told the boys. Denny pulled faces as he chewed.

When the clocks went forward, and Guy Finsey's bulbs adorned the orchard floor, Ellis and Tim got their first paid job, delivering grocery boxes for Ivan. On Thursday afternoons, after school, the boxes would be laid out on the brick floor of Ivan's shop, beneath the tiers of plastic grass.

They had a porter's trolley each, which took eight boxes, and they set out from the forge crossroads in opposite directions, Ellis delivering to Windmill Road, Morleys Road and Elsa's Farm Cottages, Tim to Scabharbour Road and Mount Pleasant. They ate a Golden Delicious as they went, pushing the trolley one-handed as they bit into it, and when Ellis returned home, three pounds richer, Mafi would call out to him in mock disgust, "French apples, Ellis O'Rourke! I ask you!"

And, often, he'd appear at her living room door and shrug. "I like them, I just do. They're nice and soft."

And if Mafi over-played her growl of disapproval, she'd cough and splutter and begin to laugh. She'd always laugh, even when she felt a little weak, even on the days she didn't have the energy to do much, which occurred now from time to time. And when she went into hospital for an operation, just before Ellis's fifteenth birthday, there was still her throaty laugh, even then.

Ellis never got a straight answer from Denny as to what the operation was, just an assurance in a vague tone: "There's nothing to be worried about, dear boy."

And whilst Denny sat holding Mafi's hand, as she waited nervously to be wheeled away to theatre, Ellis tiptoed down the lane and followed Chrissie and James into Treasure Island Woods, determined to see for himself, at last, the act of lovemaking. He had witnessed the beasts of the field doing it, he had seen pictures of professionals performing it, but no magazine could have prepared him for the transformation in two people he thought he knew, or for the noises they would not normally make or the words they would not otherwise use. He ran from his hiding place and didn't stop until he found himself in the West Wood where he walked the length of a fallen oak and perched on a bough above the ground. The West Wood was the territory, in late summer, of the Bermondsey Boys and Ellis would not have considered being here then. A coachload of children arrived in the village each August weekend from different parts of London. Children who never saw the countryside, who lived in tall blocks of flats and walked to school along the edges of main roads. Kids with weird voices. Kids with dark skin. They stayed for a week at Halls Green House where rumour had it there was a swimming pool and a snooker room and stables. There was always tension, but rarely trouble, until the last week in August when the Bermondsey Boys came and then Ellis lay low all week because there was always trouble.

This August, I'll not hide, he told himself. I'm fifteen tomorrow and I've seen things today I wouldn't have believed. I'm too grown up to fear the Bermondsey Boys.

When he got to Longspring he clambered to the top of the hay barn and lit a cigarette. He lay back in the hay and tried to come to terms with the violence of his sister's lovemaking. He wondered when he would get to do what she and James had been doing. How often do people do that? Is everyone doing it? Who of he and Tim would be the first to do it? It was bound to be Tim.

"ELLIS O'ROURKE!"

Reardon's voice boomed out from the foldyard.

"If you should ever decide, in a moment of enlightenment, that having a lit cigarette in a timber barn full of hay is somewhat foolish, then feel free to desist!"

Ellis scrambled down off the bales and took his cigarette outside.

"Sorry," he said. "I've had a hell of a day."

It was late when Denny got back from the hospital. He asked Ellis where Chrissie was and he told him she was out with James. Ellis offered to pour his dad a beer from the fridge but Denny said that he wouldn't have a drink in case he got a call from the hospital.

"What sort of call?" Ellis asked.

"No sort in particular." Denny smiled warmly to fend off further questions. He went to the fridge and looked inside. He checked inside the oven. "I'm hungry," he muttered, his face crumpling.

Ellis had never heard his dad say that he was hungry before. His dad was never hungry or tired or uncertain or anything of the sort.

"Me, too." Ellis smiled, placing his hands under his legs and sitting forward on the chair.

Denny bowed his head and took a deep breath. "You have eaten, haven't you?" His voice was stern.

Ellis shook his head.

"Your sister has done the shopping, hasn't she?"

Ellis nodded and smiled.

"Well, where is it?"

"She's not back yet."

"What do you mean, she's not back yet? It's nine o'clock."

"She rang me from the town to ask me if I minded her going back to James's for a bit. She'll be back about ten ... with the shopping."

His dad filled the kettle again and slammed it down on the stove. He threw a tea bag into his mug and sat down opposite Ellis. "And you said you didn't mind?"

Ellis shrugged and nodded. Denny repositioned his chair so that he was sideways to the table, the same way he did after a meal. He crossed his legs and lit a cigarette. His jaw muscles clenched and he looked out of the window.

"Ellis ..."

"Yes, Dad?"

"You're fifteen years old tomorrow. You are old enough to say no to your sister. You are old enough to walk over the green and buy some food and cook it. You are old enough to think of what I'll need when I get in from a day like today."

"I know. I'm sorry."

They sat in silence. Then Ellis said, "But you kept telling me everything was fine so I didn't really know today was a day like today."

Ellis couldn't sleep, not after the shouting between Chrissie and his dad. The atmosphere was strange. The cottage was not accustomed to raised voices. He went downstairs, lifted away the tablecloth that covered the television and switched it on. He imagined his dad and his sister, also unable to sleep, joining him and the ill feeling drifting away amid the magic of being up so late, the same magic that came to this room on Christmas Eve or during a power cut or on election night. And, sure enough, pretty soon, the floorboards above creaked and Ellis smiled to himself in anticipation. But the footsteps on the stairs were brisk and heavy. The living room door burst open and Denny bore down on his son, his face gripped by anger he did not want to feel. He shoved Ellis towards the door and Ellis ran upstairs. He buried himself under the sheets and fought to silence his whimpering. Denny marched in.

"I was sleeping, you selfish little bugger!" he hissed. Then he punched Ellis's arm through the bedclothes and slammed the door behind him.

From the door to the ward, Ellis and Chrissie heard their great-aunt screaming.

"They were killing him, they were killing him! They were cutting up our boy, Denny!"

Ellis peered in and saw his dad holding Mafi. She looked like a ghost. Tears streamed from her eyes.

"They were cutting up our little Ellis! Get them away from him, Denny!"

Denny rocked her.

"Just a bad dream," he said. "Just a bad dream."

A nurse pulled the curtain round and left Ellis doubting

that Mafi would ever seem the same to him now that he had seen her like that.

"Are you having a nice birthday?" Mafi asked Ellis.

They had washed her face and brushed her hair and wrapped a woollen shawl round her bony shoulders. She almost looked like Mafi again. Ellis couldn't think of anything to say to her. His fingers played with the stiff hospital sheets and he wondered what Mafi's dream had been. Chrissie answered for him.

"We all had a big bust-up last night. Dad's in a foul mood."

"She's exaggerating," Denny said. "I'm going to find some tea for us." He got up and wandered out of the ward.

"He's ruined Ellis's birthday," Chrissie said.

"I don't mind," Ellis protested.

Mafi looked Chrissie in the eye in such a way that Chrissie could not look away.

"What?" She laughed nervously.

"He's worried sick," Mafi said. "You should be thinking of him. He's only human."

Chrissie went quiet and soon she left the room. When she returned, she was holding Denny's hand and she had been crying. They drank tea. Silence took hold again but now the silence wasn't so bad. Denny O'Rourke looked at the sky. He wondered how many times the four of them would be in a room together again. Just them, no boyfriends, no girlfriends ... and Mafi.

"I think you should all go out and enjoy the sunshine," Mafi said.

"It's freezing out," Chrissie protested.

"It's an order. Go away and get some air. I do not want Ellis O'Rourke spending his fifteenth birthday in a hospital ward full of old biddies."

As Ellis stopped in the doorway to look back at his

great-aunt, his dad rested a hand on his shoulder, and as they walked along the corridor Denny left his hand there, and as they stepped into the lift and waited for the door to close he rubbed Ellis's arm where the bruise had risen. Ellis looked up at his dad and smiled. Denny leant over and kissed Ellis on the head and Ellis wrapped his arms round his dad's waist and pressed his head against him. Denny felt his heart ache with love. And he decided he would take his son to the Marsh.

They glided through a line of empty villages. As a child, when visiting Aunt Mafi on the coast, Denny had learned to recite their names in order: Woodchurch, Kenardington, Warehorne, Hamstreet, Ruckinge – where the old farm implements were laid out in a field above the road – Bilsington, Bonnington and Lympne. A dog chased the car up Lympne Hill. Ellis watched it through the back window. It barked and leapt and then it gave up and returned home. When Ellis turned round they were on the Aldington plateau and, to his right, the English Channel was a sheet of winter grey. They parked outside the castle and walked through woodland. Where the woods ended the footpath continued along a ridge, and in the field above them two wildebeest were grazing. Chrissie stopped in her tracks.

"Fuck me!"

Denny glared and winked at her in the same moment.

"Sorry," she said. "But that's a wildebeest, isn't it?"

They were at the bottom corner of the wildlife park.

"See the wildebeest, Ellis?" Denny said.

But Ellis didn't hear him. He had climbed on to a gate and was looking in the opposite direction. Beneath him was a vast, graceful sweep of perfectly flat land, offered to him like an open hand. The land was dissected by intricate veins of reflective blue water, some twisting randomly, others deliberately straight. In between these dykes were patchworks of deep green pasture. Rare amongst the pasture were fields of brown earth where shadows slept along the plough lines. The sound of sheep rose from the green carpet, joined the chack-chacking of the fieldfares and hung in the air parallel to the plateau where they stood. There was no perspective or direction to the sound here. It was gentle and yet it travelled effortlessly across great distances to them, on board a chill November breeze. For all the indescribable places Ellis had seen in the pages of *National Geographic*, the land in front of him now, framed by sea and sky and stretching out of sight, seemed the most extraordinary. It was neither beautiful nor dramatic but, as he gazed upon it for the first time, it immediately felt to Ellis like home.

"Where are we?" he asked.

"That is the Marsh," his dad said proudly.

"I love it," Ellis said. And he meant it, because fifty miles from his own village he had found a place so different it made the world feel wonderfully colossal.

"It's flat as a pancake, Ellis," Chrissie said. "Your taste gets more surreal by the day."

"What's surreal?" Ellis asked.

"You are, smelly-Ellie, you're surreal. That you, of all people, don't know what it means is deeply ironic."

"What's ironic?"

Chrissie turned in despair to her dad. "Don't worry, you've got one normal child."

"Not that I can see," Denny said.

She gave him a dirty look. "Don't tell me you intend us to go for a walk?"

"I do intend."

"On foot?"

"That's the idea."

"Do we get to sit in a pub at some point?" she asked.

"We do," he said.

A barmaid in the Walnut Tree Inn told Ellis about the smuggling gangs on the Marsh and said she was a descendant of Cephas Quested, second in command of the Ransley gang in the 1820s. She walked him along a smuggler's tunnel and when they emerged from it the sun was out and Ellis knew that Mafi was going to be all right. The November afternoon sky slanted across the Marsh, huge and magnificently blue, the biggest sky Ellis had ever seen. They headed for the sea and arrived at a peninsula where a lighthouse stood on a shingle point. Chrissie watched from the car as her father and brother ran and wrestled together amongst the fishing boats. They tumbled down the steep pebble ridge towards the sea and fell out of sight. Chrissie opened the window a little and heard their laughter buffeted by the wind. She heard a shout and then they re-emerged, hurrying towards the car, with Ellis soaked to the skin and already shaking uncontrollably. Denny sped away. Ellis lay across the back seat and felt his body go numb and his brain slow down. A smile appeared across his face so angelic that Chrissie thought he was dying.

"Hurry up!" she urged her dad. "That sea must be bloody freezing!"

"You don't say," Denny muttered.

Ellis was cocooned from their voices, wrapped in a cold numbing perfection. He felt amazing, and it was almost a disappointment to him when the owner of the sports shop in New Romney took them in and offered towels and an electric fire.

In the months that followed, Ellis took to immersing himself in cold baths. He failed to recreate that state of grace that falling into the sea in winter had gifted him but he enjoyed the baths nevertheless as a miniaturised form of transportation to another place, and he welcomed the arrival of his first chest-hairs, which appeared to be the baths' doing. As unexpected and welcome as the chest-hairs was the A star he received for an English writing project, the first time he had ever done better than a C plus in five years of secondary school. The brief the class had been given by Mr Pulman was "My Weekend".

"It can be fact or fiction," Pulman had said. "Two pages long."

The handing back of marked homework was traditionally a tepid or embarassing experience for Ellis. But on this occasion, his disbelieving eyes settled on red ink words which read, *A* Excellent. Your spelling remains atrocious, almost a foreign language, and your boycott of grammar watertight, but this is a fine piece of writing, Ellis. I enjoyed it enormously. Thank you!*

It didn't stop there. Mr Pulman announced that he was going to read an extract from the two best assignments, starting with Ellis O'Rourke's.

"Ellis's 'My Weekend' is about a boy who spends a day on a marsh-like place with his father. The description of the landscape is well written and then there's some really rather original writing at the climax, and here's a bit of that. *This is the place where the world begun. This is the land which woked up and found that it was the starting place of everything. This Marsh is a never-ending carpet. I love it most of all at dusk time when the black shapes of wind-blown bushes stand against a giant dusk sky like smugglers turned to stone by the customs men. Every single dusk on the Marsh is magical, every dawn brand new. When I am there with my dad I know that he and I have been together for a thousand years and will never die. The end.*"

The class sniggered. One girl whined, "It's a never-ending carpet where I can play with my teddy bear because I'm Ellis and I'm a baby!" This caused a ripple of laughter which Mr Pulman talked down.

"That was by far the best piece of writing in the fiction category, whilst of the factual ones I want to read you an extract from ..."

Ellis let Mr Pulman's voice recede and looked at Tim. Tim slapped his shoulder.

"That was brilliant, Ellis. Brilliant," he whispered. "Don't listen to these idiots. They're jealous of you."

Ellis was wearing his confused face and muttered helplessly back, "But it wasn't fiction."

Ellis and Denny would leave early for the Marsh, setting out when the village was a dark procession of cadaver houses and hollow-eyed windows. At shearing time, they heard the cries of ewes separated from their lambs reverberate across the flatlands and rise to them on the escarpment at Bilsington Monument. In midsummer, they listened to the hum of a light aircraft looping the loop over the Midley ruin. At dusk, Ellis saw smugglers out of the corner of his eye. They sought the eeriness of winter. The beauty of summer. The holiness of it all. At the ruins of Hope All Saints, they lay together on the grass and watched the domed sky.

"All churches should have their roofs removed," the younger O'Rourke said. "Then I'd go."

"Why bother, when you can come here?" his dad replied.

"But you go sometimes?"

"Very occasionally ... just in case."

And being of the age when threads of desire were beginning to unravel in his imagination and the romantic poets were being forced upon him by Mr Pulman, Ellis decided that the Marsh had been the birthplace of his soul, somewhere in the past.

From beneath the pall of apprehension that was the legacy of being left responsible for this boy and his sister, Denny O'Rourke glimpsed a different future when he and his son were on the Marsh. He had first seen the Marsh from on board ship, in wartime. Then, in the first warless summer of his adulthood, he had borrowed a car and gone to visit his

Aunt Mafi on the coast. The two of them had driven out on to the Marsh on a gleaming bright summer's day and every colour and detail and field and dyke and bullrush and poppy and bugloss had reflected in the mirrors and panels of the car, a Technicolor peacetime. During a picnic on the shingle point, beneath the lighthouse, Denny had dwelled deeply on the vision of a boy he had had when looking at this peninsula from his ship. He had toyed with the idea of telling Mafi about the boy but had thought better of it. And by the time he was married and his son was finally born, he had locked that vision away, out of reach. Now that he and his son were regularly visiting this same place, the future took on a new appearance in Denny's eyes. It was less solitary, with fewer battles. It was shinier, like a polished car crossing the Marsh in summer. It was beautiful.

Denny and Ellis marked the longest day of 1984 by watching the sun rise and set over the Marsh. They started at Fairfield, beneath a deep ocean sky that waited patiently for dawn. They sheltered in the shadow of the bellcote and drank tea from a flask.

"You want a bench here, really," Denny said. "Right here, tucked against the wall. Port in a storm, dear boy. Someone should do that, put a bench right here."

The first warm tones of gold and orange entered the sky and reflected in the still water of the drainage ditches. The sun appeared, showing up the lichen on the church bricks and on the tiles.

They ran with stooped backs to the Listening Posts at Greatstone, hiding from the crane operators excavating the gravel lakes. Ellis threw a pebble into an immense concrete dish expecting it to echo, but it didn't.

"They used these to detect enemy aircraft," Denny said. "Don't ask me how."

"How?" Ellis asked.

His dad lobbed a pebble at him. "Fool!" he laughed.

They stopped at the bikers' café on the main Marsh road at Old Romney and had breakfast. They were the only customers. Ellis's mug had lipstick on it and, out of nowhere, he announced, "You don't have to worry about me sitting you down and asking for sex education or stuff like that. I'm pretty well clued up on that ... from a visual angle, if you know what I mean."

Denny didn't flinch. "Good, 'cos I'm a bit rusty."

They parked at the lifeboat station beneath a fluttering ensign. Denny O'Rourke followed the caterpillar tracks across the beach to the launch. Ellis walked amongst the fishing boats. In the windows of a winch-shed he was confronted by a reflection of his dad looking out to sea. Denny's hands were clasped behind his back and from his stance Ellis knew that his dad was whistling to himself, through his teeth, the way he did when he was happy. When he was Ellis's age, the man whistling at the water's edge had presumed he would spend his whole life at sea. When he was told that he couldn't, Denny O'Rourke thought he would never get over it. But he learned to live on land and life was bearable and then he met the butterfly-lady and life was wonderful again, as wonderful as the oceans for being loved by her.

Ellis did not wish to cross the seas as his father had, but their trips together to the Marsh, though only an hour and a half away, were planting in him a desire to see those seas from all the different continents that rose up out of them, and to then, one day, live back here at the water's edge. Mafi once said to him that his mother had died of adventure. He wondered if it were possible to die of the lack of it.

They sat at the Point and Ellis noticed the wreck of a small fishing boat half buried in the sandbanks out to sea.

"This is the photograph next to your bed."

"It is," Denny said.

"I never noticed the wreck before."

"No? Maybe the tide's always been in."

"Maybe ... Did you take that photograph?" Ellis asked.

"Yes, from on board ship. On my last ever day at sea."

"Is that why you kept it all this time?"

Denny didn't answer for some time. He was distant for a while, as he toyed with the idea of telling a certain story. Then he smiled at his son.

"Sort of," he said. "Partly."

Streaks of pale pink cloud dissected the lowest horizontals of the sky and measured the sun's descent. It offered up a glow of warm, pastel colours to the shingle peninsula and a small, white, timber-clad house accepted them, becoming saturated by the evening's delicate hues. The house sat alone on the shingle, removed from the other houses there but constructed, like many of them, round the shell of an old railway carriage. It was surrounded by a wind-blown wooden fence which flapped in the wind.

"I am definitely going to live here," Ellis said.

After the sun had gone, the sky continued to repaint itself every few minutes. Their footsteps were heavy on the deep shingle, then light and silent upon carpets of moss. The power lines crackled above a shanty town of magpie traps. The lighthouse beam threw monochrome patterns on to the shingle. The wind picked up. Neither of them wanted to return to the banality of being in a car or deciding what to eat. They wanted to remain together in the incomplete darkness of midsummer. Ellis flirted with the possibility of telling his dad that the crimson sunsets above the village were his mother appearing to them, but he said nothing. The knowledge that something immense was missing overcame him. It wasn't simply that he couldn't talk to his dad about her but that he shouldn't. It had never been all right to ask. The moment was never right. He wondered if he could start by asking for the letters, the letters wedged inside the pages of Denny's blue canvas-bound naval diary and locked in the bottom drawer, the ones from his mum to his dad, in the pale blue envelopes with foreign stamps.

Dad?

Yes, my dear boy.

When we get home, could I read those letters from Mum that are in your drawer?

Of course you can, dear boy. And I'll tell you all about her.

Ellis let this imagined exchange drift away into the night. His dad was the sort of dad who gave him a day off school so that they could watch the sun rise and set on the longest day. Perhaps he shouldn't ask for more.

9

The hay was harvested in early summer at Longspring Farm. Reardon kept Ellis and Tim busy, manoeuvring the herd around the grassland harvest. The boys watched a weasel suck the blood from the jugular vein of a rat. They discussed the idea of trying drugs for the first time, without having any intention of doing so.

"We should go up to the sun barn later on," Ellis said, "browse some mags ..."

Tim's response changed everything between them.

"I'm not doing that any more. No need."

"What's that supposed to mean?"

"Nothing."

Tim meandered away towards the farmhouse.

"Why does everybody in the blooming world walk away from me when I ask them a serious question?"

"Let's make a cuppa," Tim said.

Ellis ran to catch up with him.

"And say 'fucking world'!" Tim added.

"What?"

"Say 'fucking' not 'blooming'. You're using words that don't fit the bill."

"What are you talking about?" Ellis asked.

"What the fuck am I talking about!"

"Yeah, what are you?"

"You're not expressing yourself, Ellis. You need to revamp your vocab. What the *fuck* are you talking about, Tim!"

"But what *are* you talking about?"

"What the fuck am I talking about. Spit it out, it'll do you good."

"But what the fuck *are* you going on about?"

Tim handed Ellis the cigarette he'd been rolling.

"Swearing and fucking, mate. Vital. Get them both on your agenda, pronto."

"Like you've done any fucking," Ellis sneered.

Tim lit Ellis's cigarette. "We'll have a cuppa."

Ellis seized him by the arm. "Have you done it?"

Tim smiled and headed off to Reardon's kitchen.

"You're doing it again. Walking away from me when I ask something important! It's really annoying!"

"Fucking annoying!"

They drank strong, sugary tea in Reardon's orchard and Ellis sat quietly, subdued by a premonition of being left behind. He didn't ask Tim again, for fear of sounding desperate. Beyond the shade, the day was growing extremely hot. The grass was yellow and there were cracks in the earth.

When the windfalls land on grass this pale, Ellis thought to himself, it's going to look pretty. Someone should take a photograph.

"My dad's out this evening. Come over and I'll dig out

some alcohol."

"Can't," Tim said.

Ellis drew shapes on the grass with a twig. "Please. I need you to pick a lock for me. Dad's hidden something in a drawer and locked it."

"It'd have to be early."

They walked back through the farmyard, removing their T-shirts and throwing them on to the fence. Tim stepped into the hay barn. He placed his hands on his hips and arched his back to look up at the roof girder.

"What's in the drawer?" he said, distantly.

"Nothing," Ellis answered, remaining outside on the track. "Come on."

"Not a lot of point opening it then."

"Something of mine," Ellis said.

"The thing is," Tim said, "I'll pick that lock for you if you cross the barn."

The same panic swept through Ellis whenever Tim challenged him to cross the girder spanning the roof of the hay barn. Tim had done it but Ellis knew he wouldn't be able to. He presumed that Tim was stronger than him, in exactly the same way he presumed every boy alongside him in class was more clever and every boy in the street more gifted with girls. He failed to see that he had all the same sinewy muscles that Tim had. They could hardly have been more similar physically. All Ellis lacked was whatever chemical it was that made a boy decide it would be a great idea to inch his way across a girder like that, hanging on by his fingers above a fifty foot drop. Tim possessed that chemical in bucketloads.

This moment had been and gone before, two or three times a year in the four years they had known each other, and Ellis had always withstood the suffocating process of pressure, refusal, pressure, refusal until Tim got bored or Ellis walked away. But today the balance was different. Tim was different. And Ellis wanted to read the letters inside that locked drawer a great deal. He surveyed the approach route, a stairway of hay bales stacked up to the roof at each end of the barn. He looked at the girder itself. It ran for fifty feet from one end of the barn to the other, and the same distance from the roof to the ground. In the centre of the barn, for a quarter of the crossing, there were no bales to break the fall.

"I don't want you laughing at me or winding me up whilst I try to do it," Ellis said, gravely.

"Course not! I'm going to be doing it with you anyway. You'll follow me and do exactly what I do. I've always said that. Just trust me. I'd trust you."

The trace of hurt in Tim's voice comforted Ellis. Tim ushered him forward to the bales and for a moment it seemed that he was going to offer Ellis his hand. Ellis would have taken it. Tim climbed to the top of the bales and Ellis followed. Up high, sunlight leaked in through gaps in the barn wall, illuminating particles of floating dust as if the great movie show of grown-up life was trying to burst in and play. Tim turned to Ellis.

"Just follow me across and don't stop to think. Don't stop for a moment and the next thing you know you'll be across and then you'll have finally done it and you'll feel great. OK?"

Ellis nodded. Tim wrapped his fingers round the H-shaped steel beam and stepped off the highest bale. His body-weight pulled his arms taut. He twisted his body with each extension of an arm and slid his hands along the beam, never letting them lose contact with the girder and never committing his weight to just one hand. Ellis reached up to the girder and placed one hand around it. He willed himself to move forward but his body didn't respond. He watched the veins in Tim's forearms and biceps fill with blood and he tried again to step off but his body was rigid and the two boys found themselves facing each other from opposing peaks of hay.

"You can do it!" Tim called across.

Ellis peered at Tim as if he was disappearing from view. He tried one more time to move but already knew that he possessed the wrong mind for the uncomplicated sort of boy he wanted to be. He felt the blood rise to his face in embarrassment. He looked at his friend again and was unable to stop himself asking, "You've done it, haven't you?" His voice was resigned but not envious.

Tim sighed. "I have, yeah. But, after we'd done it, I swore to myself I wouldn't be one of these guys who goes and blabs about it. She might not want anyone to know. So, don't ask me about it or about her but when I know she doesn't mind I'll tell you first. That's a promise. Who else would I tell but you? Come on, we'll go open that drawer for you."

They went to the drinks shelf in the larder as soon as Denny left for the evening. The spirit bottles were dusty and some stuck to the shelf, so rarely were they disturbed. The boys took their drinks up to Denny's bedroom, where Ellis showed Tim the drawer.

"Easy as ..." Tim muttered.

He took a leather pouch from his pocket, untied the shoelaces which held it together and rolled it open on the carpet. In the pouch were lengths of wire of different thickness, a penknife and some jeweller's screwdrivers. He took one length of wire and bent it into the shape of a square hook at the end and slid it into the lock. Then he held two thicker pieces of wire close to his eye and decided between them.

"What time you meeting her?" Ellis asked.

"Half past eight."

"That's late to start an evening. Won't you get a bollocking for being out so late?"

Tim looked hard at Ellis. "First of all, she's worth it, believe me. Secondly, of course I'll cop a bollocking but you just tell them. Or, in your case, you just tell him."

"Tell who what?"

"Ellis-the-trellis! Parents don't turn to their children at a certain age and suggest we start going out and having a good time. If you don't do it, it won't happen."

"But I do have a good time ..."

"Yeah, but you could have a better time," Tim said. "Much better! It's like this. You behave yourself, you don't act like an idiot, but you just tell him, 'Dad, I'm going out this evening and I'll be back at eleven and this is where I'll be.' And he'll say he wants you back at nine-thirty but you come back at eleven as you said in the first place and he sees you're fine and you've not been arrested or behaved like a tool and the point is that you said you'd be back by eleven and you were. He will realise he can either have a life of arguing with you and you lying to him and him not knowing where the hell you are, or he can accept that you are going to start doing your own thing and he's just got to get used to it."

Ellis didn't say anything. It sounded good in theory but he wasn't totally sure where there was to go to round here until eleven at night.

Tim returned to the job in hand. "What's in here that you're so desperate to get back?"

"Letters."

They were distracted by the sound of a car turning into the driveway. The boys watched from Denny's bedroom window as Chrissie climbed out of the passenger seat of a convertible whilst a tall, besuited, slightly older man emerged from the driver's side, wearing the sort of sunglasses that were 100 per cent reflective and Ellis had wanted to own until approximately ten seconds earlier.

"This is Dino. He's a *journalist*."

Chrissie announced this with grave reverence, mistakenly thinking it would impress two sixteen-year-old boys.

"Yeah, and ...?" said Ellis.

"Where you from?" Tim asked.

"I'm from Malta," Dino replied.

"Cool," the boys said, in unison.

"Thanks. Glad you approve."

Dino looked extremely old to Ellis and Tim and, sure enough, it soon came to light that he was twenty-nine.

"James was also much older than my sister," Ellis observed, shortly before Chrissie slapped him on the head.

They all sat in the garden. Chrissie poured herself a glass of wine and Dino a vodka and tonic.

"Don't you drink beer?" Tim asked disdainfully.

Dino ignored him and made an effort with Ellis. "Bet you miss your sister now she's living up in the big city," he said.

Ellis checkd his hair in Dino's lenses. "How much?"

Dino took off his jacket and settled back with his drink.

"Whoa!" Tim said. "Your shoulders have come off with your jacket! And you're actually pretty skinny underneath. That's weird."

"It's trendy, you hick," Chrissie intervened.

If Dino felt uneasy in the crossfire of Tim and Ellis's disdain, that was nothing compared to the discomfort caused him by Ellis's glassy silence as he drifted off into his own thoughts, achieving a vacant expression his sister and best friend took in their stride but which unnerved the newcomer.

Ellis was thinking how strange it sounded to be introduced in terms of what your job is. Dino is a journalist. Fine, sure, OK. But I'm really not bothered what his job is. How hot is it in Malta? How did he meet my sister? What sports does he play or watch? What's his room like? Can he walk on his hands like me and Tim can? How long can he hold his breath? What age did he start shaving? Are his parents divorced? What's his absolute best joke? How many times has he had sex in his life and is he knobbing my sister yet?

Somewhere between being his own age and Dino's age, it was occurring to Ellis, you probably have to decide to *do something* and what you do defines what sort of life you have. So far, he had just *been a boy* and being a boy wasn't a career option. Looming over him, all of a sudden, was the possibility that everything he had done and enjoyed up until now would soon be inappropriate or unsatisfying, and that possibility felt like a small death.

And all this change was appearing on the horizon simply because Tim had slept with a girl and Dino was a journalist.

Tim leant forward and confided to Dino, "You know those peope in Haiti that are buried alive, the living dead sort of thing, but real, like zombies? That's what Ellis looks like when he's thinking. Don't be scared. He looks the same in lessons, too."

They watched Ellis as his thoughts led him further from them. He was now considering his future. Basically, he wanted to farm but he didn't want to be like a farmer. He wanted to be a sexy farmer, and a part-time explorer. The Indiana Jones of dairy. Or Ian Botham, he'd like to be Ian Botham. The way Ellis saw it, Ian Botham was naturally talented, therefore put no real hard work into being him, had great personal skills and a tremendous social life, could hold his drink, was massively respected and knew where to buy joints, or however it is you get hold of that stuff, and was married so got regular sex. So, yes, he'd like to be Ian Botham but without the cricket. A Botham-farmer. But, wait a minute, someone else was Ian Botham already: Ian Botham. *Becoming Ian Botham* was no more realistic a career plan than *being a boy*. This was hard.

He looked up. The others were staring at him.

"Hello ..." he said quietly. Then he burst back into life. "Hey! Wait! That means you're a Malteser!"

Chrissie slumped. "Please tell me it hasn't taken you this long to come up with that? Jesus wept!"

Dino smiled, uneasily, and glanced at his watch. He and Chrissie didn't stay long. They looked in on Mafi and then, whilst Dino gave Tim a tour of his Golf Cabriolet, Chrissie slapped her arms round Ellis and forced a kiss on to his lips. He feigned disgust. In truth, he liked her doing this, although he did sometimes wonder if the cause of his conversational inertia with girls might possibly be the fact that his sister remained the second most fanciable girl he'd ever known, behind Chloe Purcell.

She led him away. "I know Dino's not your sort of bloke, but don't be horrible. He's a nice guy."

Ellis put his arm round her, too. "You're not gonna go and marry him, though, are you?"

"No way!" She stopped and faced him. "I'm knobbing him, as you'd put it. That's all."

They wandered back to the car holding hands. At sixteen years of age, nothing made Ellis feel better than a conversation like this one, where he actually got told something. A few of those conversations with his dad, he suspected, and he might not feel so out of the loop.

"What letters?" Tim asked.

Ellis watched Dino's car take his sister away, and remained looking at the empty lane long after the car had disappeared.

Tim asked again, "What letters?"

Ellis dug his heel into the driveway gravel and avoided looking Tim in the eye. "Eh?"

"Upstairs, in the drawer ..."

Ellis sighed. "From my mum. Old letters."

"Why's your dad taken them?"

"They're to him, from my mum."

"To him?"

Ellis nodded and smiled over-confidently at Tim.

"They're not to you?"

"No," Ellis said. "Please, let's get on with it. I just want to read the letters. It's OK. It's fine. He wants me to read them."

"Then why has he locked them up? They must be private."

"He lost the key ages ago."

"Sure," Tim muttered unconvincingly. Now it was his turn to bow his head and study his feet.

"Come on!" Ellis urged him.

"But they're not yours."

They stood in silence. Tim looked at his watch and wore the pained expression of a friend who didn't want to pass judgement.

"It's getting late. I'll be late for her."

He started off down the driveway.

"It can't be half past eight already!" Ellis pleaded.

But Tim was gone, walking at speed on to the lane without looking back, the leather tool pouch wedged into his back pocket.

Ellis sat on the front lawn. His mother's handwriting turned to ribbons of ink and snaked away from him into the evening, leaving his world poorer and prompting him to see things anew. He saw the garden for what it was, a series of impenetrable borders camouflaged by wild flowers and birdsong. He pictured the lady living here with them and realised she was a generation too old. Mafi was the sort of relative Ellis should be visiting from time to time, not living with. The only woman in the world he could be held by and laugh with, and love one minute and hate the next, had left him for London and was dragging home bores who wouldn't know how to talk to him. And his father continued to torture him by being the loveliest, loneliest, least penetrable of men.

Ellis dragged himself inside and told Mafi that he was going out with friends and would be back at eleven o'clock. He left the room before she could answer. He didn't know where to go. All that mattered to him was that he was not in the cottage when his dad got home and that he arrived back no earlier than eleven.

He wandered towards Sedgewick's land at Dale Farm from the back fields above Wickhurst lane, avoiding the roads in case his dad was driving back into the village. Sedgewick, who was high up in the council, had sold a meadow to a developer who started to build a small, highly unpopular cul-de-sac of commuter houses there. There was a rumour in the village that every time the builders started to work there the site was vandalised, but Ellis and Tim hadn't been to investigate. Now, Ellis climbed the site fence and found the burnt-out shell of an excavator and footings that had been set about with a sledgehammer. Some weeds and crops were coming up through the concrete.

He walked slowly out of the valley to the bridge at Hubbards Hill. He sat beneath it, watching the traffic on the bypass. When Harry Lyle, the son of the people who owned the post office, ran away from home, this is where they found him, huddled up beneath the concrete buttresses. Most children in the village ended up here at some point in their life, watching the traffic, having their first grope, avoiding PC Bachelor, running away from home or just feeling bored. Ellis had spent some time hiding here after he shot Des Payne, and now he was back again. He watched the cars and guessed at the time. He tried to calculate how long he'd been gone, how long it had taken him to cross Dale Farm and how long he had been sitting here. Another half-hour here would probably do it, he decided, and then a slow walk home. That should make it eleven o'clock.

In a rare lull in the traffic he heard a whimpering from nearby. He looked around but could see nothing. He heard it again, this time stronger and, he realised, from further away than he had thought. He looked across the road and as a fresh wave of traffic stole the silence back he saw, tucked under the bridge, Tim Wickham and Chloe Purcell, their arms and legs wrapped round each other. They shared kisses, more tender than the ones Chrissie and James had shared. Her eyes were closed and her face wore a depth of passion Ellis could never have imagined her capable of. He felt his legs buckling as he got to his feet and hurried away without being seen.

He was disgusted at himself. He cursed his naivety. He was sick of being the viewer. Sick of watching. Sick of wondering. Angry at never knowing.

He had always felt that of all the girls he knew, Chloe Purcell was the plainest and most quiet. He had presumed he would end up with her because she was so plain and he was so useless. And, despite himself, he'd always thought she liked him. She had once said she wanted to fly away with him, after all. Now, presumably, Chloe and Tim would laugh at how Ellis had gone to a barn dance with her and not spoken a word or made a move.

No one, he told himself, ever tells you what's really going on. I have to do my own thing and have my own secrets, otherwise I'm just a baby. One day I'll show them. I'll be gone. I'll meet people who don't know me and I'll be different with them. I'll have lots of friends and I'll get letters and phone calls. My girlfriend will be a prettier version of Chloe and she'll get up out of bed in the mornings and walk naked to the kitchen and make us tea and bring it back to bed.

But as he marched furiously back into the village, another part of him said, "That won't ever happen to you."

He found Mafi in her kitchen. She asked him if wanted a cup of tea.

"Are you having one?" Ellis asked resentfully.

"Yes."

"Yes, please, then."

He moped into Mafi's living room and threw himself down on to the armchair his dad usually sat in. He looked at the ship's clock that a great-uncle he had never known brought back from his voyages. It was only half past nine.

"Bollocks," he muttered. "Fucking virginal tatty bollocks."

He sighed dramatically and listened to the ticking of the ship's clock take over the room.

"Can't be that bad ..." Denny's voice came from behind Ellis's head.

Surprised, Ellis looked round and saw his dad standing at the window, smoking a cigarette and watching the night sky.

"I didn't see you."

"I guessed that." Denny laughed under his breath and laid his hand on Ellis's shoulder as he passed him and took a seat in the corner of the room. Between his thumb and forefinger, he played with the length of wire Tim had left protruding from the lock of Denny's drawer.

"Oh ..." Ellis sighed, involuntarily, when he saw it.

They sat in silence for a while until Denny said, "I'm not angry with you, Ellis," and smiled cautiously.

"Well, I sort of wish you were."

"Why?"

"Then I could get angry too."

"I don't want either of us to be angry. There's no need, no need at all. But some things of mine are not for sharing. It's private, Ellis. It's very private."

Ellis stared at the floor. "Now I am angry," he said. "Private ..." He muttered the word bitterly. "There's nothing I hate more than bloody private. Everything is private. I'm not allowed to know anything."

"We have a good life, Ellis, everything we need."

Ellis felt unable to breathe and rose to his feet.

"That's a stupid thing to say to me," he said, and walked out.

Tim left school without finishing and went to work full time for Reardon. Chloe spent every weekend at Longspring. She remained quiet and plain and incapable of laughter, but the smile she smiled where others would laugh still overwhelmed Ellis.

Ellis kept himself to himself. He stayed in the cottage and returned to Treasure Island, surprised that no younger boys had made it their own. Once, he set out for the goat-lady's house but turned back halfway.

He read *National Geographic* and imagined a score of different lives for himself, his favourite being the one in which he was a world renowned, hugely respected and sexually sought-after roving farmer, an international agricultural trouble-shooter, a genius with instincts for farming in any country and climate and an ability to read the landscape that inspired the awe of those who witnessed it. He slept out under the stars, on hillsides, by riverbanks and on beaches and saw things that no one in Kent had ever seen. When he imagined this life the technical details of his genius were omitted, as was the training and experience which would be required of him to attain it. He thought purely in terms of sensory pleasures; fresh air, travel, Eden-like views, excitement, being admired, looking rugged and, of course, indulgent women.

He tried to tell Denny little, to curb his lifelong instinct to share all his unedited thoughts and ideas with his father, in the hope that this would be the start of his being a grown-up. He attempted to create an illusion of there being much that Denny didn't know about in Ellis's life, even though this wasn't true. He tried to smile and laugh less with his dad too, but repeatedly found himself looking back on the day and realising he had forgotten to do so.

It's hard, he had to admit to himself, pretending you've some interesting secrets when you haven't.

In the February of 1985, winter tightened its grip on the landscape for a few more weeks and Ellis heard from Michael

Finsey that Chloe Purcell was going to run a livery yard for
Reardon when she left school, and that her parents were
furious she wasn't going to college. The hurt poured into
Ellis. He hadn't been to the farm since Christmas, nor had he
seen Tim, a feat that Mafi rated as "quite an achievement" in
a village so small. At Easter, Tim phoned and persuaded Ellis
to go for a drink.

"Just the two of us," he assured him.

In the twilight of half-drunkenness, Ellis told his friend
a half-truth. "I suppose I felt a bit annoyed 'cos you were
always with your girlfriend, so I decided I'd come over a bit
less."

Tim laughed. "You disappeared!" His eyes sparkled and
laughter-lines cradled them in optimism.

"You didn't come looking for me," Ellis said.

"I was in love. Girls do that. I'm sorry."

"Anyway," Ellis said, "that's that sorted out."

They left the pub with their arms round each other and
drove when they shouldn't have, through the back lanes into
the Rother valley. From the top of Catt's Hill they saw an
electrical storm heading inland off the Channel. At Fairfield,
they ran in great circles as curtains of rain swept across the
Marsh and soaked them through. When the lightning came
it lit up the flatlands, silhouetting the lonely church and the
wind-bent thorn bushes. They chased after lightning bolts
and goaded the thunder. And when the storm had become
a silent slither of white light above the ridge, they wandered
aimlessly in the darkness, catching their breath and feeling
the blood race around their bodies. They drove up the lane to
the turkey farm at Becket's Bridge and parked in the Dutch
barn. They slept in the car until Ellis was woken by his own
shivering, shortly after five.

They were at Reardon's by seven. Ellis stood at the
highest point on the farm and surveyed his village. It felt
good to be back at Longspring, but it felt different too. A few

months' absence made him feel like a visitor now. He liked the idea of being a prodigal son, to his family, but most of all to Tim, and through him to Chloe. He wanted to be missed. He wanted to be a mystery. This morning, his ambition took no more form than that. He didn't know what to do or where to go. But he knew now that he wanted to leave and go to that fictitious place where his daily struggle to communicate and to concentrate was cured. He would return regularly to see his dad and they would meet on the Marsh often. His dad would be proud of him.

Shivering and tired, he went home, resolved to force his way out of a life that threatened to consume him with disappointment, now that Chloe loved Tim. As he waited for the bath to fill, he looked at the framed poster on Mafi's wall of a painting called *Nuit d'Eté* by Winslow Homer. In it, two women dance happily together on a moonlit beach. Silhouetted against a rough, silvery sea is a cluster of onlookers. A pale blue trail of moonshine beckons the dancers towards the horizon.

Denny appeared at his son's side, just when Ellis wanted to be alone. "What's up?"

"Nothing much. I'm just bored." He pressed his index finger against the picture and said, "I want evenings like this. I want to go places and see things."

Denny sighed heavily. "It'll happen, dear boy. But there's no hurry. You've plenty of time. Please, dear boy. Please."

Later, after Ellis had bathed and eaten porridge with golden syrup, he saw from his bedroom window that Denny was in the far corner of the orchard, sitting against an apple tree, staring at the sky. He looked scared, as unlike Denny O'Rourke as Ellis had ever seen him look. And Ellis could hear his father's voice in his ear: "Please, dear boy. Please."

10

Katie Morton was the first. She was neither his girlfriend nor his lover but she was the first. He met her in the spring of 1985 when his school career was petering out a year short of the finish line and Chloe's presence on Longspring Farm had made it yet another place where he fumbled for words, doubted himself and, consequently, no longer ventured. Katie Morton lay sunbathing on the green on the day her parents moved to the village. She was tall, with tight curly black hair and braces on her teeth. When she walked, her arms were folded across her chest, like a schoolteacher. She was nineteen. What a catch it would be for Ellis to go out with a girl two years older. Lazily, and without meaning it for one minute, he told Chrissie and Bruce, his sister's current boyfriend, that he was going to go out with the new girl.

In June, Ellis's headmaster wrote to Denny O'Rourke questioning whether there was any point in Ellis returning to school for his final year. He enclosed a questionnaire that all the pupils in Ellis's year had completed.

Question 6: Where would you like to be in five years' time? Ellis's answer: The late eighteenth century. Question 4: What would be your chosen career if you were to decide on it now? Freelance contraband smuggler, self-employed. Question 20: What single change would most directly improve the world you live in? This test stopping at question 19.

Denny heard himself chuckle. The sound reminded him of his wife and suddenly, again, the bed he was lying on was enormous. A few yards away, Ellis lay on his own bed in deeply self-critical mood. What sort of seventeen year old daydreams they are a Marsh smuggler, he berated himself.

My peers are daydreaming about having sex with Joan Jett or Bananarama.

He was too restless to sleep.

Smugglers would have got a lot of sex, his inner voice continued. Although women had brown teeth in those days so it can't have been much fun. There again, men in those days had no concept of women with white teeth and you can't miss what you don't know.

Yes, you can, he remembered.

Fearing his mind could implode, he slipped downstairs and poured vodka into a glass and took it to bed.

Chrissie came for the weekend and brought with her some concert tickets and many questions.

"Have you asked the new girl out yet, Ellis?"

"No, but I saw her today."

"What, you went to her house to see her or you saw her half a mile away?"

"We walked past each other on the footpath."

"And what did you say to her?"

"Hi Katie."

"And what else?"

"Just 'Hi Katie'."

"That was it?"

"When two people walk past each other there's only a couple of seconds of actual talking time!" Ellis protested. "You can't fit many words in."

"You can if you stop walking."

"And what if she doesn't stop when I stop? I'll be left standing there, looking like an idiot!"

"Ellis! What on earth – what on God's earth! – makes you think that Katie Morton would walk past you if you stopped and said hello?"

Ellis didn't say anything.

"Don't worry. I come with a plan," his sister continued.

"Please don't humiliate me in front of her," Ellis said. "I have to live in this village, you know."

"Well, you're seventeen so that's not strictly true."

She handed him two tickets. "Bruce got hold of these for you."

Ellis read them: *Finsbury Park Rainbow – Friday 11 June 1985 – Whitesnake plus support band.*

The Whitesnake album Bruce had taped for Ellis was his current favourite, a fact he hid from his contemporaries at school, who loathed hard rock. Many of them had started going to concerts in London. Their treks to the Astoria or the Brixton Academy were the stuff of legend in Ellis's mind. How on earth, he wondered, did they know how to use the Underground system? How did they know where to go to find their seat when they got to the venues? How did they get tickets in the first place? How had any of them returned from London with their lives?

"What have these tickets got to do with anything?" he asked, dreading the answer.

"You're taking her to the gig," Chrissie said.

"Who?"

"Mother Teresa of Calcutta! Katie Morton, you nitwit."

Ten minutes later, Ellis was out of excuses and Chrissie had got Katie's number from the operator and marched Ellis upstairs to the privacy of the phone in Denny's bedroom. Now, Ellis found a cold sweat upon him as Katie Morton herself answered the phone.

"Hello, it's Ellis here, from down the lane."

"Hello Ellis from down the lane."

"Hello. How are you, Katie?"

"I'm fine. How are you Ellis from down the lane?"

"Fine thanks."

"What do you want?"

Ellis physically recoiled from so blunt a question. Chrissie pushed the receiver back towards his mouth.

"What do I want?"

"Yeah."

"Er ... I just wondered if you fancied coming to a concert with me?"

Chrissie mouthed the word "gig" at him.

"I mean a gig," Ellis corrected himself, at the exact moment Katie Morton said, "What's the concert?"

"Sorry, what?" Ellis asked.

"No, go on. What did you say?"

"Nothing. What did you say?"

"I just asked what the concert was. What did you say?"

"I just said it was a gig not a concert."

"What's the difference?"

"I don't know," Ellis faltered.

"What band is it and when is it?" Katie asked, in her shopping list kind of way.

Ellis went silent. At that moment, he realised that there was no way Katie Morton was going to want to go with him to a Whitesnake concert. She wouldn't want to go to a Whitesnake concert with anyone and she would not want to go to any concert with him. The situation was peppered with negatives.

"You there, Ellis?" Katie asked.

"Talking Heads ..." he replied blankly.

Chrissie looked confused.

Katie became animated. "Talking Heads! Really? Very cool. When?"

"I don't mind," Ellis muttered distantly, knowing he had screwed up.

Chrissie cuffed him across the back of the head.

"You don't mind? How about David Byrne, does he mind?"

"Who's David Byrne?"

"*For fuck's sake!*" Chrissie mouthed, collapsing back on to the bed.

"Are you drunk, Ellis from down the lane?" Katie asked.

Ellis pulled himself together. "No. I'm not drunk at all. Sorry, I was distracted, my sister walked into the room." He picked up the tickets. "The concert is on Friday June the eleventh at the Finsbury Park Rainbow and I would really like you to come with me."

"That's next Friday. I'll think about it and call you back, OK?"

"OK."

"It's really sweet of you to invite me and I really appreciate it. I'm just not sure what I'm up to that evening."

"OK."

"Bye, Ellis." She hung up.

Ellis held the receiver against his chest and smiled. He had crossed the threshold. He had invited a girl out. It hadn't gone quite to plan and she wouldn't accept, but the ordeal was over and he could now say he had done it. He felt elated. He flopped back on to the bed, alongside his sister, emotionally exhausted.

"Talking sodding Heads?" Chrissie whispered.

Ellis shrugged. "There's no way she'd go to a Whitesnake gig."

Ellis sat in the living room, hoping the phone wouldn't ring. Denny turned the lights off and he and Ellis watched the horizon catch fire. The sky arched its crimson back across the village. Its blackening ribbed patterns reminded Ellis of the markings of the *Cheiracanthium* species he had been forced to read about during the truces.

What, he asked himself, if the entire world is the belly of a huge spider and we're all inside it? Beyond our universe is the outer body of a spider bigger than known existence and beyond that spider we call the universe are a trillion other spiders. And those trillion spiders live in just one spider well and there is a world full of wells.

"Spiders are little and we are big, they are big and we are little. It makes no difference either way round."

"None at all," Denny agreed.

And if it makes no difference, Ellis resolved to himself, it makes no sense to be scared of anything.

In the near darkness, he looked at the shape of his father's body and a faint glow of dusk on his face.

"Dad."

"Yes, dear boy?"

"You know ... I am going to do new things." His voice was gentle and strong. It was a new voice and it was as alien to him as it was to his dad. "I'm going to travel and seek out things. You know that, don't you?"

He got no response. Denny was motionless. There was more movement in the sky beyond him, as it gave up its last colour and detail to darkness.

Katie Morton rang three days later and said yes. Ellis was devastated.

"You have to tell her immediately that she's not going to see Talking Heads," Chrissie told him.

Ellis agreed absolutely. Definitely. Obviously. But kept putting it off until, suddenly, it was Friday and Katie was waiting for him at the foot of her parents' driveway on Wickhurst Lane. She opened the door to Mafi's car before Ellis brought it to a standstill, and was in a hurry to get away. Her parents, she said, were in a "foul mood, as usual".

Ellis had memorised the map of the London Underground during the week. He found it easy thanks to the colour scheme, which his brain could immediately make sense of. He did a last dummy run to calm his nerves as the train approached Victoria station. On the pale blue line, they sat opposite a row of seven long-haired men, all of whom wore Whitesnake T-shirts. Katie Morton looked at them curiously and turned to ask Ellis a question, but he cut her off.

"Where did you live before?"

"Near Brighton," she replied.

"I'd like to go to Brighton," Ellis said.

"It's great."

"Do you miss it?" Ellis asked.

She shrugged. "I'm not too bothered for now. I'll tell you something that no one is meant to know," she said, leaning close to his ear. "My parents would kill me if they knew anyone knew."

"What is it?" Ellis said.

"My brother's in prison. That's why we left Brighton."

"What did he do?"

"Not much. He's only in for a year."

Ellis didn't know what to say. He wanted to know what the crime was but feared that to ask again would be immature. Maybe everyone except for him knew someone in prison. If so, he shouldn't find it too amazing. But it was amazing, so would she think him dull for not asking more about it?

More David Coverdale lookalikes boarded the train at Highbury and Islington and Ellis decided it was time. He pulled the carefully resealed envelope from his pocket and ripped it open. "Jesus!" he said. "I don't believe it!"

"What?" Katie Morton asked.

"They've sent the wrong tickets!"

As Katie Morton studied the tickets, Ellis doubted the wisdom of messing with a criminal's sister. She laughed. It was a laugh Ellis couldn't begin to decipher. He didn't say anything else about it and neither did she. At the entrance to the Rainbow, he asked her again if she wanted to go for a drink instead or to just go home and she pushed him towards the door with the same knowing smile.

They saw a support band called Redfoot but they never did get to see David Coverdale's Whitesnake. As they waited for them to come on stage, a very large woman stood alongside them, drinking vodka straight from the bottle. She was huge, more than six feet tall, broader than Ellis and fat; very, very fat. Her hair was long and bushy and dyed black. Her skin was talcum-powder white and she wore dark make-up around her eyes and black lipstick. Ellis saw that she was crying as she swigged from the bottle, as if the vodka was streaming out of the pores of her skin. She smiled at Ellis and Katie through maroon mascara tears and pulled down her leather jacket to reveal a denim jacket beneath, and on the back of it an intricate spray-on picture of a smiling young man holding a guitar. Around it, in metal studs, were the words *Ronnie, 1961–1983, Gone But Still Loved.*

"This is my first concert without him," the enormous woman said, hauling the leather jacket back across the vast expanse of her rounded back.

Katie Morton placed her hand sympathetically on the huge woman's arm. When she did so, Ellis had no idea that Katie was drunk, but moments later he found out just how drunk she was.

"Did you eat him?" Katie asked the woman.

With four thousand people pressing against them, Ellis's world, miraculously, fell silent. His mind sank into a numbing incredulity at what had just been said. The woman turned, it seemed to no one in particular, and screamed, "Bunny!"

"She's sorry!" Ellis said urgently.

"BUNNEEEEE!" Her face contorted with anger.

Ten feet away, a tall, Caucasian version of Mr T heard the huge woman's call of distress. His face sank immediately into a darkness, as if already expressing regret over what he was yet to do to whoever had upset his friend.

"Did I say something?" Katie shouted.

Bunny moved towards them.

"We're leaving," Ellis yelled, pushing Katie away as the huge woman lunged at them so drunkenly that she seemed to be aiming to simply fall on top of them and squash them to death.

This was the first time Ellis had taken the initiative with a member of the opposite sex. He held Katie's arm so tight he was almost lifting her, and as Bunny chased them through the syrup-thick crowd Ellis took advantage of being half the width of his pursuer and weaved and ducked himself and Miss Morton out of the arena to the now empty bar, from which they ran without looking back. The Seven Sisters Road would never look so attractive again, nor would the air of Finsbury Park ever taste so fresh. On the tube and train that carried Ellis and his liability of a date back to the garden of England, it occurred to Ellis that a trip up to London to see Whitesnake had been in no way diminished by not actually seeing Whitesnake. His attachment to hard rock and big-hair bands was, he concluded, a little cosmetic. He would check out this David Byrne bloke tomorrow.

The lights of the village nestling in the valley were benevolent and welcomed Ellis home.

"You can't drive down to the house," Katie said. "My parents are arseholes."

Ellis parked by the primary school and walked her home. As they crossed the top of the village green, a truck drove past, catching the couple in its headlights. It sounded its horn in friendly recognition.

"Who was that?" she asked.

"Haven't a clue."

They picked their way across the rutted surface of Wickhurst Lane in the darkness. She stumbled and took hold of his hand.

"You don't like London much, do you?" she said.

"Scares me rigid."

"Just remember, all those terrifying-looking people in London would be scared stiff walking down here in the pitch dark. They'd shit themselves at every animal sound."

He dared to stroke her hand with his fingertips, in a way

149

that could have been accidental if she objected.

"I liked the way you didn't try to hide how scared you were up there," she said.

"I did try to hide it," he said, "all evening."

Katie Morton smiled but Ellis couldn't see it. They parted at a small stone bridge that crossed a stream at the foot of the Mortons' driveway. Ellis told her that at this time of year, if she walked a hundred yards up the stream to the line of pollarded willow, and if she waited in the stream downwind of the line of exposed tree roots as evening fell, she'd see badger cubs playing.

"Have you seen them?" she whispered.

"Yes, every year," he said. "I know this village like the back of my hand."

"Now *that* I do believe," she said. "I think you and I should just be friends, don't you?"

"Oh, yeah, definitely. I agree," Ellis said.

As he stepped into Bridget's shop the next afternoon, Ellis was scolding himself for talking to Katie about badgers when she might have been waiting for him to fondle her. Perhaps it was this that had put the kybosh on things between them. The bell above the shop door was still ringing when Bridget's voice met him like a physical barrier.

"Here comes lover-boy. Better luck next time."

Mrs Hawking was at the counter, dropping loose change into her purse. She winked at Ellis, saying, "She's too old for you. You're a nice boy."

"I've forgotten my money," Ellis stuttered, untruthfully, and left.

Emotionally and mentally exhausted by the aftermath of going on a date, Ellis was happy to lie low at home and do work on the cottage for his dad. He went into the town to collect floorboard pins and varnish, and in the window of the

Small World Travel Agency a poster told him that for £126 he could buy a train ticket that would take him anywhere in Europe for a month.

"Oh my God ..." he muttered, as he stood inside the travel agents reading the leaflet. And he began to shake with excitement.

A truck arrived on the Saturday morning and hoisted antique floorboards on to the driveway. For a decade, Denny O'Rourke had wanted to replace the flooring in the downstairs of the cottage and his pleasure at the job ahead made him eager and boyish. Mafi sat in the garden and watched Denny and Ellis as they worked side by side, co-ordinating instinctively, rolling up their sleeves in the exact same way and sharing mannerisms as if they had handed them to each other from a shared tool box at the start of the day. Their thoughts, however, were not in harmony, for Ellis could think only of the rail map of Europe he had bought and of the thin black lines that spread across the continent, some solitary and remote, others converging in thick swirls on Madrid and Munich, Paris, Rome and Milan.

On the Monday morning, when his dad had left for work, Ellis shoved the small, folded document with its orange boxes under Mafi's nose.

"It's just to do with the summer and work experience and everything ... I forgot to get dad to do it," Ellis said rapidly. "I'm really late, Mafi. Just sign it there."

She signed inside the orange box, unwittingly confirming herself as Ellis's next of kin.

The next weekend, they ate a Sunday roast outside, by the side lawn. The living room windows were open and a smell of floorboard varnish laced the air.

Denny breathed deep with contentment. "We've been here ten years and it's taking shape ... on a perfect day. It's never finished, but today ... it feels great."

And Denny O'Rourke did, indeed, feel truly great for a

few seconds more, until his son spoke up, with the exquisite mistiming of a teenager.

"Dad ..."

"Yes, my dear boy?"

"I'm going inter-railing in Europe this summer. For a month. On my own."

"No. You're not."

"I am."

The afternoon changed.

"Maybe next year."

"I want my life to get going," Ellis complained.

"Don't be dramatic," his father said.

Mafi smiled at Ellis and faintly shook her head, to steer him off the subject.

"If you're feeling desperate to go abroad for the first time, then we'll go somewhere together this summer. How about that?" His dad smiled encouragingly.

Ellis slumped. Just when he needed his dad to create a rift between them, from which Ellis could justify escape, he did just the opposite.

"I've already got a ticket," Ellis said, without defiance.

"How? You can't have," Denny said, trying to sound unperturbed. "You're only seventeen. You'd need my permission."

"You're wrong and I've got one."

There was silence. "How?" his dad finally asked.

Ellis shrugged his shoulders.

"I know how, don't I, Ellis?" Mafi said.

"It doesn't matter how. What matters is I'm going."

"If you think I am going to let you walk out of here when you're still just a child and get yourself ripped off or hurt or killed in some foreign country then you must think that being your dad is some part-time hobby I don't give a shit about, which makes you just about the most stupid little bugger I've ever met."

Denny marched inside.

"Could he possibly have a more negative view of the world?" Ellis muttered.

"I can't believe you tricked me like that, Ellis. I really can't."

"It doesn't matter about that. It's just important that I get going somewhere."

"You're not even going to apologise to me?"

Ellis looked at his feet. "I'm sorry. But he'd sailed round the world four times before he was twenty-one, that's the ridiculous thing!"

"He wasn't on his own," Mafi reminded him.

Ellis went to his bedroom and found his dad there, looking through his belongings.

"Where's the ticket?" Denny asked softly.

"I'm not giving it to you."

They both sat on the bed in silence.

"You're not to go. Do you understand?"

Ellis said nothing.

"Please," Denny said.

There was that word again, sounding strange coming from his dad.

"Ellis ... if anything ever happened to you, I would be devastated."

"If nothing ever happens to me, I'll be devastated."

"You've a clever answer for everything today. You're not ready. I do not want you to go." Denny let his voice trail away.

"Then I won't go," Ellis muttered.

"So, give me the ticket."

"No."

"Ellis ..."

"I said I won't go. That's it. If you think I'm not ready, that's one thing. If you think I'm untrustworthy, that's another. I'm giving you my word."

In the silence, the air between them calmed. Denny felt relief so close to elation that he had to control himself not to show it. "I trust you," he said, and left the room.

That day, and the sixteen that followed it, Ellis tried all of his magic places in the village: every tree he loved to climb, every field he loved to sit in. Each of these places was a favourite and familiar face and every one of them looked Ellis in the eye and reminded him that all other seventeen year olds were having the time of their lives.

On 1 July, Ellis packed and stood in his bedroom perfectly still, clutching the bag, as if he were a photograph of himself, taken moments before leaving the room. But he didn't leave the room, because he was terrified. That night, he couldn't sleep for taunting himself that his life was destined to be a small, monochrome one. The morning brought with it a morsel of courage, fed by nothing more substantial than the comfort of daylight, and he convinced himself that if he hesitated again and failed to embark on this small adventure, then he would never embark on any.

He gave himself the hour-long train journey to Folkestone to justify his going. His fear of inertia was real but not reason enough to inflict this agony on his dad. But, just when he needed her, his mother flew to his aid. He knew nothing about her. He had been dissuaded from asking all his life. This failure on Denny's part, as he suddenly felt able to see it, was his excuse for going and it was strong enough to withstand the increasing nausea he felt at every revised point of no return, as he boarded the ferry, as the ropes slid from the quayside, as the hull passed the line of the harbour walls on to open sea.

By dinner time he was in France, his only companions the taste of salt air and the smell of ferry fuel. He was hungry but having booked into a room in a drab area near to the harbour he was too nervous to leave it. In the darkness, the idea of justifying his trip with the memory of his mother crumbled before him. It was irrelevant. He had never pushed for information about her. He'd never truly confronted his dad and demanded to know. He had taken little dissuading from the subject because he was happy if his dad was happy and his dad was not happy when they talked about his mum.

Once again, the arrival of morning boosted Ellis. Great journeys must be planned at first light, he realised, when the heart is fearless. He rang Chrissie from a call box in Paris and after he had spoken to her he stepped out on to the boulevard de Magenta and, for the first time, the adventure began to outweigh the fear. Europe beckoned. If he stayed four weeks then he had six pounds a day to spend. He would sleep on trains and in train stations to make the money last. This, he had read, was what everybody did. On the train to Nice he slept in the heat of the window. He took a roll-up mattress on the roof of a youth hostel where the dormitories were full. The roof was a free-for-all for latecomers and Ellis watched through the gaps of his folded arms as grown men and women undressed and slept within sight of him. He felt the unfamiliar musty, warm air of the Mediterranean cling to his skin and climbed out of his sleeping bag and lay on top of it in his jeans and T-shirt. At midnight, he woke and imagined how angry his dad was and bitterly regretted not calling him. When he had called Chrissie instead, she had laughed and told Ellis he was going to get "the bollocking of all time".

"... so you might as well enjoy it," she had concluded.

"Might as well," Ellis had replied unconvincingly.

Chrissie had agreed to tell their dad where Ellis was on the condition that Ellis called home within two days. He was looking ahead with dread to that phone call when a woman in her late twenties laid a mattress down alongside his.

"Bit of a latecomer," she whispered, with a twang in her voice.

Ellis smiled and lay back, resting the back of his head

in his clasped hands. The woman laid a white sheet on the mattress and removed her clothes, lying down on the mattress in her underwear. She smelt of suntan lotion. Ellis became aware of his own breathing. His toes tensed up and he wiggled his ankles.

"Mind if I have a smoke?" the woman said, sitting up on her side.

Ellis smiled and shook his head. He stole a glance. She was tanned and had long, straight, straggly blond hair. Her face was angular. She wasn't pretty but she was handsome and healthy-looking and almost her entire body was visible and lying inches away from him. He forgot his fears. He forgot his home. The woman offered him a cigarette. He declined and pulled out his tin box and rolled one. She approved of this.

"Where you from?" she whispered.

"England. Kent," he said, shyly.

"New Zealand. I've been travelling for three years."

Ellis's mouth dropped open. Three years! She smoked one of Ellis's roll-ups after she'd smoked her cigarette and then she turned on to her back and slept. When the cathedral chimed for three o'clock, she moved in her sleep and her foot came to rest across Ellis's calf muscle. He savoured the sensation and soon afterwards he fell asleep.

Mostly, they lay on the beach and read and went swimming, taking it in turns to watch each other's belongings. She sunbathed topless and asked Ellis to rub lotion into her back, which he did with growing confidence. They swam together some of the time and he grew accustomed to the sight of her breasts. Accustomed, but not blasé. They were as magical and wonderful to him on their third day together as the first. Her thighs were strong and her calves defined. She could have been an athlete or a swimmer, or a manual labourer. A farmer, even. Her skin was extraordinarily tanned. He didn't feel the need to speak much. She wanted to do the talking. After three years away she was feeling homesick and was thinking of going home. On their last evening, they ate a picnic on the beach at Menton and got blind drunk whilst she told him what she called "her life story".

"Ours is a perfect friendship," she said. "After tomorrow, nothing can ever damage it."

To his surprise, Ellis realised that he wasn't in love with her, even though he'd rubbed oil into her back. He didn't idolise her, even though she was prepared to give him the time of day. He wasn't aching with sexual desire for her. He just liked being with her. They slept side by side on the beach in sleeping bags that last night. The stars spun above Ellis's head. He heard the woman crying to herself. She laid her head on Ellis's chest and slept there. The weight of her body against him brought sobering stabs of joy to him. They swam in the morning, before they said a word, and their hangovers eased. Ellis swam only briefly, deliberately, so that he could sit on the beach and watch the woman from New Zealand walk out of the sea towards him one final time. He locked the image away for keeps, where it remained more fresh and magical than many of the more intimate moments since.

At the train station she said that they should not exchange addresses, that they would part now with their friendship untainted. They hugged tight but they didn't kiss.

"I have a wonderful life," she said.

He couldn't speak.

She climbed the steps to the station and he watched until she was taken by the crowd. He made a wish for happiness to be with her all her life and as he walked down the Boulevard Gambetta towards the hostel, he felt lonely and burst into tears.

The phone call was made from a train station concourse.

"Dad, it's me. I'm in Italy and I'm fine. Please don't be angry."

"Where in Italy?"

"Verona."

"Is it nice?" his dad asked, in a disarming, clipped monotone.

"Yes ..." Ellis faltered.

"Are you safe?"

"I'm safe and well and I'm planning to ..." Ellis heard the receiver being laid down on the small bureau desk by the front door. He waited for something to happen. There were footsteps and then his dad spoke in the same foreign monotone.

"I was looking for Mafi so she could talk to you but she's gone for a drive with Chrissie."

Silence fell between them.

"Right then ..." Ellis said, after some while.

"I want you to do something for me, Ellis," Denny said.

"Yes? Anything."

"I want you to ring Mafi every other day so that she knows you're safe. She worries about you and that's not fair on her."

His voice was taut and brittle in its show of strength.

"You can call during the day, there's no need to wait until I'm back from work. It's your great-aunt who worries."

"OK."

There was no fight. No argument. None of the things Ellis had prepared for. Just coldness.

He's good at this, Ellis thought.

The finest part of Ellis's adventure was already over. No one and nothing would quite compare to his friend from New Zealand. He didn't care too much. All that mattered to him was that he had gone away. He had had an adventure. He had done something that Tim hadn't, and that Chloe might want to. But, for all the new ground broken, Ellis also discovered that it was still his father he wanted to share this with. In the evenings, it was Denny he imagined talking to about the day, and in moments of awe and adventure it was Denny he wished could see him there.

He rang Mafi every few days and she asked him excitedly about where he was. He saw Florence and Siena and got knocked over by a moped in Lucca. He slept in the giant tent in the botanical gardens in Munich with hundreds of others like him. He got so drunk in Munich that he boarded a night-train to Vienna and woke in Koblenz. He walked in the mountains above Innsbruck and stood at the top of the Olympic ski jump in its snowless state. He slept in a meadow of long grass and wild flowers where the temperature dropped and breathing felt like drinking fresh water. There, he felt a yearning which has been in him ever since, which never dilutes, never increases, but is ever-present, sometimes gentle, other times desperate. The possibility of fulfilment? The promise of joy? A glimpse of heaven? He doesn't know. Perhaps it was no more than the clean mountain air.

11

The village looked small and altered. It would take a day or two for it all to look familiar again. William Rutton the butcher waved. Denny's bedroom curtains were drawn against the sunlight. Ellis saw him peer out and withdraw again. Mafi rained kisses on him. The stairs seemed shallower and the cottage smaller.

Ellis sat beside his dad on the bed and touched his arm. Denny feigned waking and put on his glasses. His breathing was loud and slow, through his nose. He raised Ellis's hand into the air and let it drop limply on to the bed. He got up and walked out of the room, shutting the door gently behind him. Ellis listened to him descend the stairs and his eyes settled on the imprint of his father's body on the sheets.

Chrissie came home for the weekend. "You look like George Michael with that tan."

"Why thank you," Ellis said courteously.

"Wasn't a compliment," she said. "What's going on?"

"He's not talking to me."

"What? Not much? Not at all?"

"Not a word," Ellis said.

She found out for herself at dinner. "This is ridiculous," she told her dad. "You can't just not talk to someone."

"What would you like me to talk about?" Denny asked.

"Anything," Ellis said.

"Shall we talk about trust?"

Ellis looked away. "No."

"Lying to my face. Shall we talk about that?"

He got no answer.

"OK then, Ellis. Shall we talk about what it feels like to lie awake for twenty-nine nights waiting for the phone to ring with a foreign voice on a distant line telling me where I can come and identify my son's body? Let's talk about worrying myself sick about you, and losing the ability to eat or think straight. Let's talk about my happiness being at the mercy of whether or not you've managed to spare five minutes of your precious time to call Mafi to let her know how you are."

"You didn't want me to call you!"

"Which of those things do you want to talk about, Ellis?"

Ellis shook his head.

"WHICH OF THOSE?" his dad raged.

"I don't want to talk about any of them," Ellis whispered.

"Well, there's nothing else I'm interested in talking about with you."

Ellis went to his room and emptied his rucksack, in the

hope that his perfect friend had broken her own rules and left him a note with her number in New Zealand, amongst his belongings. But she had not.

Denny began renovating the dining room walls. It gave him reason to shut himself away. He cut out areas of rotten lath and plaster and pinned in new strips of chestnut which Terry Jay had split for him. Two post-beams were rotten. Dark slithers of wood crumbled between Denny's fingers.

"Can't make that out ..." he muttered.

The wheat at Longspring Farm had been harvested. Ellis sat in the east field and admired the farmhouse. In the half-light, further down the track, he thought he saw Chloe Purcell step out of the herdsman's house into the shadows of the lime trees. He told himself it couldn't be her. Whoever it was standing in the shade, she rubbed her neck wearily and returned inside, leaving the door open for Michael Finsey's return.

Ellis wandered aimlessly away. Back on the village green, he sat on a bench in front of the primary school. He ate an ice cream then drank a can of lager and contemplated how poorly the two mixed in the palate. Katie Morton appeared from the top of Wickhurst Lane and joined him.

"Look!" she said, flashing him a toothy, white smile. "Braces off!"

Ellis nodded his approval.

She looked impatiently at the darkening sky and asked, matter-of-factly, "So, did you lose your cherry on your travels?"

"No," said Ellis.

"Isn't that what these trips are for?" she asked.

"Why aren't you at work?" he retaliated.

She pulled a face at the clouds. "Came home early to sunbathe but that's buggered." She settled down next to him.

"At a loss what to do now," she said. "Might go for a dip."

"Where do you go?" Ellis asked.

"The pond at that farm on the hill, whatever it's called."

"Dale Farm. I wouldn't."

"I've swum there before."

"I hope not. There's an open pipe goes into that pond, full of you know what."

"Is there?" Katie pulled a face. "Bloody hell ..."

Ellis looked blankly across the village green. Katie Morton studied the sky and watched her hopes of a tan evaporate.

"I wouldn't know how to lose my virginity," Ellis murmured.

She didn't respond and Ellis became more self-conscious the longer they sat in silence.

"Well ..." Katie Morton said, eventually, with the pragmatic air of someone who didn't want to waste an afternoon, "you're not going to lose your virginity to me, Ellis, but if you like I'll give you a guided tour."

Ellis kept his eyes fixed on the grass and wondered what she meant. Katie Morton stood up and offered him her hand. "I'm taking you home ..." she said.

She stirred because Ellis had moved in his sleep, muttering someone's name.

"Who's Jo?" she whispered. "Not that I'm bothered."

"Uh?" Ellis moaned sleepily. His head swam in a syrupy daylight. Semi-conscious, he dragged the sheet up to cover their naked bodies. Beneath that sheet, his body felt the indelible touch of another naked human being lying warm beside him for the very first time. Katie Morton pulled the sheet away again and placed Ellis's hand on her tummy. He breathed the strange and subtle aroma of her unperfumed skin and he drank in the sight of her pale stomach and the wiry hair, unable to fully take in how wonderful life was becoming this summer.

"You said 'Jo' in your sleep," she said.

"She was from New Zealand," he said. "Rotorua."

"The woman you didn't lose your virginity to?" she teased.

He shut his eyes. "I think you know full well by now that I've never made love to a woman."

This made her smile. "Yes," she said.

He breathed in lazily and she moved her head across to his chest. She pressed her feet against his and they flexed their toes against each other's. Then the bedroom door opened. Ellis was not aware of the door but of Katie's body becoming rigid against his. She sat bolt upright. The middle-aged woman standing at the foot of the bed was shaking and her shoulders started to heave. She was a strong woman, Ellis soon learned, with her daughter's height and the added bulk of middle age.

Ellis's passage out of the house bore the sensation of being propelled without touching the floor. It happened too fast for him to become concerned. He was aware only of the strength of Mrs Morton's hands as they somehow made a handle out of the flesh on his shoulders with which she threw him out.

He found himself standing on the Mortons' lawn. The front door slammed shut with a thick, substantial thud. On a day of new experiences, the latest was that of being naked outdoors. In itself, it was possibly a lovely sensation, he thought, but weighed against it right now were some powerful negatives; chiefly, that the most populated part of the village lay between his naked body and home. He heard footsteps on Wickhurst Lane. Miss Spinazi, the primary school infants teacher, was walking home. The wiry spinster stopped and stared.

This, Ellis told himself, is probably the only adult in Kent less sexually experienced than me. It had to be her who came along.

"I got kicked out," he explained weakly, thumbing towards the Mortons' house behind him.

Miss Spinazi's mouth dropped open.

"It was like going through a wormhole," Ellis added. "Are you on your way home, Miss?"

She nodded and swallowed fearfully. Ellis pointed in the direction of her small, terraced cottage and nodded encouragingly.

"I don't suppose there's any chance that I could ..."

And at this she scurried away. Ellis returned to the Mortons' front door and called through the letter box.

"Please could I have my things?"

He could hear nothing from inside. He stepped away and looked for a place to hide in the garden until he was reunited with his clothing. The front door burst open. Mrs Morton marched towards him and sent him down the driveway with a series of rough pushes to the chest.

"You are not getting any clothes back, you beast! If you don't leave immediately I shall get the PC."

The last shove sent Ellis sprawling on to the loose gravel of the lane Katie had led him along a few hours earlier. He landed badly, cutting the palms of his hands and grazing his knees. He stood up, dusted the clinging stones off his skin and watched Mrs Morton march back into the house. Now he was shaken up, not so much by the playground cuts and grazes as by the realisation that he was going home naked. He was also alarmed by how small his penis suddenly seemed to be. He had two choices. To hack across the fields to Longspring Farm or to cross the village green to the cottage. The latter option was infinitely quicker. In fact, if he put his head down and ran, he could do it in two minutes. But it meant going through the centre of the village. The route to Reardon's was comparatively long but it was possible that Ellis could get there without being seen by another human being. Better still, he realised, and closer, would be to cut

across the fields to Tim Wickham's house. Then his heart
sank as he realised that neither Reardon's nor Tim Wickham's
was an option. If Ellis had to list the three people he could
least afford to be seen naked by, they would be, first, Tim's
mum – due to an adolescence filled by fantasies of her which
still had the potential to stir an ill-appreciated erection.
Second, Chloe, who could well be at the Wickhams' house
or Reardon's and would probably have the opposite effect on
Ellis's penis precisely because he wouldn't want her to; and,
third, the goat-lady, whose cottage Ellis would have to pass
by. It was just too scary to contemplate being seen by her.
She might ask him inside, offering to help. He'd be scared
of entering her house with armour on. Naked didn't bear
thinking about.

"Shit!"

Another sub-dilemma presented itself. Did he run freely
and go for speed, thereby allowing his genitals to move
however genitals moved when unsupported by underwear,
or did he hold on to them with one hand? Freestyle, he
decided. Because speed was paramount. And realising that his
situation was not going to improve whilst he stood there, he
started to run. And the faster he ran the more free he felt, and
he understood that if he chose not to care then he didn't care;
if he chose not to be embarrassed then he wasn't; if he chose
not to feel the pain on the soles of his feet then he didn't
feel it. He stuck two fingers up to his own instincts and ran,
leaving Wickhurst Lane behind and fixing his sights on the
far side of the village green as he stormed across it, oblivious
of everything and everyone outside his tunnel vision. He
ran faster than he had ever run. To do so in bare feet felt
wonderful. Natural. Easy. To do so naked changed him, in
the course of a few hundred yards, from a circumspect boy
to a young man. For the first time in his life, that part of his
brain that had often whispered, "You'd better not, Ellis,"
now murmured, "Fuck it, Ellis, why not?"

Suddenly, he was over the garden fence and scrambling through the conifers, the harsh branches scraping his skin until he stumbled out on to the side lawn where Denny was carrying rotten lath to the bonfire heap. Ellis bent over to catch his breath and work out what to tell his dad. When he looked up, his dad wasn't there. Ellis waved innocently to Mafi as she stared from her living room window. Denny was at the washing line, unpegging a towel. He wrapped it around his son.

"You're bleeding ..." he said, unable to mask the tenderness.

"Just a stupid dare with Tim, Dad. Just stupid, got a bit out of hand. I'm really sorry."

Denny picked off the stones embedded in his son's arm.

"Dad, I'm sorry," Ellis repeated.

"Make sure you get your clothes back," Denny said, sidestepping the infinity of his son's apology.

"I'll take care of it," Ellis said and thanked God his dad was talking to him again. "I'm such an idiot," he added innocently.

Denny nodded in agreement and although his head was bowed as he attended to his son's cuts, Ellis saw him smile.

Ellis slept and bathed and dressed and put what cash he had in his pocket. He was going to find Tim Wickham wherever he was and take him for a pint. It had been an incredible day and he didn't want it to end in a hurry. He wanted to go out. He wanted to sit in a pub and smoke and nurse a pint and, hopefully, look as good as he felt. If Chloe was with Tim then fine, he didn't mind at all. He had his own private life now and they were welcome to theirs.

The phone rang. Ellis looked for a pair of shoes that weren't sprayed with dried mud, and the phone kept ringing. Ellis never answered the phone, neither did Mafi, unless they were walking past it as it rang. It was unusual for Denny to let it ring. Ellis stamped his feet into his shoes and went down the landing to his dad's room and picked up the phone by the bed.

"Hello," he said.

"Ellis?"

"Katie?"

"Yeah. Christ that wasn't funny!" She laughed. "They've freaked out. I don't know where they've gone."

"Who?"

"My parents, who else? They're not at yours, are they?"

"No. Your mum's pretty strong."

"I'm so sorry for what happened."

"I don't mind. It was worth it."

"You wanna meet?"

"OK."

"Don't sound too enthusiastic. Meet me up by the bypass, in Morley's café, in an hour."

"OK."

On his way downstairs, from the small window on the half-landing, Ellis saw Katie Morton's parents walking down the driveway to their car. He found his dad sitting at the dining table. The two chairs opposite him had been pushed away and come to rest like a car crash beside the wall that Denny was gutting.

Ellis's tendency to make the wrong observation at the wrong time kicked in. "Can you believe they drove here when it's a five-minute walk?"

Denny's face was set angrily in thought. Ellis fought the urge to continue out of the cottage and took a seat.

"I'll go if you don't want to talk," he offered.

"You'll do what pleases you," Denny muttered bitterly.

"Whatever that's meant to mean," Ellis added.

There was a long silence. Then Ellis started to get up.

"It means," his dad hissed, sending Ellis back on to his chair, "that if you stopped and thought about me let alone bothered to think for one second about your mother even, then maybe you'd just ..."

His voice faltered into silence.

"Maybe I'd just what?" Ellis asked. "Think what about my mother?"

Denny O'Rourke fixed his angry gaze at nothing.

"Think what about my mother?" Ellis repeated accusingly. "I know diddly-squit about her. Except that she's dead."

"Exactly," his dad whispered.

Ellis leapt to his feet. "WELL, WHAT THE JESUS IS THAT SUPPOSED TO MEAN?"

"Don't shout at me, boy!"

"What is it supposed to mean, I said! Now fucking well answer me!"

"Ellis!"

"Because just what the fucking hell I am supposed to think about my mother beats me. I know nothing about her, do I? How dare you tell me to think about someone you've spent my whole life pretending never existed!"

"SHUT UP, ELLIS!" Denny bellowed.

But Ellis ploughed on. "You've kept her from me all my life and now you want to use her as an example! Of what? I don't know anything about her! You're useless, you've always been useless and bringing her up now is just about the most useless you've ever been!"

Denny O'Rourke fell back on to his chair. His hearing and vision became distant and unfocused. When he managed to raise his head again, he was alone.

Morley's café and truck stop was spread out on a plateau above the main road. From here, Ellis watched the toy houses of a miniature village in the soft, low, late afternoon light and scoured the lanes and fields for a sight of Katie Morton. He wandered across to the café entrance. Steam had obscured the warm orange windows, making indistinct silhouettes of the few people within. Ellis peered through them as best he could. Katie was not inside and Ellis was too intimidated to go in alone. In the car park, he noticed the driver's door of a large decrepit Mercedes open. The interior light came on and illuminated a small, rounded, curly-haired man as he took a last drag on a joint and threw the roach away. As he passed Ellis and pushed open the café door, he smiled vacantly. "Going in?"

"Nah," Ellis said casually. "Waiting for my girlfriend."

He walked away and sat on the fence at the far end of the car park. He listened to the metallic flashes of sound as cars sped by on the main road.

He was used to being in the dark about the transactions that occurred between people. This evening it was different. Only he and Katie Morton knew what they had done. The others thought they knew. They presumed the obvious, and Ellis saw his dad diminished in some small way by his ignorance.

"We began with a lie, you and me," Katie had said to Ellis, as she led him upstairs six hours earlier. Ellis didn't understand what she meant. "Oh Lord! They've sent us the wrong tickets!" she mocked.

In the bathroom, she asked him to remove a medium-sized *Tegenaria saeva* from the bath and run the taps. She took a pee in the toilet next door whilst Ellis's resolve to cup the spider in his hands and place it on the window ledge failed him and he ushered it, with a loofah, down the plughole, convincing himself that it would have plenty of time to escape through the pipes before the bath was emptied. There were protests, but he turned a deaf ear.

Katie added bubble bath to the running water. "But we'll not tell any lies today. I'll tell you whatever you want to know and I'll be truthful."

"So will I," Ellis said, not knowing what the hell she was talking about.

She told him to sit down on the chair beside the bath and

then she undressed.

"We aren't going to have sex. I don't want to go out with you or to cop off with you. I don't find you especially good-looking or fascinating. But I like you more than other boys I can think of, three of whom I have slept with I might as well tell you. I'm not planning on adding to that number in a hurry."

Ellis listened obediently and found, to his surprise, that he didn't particularly want to 'cop off' with her either. He just wanted to be exactly where he was, listening and watching. He was happy not to be expected to do anything. She was naked now and he was aware of the sound of his own breathing and swallowing in a way he had never been before. She turned off the taps and felt the water. Her body could not have been more different from the woman from New Zealand's.

"Don't you tan?" Ellis asked.

"Don't I what?"

"Tan? In the sun."

"Not spectacularly," she said. "But it's not for the lack of trying."

She climbed into the bath and told Ellis to kneel alongside. "You can look at me and you can ask anything, but you can't touch. I'll place your hands where I don't mind them going."

"OK, thanks," Ellis said, as if being given road directions.

She cleared the bubbles away from her breasts and placed his right hand on them.

"Mine are rather small, Ellis," she said. "You'll decide what you like as you find out."

"I'm going to like big ones," he said immediately, without thinking.

She burst into laughter. "Honest Ellie, that's you."

Ellis withdrew his hand, though not abruptly. "Please

170

don't call me Ellie," he said gravely. "Only my mum called me Ellie."

She was taken aback. "You're an odd fish," she said.

"And you're not?" he replied, stretching out his arms to remind her where she was and what she was doing.

The affection in her face gave him confidence enough to say, "I can't see your body for all the bubbles."

"Soap gets rid of bubbles," she replied.

He took a bar of Mr and Mrs Morton's not inexpensive soap, dunked it in the water and rubbed it between his hands, allowing the lather to drip from the bar and fall on the bubbles. The bubbles fizzed as they dissolved. Katie Morton raised one leg out of the water and presented it to Ellis. He washed her legs and her tummy and her breasts. The bubbles crackled all the while and soon he could see her, through the milky water.

After that, she led him to her bedroom and she removed his clothes and told him not to worry about his erection. They lay on the bed together and hugged. She took his right hand and placed it on her tummy and then she slid his hand down until it rested on her pubic hair. He stared peacefully at her body and never thought to explore or probe further. He had no urge to lie on top of her, or to fondle her or to penetrate her. He did not burn with the stabbing, restless desire he felt when he and Tim used to go to the goat-lady's place. What Katie and he were doing was just right. It was peaceful and tender and it placed no pressure on him to know more than he knew.

And all the while he kept telling himself, What a summer! What a summer!

An ivory glare emanated from the cloud cover and flooded the room with smooth light. Ellis smiled inwardly at the bright new world appearing before him.

"It's like watching underwater films," he said, blissfully unaware of speaking.

"What is?"

"A woman's body."

"Like I said," Katie stroked his arm, "an odd fish."

And then they fell asleep.

The village had sunk into dusk. In that gloom, beyond the charcoal fields of Elsa's farm, Ellis could no longer place the once infinite joys of village life: the avenue of lime trees at Longspring, the view of the Downs glowing crisp and blue in the frost of winter, a peek at Kerry Moscow's knickers as she climbed the gate to the Rumpumps when they were both nine years old, a meringue handed to him by Mrs Brown at Forge Cottages as he waited with his sister for the 454 bus, helping his father cut the grass in the orchard, handing a cigarette to Tim Wickham as he handed one back with the greater part of the day still ahead, the field at Long Barn a ripple of tall, swaying wheat. All these and a thousand other delights lay discarded in the corner of Ellis's restless mind, like neglected toys in a bedroom cupboard. The smallness of the place was what he saw now, and the lights of the bypass and distant towns which rose out of the settling darkness and glimmered and twinkled with their own imprecise promises.

Sometimes, as a very small boy, Ellis looked close up at his hands, at his fingerprints, at the faint pathway of a vein beneath his skin, and he had the sensation of being newly born, immediately out of the womb, a few hours old, the process of his cells dividing and his body forming still ongoing, but with no one watching, no one gathering him up to wrap layers of clothing around him. The feeling of living inside a space suit and instead of the sound of your own breathing all you can hear is your own voice wondering aloud what happens next.

"Still waiting?" The man with the Mercedes stood nearby beneath a street light. He was short and unshaven, in his early forties, with a beer gut and Marty Feldman eyes. By the looks of him, Ellis thought, possibly a Whitesnake roadie. Behind him, the café was in darkness.

"Women!" The man had a lazy East End accent. "Need a lift?"

Ellis looked away. He watched the sodium lights that snaked around the valley and out into the world. He felt the breeze that followed the cut of the main road blow against his face. This moment was open-ended and it was his own. His own adventure, his own story, his own mistake.

"OK," he said.

They travelled in silence at first and Ellis stole glimpses of the man's head rolling back and forth as he drove.

"Do you toke?" the man slurred, bringing himself back from the edge of sleep.

"Do I what?"

"Toke," the man repeated. He leant across Ellis and opened the glove compartment. Ellis looked at the cigarette papers, small blocks of hash and ready-rolled joints. He said nothing. He had been contemplating trying pot for some months now but had done nothing about it. Now, he suspected, was not the time.

"I'm a roofer," the man said, reaching for one of the joints and lighting it. "Roofer and builder. Build roofs."

He took a few tokes and then handed it to Ellis, who accepted it, vowing to embrace a non-inhalation method. The smoke tasted sweet and beguiling and he broke his vow on the third toke.

"That's nice and mild," the driver said, "you'll be OK with that. I never smoke anything major when I'm driving. I don't like people who do."

Ellis took another drag and handed it back. "It's very nice," he whispered, although he had intended to say it aloud.

"Never smoke anything that mashes your brain when I'm

behind the wheel," the man repeated. "Just a little toke on something mellow."

"Probably wouldn't pass as a road safety campaign, that," Ellis said.

The man looked confused, then changed the subject.

"Employ loads of people, I do. Good money in roofing."

Ellis felt a ripple of nausea. He rested his head back and closed his eyes.

"Know anything about roofing?" the driver asked.

"No," Ellis said.

"You can start tomorrow then!" The driver wheezed a laugh to himself and handed the spliff back to Ellis. Ellis defied his own instincts and smoked the rest of it.

"Road safety campaign ... yeah ..." the driver slurred to himself, confused. "Yeah ... nice one."

Ellis was woken by the seagulls. It was morning and he was in the Mercedes. It was parked in a dead-end street beside a large, bleak-looking pub called the Harbour Lights. A blanket was wrapped around him. Opposite the pub was a sea wall and the tide was high the other side of it. The beach was shingle and to the left was a harbour with a tall, blue-grey tower. Mist was burning off the water and a large cargo ship manoeuvred through the harbour entrance. Somewhere out to sea, an invisible vessel boomed a low signal that made the windows of the pub vibrate.

Ellis hauled his shivering body on to the sea wall. A young man appeared, tall and lanky with long dyed-black hair. He looked as though he got no daylight.

"There you go." He handed Ellis a mug of tea.

"Thanks," Ellis said.

"Mick says you can start today or leave it till tomorrow if you're knackered."

Ellis watched the young man go back inside the lifeless

174

pub. He sipped the strong, sweet, piping hot tea and looked out across the water. Contentment swept through him. He wondered where he was. He looked around. From the top of Coastguards Alley, a phone box stared accusingly at him. The red paint had faded to matt pink. One pane of glass was broken, low down, an impromptu cat flap. He rang Chrissie and told her that he was on the coast and that he had work. He asked her to tell their dad. She refused and told him to go home, but he knew that she would call Denny immediately. She loved to break news.

He returned to the sea wall and rolled himself a cigarette and vowed not to go back home for one whole year. That would be amazing, he told himself. That would make him mysterious and desirable. That would mean he had his own life. OK, this place was not like the photographs he had pored over in the pages of *National Geographic*, but it was something new and that felt good. The phone box in the alley glared at him again. He rehearsed a phone call to Denny but even in his imagination the conversation strayed into argument.

It's private, Dad, Ellis imagined saying. See how you like it.

12

The flat above the Harbour Lights pub had four bedrooms. One was used by Sapphire, the barmaid. Mick and his crew slept in the others. Ellis had to wait until the men finished watching videos in the early hours of the morning before he could brush the food and roaches off the sofa and use it as his bed.

"See these stairs here?" Mick said, giving Ellis a tour.

"These two steps?"

"Yeah." Mick stood over them, the way TV detectives stand over a corpse. "These two steps down to the kitchen and living area mean that the flat is split-level. Right?"

"With you so far," Ellis said.

"And you know what that means, don't you?"

Ellis shook his head.

"That it's a maisonette, not a flat."

"Right." Ellis nodded.

"That is to say, it's a maisonette as opposed to being a flat, if you get me."

Ellis could only wonder how a man with such a slavish devotion to mind-enhancing drugs had been left so cruelly unenhanced.

Mick put Ellis into the care of Jed, his foreman on a house renovation at Joy Lane Beach. Jed was softly spoken and quick-witted, handsome and strong, with small, piercing eyes. He was twenty-four and already tanned and marked by eight years' labouring. Ellis stuck close to Jed, did what Jed told him and spoke hardly a word, using the first two weeks to weigh up the new sort of people around him. His first pay packet consisted of ten five pound notes, a carton of French cigarettes and a block of hash. He bought jeans, a T-shirt, underwear and a toothbrush.

High above the town, from the rooftop at Joy Lane, they watched students hitching to summer jobs in Canterbury and Margate, dressed in dungarees and torn jeans.

"It's like a Dexy's Midnight Runners convention," Jed said.

Dark clouds brewed out to sea and the downpour came in heavy sheets. The crew took cover inside the house and smoked spliffs and turned up the radio, above the sound of rain peppering the tarpaulins. One guy cursed a Madonna song and said she was "shit" but added, after further contemplation, that "he'd give her one, though, if she begged". Another man announced that he was "too fucked to raise a finger, let alone walk home".

"You should go for a swim," Ellis said. "It'll freshen you up."

The crew turned and stared.

"It talks," one of them muttered.

They carried Ellis's wriggling body across the beach and threw him into the sea. He floated away on his back, a sodden spliff between his grinning lips. The men laughed and splashed in the water. In time, they dispersed. Slithers of lightning shot from the underbelly of black clouds out to sea. The storm moved eastwards, parallel to the coast. The lightning was silent, the waves gentle and unperturbed, but black, jet black. Ellis laid his wet five pound notes on the sea wall, pinning them flat with pebbles. He lay on his back in his soaking clothes. It felt good to have a little money.

He learned how to re-bed ridge tiles, use a slater's ripper, lay bricks, bake hash, spike a B-bomb and brew home-made honey oil. And, seven weeks after leaving home, he lost his virginity to Sapphire, the barmaid from the Harbour Lights, real name not known, and an event which he had expected to transform his life and propel him into a state of supreme wisdom passed without ceremony or pleasure, leaving him crushed by the disappointment of their loveless encounter on the beach.

"You could do with a proper girlfriend," she told him, as she stepped back into her knickers, snagging them on the soles of her Dr Martens. "Someone you really like. I'm not going to do any more fucking until I meet someone I actually fancy."

He nodded purposefully, to paper over her comment.

"Can I say something blunt?" she asked.

"Blunter than what you just said?" he asked back.

"You have it all to learn in the sex department. Get an actual girlfriend and you'll improve your technique."

Ellis thought about this. Just getting to do it in a bed might help him, he thought.

"You'll crack it," she added. "Pardon the pun."

He smiled bravely, and wondered what the pun had been.

Next day, hungover and grieving for his stillborn romantic dream, Ellis was in no mood to go to work and knowing that Jed had a day off he wandered around the bay to the foreman's mobile home.

"I'm not working today, I'm too depressed," Ellis announced, at the doorstep.

"Depressed? How exotic. Have you told Mick you're not turning up?"

"No, I'm just taking the day off."

"That's a stunningly bad idea."

They walked across Graveney Marshes as far as Horse Hill, to pick mushrooms.

"I used to pick mushrooms at Reardon's," Ellis said. "For breakfast."

"Not mushrooms like these you didn't," Jed said.

No, not mushrooms like these.

"I've never had anything like these before ..."

"Yeah," Jed said, watching Ellis vomit at the foot of one of his bird tables. "They do taste a bit cheeky. We might be a tad premature eating these. Probably need some Daddy's sauce."

"Sweet Jesus!" Ellis groaned, as the garden folded in on him. "I'm gonna go to work."

"Another remarkably bad idea."

Ellis wandered away and was sick again on the beach. He

waited for the spiralling to go. He felt lonely. He slept and he was cold when he woke so he walked at a pace. He crossed the footbridge over the rail line and climbed through the allotments to the Rose In Bloom pub. Specks of rain dappled his face and made him smile. He looked at the greying sky and saw that the droplets of rainwater had begun their journey in another sphere, somewhere between the skies and outer space, in a world not detectable to the human eye. It was a world of flat water, moving horizontally in sheets between beams of starlight, a world of iridescent blue, more mysterious than the base of the ocean. The rain came from this world and he welcomed the droplets on to his face. They fell in slow motion towards him, each one distinct and crystal clear, and as they permeated his skin and entered his body he felt that he belonged to that other world.

He looked across the road to the bungalows stacked neatly on the hillside. A man and a woman emerged from either side of every bungalow. They held their palms up to the sky to check for rain, blew kisses to each other and returned inside, hovering a few inches above the ground. The women wore clogs. There were goats grazing all around. Everything was vivid on the surface and uncertain beneath.

At the disused brewery, Ellis found Mick and smiled at him innocently, with bright, trippy eyes.

"You're five hours late."

"Oh dear."

"Fuckwit! Go up to the top floor and hose it down and do it quickly so I can get these boys back to work underneath you. Then make me a fucking cup of tea."

Ellis trudged up five flights of stairs inside the gutted building, immediately losing his grasp on what Mick had asked him to do. The floors had been ripped out and Ellis could look down through a skeletal run of scaffolding planks on each level to the ground. At the top of the building, white paintwork had peeled from the walls, taking chunks of plaster with it. Ellis rested and looked at his surroundings. He thought he saw his father out of the corner of his eye, but when he turned there was no one there.

"Sorry," he called out, just in case.

He was shaking and his throat was dry but his physical weakness worried him less than a dawning sense of crisis. He looked at his feet and found himself unable, or unwilling, to look up again. A flurry of panic came towards him. He tried to recognise it but was distracted by Mick's voice, screaming at him from outside.

"ARE YOU FUCKING DEAF OR WHAT?"

Ellis peered out of a glassless window. Five floors below stood Mick, nostrils flaring, eyes bulging.

"Eh?" Ellis thought he was going to faint.

"I've been shouting to you for fucking ages, you wanker!"

"Have you?"

"Yes! Take the fucking hose!" Mick jabbed his hand angrily towards the wide open loading doors. Ellis stepped out on to the hoisting platform and took hold of the pulley rope and the hose that had been tied to it. He pulled the hose into the room, stood motionless and tried again to place this feeling of impending trouble.

"ELLIS!" Mick shrieked.

Ellis tiptoed over to the platform and felt a fit of giggles imminent. Down below, Mick was turning purple with rage. "What the fuck are you doing now?" he yelled.

"Nothing!" Ellis chose, unwisely, to answer.

"Ellis, are you taking the piss because I'm in the mood to smack the shit out of you if you are?"

"Whaaaat?" Ellis whined, confused.

Mick composed himself and faked a smile. "Please, old chap, hose down the ceiling and walls, like I asked you to twenty minutes ago, so that all these boys can get back to work underneath you. Please, pleasey-weasey."

"I need chocolate," Ellis said.

Mick exploded. "YOU DON'T NEED FUCKING CHOCOLATE, YOU CUNT! YOU NEED A HOSE AND YOU'RE FUCKING HOLDING ONE!"

"All riiiiight!" Ellis started to giggle. He stepped back inside and picked up the hose, studied it, laid it down again and fell to his knees. Then he saw them, all around him, cobwebs stepping forward into his line of sight one by one, the way stars appear in the sky at the margins of darkness, coming from nowhere to dominate the view. They were in the apex of the roof, under the sills, across the shattered windows. And hiding somewhere inside them were millions of spiders. Spiders Ellis couldn't see but that his weary, confused, tripping mind insisted were there.

"Oh bollocks," he moaned, and hid his face in his hands. "I'm too grown up for this rubbish. Please just go. I've got to hose down the place so you have to go. Not that you're here. You need to get organised and evacuate."

They responded sympathetically in the same voice as in the old days. "We're not here, Ellis. We haven't been here for a long time, not since they started all the work. You need some sleep, Ellie-boy."

"Don't call me that," Ellis replied wearily. "This is a pain in the arse."

He stood up as resolutely as his jelly legs would allow, grappled for the hose and set to work. "You're not here. They're not here. It's ridiculous."

Jed marked the arrival of his first video player by renting *Badlands* and *A Nightmare on Elm Street* and inviting a few people over. Ellis slept in the spare room and the next morning, whilst cooking breakfast, Jed said, "The room's yours for forty quid a month, if you like."

Jed's mobile home was on the edge of a caravan park at

the far end of Joy Lane Beach. He had surrounded it with home-made bird tables and feeders, which he filled every morning before work. Joy Lane was on a plateau running out of the town, parallel to the sea. To the south of it, modern bungalows were stacked in neat rows of Lego on the hill, gazing permanently at the tides. To the north was the London to Ramsgate line and then the golf course and then an arc of beach huts and then the sea. A railway bridge connected the lane to the short no through road which was Joy Lane Beach. Nine sets of steep steps led down to nine white-painted dwellings on the water's edge and beyond them was the caravan park. The beach was quiet and empty. It yawned wide open at low tide, a vast mud expanse dotted with mussel beds and small wrecks.

Ellis accepted Jed's offer and couldn't believe his luck.

There was masking tape in Jed's shed and Ellis used it to seal the gaps in the walls and window frames of his new bedroom. He knew, better than most, the wealth of spider-life on a beach and it was cold enough for them to be driven inside. He didn't want to dwell on the fact that he was beginning to worry about them again.

A photograph of a six-year-old boy smiled from the kitchen wall. Jed told Ellis that the boy was his baby brother and offered no more detail. Near to the boy, suspended from the ceiling, was a rusty Victorian saucepan rack with a row of fishing hooks from which hung large, dome-shaped mushrooms. The mushrooms were amber-brown and each stem had a black line around it near the dome. The domes were tainted by grey warts.

Nothing seemed to ruffle Jed. He had an on-off love affair with the landlady of the pub that jutted out into the sea. She was eleven years older than him. People viewed him with respect and began to notice his young sidekick too, struck that a near mute should have such bright blue eyes as Ellis O'Rourke had.

Ellis wrote to Chrissie to give her his address. He described the view of the coastline from his bedroom window. He asked her to send his love to Mafi and his dad. The day was crisp. Out to sea, the decaying army forts on the Shivering Sands were clearly visible. Men working the mussel beds were a silent film but for the thin calls of wading birds. Joy Lane Beach was living another day in its own separate world. Ellis wished his dad could see him.

What shocked Ellis about the Buckingham green Triumph Herald 1200 for sale on Cromwell Road was not the surprisingly low mileage of a twenty-year-old car – which the owner put down to having used it "just for nipping to the shops", hearing which his brother suffered an attack of the giggles – nor was it the strange bubbly effect of the paintwork, or the liberal use of electrical tape to hold together the pvc seats, or the absence of a rear bumper. No, what struck him most of all was that this splendid vision of mechanical beauty cost a mere one hundred and fifty pounds. When he considered the hundred pounds sitting in his Post Office account and the fact that he was earning decent cash, it dawned on him that it was now entirely plausible that he could own a motor car. If moving from Mick's sofa to Jed's place felt good, just imagine how fantastic life was going to feel if he owned a car. He would be mobile and grown up and unbelievably cool. His social life and sex life would quickly move on to a par with Bruce Springsteen and that bloke in Dynasty with the quiffy hair. He simply had to own this D reg Triumph Herald. All he needed now was his driving licence and his blue Post Office Savings Account book, and they were back home.

It was a Thursday morning. He had an hour. His dad was at work, of course, and Mafi would be having her hair done at Carrie Combe's and then having a drink in the Windmill, as she did every Thursday. The cottage was cold and hollow. He listened to it creak and groan, surprised to discover that in the middle of the day it sounded like the dead of night. He went to his room and got what he needed. He took his matchbox as well, the one with his mum in it.

He looked out at the front garden and recalled his dad buying a Mountfield lawn mower the first summer here. The noise of the engine had startled Ellis. He remembered burning his forearm just above his wrist on the mower that same summer. He thought of the first time he cut the grass for his dad, when he was twelve. He could feel the weight of the machine as his undeveloped body struggled to heave it around. He saw his dad in a ragged gardening sweater, stooping beneath low-hanging branches as he cut the grass. You always started in the orchard, mowing crossways from the fence by the working men's club downhill towards the cottage. Then you cut the small patches of lawn around the quince bushes and Mafi's garage and round the back of the cottage beneath Mafi's living room window. Then, up on to the side lawn, raising the height of the blade a notch so as to keep the grass lush and soft. You mowed the side lawn lengthways, up and down the slope. Then, to finish, the front garden, starting at the bottom, in the wet areas around the weeping willow, and finishing on the neatest part in front of the house. In the summer, Ellis liked to time it so that he was finishing the last lines of the front lawn as his dad returned from work. His dad's face would break into a smile from behind the wheel.

"Wonderful, dear boy," he'd exclaim, getting out of his car. "Thank you very much."

One summer, they returned from a summer holiday and the grass was so long that Ellis had to march up and down a few yards in front of his dad, stomping down the grass for Denny to mow. Another time, it started to rain and Mafi came out with a bright red umbrella and held it over Denny as he mowed. Ellis took a picture. His dad is laughing.

He drank hot chocolate on the train because he felt weak. He felt weak because he had lingered too long in the cottage and, suddenly fearful that Mafi would walk in on him, had left in a hurry, agitated by the sensation of being chased. He had felt she was watching him for the three miles he walked across the fields to Hildenborough station.

The train window played a movie of hop fields and pasture. Ellis wondered whether the cottage had always been that desolate when everyone was out, or whether his leaving had created the void. Was it his fault, the hollowness that now prevailed in the rooms, the sense of something lost?

Nothing is ever motionless, he told himself. The day you arrive somewhere new is the day you start towards leaving that place. Time never stood still in the cottage for us to just be, to just exist. It was running out from the moment it began. Every day of your life is lying in wait for you.

I thought I would cut the grass for him for ever.

Jed left Mick's employment and took Ellis with him. The green Triumph Herald with its home-made wooden roof rack laden with paint pots and ladders became a recognised sight in the town. By day, Ellis felt warmed by the adoring company of the old ladies whose houses Jed sent him to paint. By night, he haphazardly sought the company of young women, but when he found it there was rarely the affection he dreamed of. He escaped from these regrettable encounters to the beach where the winter winds were scorched by Scandinavian ice and the rains were horizontal.

As the year grew old, there were few days when the ibotenic acid of the fly agaric mushroom was not canoeing leisurely around Ellis's system. The after-effects of alcohol, cannabis and amphetamine sulphate could all be diluted by retreating to the beach, unless the binge had been extreme

185

enough to render Ellis unconscious or sick. His body always recovered, with a little time. Harder to treat was the self-loathing that overcame his psyche whilst his body bore the brunt of his prodigality. Even that, though, he'd forgive and forget when the high of recovery embraced him. This was usually on the second morning, when he would wake to find the sickness replaced by the head pains of dehydration. He would eat well, drink sweet tea and be filled by a feeling of profound love for everything and everyone around him, unaware that this feeling was there simply because yesterday he had felt so ill and today he did not.

On the evening he had a date with Shelley Neame, he got home from work sweaty and caked in dust, and went immediately to run a bath. The large house spider waiting beside the hot tap ruined his plans. He knew instantly from the once familiar ripples inside his stomach that he would not be able to reach towards the bath tap.

"Come on, Ellis," he groaned, "this is baby stuff."

But there wasn't time to think about it. All that mattered was meeting Shelley Neame and there was no way he could do that without washing. It was the lowest of all possible tides. He walked for twenty minutes across the mudflats to the sea, wearing Jed's bathrobe and a towel around his waist. He carried a bar of soap, a bottle of shampoo and a tall wooden pole. When he reached the water, he planted the pole into the mud, hung the bathrobe and towel from it and hurried into the water until it was deep enough to bathe in and wash his hair. He arrived in the lounge bar of the Victoria pub in Victoria Street very clean, if a little salty, and very late. Twenty-five minutes late. Shelley Neame had been and gone.

He called her from the phone box on Harbour Street. She was prickly and offended at being stood up.

"Is it because I'm bisexual?" she asked.

"No. Not at all. I had no idea you were. I really want to see you. Do you mean you used to be a man?"

"No, dickhead! That's not what it means."

"Good. That'd be a bit freaky. What does it mean?"

"If you're that wet behind the ears it's probably best we're not hooking up."

She was gone and Ellis was pissed off. He really fancied her. She drank Guinness, and he found that indescribably attractive in a woman.

"Bollocks!"

He moped his way across Middle Wall and Island Wall to the pub on the beach, where he removed himself to the corner of the downstairs bar and drank. Really drank. For the first time in his life. He drank pint after pint and when he was drunk enough, he let the spiders know that he blamed them for his foul mood.

"I fancied her, as well you know!"

"You should be thanking us! We've saved you from an evening with a bisexual!"

They were taking the piss and he knew it. They just wanted him to admit he didn't know what bisexual meant. He refused to discuss it with them any further and watched, with sullen detachment, the crowd of students, would-be artists, casual labourers and opt-outers that gathered here every night. He questioned whether, in their zeal not to conform, these people were merely embracing a different flavoured regime. How open-minded were they really, he wondered. If one of them had turned up this evening not wearing the clothes, body-language and politics agreed amongst them, would they have been welcome? They were in each other's company constantly. When did they encounter something else? They talked about the same things every night. They slept with each other, gradually crossing off every permutation. They despised people with money and constantly bemoaned their lack of it. None of them seemed to go anywhere and yet they spoke of routine as if it were a disease they couldn't catch.

Ellis's evening became a blur of drink and unconvincing resolutions. He would look for farm work inland and discover a new heaven similar to Longspring. He would visit Tim Wickham. He would make it through a whole year before going back to his dad and would make something of himself before then. He would read some novels. He would write to his dad once he had a farm job. He would never get this drunk again.

He drank slowly and unremittingly until it was dark outside and he was more drunk than he could have imagined it possible to be. Unaware of the people he was falling into, he made his way out of the pub. The sea air seemed to free up his brain and the information he had been straining for earlier in the evening suddenly came to him. He hurried back and threw open the pub door to share his enlightenment.

"I've got it!" he shouted, silencing the downstairs bar. "A bisexual is a one who sleeps with men and women and women and men, right?"

Stumbling home along the sea wall, Ellis fell, and in a moment that was to make him, fleetingly, a local legend, he nose-dived through the driver's window of a parked car and fell asleep with his face wedged against the handbrake and his legs sticking out of the window.

Longspring was pale and silent and perfect. The sea is never silent, Ellis told himself. He watched Tim emerge from the milking shed and walk down to Michael Finsey's house. Chloe opened the door, stepped into the garden and took washing from the line. She waited for Tim to reach her and they walked inside together, without touching. Ellis watched this scene play out against the sound of crows in the treetops and shock in his heart. So, it had been Chloe he had seen stepping out of the herdsman's house that evening. But it was no longer Michael Finsey's house, it was Tim's. It was Chloe's and Tim's. He was not, after all, to be met here today by the twelve-year-old Tim Wickham he had been missing.

"Why have you got two black eyes?"

"I fell into a car."

"You look like shit."

They walked up the track with their arms round each other. In the hay barn they handed each other a rollie.

"I've missed you," Tim said lazily.

"Same here. Where's Reardon?"

"Ireland. For a week."

"What happened to Michael?" Ellis asked.

"Got Fincher's herd at Rolvenden."

"You're young to have your own house," Ellis said.

"Young to have my own herd," Tim said, laughing under his breath. "It's fucking excellent."

Tim laid logs in the stove and they sat at the kitchen table. They opened a bottle of red wine at the end of the afternoon. Tim showed a brief interest in Ellis's life on the coast before conversation settled on familiar details of the farm. Ellis stole glimpses of Chloe, who was subdued. She had grown heavier and filled out and was infinitely more attractive and feminine to Ellis than the pale, skinny fifteen year old he had once hoped might settle for him. She and Tim seemed to be playing at being adults. And they were not convincing, other than resembling a couple who had been together a long time.

"I haven't learned how to cook, before you get your hopes up," Chloe said.

"She's not joking," Tim said, pinching her waist and provoking a rare smile.

They got drunk over dinner, drunk enough for Ellis to tell Tim he'd help with the milking. Chloe went to the stove and, with her back turned, asked Ellis about his 'love life'.

"There's no one really ..." Ellis said half-heartedly.

She opened the stove door and the three of them watched the flames.

"We'll have to find you a good woman," Chloe said, without meaning it.

She wrapped a coat around her shoulders and stepped outside. Through a doorway that seemed narrow and hunched, Ellis watched her sadness beam its distress signal silently into the night, before she wandered away to share her secrets with the horses.

It was the sound of a mug grazing the teak blanket chest beside his bed. Before he fully regained consciousness this sound breached the defences of his memory and unveiled ephemeral glimpses of mornings when his dad woke him before sunrise. Momentarily, he thought that they were heading to the Marsh. Love for his father and for those times seeped into his heart and he was sure that his dad's fingers were stroking the hair off his forehead. He opened his eyes. Chloe was sitting on the bed. She smelled of sleep and her body emanated heat in a cold room.

"Wake up, sleepyhead," she whispered. "There's a cup of tea for you."

He felt the mattress rise as she left. It was pitch black outside.

Tim applauded Ellis as he sleepwalked into the kitchen. Ellis grunted and threw cold water over his face. He ran to join Tim on the track to the top field and together they brought in the herd.

The more tired Ellis became the more he felt that he was standing outside himself, watching the day pass. The times he had spent at Longspring seemed unclear and this saddened him. When they stopped for a break in the hay barn, he could have slept instantly.

"Your girlfriend is the only woman I've met in the last four months who doesn't smell of joss sticks," he said.

Tim smiled and handed the hip flask over. Then, after a silence that had almost stolen Ellis to sleep, Tim said, "My wife."

Ellis sat up. "Come again."

"Wife, not girlfriend."

They were silent.

"I didn't know how the fuck to find you, otherwise you'd have been my best man."

"Fair enough," Ellis muttered.

"There were nine guests. You'd have made it a good round number."

"Who was your best man?"

"My dad, and Reardon gave Chloe away. Her parents wouldn't show."

They smiled warmly at each other, but Ellis felt shocked by the disappearance of the boy called Tim.

It was exactly the same. A faint, scraping ceramic sound. Followed again by the sensation of her weight on the side of the bed. Ellis woke beneath heavy, closed eyelids. He had slept deeply and his body tingled in the warm frailty of waking prematurely. He couldn't feel where his back touched the mattress, so perfectly melted together were his body and the sheets. He opened his eyes. Her white nightdress was ghostly visible in the near dark. He could make out the contours of her face but not the expression. His left hand found her right hand and they held tight, pressing their fingertips into the other's knuckles. He felt the weight on the mattress shift as she climbed across him. She pulled the blankets away and cold air brushed his legs. She unbuttoned the top of her nightdress and the hem settled across his chest. He touched her warm skin and the cotton brushed his knuckles as he stroked her ribs and allowed his thumbs to stray to her breasts. For the first time in his brief and woeful sex life so far, Ellis felt the body of a woman who was rounded and fleshy and whose movements of lovemaking were not clinical. She fumbled in removing his underwear, then drew the blankets up around them and lowered herself on to him. They kissed tenderly. She had seemed so tiny when they were growing up, and now she was upon him, the warmest, softest, most sensual woman he had touched, with breasts that made him want to kiss and suck and sleep. Her skin smelled of heat, as it had the previous morning. It brought him comfort and yearning in equal measure, as if they were feeding and stealing from each other. Only at the very end did their bodies become urgent and forceful and only then did her hands cease caressing his skin and instead grip it tight. Their kisses guarded each other's mouth to ensure the near silence. For a few ecstatic moments afterwards, Ellis gazed at the faint details of her body in the tantalising half-darkness and felt enveloped by skin and the wetness of inside her. Then, on the brink of sleep, he felt her body lift away and a desperate longing came over him, like the desire for hope within grieving.

He slept briefly and woke to the half-light. He found Chloe in the kitchen cooking breakfast for her husband and her lover. He didn't stop. He had put his boots on in the bedroom so that he didn't have to. Although he was hungry, very hungry, he moved straight through the kitchen, pulled his jacket off the peg and left the house without saying a word. He knew that Tim would still be in the milking shed. He couldn't think about it. He just had to drive away. And that's what he did.

It was mid-afternoon when he saw the coast again. For the first time, the familiar sweep of houses on Borstal Hill and the tower in the harbour and the glistening sea failed to inspire him.

I am for ever the person who did that. No matter what happens in all the years, I can never undo today.

He sought the quickest route he could to numbness with

what he had in his tin. In the dream that followed, he was sitting on a hillside overlooking a great desert. Far away, alone on the great plain of sand and rock, was a gigantic nuclear power station in meltdown. It looked like a chewed toffee. Snowy the dog appeared at Ellis's side. They watched a tame sparrow on the ground. Ellis tried to pick the bird up, to stroke it, but couldn't get a proper hold of it. He fumbled and the sparrow disintegrated in his hand.

He woke and it was already dark. He smoked a spliff and the savage self-loathing washed over him again, leaving in its wake a residue of disappointment. Disappointment at the discovery that he was who he was. He smoked more and curled up on his bed and drifted in and out of sleep. Later, a shiver of cold disturbed him and he pulled the blankets across his body. Then he slept deeply and a curtain appeared in front of him. The curtain was amber and made of millions of wasps. He stepped closer and peered through the droning curtain and saw himself and his mother lying together. It was very hot and the whole world was swamped by a deep orange hue. Ellis's right forearm was swollen and hurting. The skin on his arm broke open and thousands of spiderlings emerged. They poured out of his arm and converged on his mother and ate her. He woke abruptly, his back prickling with sweat. He was thirsty beyond measure. There was a weight pressing down on his forehead. Opening his eyes, he saw a spider resting on his face. It was the size of an adult hand. The palps were sunk into the soft crease between his lips. The spider didn't move and neither did Ellis. He breathed through his nose and kept his mouth shut tight. He remained motionless for hours. His vision was obscured by the spider's abdomen but he began to sense light appearing in the window. The ceiling became washed with daylight. He heard the incoming tide reach the shallow rim of pebbles at the top of the beach. The waves dragged a little of the shingle away and then, in time, retreated to the silence of the mudflats. The day moved slowly from one period of intense thirst to another. In the peace of crystal clear crisis, Ellis felt calmer than he had for some months.

Late in the afternoon, he felt the spider move. He held his breath. The spider walked away. When he was sure it had gone, Ellis rolled on to his side and curled into a ball. He heard his own voice some way away. It was the faintest of whispers. A single word, dissipating into the air.

"Daddy ..."

13

Late one night there was a car crash on Graveney Marshes in which three young men were killed. The local radio was full of it next morning and Ellis woke to find a man peering in through his bedroom window. The man was in his seventies, wore old-fashioned tweed and had the look of a Victorian gentleman. He was giraffe-like, tall and thin, with tight waves of grey hair. All of which made him noticeable, but what made him appear positively strange was the way his hands were cupped together in front of him.

"What are you doing?" Ellis called, through an inch of open window.

"Ah, excellent," the man said.

"What's excellent?"

"That you're alive and well. All in one piece, thank God."

At that moment, a frog leapt out of the man's hands.

"Damm!" he said, and scrambled after it.

Ellis threw on some clothes and followed the man – who followed the frog – off the beach, across the railway bridge and on to Joy Lane. At the bottom of Medina Avenue the man stopped to straighten up a wonky road sign, whilst the frog continued up the avenue to the furthest house. The road sign was home-made but convincing. It was a triangular warning sign with a red border, inside which was a frog.

"What's that sign for?" Ellis asked.

"Ah!" the man exclaimed. "Excellent! Excellent!"

"What's so excellent now?"

"That you're here."

"You've got to be the tallest man I've ever seen," Ellis said.

"Got to be," the man replied.

"How tall are you?"

"Six seven."

"And is this your sign?"

"Yes."

"What's it all about?"

"It's all about the fact that I am a preserver of frogs. Rare frogs. They come to my pond and I protect them. They are wild. They are free to come and go. Those that want to come and go near the road need protection." He gestured to the road sign, then smiled benevolently. "I am glad you followed me," he added. "I like curiosity in youth."

"Why were you peering through my window like a pervert?"

"Just checking you and your chum were unharmed. More neighbourly than perverted, I hope you'll agree. Come on, I'll show you the clan."

"It's OK." Ellis retreated. "I don't want to disturb you."

But the old man was already walking away, his long back stooping noticeably. "It's no bother at all. We'll have some tea. My name is Hedley, unusual nowadays I know, but it was fashionable once."

Ellis followed the man to the furthest bungalow, keeping his distance. It was the one house that backed on to fields. Hedley led Ellis down the side of the house and straight into the garden and, as promised, Ellis's eyes and ears fell immediately on a colony of frogs in a corner, where a pond nestled in the shadow of a scarlet willow.

A lady appeared. "Would you chaps like some tea?"

She seemed unsurprised to find Ellis there.

"Yes, please, old thing," Hedley said. "Darling, this is Ellis."

"Good-oh. Hello, Ellis."

Framed by a chorus of frog-song, Ellis managed a bemused smile.

"Make yourself at home," the lady said. "I'm glad everything's all right."

Amusing though it was to discover that there were people who actually said "Good-oh", Ellis felt uneasy. He didn't know why. He lit himself a cigarette. Hedley pulled two garden chairs out of the shade. Both men sat and looked across the layered bungalows at a view of the sea.

"Bit cold for tea on the lawn but I don't expect you want to come inside," Hedley said.

"This is fine," Ellis said defensively, exhaling smoke.

"Can you spare me a cigarette?" Hedley asked, and proceeded to puff it in the manner of a man who has never smoked a cigarette in his life.

This does not add up, Ellis told himself.

"Well, I like your frogs," he said, feeling uncomfortable with the silence.

"Thank you. I won the MBE for them."

"I don't believe in all that."

"Neither do I."

"Then why did you accept it?" Ellis asked.

"For the experience. Life's too short to dodge them."

"A bit hypocritical."

"I'm sure you're right."

Soon after, having discovered that in Hedley he had met his match when it came to carving out long silences, Ellis left. It was hours later, when he was slipping from rational thought into hallucination, that Ellis realised why he had felt perturbed by the old man. When Hedley had introduced him to his wife, Ellis had not, he was quite certain, told him his name.

Ellis gave Jed six months' rent in advance when he broke the news that he could no longer work for him.

"Why can't you?"

"Too many spiders. It's coming back a bit."

"What is?"

"Nothing. I just need a different sort of work."

His money lasted three weeks, at which point he sought credit at the shop on Joy Lane for the first time.

"You look like shit," said Raj, the shopkeeper.

Ellis realised that he was being watched by Hedley, the frog-man, from behind a carousel of KitKats. He ignored him.

"It's just the once, Raj," Ellis said.

"Yes to the milk, eggs, potatoes, onions and corned beef, but no tobacco and Rizlas on credit. If you're too broke to pay you're too broke to smoke that shit!"

Hedley joined Ellis at the counter.

"Excuse my language, Mr Wilkinson," Raj added.

"Quite all right, Raj, couldn't agree more." Then Hedley smiled at Ellis. "Good morning."

"Hello." Ellis was guarded.

Hedley laid down his shopping basket on the counter and removed his wallet from his jacket pocket in his own unhurried manner.

"Wait for me outside, young man," he instructed Ellis.

Ellis left the shop and stood on the kerb, in two minds whether to stay or go.

He can't molest me on the street, he told himself. So he stayed.

When Hedley emerged, he tossed a packet of cigarettes at Ellis with a flourish.

"Asking for tobacco and those other fiddly things would have lacked subtlety on my part, so you'll have to make do with those," Hedley said, and wandered away to his bungalow.

"Er ... thanks," Ellis called out, uncertainly.

Three days later, Hedley was back, standing amongst the bird tables in torrential rain, unnaturally tall despite his stoop, under a large black umbrella with brass tips and a polished wood handle. He wore a shin-length raincoat, more suited to a Manhattan sidewalk in the fifties. The coat was immaculate and without a crease, even in the wind and rain. Hedley smiled and made a half-wave and Ellis went to the door.

Hedley raised his voice above the downpour. "I won't come in, but I needed to talk to you."

Oh, Jesus! Ellis thought.

"My wife and I need someone to do some paid work whilst we're on holiday."

"Oh, yeah?" Ellis smiled, unaware of his own pained expression.

"Frog-sitting. It'd be four hundred pounds a week and we'll be away for two weeks. I make that eight hundred pounds."

Ellis's mouth dropped open.

"Are you interested?"

"It seems a lot of money," Ellis said.

"It's the going rate for a qualified frog-sitter."

"I'm not a qualified frog-sitter," Ellis said, raising his voice as the wind picked up. "I'm not a qualified anything."

"You have a backside, don't you?"

Ellis glanced at the heavens and wondered if he ought to invite his unfathomable visitor in.

"And, presumably, you know how to sit on it?"

"I know how to sit on my arse, yes."

"Splendid!" Hedley triumphed. "I'm going to stick my neck out and say you'll be able to perform the dual role of sitting and frog-watching."

Feeding the cat would have been more strenuous, though less time-consuming. If any frogs left the garden and headed for Joy Lane, Ellis was to stand in their way. They would, Hedley assured him, "hop back home" when he did.

"If it's terribly rainy, I suggest a large golfing umbrella as the garden shed is somewhat riddled with creepy-crawlies."

"Right ..." Ellis said, struck yet again by the sense of things not adding up with this man.

"Some people are averse to creepy-crawlies," Hedley added. "If you're not, then by all means take shelter in the shed. But I suspect you might be."

Hedley advanced him one hundred pounds. Ellis's hours were nine in the morning until noon and two in the afternoon until five.

"Do they understand they're not supposed to hop off during the two-hour lunch break?" Ellis asked, his bemusement undiluted.

Hedley ignored the question. "Bring some kind of contraption for your cigarettes with you. I don't want cigarette butts all over the garden."

"Are we talking about an ashtray?" Ellis replied.

He watched the frogs do nothing, read an account of Cornish wreckers and pored over a book of Cornell Capa's photographs that inspired him to buy a Kodak Retinette camera from a junk shop in Swalecliffe, in which his first film became irretrievably jammed. On three occasions in the fortnight he walked alongside a frog as it made an excursion on to Medina Avenue and back. Ellis couldn't be sure whether or not it was the same frog each time but he liked to think it was. A lone voice of dissent. A troublemaker.

Hedley paid him a hundred pounds in cash on his return and the remaining six hundred pounds he wrote out as a cheque. "You do have a bank account, I take it?"

"A Post Office book."

"Fine. Just pay it in and use it steadily. And eat something healthy from time to time, I implore you."

It was a fortune and nothing could convince Ellis that what he had done was deserving of it. In fact, he wasn't convinced that it had been necessary to have him, or anyone, babysit the frogs at all.

"What do you normally do when you go away?" he asked.

"Don't worry about that. I've got you now," Hedley said.

In the winter, Hedley found Ellis a succession of small and largely unnecessary tasks, for all of which he was overpaid. Occasionally, Hedley would be sitting on the sea wall outside Jed's place and Ellis would join him and they would look at the estuary together and have a chat. Hedley would always ask Ellis if he was all right and in good health before leaving.

"You can turn to Mrs Wilkinson and me if you are in trouble," he once said. "Any sort of trouble, or no trouble at all. Turn to us for anything."

A towering sky arched across the coast, revealing the earth's curvature to those who cared to stop and look. Far out on the low tide the noises of the town were distant and mottled, as if the world were underwater. The houses on Joy Lane Beach seemed no more than a raised scar on a muddy skin. Ellis roamed amongst the stooped bait-diggers and nervy oystercatchers as thin streams of seawater trickled across the bay, painting the estuary floor with silver streaks of reflected sky. Then he saw a man crossing towards him.

The first blow was graceful. It flew not from an isolated

fist, but from Tim's entire, momentarily airborne, body. Ellis peeled himself out of the mud and up on to his knees, where he received the second blow. Thereafter, he made no attempt to defend himself as Tim kicked and punched him to the edge of consciousness. His only retaliation was to show nothing. When it was over, Ellis rolled on to his back. His ribs contracted and groaned and he felt his eyes closing over. Tim pressed his boot down on Ellis's head, inviting the earth to swallow him. A mussel shell, lodged in the mud on the sole of Tim's boot, pierced Ellis's skin and made a tear in the vein on his temple.

"That wasn't about her," Tim said. "If it was about her, I'd keep going till you were dead and then I'd bury you. That was just about you and me."

The redeeming quality of being kicked half to death, it occurred to Ellis, as ice-cold water trickled from the mud around him into his clothes and his ears, was that so much pain invades your body so quickly that the rest doesn't hurt at all. It damages, but you barely feel anything.

Tim had gone. Ellis was deaf and almost blind but he knew that he was alone. He stared at the sky through slit eyes and felt his way through rolling a skunk reefer. With short, sharp breaths he lured himself to the threshold of comfort and became oblivious of the freezing bed of mud he could not rise from. It occurred to him that spiders the size of pylons might be advancing towards him across the flats. He plastered the ash-coloured mud over his face, and they passed by without seeing him.

Some time later came the chugging of a diesel engine and the sensation of being lifted. His body was laid down on to something hard and he wondered if he was dead.

"Hello, Mr East," he heard himself slur, from somewhere beyond his own body.

Baldie East, the whelk-man, peered down at him. He was

old and shrunken. His face was lined and his eyelids were creased and his head was crowned with thick, snow-white hair. The smell of mussels and whelks streamed into Ellis's nose and he lay blind again as his body jarred and rattled with the movement of the trailer on which he lay as Baldie's tractor dragged it back to shore.

Still caked in mud, Ellis found the Welsh boys in the Rose In Bloom pub on Joy Lane. There were seven of them and they lived together in a two-bedroom flat above the sweet shop on Harbour Street. They drank heavily every night and impersonated Richard Burton whenever they were close to passing out, which was often. Four of the seven were called David Jones. They were distinguished as Dave, Davey, Jonesey and DJ. All seven men were mighty drinkers.

"You're looking pretty this evening, O'Rourke," Skip Williams said. He was the calmest of the seven.

"You look like a corpse covered in crap," Davey said.

"Lowering the tone, you are, O'Rourke ... lowering the fucking tone!"

"Nose suits you, spread over your face like that."

"It's been there once before," Ellis said. "I'm only stopping for one. I'm freezing cold. And I need crisps, loads of the fuckers."

By ten o'clock they were drunk. The roar of their laughter and foul language carried to every part of the pub, intimidating the regulars and provoking two warnings from the landlord. If Hedley and his wife had been pubgoers, this would have been their local. It served the gentlefolk who inhabited the sea-view bungalows on the hillside above Joy Lane and the gentlefolk were not happy.

Two empty pint glasses fell from the table and smashed across the floor.

"Put those anywhere you like!" Jonesy cried out.

The boys roared and the landlord stormed over.

"Another broken glass and you're barred, the lot of you! Last warning! And you can cut out the swearing as well or I'll be down on you fellers like a ton of bricks!"

Ellis climbed on to the table, stopping halfway to steady himself, with his bum stuck out like a novice surfer. He regained his balance, stood atop the table, looked down on the clientele and beamed them a smile.

"FUCK! BUGGER! WANK!" he announced, raising his pint glass to them before draining it and smashing it on to the floor.

They went quietly.

Ellis woke lying star-shaped on the beach. The morning sun levered his swollen eyes open as far as they would go. He heard footsteps on the shingle and squinted to see the silhouette of someone standing over him, their hands rammed into the pockets of a long, fashionable-looking winter coat. He raised his hand to the sun and as shadow covered his eyes he saw his sister. She winked at him, as if they'd seen each other yesterday, and he laughed to himself, which hurt his ribs.

"How did you get here?"

"I got a lift. You look like a shipwreck."

They sat shoulder to shoulder on the breakwater letting the sun soak their faces. Ellis suspected that pneumonia was lurking somewhere beneath his hangover. Two of the Welsh boys were passed out on the beach. At some point in the night they had cuddled together against the cold and they were still stuck to each other, like sleeping lovers. Ellis wished he had a camera.

"I'm surprised we never came here with Dad on one of our days out. It's pretty nice," Chrissie said.

"How is Dad?"

She looked at his bruises and didn't answer. She ran her finger across the scab on his temple.

"Tim?" she asked.

He nodded and his lips trembled.

"So its true you knobbed his wife?" she said.

His shoulders slumped and he bowed his head. He walked a few paces away and looked out to the sea forts on the horizon. For a moment, he thought he was going to throw up.

"Yes," he muttered. "It is true. It's the truth. It is a true fact. Coming to you straight from the planet Truth, after a quick stopover in the galaxy of Unforgivable Fuck-up."

He watched the waves and she watched him and they didn't move and they didn't speak. The tide was turning. Baldie East would be preparing his nets and cages in the harbour before moving out to the whelk and mussel beds as the receding tide unveiled them.

"You are so useless with women, Ellie-boy," Chrissie said affectionately.

"Don't call me Ellie-boy," he whispered.

She lobbed a pebble towards his feet.

"It is unforgivable," she said, without reproach. "And you look so awful."

In the fish and chip shop on Harbour Street, in the restaurant area at the rear of the shop, amidst the Formica tables and the wood-panelled walls, hidden at first by the clutter of sugar shakers, ketchup bottles and mustard pots, was Mafi. Ellis sat beside her and kissed her. She gasped at the bruises on his face.

"Who did this?" she asked.

"I did," Ellis said.

She gripped his hand.

They sipped tea and then Ellis excused himself politely and walked outside. He crossed Harbour Street, hurrying to the corner of Sydenham Street, and threw up on the Jubilee rose bed. He returned to the table and nothing was said about it. In the silence, it occurred to Ellis that they might have come with bad news.

"Is Dad all right?" he asked.

"Yes," Mafi said.

Ellis looked at the familiar contours on her face and the liver spots on her skin and thought how much he loved her.

"That's not why you've come? Nothing bad has happened?"

"Nothing bad has happened," Mafi assured him softly. "It's just a day out for me. I wanted to see my boy."

They sat in silence for a while. Ellis's mind wandered and he thought of the spiderlings pouring out of his arm and taking his mother.

"Did I do something to harm Mum?" he said.

Mafi and Chrissie looked appalled.

"What would make you ask that?" Mafi said.

"Just ..." He was distant. "Just a thought ..." He rubbed his eyes and smiled brightly. "And, you know, Chrissie's been reminding me how useless I am with women and it's probably true, I am crap at most things. I suddenly wondered if I did something. That would be why no one will ever tell me what happened. If it was my fault."

"If what was?" Mafi asked.

"Mum."

"No!" they replied in unison.

"I'm a woman and you're not useless with me," Mafi added.

"He did trick you into signing his inter-rail ticket," Chrissie reminded her.

Mafi ignored her. So did Ellis.

"He just thinks that there's a lot of her in you," Mafi said.

The words hung before him. It was nice for him to replay them in his head. A brief sentence, unannounced and unheralded, but explaining much and promising more.

"What happened to my mum?" Ellis asked.

Mafi smiled to herself in a way Ellis couldn't fathom. Absent-mindedly, she stroked Ellis's arm, as if she thought it was her own. Three plates of buttered toast were placed on the table. Chrissie looked affectionately at Ellis but didn't say anything. Ellis pushed his plate away calmly.

"What happened to my mum?" he repeated. He placed his hand on Mafi's cheek and gently turned her to face him. He nodded at her and whispered, "Now's the time ..."

Mafi took his hand. "One day, all of a sudden, your mother panicked that she could see the rest of her life stretching ahead of her with no more surprises. You were four years old. She was subdued for a long time, for months, then she admitted how she felt. Your dad believed that she should do something about it sooner rather than later. He was scared that if she didn't, she'd tell him something worse one day, when you and your sister had grown up and moved on. He didn't want to be left alone. Your mother and you were great together. She loved you. There were no problems with you. She just had an accident and if she hadn't had an accident she'd have come back home to you all. You had a mother and she loved you and she died. It wasn't your fault at all."

Mafi sipped her tea. Ellis glanced at Chrissie. She smiled innocently back at him and took a piece of toast, concentrating on it exaggeratedly. He stretched out his leg and tapped her shin with his foot. Without looking up, Chrissie said, "Keep going, Mafi."

Mafi licked the tip of her index finger and used it to wipe away the tea stain on the lip of her mug, something she had never done before and would never feel the need to do again.

"She went on an adventure with a girlfriend from school. Your father saw her off and she wrote to him often. She swam in the Arabian sea. She went to the holy lake of Pushkar. She was young and she was confused and she felt that she had missed out on a whole way of living and that soon it would be too late. She wrote long detailed letters to your father about what she was seeing and feeling. And she went to a place called the Golden City and she met a man. She liked the man and she fell out with her friend over him. The man liked her too and they had an affair ..."

Mafi faltered. She had resolved to talk through this moment, to downplay it as far as possible, but had been brought to a halt by the words "they had an affair". She needn't have worried. Far from being crushed by the revelation of his mum's infidelity, Ellis welcomed any detail about her. He felt particularly unselective and non-judgemental about it. He just wanted to know anything, everything, there was to know.

"It lasted a week and then she left him. She set off alone to escape him and return home. She missed you and your sister dreadfully. She wanted to be with your dad again. She took any lift or bus she could and headed for a place called Jaipur because she knew how to get home from there. She wrote to your dad. She told him everything. She apologised and told him the truth and she said she was desperate to come home to him and the two of you. And ..."

Mafi's voice trailed away.

Ellis smiled at her. "And?" he asked.

"And ... she took a ride in some old truck on some rotten old road and it crashed off the road and that's where she died."

"In India ..." Ellis whispered.

"In northern India," Mafi confirmed.

"Northern India," Ellis repeated, to accustom himself to the idea. "That's a long way from home."

Chrissie leant across and held Ellis's hand. He felt fine and he gave her a wide-eyed smile to let her know. His priority was to take in his surroundings and to create a snapshot in his mind's eye, so that he would never forget the moment when he found out. As for the details of what he'd been told, and how he felt about them, well, he had the rest of his life to think about that. All that mattered for now was that he had been told. Finally. On 2 November 1985, in the Harbour Street fish and chip shop.

"Poor Dad ..." Ellis said.

"Do you remember when Mafi first came and stayed with us in Orpington?" Chrissie asked him.

Ellis shrugged. "Sort of."

"That's when Dad went out there. He scattered her ashes in a place she had written about in a letter to him because she said it was the most beautiful place she had ever seen."

"The reason you've no relatives on your mum's side of the family," Mafi said, "is they've not spoken to him since he decided not to bring her body back home."

"We should go there, one day?" Ellis urged his sister.

"Maybe. But when we're older, after Dad's gone."

But that, Ellis knew, was a time so distant that it needn't exist.

"We'll be too old then. We should go, now, with Dad."

On the sea wall, alongside the Red Spider café, Ellis stared at the waves. He shut off his mind and the storm of thoughts within it and filled his head with the colour of seawater. He lost his bearings and drifted, anchorless, for a while until Mafi broke the silence.

"Any day you see the sea is a good day," she said.

It was too cold for her to sit outside for long. She shuffled along the sea wall to the pub and found a seat next to the radiator. She sipped a glass of barley wine and watched her great-niece and great-nephew from the window. This evening she would be able to tell her nephew that she had seen his son and that he was safe. She looked at the arthritic swelling on her hands and at the knots in the floorboards.

She unbuttoned her overcoat and sat back. She felt happy to be on the coast again and at ease with the knowledge that her time was winding down. Today was a great adventure, perhaps the last. She was quite content.

Ellis watched Mafi's Morris Minor disappear round the bend at the top of Nelson Road before setting off purposefully to the call box on Coastguards Alley. He took a deep breath and dialled the only London number in his diary apart from his sister's, and asked to speak to Mr O'Rourke.

"Who shall I say is calling?"

"His son."

The line was silent. Ellis covered the mouthpiece whilst he swallowed and cleared his throat. Then the tone of the silence changed and Ellis knew that his dad was there. Ellis allowed himself to breathe, inviting his dad to speak. Denny declined the invitation.

"Dad?"

Still there was silence.

"It's Ellis."

"Hello, Ellis."

"How are you?"

"I'm fine, son. How are you?"

"Pretty good."

"Good."

His dad's pitch was perfect. It carried neither anger nor a crumb of tenderness.

"I just called to say I've seen Chrissie and Mafi today and that I'm going to call you every Friday evening from now on."

"Did you know Tim Wickham and his wife split up?" Denny O'Rourke asked.

Ellis slumped and looked across the bay. "That's probably because I slept with her," he said solemnly. He knew that his dad wasn't going to speak again. "Bye, Dad," he said, tenderly.

Ellis and Jed shared a spliff on the beach that evening. The sea ripples rolled in softly at perfect intervals. The moonlight rode them like a folded paper boat. Ellis thought of his dad's voice. Jed thought of what he and the little boy he called his baby brother might do together this weekend.

"The European water spider is the only spider that has evolved to live permanently under water," Ellis murmured.

"Go on," Jed said.

Ellis did so, gazing at the lights on the headland across the estuary and whispering, as if Jed were a sleepy child.

"It lives in ponds and streams, slow-moving streams. It spins a dome-shaped web and anchors it to a plant. It comes to the surface of the water and gulps down a bubble of air and takes it to the web and releases it. Gradually, it fills the web with air until it is like an air-filled balloon. It lives in the balloon, under the water."

"I don't know where you get it from," Jed said, dragging deeply on the joint.

"I read it in a book," Ellis said.

14

Hedley Wilkinson knocked on Ellis's door on Christmas Eve. "A strange thing," he said, "but fortuitous, in a sad way."

"What?" Ellis said, wondering if the old boy had finally lost his marbles.

"I was walking, not five minutes ago, past the phone box on Joy Lane when it rang and I picked it up and it was a young lady saying she wanted to speak to you."

"Me?"

"Yes, you, and did I happen to know you? I said that I had that honour and she requested that I give you this message. Your aunt Mafi is sick and she may die any time, tonight probably. You're to go home straight away. Would you like to borrow my car for the Christmas period?"

Ellis stood bemused. Hedley's role in his life was becoming more odd. "No, thanks. I've got one."

"But is it reliable? A good runner? This is important."

"Was it my sister?"

"Yes. Oh ... I suppose so. I don't know. It would have been, I imagine. How would I know? Do you have one?"

Ellis thanked Hedley and ushered him out.

"Ellis!" Hedley's eyes appeared at the letter box.

"What now?"

"You will go, won't you?"

"Yes."

Although he had never sat beside a human body so frail, Ellis adjusted swiftly to the sight of her. Mafi had grown old at a steady pace. What he saw now wasn't a marked decline, just further erosion taking her to the brink.

He knew he should have gone straight to his father but something fear probably had propelled him directly up the stairs to Mafi's room. This was, he already sensed, yet another error of judgement on his part. Before he had time to rectify it, the door opened and Denny tiptoed in, pressing his forehead against the door as he closed it noiselessly. Only then, as he stepped towards the bed, did he see his son. His face tautened to anger and he left the room immediately. Ellis cursed himself and rested his head on the bed. He listened to Mafi's breathing whilst her hand made circles in his hair.

"Imagine this ..." Her voice was faint and very slow. "There was a meadow on the edge of the Marsh. Your daddy was walking there when he saw her standing among the campions and poppies and when she ran her hands across the tips of the meadow grass up flew butterflies, hundreds of butterflies, white and red and brown and pale blue. They danced and fluttered around her head. When she laughed they flew away. Disappeared into thin air. Your daddy knew that he wanted to be with her for ever."

"Was that my mum?" Ellis asked.

"It was," Mafi said.

"Did it really happen?"

"Yes."

"How do you know for sure?"

"Because I was there. And it feels like yesterday to him. He never wants you or Chrissie to have a broken heart, that's all."

"I don't think he's very pleased to see me."

She tugged sharply on Ellis's hair, causing him to sit up. "If only you'd talk to people, properly, the way you talked to your spiders when you were little," she said.

Ellis walked downstairs and from the kitchen doorway he watched his father making a pot of tea. For the first time ever, he glimpsed the unbroken entirety of Denny O'Rourke's life and he saw a man still in love with the butterfly-lady, still missing her, still hurt by her.

"Hello," Ellis said, with all the apology he could invest in the word.

Denny pressed a mug of tea down in front of him and left the room without speaking.

Chrissie arrived from London and pulled the Christmas tree out from its hiding place in the corner of the living room. At three o'clock, she and Denny left Mafi's bedside and curled up together in the dining room window to listen to the carols from King's College. Ellis was outside turning over the vegetable patch with the pickaxe. He stopped for a cigarette and clambered over the fence to the working men's club, which was boarded up. A planning notice detailed the three small houses to be built in its place. As the day faded, Ellis lit a bonfire and burnt off the tree brash his dad had cut in the autumn. He regretted that nightfall would force him back inside. His dad had not spoken to him all day nor remained in the same room as him.

He sat with Mafi, who was too weak to speak now. Later, he bathed in deep, steaming hot water and smelled Chrissie's fish pie in the kitchen. When he appeared for supper, clean-shaven and wearing the only shirt he possessed that had a collar, his dad finally ended his silence.

"You've used up all the hot water, you selfish little bugger."

Ellis went upstairs and packed his bag. Chrissie followed him and persuaded him to stay.

"You'll never undo it if you go now," she said.

She took Ellis's boots downstairs and placed them next to Denny's gardening shoes. Ellis switched the light off and lay on his bed and returned to the butterfly meadow. It was not so long ago, he reminded himself. That man downstairs is still the man in the meadow. He didn't come into being on 17 November 1967 when I was born. He wasn't put on this earth just to be my father.

On Christmas morning, Denny took a pot of tea and a jug of water up to Mafi's room and did not acknowledge his son. Chrissie gave Ellis a camera. A Pentax K1000. He was thrilled.

"My friend Milek is a photographer and he says this is the ideal first camera for you."

"Knobbing him?"

"Negative."

Ellis took Chrissie out to the car. Wrapped in a blanket and sticking out of the back window was a large mirror, almost full length. Ellis had made it himself out of pale driftwood from the beach. There were tar marks in the grain and the words "Le Havre" burnt into the wood.

"I love it. I absolutely love it," she said.

They sat in the back of the Herald and shared a cigarette. The day was cold and still and the sky pale grey, the sort of grey that looks a mile deep.

Denny refused to acknowledge his son over Christmas dinner and Chrissie winced at the tension. Ellis grabbed the bottle of red wine from the table and marched out. He drank as he walked up the path to the green. He read the village notices on the school railings. There was a meeting in January to organise the campaign to save the post office from closure and there was a call to sign the petition to fight the reduction of the 454 bus service.

He sat on a bench on the green and, with a lack of imagination that was becoming habit, decided to get stoned.

The cherry-faced man whose arm was always in a sling crossed the green and entered the Methodist chapel. Ellis had never known his name nor the reason for the sling. He wondered what ribbon of circumstances had left the man alone on Christmas Day. Then a pair of giant hands covered his face. The skin was coarse and the fingers were fat and brutal and pressed hard against his eyes.

"Guess who?" It was an effortlessly menacing voice.

"Don't know."

The voice laughed and the hands lifted. Ellis turned and found Des Payne taking a seat beside him.

"Happy Christmas," Des said, sincerely, and laughed.

Ellis laughed nervously. "Jesus, Des ..."

"Had you going," Des said. He leant forward in his skin-tight jeans and pulled a half-bottle of brandy from his Parker coat. He offered it up. Ellis took a nip and, having lit the spliff, handed it to Des.

"Dog's bollocks," the big man said appreciatively.

"Always go for a walk on Christmas Day when my uncle starts picking on my dad. Tradition."

Ellis had never credited Des Paine with a real life. He was just the overgrown skinhead from Morleys Road who had kindly declined to kill him once.

"I'll murder my uncle one of these Christmas Days."

"Why?"

"Takes the piss. Always scrounging off my dad, always eating the fucking turkey my dad pays for, getting pissed on Dad's booze and then he starts bullying him. Dad doesn't like an argument but I could kill my uncle without breaking sweat or giving a shit."

They toked and gazed at the grass as if it were entertaining them.

"Not really," Des muttered, as an afterthought. He pulled out his cheeks and sighed, weakened by the weed. "Where did you run off to then?"

"The seaside," Ellis said.

"Fuck me! That's all right, isn't it?"

"Yeah, I like it."

"Fuck me! Gotta hand it to you." Des smiled and nodded to himself, impressed. "So, you just left here and went somewhere else?"

They fell quiet whilst Des toyed with the idea curiously. They both felt quickly stoned.

"Must be cold by the sea."

"Sometimes it's colder, sometimes it's warmer."

"Is it? Fucking hell! What are the pubs like?"

"Pretty good."

"And there's loads of this flying about, is there?" Des waved the joint at Ellis.

"Plenty."

"Fucking hell." Des breathed out smoke and handed the dog-end to Ellis, who sucked the life out of it, felt the burn of the roach and tossed it away.

"You've done all right for yourself," Des said. "Yeah ... you just left here and went somewhere else." Des whispered the words, as if repeating a riddle he couldn't make sense of. He stretched his legs out and let his arms hang lifelessly. The energy had drained from him and so had the desire to crush his uncle.

"You still scared of spiders?" he asked.

"Not sure at the moment," Ellis said.

"My girlfriend's pregnant," Des said. "Mum's going to bring the baby up. We can't handle it. Bionic balls, me."

They sat in comfortable silence until Des laughed under his breath and muttered, "Fuck me." It was his mantra. It's what he would have said if he'd discovered America, or gravity.

Ellis crawled off the bench and lay flat out on the grass. A few gaps appeared between the clouds and beyond them glowed a reddening sky.

"Your dad put a note up in Bridget's shop saying that you'd fucked off and if anyone heard anything to let him know. Then he put another note up saying you were all right."

"The goldfish bowl ..." Ellis muttered.

"I wouldn't rush into Bridget's, by the way. She don't like you one bit."

"What's it got to do with Bridget?"

"Fancies your dad. Always has. No, I definitely wouldn't go in there unless you're really desperate for bread or milk or something. Even then I'd just borrow off someone, you know? Or pay a child to go into Bridget's and get what you need and wait round the corner, except if you want cigarettes 'cos Bridget's clamping down on selling them to kids. I think she was warned."

"Des! Shut up, man, you're stoned."

"Oh ... Yeah ..."

Ellis returned to the bench and took another joint from

his pocket. He dangled it in front of Des. "Up for it?"

"Fuck me, yes!"

Des stood up and shook his head and torso to wake himself up, the way a dog shakes itself dry. Then he sat down and wrapped a huge arm round Ellis and looked him in the eye, as if he were going to kiss him or kill him. Ellis recoiled.

"I'll tell you something," Des growled.

"What?" Ellis swallowed.

"I was in Bridget's when your dad came in ..."

Des went quiet. His eyes pierced Ellis from close range. He breathed deep into a chest carved from stone.

"He looked like a dead man. I shan't forget it. He looked like a ghost. Made me want to say something to him, say something nice ..."

Ellis found that by tensing up his neck and flaring his nostrils he could prevent his eyes from welling up. He walked away and lay down again on the grass. He watched the clouds close rank and darken. Des lay beside him and took the spliff from Ellis's fingers and lit it. He toked, then placed the joint between Ellis's lips. Ellis drew heavily and felt the drug rise behind his eyes.

"Sorry for shooting you in the head."

"Sorry for stuffing gum up your nose."

Their laughter rang out across the village green to the old man inside the Methodist chapel, who mistook it for the laughter of children. It drew a smile across his face and he returned his polio-ravaged body to his empty house on Glebe Road with an uplifted heart.

Denny emerged from Mafi's room late on Christmas night. He said to his children, "It's nearly time, I think."

Mafi's skin seemed paper thin, as if the life had already slipped away beneath it. They sat with her, deep into the night, until tiredness overcame them all.

Denny slept late for the first time in many years. He was woken by the sound of Ellis shuffling sleepily along the landing corridor to Mafi's door. He heard his daughter's bedroom door open and moments later she appeared in his room and sat on his bed.

"Would you like a cup of tea?" she asked wearily.

Before Denny could answer, they heard Mafi's bedroom door burst open. Ellis thundered in.

"Can you come!" he gasped and ran out again.

Denny bowed his head. Dignity was a priority for him from this moment on. Chrissie waited. There was no need to rush. Their eyes met and he nodded, with the faintest of smiles. When they entered Mafi's room, Ellis was plumping up the pillows and Mafi was sitting bolt upright in her bed. She beamed her nephew a rosy-cheeked smile.

"You know what I fancy, Denny? A lamb chop."

Ellis felt Mafi's forehead. She found it irksome and waved his hand away.

"With peas and potatoes, preferably."

"Right ..." Denny replied, unsure.

After she had eaten, Mafi talked, without significant pause, into the evening. Then she slept.

Ellis drove Chrissie up to the town, where she was getting a lift back to London with an old school friend. On his return, he parked his car facing down the driveway so that he was ready to head off next morning. He breathed the cold air deeply, gave thanks for Mafi's return to health and smiled in anticipation of his return to the coast next day. As he walked towards the kitchen door, he readied himself for a final evening at the sharp end of his father's resentment. He stepped inside the cottage and, behind his back, the first flakes of snow began to fall.

He woke beneath a bedroom ceiling that radiated light, and he knew that he was trapped.

The garden and rooftops were thick with snow. Ellis stomped his feet into his boots. When he reached the car the snow was up to his knees. He wandered around the cottage, inspecting the depths of the drifts. On the front lawn, he encountered his father doing the same. Denny ignored his son but, momentarily, they were shoulder to shoulder beneath the old cobnut tree and wearing identical clothes, Denny in his current winter coat and hat and Ellis wearing Denny's old ones, relegated now to gardening use. Mafi's voice rang out from her bedroom window.

"Yoo-hoo!"

She held Ellis's new camera to her eye and took a picture of the two men, staring up at her, incredulous of her recovery.

Mafi held court, a glass of whisky cradled in her porcelain hands.

"I kissed a German," she told them, out of the blue. "I was picking hops at Boughton in 1941 and a German plane appeared, firing at vehicles on the main road. It swooped over the farm. Everyone ran for their lives except me and Doris Uden. I saw him as clear as if we were dancing together at the Leas Cliff Hall. He was a handsome devil and he flew right at us. I blew him a kiss and he blew a kiss back."

Denny went downstairs to cook the lunch.

"Don't be stingy, Denny, I'm hungry as a horse," Mafi called out. "I might meet that handsome German in heaven when I die," she confided to Ellis.

"You're not going to die now."

"Don't be so silly. This is pure willpower. A parting gift." She winked at him. "The day you returned from Europe, your father sat at his bedroom window all day, peeking out from behind the curtains, waiting ..."

"He was fast asleep when I went up to see him," Ellis said.

"If you believe that you're a fool," she told him. "Anyone can lie in bed and shut their eyes."

Denny O'Rourke sat with his aunt all afternoon. Ellis split cherry logs in the back garden and shovelled the snow away from his car in a futile gesture of intent which ignored the reality that the village was cut off. Every now and then he stepped inside and could hear muffled conversation and laughter from Mafi's bedroom.

Ellis took a glass of whisky to his bedroom and hid from his father there. When he was sure Denny had gone to bed, he watched a film on television and smoked cigarettes throughout, having not had one all day. In the early hours, he put on his boots and his dad's old coat and walked into the village, through deep snow. Footprints mapped everyone's movements, from their front doors and back again. There were no secrets in a snow-bound village. The night was still and stingingly cold. Ellis felt the tops of his ears burn and his lips and jaw became numb. The village green was a lake of bright, reflected moonlight. Ellis's breath billowed towards the star-flecked sky, a smoke signal for a soul on its way.

He looked in on Mafi. The moonlight was pale blue on the walls of her bedroom and on her skin, taking the blemishes of age away from her face and hands, leaving her ancient but flawless. Beautiful. He studied the rise and fall of her breathing the way a parent watches their newborn child.

When Ellis woke he sensed he had slept late. The sky was a single enormous pearl light bulb emitting soft, even light. He listened carefully to the quietness and in it he detected sound. It was the discord of absence. The afterglow of departure.

His dad pushed the door open delicately. He placed a mug of tea down for Ellis and sat on the side of the bed. He looked his son in the eye. The grave censoriousness had left his face.

"Mafi died an hour ago," he said.

Ellis nodded and smiled at his dad. Then he fixed his gaze on the bedroom door as it moved back and forth in a draught.

"Were you with her?"

"Yes."

"That's good."

They sat for a while not knowing how to cross the few inches that separated them. Ellis's gaze moved from the door to his dad's hand, resting on the blanket beside him. He considered laying his younger, thinner hand upon it but couldn't.

"I don't want you to be upset," Denny said sternly. It was almost an instruction.

That's right, Ellis thought, you don't. You don't want me to experience grief or harm or heartache. That's all you've ever tried to deny me.

Ellis waited for Reardon at the foot of the green. The sun dazzled from a cloudless sky but there was no thaw. Russell Grey stepped out of his back door and sucked on a cigarette. He was wearing a dressing gown, long johns, combat boots and a woolly hat. They watched as Katie Morton's father appeared at the top of Wickhurst Lane in his suit and overcoat, with a scarf throttling him and a Russian-style winter hat pressed down on his head.

"Dressed by his wife," Ellis said, loud enough to be heard.

Mr Morton stepped gingerly across the ice, scowled at Ellis and bade Russell Grey a good morning as he began a four-mile walk to the mock-Tudor-fronted office he had moved his insurance business to after his son's imprisonment. The two men watched Mr Morton struggle up the ice slope out of the village.

"Mad," Russell Grey murmured.

"Not when the alternative is staying at home with Mrs Morton," Ellis said.

"Their daughter's not exactly Meryl Streep, but fair play to you, they all count."

This observation aired, Russell Grey returned indoors to his flat above the post office and to the wife who still sported the beehive hair-do that had scared Ellis as a child, although she no longer dyed it blue.

Ellis jogged on the spot and cursed into his scarf at the cold until Reardon's tractor appeared. It barely slowed at all as Ellis leapt on to the trailer. It was the first vehicle to get out of the village since the snow came. Mr Morton politely declined Reardon's offer of a lift as they passed him. They came to a halt at the top of Hubbards Hill, on the edge of the common. Shaded from the brilliance of the sun, the common was frozen over. Through a labyrinth of white-capped branches, Ellis found four slow-moving figures in black. He saw their top hats first and then the thick fur-lined boots into which their trousers were tucked. They carried a polished cherrywood coffin, upon the lid of which were four pairs of immaculately polished black shoes. On the far edge of the common, a hearse was parked up where the snow dunes had swallowed the road.

The coffin lay on the dining table whilst the men prepared Mafi's body upstairs. They carried her down in a large sling and this, in particular, Ellis and his dad made sure they didn't see. The coffin was returned to the trailer. Denny O'Rourke and his son sat alongside it with three of the men whilst the head undertaker went on foot, ahead of the tractor. At the church, they left Mafi's coffin on trestles in front of the altar. Denny O'Rourke went into the garden as soon as they got back. He was mute and impenetrable. Ellis went to Mafi's kitchen and took a Mackeson's bottle opener from the drawer and placed it in his pocket. It was all he wanted of hers.

He screwed two planks of wood to the wheels of the hay cart and pulled it out of the valley. It took him two hours to reach Hildenborough station. The train from London was pulling away and Chrissie was standing on the platform, a suitcase and half a dozen carrier bags of food at her feet. They loaded the bags on to the cart. Christmas-tree lights shone from the windows on Scabharbour Road as Ellis and Chrissie trekked back towards the village. They stopped at the five-bar gate opposite Mackley Farm and looked across to the Rumpumps. The snow blanket on the landscape glowed in the dusk and, already, Ellis couldn't remember how the village looked without it.

"I'll be glad when this is over," Chrissie said.

Ellis wondered if the lame, lonely widows and widowers inside the almshouses on Glebe Road ever looked out of their windows at this view and thought the same thing.

I'll be glad when this is over.

The horror of growing old shot through Ellis's young mind for the first time.

"Jesus Christ ..." he muttered.

They wrapped their arms around each other and Chrissie had her cry.

There was a note on the kitchen table from their dad. He had returned to the church.

"Dad's not taken the torch, Ellis," Chrissie said. "Go and meet him halfway so he's not walking back in the dark. Please."

Ellis turned each corner expecting to see the shape of his father against the snow, but reached the church without encountering him. The nave was in darkness and the altar lit by a single, harsh bulb, high above. Silhouetted by this light, Denny O'Rourke stood rigidly beside his aunt, his hands pressed down on the coffin lid, his head bowed.

Ellis watched with a certain reverence. This could be any

moment in time, he realised. Any moment in any year since 1971. His dad had been standing here ever since that date. When he held Ellis in his arms, when he carried him on his shoulders, when he led him across the Marsh, when he smiled at him and laughed with him, when he resented him and ignored him, through all these times Denny had also been standing at a coffin, head bowed, presuming no one could see.

Ellis felt suddenly agitated by his invasion. He feared that if his father saw him now then he would never look his son in the eye again, never forgive him for being here. So Ellis crept away, but as he reached the door he heard a sound which compelled him to turn back. He saw his father look to the heavens and fight back his tears with a sharp intake of breath. He pressed harder down on the coffin, bowed his head again and gasped for air. Then the sobbing came. His shoulders heaved and cries battled their way out of him. He inhaled again, fighting valiantly, but the battle was lost and the tears and sobs burst out of his shaking body. His dignified, upright frame buckled and he slumped forward on to the coffin, resting his forehead against it as he wept. Ellis stared open-mouthed. He was seeing the unseen, touching the unknown. He was watching God. Then the panic returned to him, for if his dad knew he was a witness to this, their estrangement would be complete. His heart raced as he tiptoed to the door and slipped away.

Chrissie knotted Ellis's tie for him.

"Got some news," she said.

"You've worn out your G-spot?"

"Good news for you, what's more. Or could be."

"What?"

"I've hooked up with Milek."

Ellis let this hang for a moment.

"Milek the photographer?" he checked.

"How many Mileks do we know?"

"When you say 'hooked up' I presume you mean spread your legs, wide open like a giant clam?"

"You presume correctly. Extremely pleasant it was too."

"Why didn't you say so before, when you gave me my camera?"

"Because we hadn't hooked up then. This is very fresh Yuletide news."

"And why does this news relating to your rarely unshared bed concern me?"

"Because he's a photographer and he might give you some work."

"Carry on knobbing."

She hushed him, seeing her father appear.

"Time to go," Denny said brightly. He had equipped himself with an armour-plated smile to see out the morning.

From the window, Ellis saw Gary Bird's mother and her neighbours emerge from the cottages across the lane. They were dressed in their best and tiptoed through the snowdrift to the middle of the road, like farmyard geese. Mrs Bird held her palms upwards and grimaced at the sky. Ellis, Chrissie and Denny walked through the village and up to the church. Some of the villagers waited at their gates holding sprigs of holly and fell in line behind the O'Rourkes. An hour later, when they followed Mafi's coffin across Glebe Road into the new cemetery, the world was a blinding whiteness again and the snowflakes were like feathers.

Denny O'Rourke changed out of his suit as soon as they returned home. He clambered into the hatch attic where the thaw of the previous night was dripping in. Ellis found him contorted beneath the low roof, repositioning buckets.

"Dad, I'm off now," Ellis said.

"Doesn't make sense," his dad replied. "These drips aren't the drips we're getting downstairs."

"So, what's new?" Ellis sighed. "I have to go, Dad, the snow's settling again."

"Drive safely," his dad muttered, monotone, without looking at his son.

The seatbelt pulled tight against Ellis's chest. He watched the weeping willow at the foot of the garden become ghostly then disappear as snow covered the windscreen. Within this white veil, he pictured his father on his knees, his shoulders bearing the weight of the immense slanting roof. He started the engine, flicked on the wipers, and drove away.

Denny O'Rourke remained on his knees in the attic, arguing with himself between action and inaction. He crept towards the attic door then stopped and stared at the aperture to the outside world, paralysed by indecision.

Chrissie lay on her bed with headphones on, listening to Mafi's favourite tape of Delius. Tears streamed across her cheeks.

The patch of snowless ground, where Ellis's car had been, glowered at Denny. He followed the wayward tyre marks across the ice and on to the lane. He looked across the cottage's vast cat-slide roof to the virgin white slope of Hubbards Hill above the village. In the lost perspective of whiteout, the hill seemed vertical. Mountainous. Dangerous.

Ellis's ascent out of the valley was slow. He crawled the car slowly around the patchy snowdrifts on Glebe Road and the packed ice alongside the war memorial, but at the mid-point of Hubbards Hill, where the bridge crossed a deserted, snow-strangled main road, the wheels spun and the car slid inexorably backwards. It was a silent, serene sensation and although his heart sank at the prospect of further captivity within the village, Ellis made no attempt to fight the slide. There was no point. He was no longer the driver but the passenger, on board a smooth-moving ship, gliding across mirror-calm water into a port not of his choosing. The surrounding trees and fields were silent but complicit. They folded in on him as he slid homewards. As the car came to a halt, it spun gracefully. The valley panned through Ellis's windscreen and he was left facing the village. He looked at the cloudless blue sky and heard a girl shriek with laughter. In his wing mirror he glimpsed a boy and a girl playing in the snow, disappearing behind the toll cottage by the bridge. Smoke billowed from the chimneys. His eyes drank in the panorama of whiteness and the punctuations in the snow of cottage, farm, tree, gate and fence. The children laughed again, this time from a distance. The sound seemed to echo and then the world fell silent and cold. The car slipped again, skating a little further and coming to rest against the hedgerow, a yard inside the village sign.

"Fair enough," Ellis whispered, "fair enough."

The snow was dense, even though the flakes looked as light as dandelion clocks. It settled in sheets again on the windscreen, entombing Ellis in a white cubicle where he sat motionless and blank, increasingly oblivious of the blizzard as he prepared to harden his heart, for the sake of his self-preservation, before returning to his father. He sat for almost an hour, alone in the void, coming to terms with the arrival of transience in his world that Christmas. To find himself alone was not something that concerned him, but to feel so lonely came as a shock.

Then the white screen in front of him began to disintegrate. A hand broke through the snow, clearing the windscreen. Behind it appeared Denny, wrapped up against the cold. With large gardening gauntlets on his hands he brushed the snow aside. He didn't look his son in the eye, not even when he opened the driver's door and pulled out the ignition key.

"Not today," Denny said, ushering Ellis out of the car. "You're not leaving today."

They walked in silence down the hill, watching their step through the blinding flurries and dodging the sheet ice. They passed beneath the church tower and stopped to survey the village below. Neither of them looked left towards the new graveyard.

Then Denny spoke with his old voice, the voice that had raised Ellis and made him feel the most loved boy in the world.

"You didn't have to leave the church last night, Ellis. You should have stayed with me. We could have walked home together."

Denny wandered on, taking care on the icy slope. Ellis didn't move for some time. He sucked the cold air into his lungs and allowed his eyes to fall out of focus in the snow. He was suspended by the purest feeling of happiness and love, and a sense, suddenly, that anything was going to be possible in the future.

15

The future began with a job interview at the Bullet Photographic Agency and, an hour beforehand, a rendezvous with Chrissie at her office where Ellis was introduced to Milek, professional photographer and broker of this life-changing career opportunity. Ellis allowed Chrissie's pre-interview lecture in how to behave in front of grown-ups to pass without protest, but when she came at him with a hair brush he drew the line.

There were two women and one man at the interview. Ellis tried to describe them to Jed that evening but it was difficult because they didn't talk the way he was used to people talking. When they asked him a question they seemed to answer it for him and then invite him to agree.

"How long have you been passionate about photography?"

asked the man, a Spandau Ballet lookalike. "For ever, or for ever and a day?"

Ellis looked to the women for help but they seemed to think this a reasonable question too, judging by their expectant faces.

"Well," Ellis ventured, "I'm not 'pash ...'"

He discovered that "passionate" was not a word he could finish. It just sounded so wet.

"I'm not pash ... about it yet. Really. Not yet. I've only just got my first camera ..."

"What you got?" interrupted the man.

"Pentax K1000," Ellis smiled.

"Amateur hour, my friend. Don't show your face in public without a Nikon."

Ellis smiled submissively and kept his opinions to himself. "I'm keen on photography," he continued, deciding that "keen" was a perfectly good substitute for the p word. "Anyway, you only want someone to make tea and catalogue slides, don't you?"

The two women smiled in unison. The junior one muttered, "Priceless ..."

"We call them trannies, not slides, but it doesn't really matter," the man said.

Then why say it? Ellis refrained from asking.

"You would also, in time, be going out with our staff photographers as their assistant. You need to at least *like* photography to be good at that," the boss woman said.

Ellis sensed that he had strayed from Chrissie's directive that he portray himself as "highly motivated".

"I do," he said, injecting some enthusiasm. "I really like it a lot."

"What, in your view," asked the younger woman, "is the hallmark of an iconic image?"

"I'm sorry, I don't know what the question means. I understand depth of field though. Milek took me through it, if that's any help."

The man jumped back in. "Look. Point is, my friend, you have to get your head around the diversity factor. Follow? One moment you might be holding a negative crafted by one of the finest photographers in the world, the next you'll be making the tea or taking my laundry to the dry cleaners."

The room fell silent.

"Do you follow?" the man asked, expectantly.

Ellis smiled politely. "Um ... I don't want to seem rude but I can tell you for free that I will not be taking anyone's laundry anywhere."

Again, there was silence. The three Bullets fixed their attentions on separate fictitious objects in the middle distance over Ellis's shoulder and did a passable impression of being lost in thought.

"I do feel passionate about photography, by the way," Ellis said, meekly. "I don't know why I said I didn't earlier."

"Good lad," Spandau-man said, pressing his blue-rimmed specs up on to the bridge of his nose. "Good lad."

Cunt, Ellis thought.

Ellis rang his sister from the call box on Joy Lane.

"They've given me a form to fill in and it says I have to write a letter of intent."

"They're bastards to get right, those sorts of letters," Chrissie said. "Just tell them it's exactly the job you're looking for and that you've a passion for visual media."

"OK, I'll do my best."

"Keep it short. Half a page."

"OK."

"Ellis, there's something else."

"What?"

"He read your letter."

There was a little silence.

"I found him sitting on the bed folding it up. He cried on

my shoulder."

"Oh."

"Ellis?"

"Yeah."

"Thank you."

"What for?"

"Letting me see Dad cry. I've never seen him cry. I wish you could have seen it too."

The image of his father at the altar came to him. He suspected Chrissie would resent Ellis for that moment, if she knew.

"I'm glad you saw," he said.

He sat on the beach and pictured his dad reading the letter. Ellis had left it by Denny's bed, propped against the photograph of the lighthouse shore. He imagined the words entering his dad's eyes and mind and heart. "*Dear Dad,*" he whispered to the white horses crossing the estuary, "*I will always be grateful that you brought Mafi into our home. I have loved growing up with Mafi there. You are a private person for your own reasons and you have made me into one too. But that doesn't mean that I do not feel the need to tell you how much I love you. I will be thinking of you there without Mafi and I will never forget her. I love you, Dad.*"

He smiled to himself and nodded with satisfaction.

Awaiting him on the doormat were the first photographs from his new camera and, amongst them, a picture of himself and Denny, side by side in the snow, wearing identical clothes and expressions of disbelief. He heard Mafi's voice call out. "Yoo-hoo ..."

It surprised and pleased him how similar he and his dad looked. They had the same set of lines arching across their faces towards high cheekbones and large, bright eyes. They stood shoulder to shoulder these days, the greying hair and deeper lines on Denny's face the only notable differences between them. Mafi's camerawork had almost left Ellis with a picture of snow and nothing else. She had cut Ellis and his dad off at the chest and placed them in the bottom corner of the frame, devoting the majority of the photo to the whiteness. Her frail, shaky hands had also conferred a slight blur on the image. Ellis placed the photograph beside his bed and decided he would post a copy of it to his dad. He laid the job application form on the table beneath his bedroom window. Beside it, he placed blank sheets of paper, ready for the moment he felt inspired to write his letter of intent. Outside, a posse of Jed's friends were dragging timbers across the beach to a huge bonfire stack. A barge bringing timber from Malaysia for the rebuilding of the sea defences had shed its load in a storm. Timber had been washed up along the shoreline between Margate and the estuary for days on end. It was going to be a big fire. It was going to be a big night.

Ellis never read in a book that sandwiching sixty micrograms of acid between skunk blowbacks was a bad idea, but he probably should have worked it out for himself before finding himself face down in the shingle struggling to breathe. Someone had placed his head in setting concrete but he dared not move in case whoever had done it was still in the room. On the point of suffocation, he panicked and flipped over on to his back where he was met not by the face of his fictitious attacker but by plumes of his own manic breath rising into a starry sky. The crackle of the bonfire and the buzz of conversation and laughter were nearby. He knew he had to sit this one out and wait for his organs to return to his jurisdiction. His vision was shooting all over the place and he felt sick as well as paranoid. When he regained the use of his legs, he returned to the bonfire and sat on a railway sleeper watching the flames. His mind settled and he saw, hovering in the sky across the bay, a great waterfall, a mile wide, with crystal-blue water cascading down it. At the foot of the falls, a gathering of strange green creatures sat on the water's surface fishing with brass curtain poles. Ellis recognised the creatures from previous Dr Seuss dreams. He smiled gormlessly at them and didn't care that they probably weren't there at all. It was just good to see them again.

A friend of Jed's, called Marianne, stood over Ellis and asked him if he'd like a cup of hot chocolate. She took a mug from the tray her girlfriend was carrying and placed it in Ellis's hands, securing his fingers around it. Ellis watched her hands on his and felt happy and vivid. He sipped the sweet hot drink and decided that now would be a perfect time to write his letter of intent.

He knelt at the table in his bedroom and placed a blank sheet of paper in front of him. He felt inspired and clear about what he was going to write but struggled at first, until he realised he was writing with his left hand. When he started again, using his right hand, the words poured forth and a letter which had threatened to be difficult to compose was suddenly the easiest thing in the world. His only reservation when he knelt back and surveyed the six pages he had produced was that his black biro had run out after four and a half and he had found only a blue pen to replace it. Taking into account the red pen he had used for the illustrations, there were three different colours on the page. He worried it might look messy or indecisive. Conversely, it might look passionate, which was a good thing. That presentational issue aside, it was a job well done. He put the letter and the application form in the envelope provided.

It was the start of a beautiful morning beneath a bright winter moon. Ellis guessed at six o'clock. He stopped at the post box on Joy Lane, kissed the envelope once for good luck and despatched it. He walked up the hill, past Hedley Wilkinson's frogs, across the fields above Medina Avenue, and on to the Thanet Way, where he jogged through the gaps between fast-moving lorries on the dual carriageway. When he reached Mac's Café, the truck stop on the London-bound side, he looked back and wondered why the lorries had sounded so angry with him.

Ellis had placed his order. The lady behind the counter was staring back at him, trying not to laugh, and Ellis was confused. He looked at the lorry drivers at their tables. Each one was looking at him with amused curiosity.

"That didn't make a word of sense, my love. Do you want to try again?" the lady said.

Ellis took a deep breath and repeated himself. "All the ... 'n' thing talkie 'bout, foodum you know, like freedom."

He smiled, secure in the knowledge he had asked for the set breakfast for a second time.

"Like before, darling, I'm not getting you."

"And a hottie," Ellis added, "like Marianne did."

The lady smiled kindly and the giggle she was trying to suppress crept out. Ellis smiled back wide-eyed. He looked like a child. He turned to the men in the café, his big blue eyes dilating merrily.

"Shame Marianne herenay, ain't she?"

One of the men stood up and approached him. He was fat and hairless and gummy. He put his flabby arm round Ellis.

"You – want – to – eat?"

Ellis nodded and pointed to the lady behind the counter with an expression of despair.

"No, it's not her fault, you were talking gobbledygook. You aren't making sense," the big man explained.

Ellis smiled. "Oh ..." He nodded thoughtfully.

He walked across to a table where four men in boiler suits were eating and pointed to a mound of baked beans.

"You want beans?" the big man asked.

Ellis nodded, like Harpo Marx.

"He wants beans," the man said to the lady.

Ellis pointed to the fried eggs.

"A fried egg? How many?"

Ellis lifted his index finger.

"One fried egg."

Ellis withdrew his finger then stabbed it into the air again.

"Two fried eggs?"

The lady behind the counter took down the order. As the set breakfast came together item by item, the other men around the café willed Ellis on, nodding their heads without realising they were doing so, and when Ellis drew a line through the air to signal that his order was complete a round of applause rang out from the tables.

Strange bunch, Ellis thought to himself.

He took a seat in the corner and tucked a white paper napkin into his shirt. The lady brought him a mug of tea.

"Will Mac be cooking my foody?"

"Who, darling?" she asked.

Ellis looked at her in amazement and then pointed to the neon sign outside.

"Oh!" the lady said. "Mac! Yesss! He's cooking it right now, sweetness ..."

Ellis nodded his approval. There seemed little point going to a café called Mac's if Mac wasn't going to cook your breakfast. When his food arrived seeing the baked beans seemed to spark an idea.

"You know what I find not-ly good about the Buddhists?" he called out.

The café fell quiet. By the looks on their faces, none of the men there did know what Ellis's objection to the Buddhists was.

"Are they the ones who believe in reincarnation?" he checked. "Well, whoever it is that do, they're just as bad as the rest of everyone else. See, everyone slags off Christians for being all clever about everything and, you know, like you tell them how stupid all their stuff is and doesn't add up to two plus two and they say 'But we've got faith so we know anyway even if no prove' and so there's not a lot you can say to that really. Is there?"

There was no reply.

"Is there?"

Silence reigned. A number of plentifully loaded forks hovered just outside the mouths they were aimed for.

"Like picking a fight with fresh air. Religion. Same with recarnation milk. We believe you borny gain as another shrub and don't remember the last time. Bingo and don't forget the custard! You can't argue with it 'cos you don't remember the before. I was Horatio Nelson and you can't prove I was not. Don't mind the shaved-headed vibe and the robes though. It's all bollocks. Who's with me?"

This was a tough audience to warm up.

"Anyone else feel the same way?"

He awoke in a tight, windowless box-bedroom, on a narrow bed surrounded by blue-grey walls. In one corner, within reach, was a wash basin and a single towel hanging from a rail beneath it. In the other corner was a small wooden chest painted thick with white gloss. A drawer was missing. On top of the chest was a small red book. The words "Holy Bible" were in gold on the front and side and a purple silk page-marker extended from the bottom of the red gilded page edges. There was a sound of ticking, but Ellis could see no clock. The blue-grey paintwork was so thick and featureless that he couldn't see the join between the walls and the ceiling. A lady entered. She was middle-aged and wearing the same sort of pink and white apron as the lady in Mac's Café. She placed a mug of tea beside the Bible and sat on the edge of the bed. Her skin was shiny and there were greasy spots on her cheeks which led to her dimples. She smiled and her top front teeth protruded slightly and rested on her lower lip.

"Do you know the Mockingbird song?" Ellis whispered.

She shook her head and felt his forehead. Her hand was cold and clean and slightly pudgy.

"You're not her, then ..." he muttered.

She did his coat buttons up for him as his hands were shaking. As they left the room, Ellis saw a small Tupperware container on the floor catching drips from a radiator.

"Oh!" he said. "It's not a clock."

"It's a radiator," she said.

She navigated Ellis through a maze of faceless corridors to the outside world. He stood in the early evening darkness and came to terms with the fact that the day had passed without him. Mac's Café flashed in neon in the corner of his eye. He felt disorientated and weak and he couldn't think straight. The lady held on to his elbow until there was a big enough gap in the traffic for Ellis to cross the dual carriageway. He looked back and she disappeared behind the crossfire of lorries.

By the time Chrissie came for him, the snow had gone but the pebbles were still freezing together at night. Ellis spent the morning lying with his face against the shingle, listening to the distant church bells on Borstal Hill and watching the sunshine thaw the beach. His eyes were as close as they could be, whilst remaining focused, to two small pebbles frozen fast together. He set his heart on seeing the pebbles part in the thaw, on witnessing the exact moment their frozen bond evaporated. But no such drama unfolded and, in time, he realised that a paper-thin gap had appeared between them without his noticing.

Jed walked past, heading into town.

"What are you doing, Ellis O'Rourke?"

"Waiting for two pebbles to part."

"Some might argue you are pissing your life away."

"Nonsense! I'm waiting to become a great photographer."

"Will you be rich?"

"Very."

"Then you can buy me a pint at lunchtime. I'll see you in there."

"Talk to my secretary."

As he took his seat in the pub, Ellis thought to himself how similar to his sister the woman on the sea wall looked. He started his burger and chips and had got halfway through his pint when he looked again and realised that the woman on the sea wall was his sister, staring back at him.

"Why?" Chrissie said to him, as he walked towards her.

"What you doing here?" he asked, going to embrace her.

"Why?" she repeated.

Her monotone stopped him dead. "Why what? What's up?"

"Why?" she persisted.

"Why what?" He laughed nervously.

"You must hate me. I can't think of another reason."

"Chrissie, what are you on about? I mean, what's up? Why are you here? Has something happened?"

She pulled a fistful of papers from her coat and held them up for him to see. The writing was childishly erratic and interspersed with little sketches. He let out a faint, involuntary gasp, but nothing specific came to him, just ominous warning signals flashing around his brain.

"I feel like ... something is familiar, but, no ..."

"I thought so," Chrissie said. "I thought you just might have been so pissed you wouldn't remember. It doesn't make it any less shitty on your part, you little wanker."

"*What?*" he implored.

She held up the sheets and read aloud, struggling to navigate the misspelled, unpunctuated mess.

"*Dear Bullet Photographic Agency, Letter of Intent from*

Ellis O'Rorck – you've actually spelt your name wrong there – *First thing I should point out clear is that I am not an Irish. Many make that mistake and yes, with a surname like mine, somewhere way way way back of course, but I am not allowed a Irish passport and I have never visited the Emrold Isle or the Emrold Forest, subject of John Boorman's very very very fine recent film which I took the liberty of catching at the Cannon Cinema in Herne Bay which offers admittens* – which you spelled like kittens – *for one pound on Monday nights. Secondly, I was concerned at how pale you all looked, a Irish affliction as it goes. You might consider trying beach life. It does wonders and excellents for the skin.*

"*About the interview, it struck me that ...*

"Then," Chrissie said, "there's just a scrawl. Your writing becomes a sort of cardiogram for a page or two."

"My writing?" Ellis protested.

Chrissie ignored him and continued reading.

"*We are having a bonfire this night. I'd ask you to photograph Marianne for me but you'd only steal her soul. Passion! Passion! Passion! Do I have a passion for photographs, you ask me? Well, yes, but not for photographs which people like you wrote 'processed peas down to 29p' all over, if you get my drift. My O'Rourke's drift! Ha! Never noticed that one before.*"

Chrissie took a moment to shake her head in disbelief.

"*Anyhow, I wish to be considered for the post as ... thingy, you know, the job. I could do some hanging out in London and up my social life huge notches. I am feen and kit* – I suppose you meant keen and fit – *alert, stealthy, rarely steal from others and have a talent for taming seals. I know the location of every dried food item in the supermarket and speak fluent barcode.*

"*Now, some seemingly random facts from modern world history for you just on the off chance I discover that you have employed Mr Townsend, my history teacher from school, to assess this application form: Irish Free State, 1921. French Revolution, 1989* – it was 1789 actually, Ellis. We haven't had 1989 yet – *Normandy Landings, 1944. First ever episode of Starsky and Hutch 1973. That's it, that's all the dates I can remember.*

"*In conclusion, photography can be used for the greater good, for exampley, you know that picture of the girl running away in Vietnam and that picture of Gandhi with his legs crossed. I'm making that up but somewhere there just has to be a famous photograph of that man with his legs crossed cos he was forever crossing his legs. Or the photographic art can be abused, like, you know, those photographs of what they call in the porn trade sticky cum-whores lap-it-up moments and also photographs of sunsets used to sell people pensions.*

"*So, my plea to you is to leave the office, get some sea air (trains run from London to this part of the world twice an hour and you can walk at the beach in fifteen minutes if you take Station Road and Cromwell Road and Oxford Street – no not that Oxford Street derr-brain! – Nelson Road, Island Wall and Edwards Alleyway. Return to your place of work refreshed and inspired to work for the common goody goody two shoes of man. Study human rights legislation in the evenings and you, the bloke on the right as I looked at you, stop wearing those ridiculous blue specs and stop patronising job applicant people, and you, the woman in the centre, return your breasts to the inside of your clothing where tradition dictates they should be during daylight hours. You are too late for the French revolution my dear* – there is absolutely no punctuation here whatsoever, Ellis – *My name is Ellis O'Rourke. I really want this job and I hereby announce my contemplation to be chosen as the astronaut to pilot the Bullet photographic agency crusie ship into the second half of the 1980s. Good evening.*"

Chrissie fell silent for a moment before erupting into mock animation.

"Ooooh and look Ellis! You've done some illustrations to bolster you chances! There's a sketch of your house on the beach, there's the man's spectacles with a bullet hole through them and, look, there's the two ladies from the interview in what I guess is one of those cum-whores lap-it-up moments! And they're in red, which is lovely!"

Ellis remembered some of this now but not much of it.

"It wasn't really me," he pleaded. "It wasn't ..."

He lowered his head and waited for the torrent of self-criticism to engulf him but instead he found himself thinking that some of the letter had really been quite amusing and well written, especially when one considered the state he must have been in when he wrote it. He didn't dare ask how Milek felt about all this.

"I think I need a drink," he said, nodding towards the pub.

"I think that's the last thing you need," she muttered.

He took his pint to a spot where Chrissie wouldn't be able to see him from outside. There, he drank his self-loathing. Trying to piece together the night of the bonfire party was hopeless. He and Jed had both tried that in the previous couple of weeks without success

The unpalatable thing for him was that he knew that he had written the letter simply because it was just the sort of thing he would do. The letter itself wasn't what bothered him. That was a one-off. He could move forward from this point in time fairly confident of never writing a letter like that again. But the idea of Ellis being so off his face that he wrote a long, detailed letter which he then forgot the existence of, that was pitifully like him these days.

"I'm a bad person," he said to a man nearby.

The man picked up his pint and walked away. "I didn't come here to listen to your whining, you middle-class cunt."

Ellis laughed to himself.

"Did you laugh at me?" the man said.

"No," Ellis said softly. "I did not." He met the man's stare and didn't flinch. The man curled his lip and let it go.

Ellis lit a cigarette. This moment is recoverable, he told himself. I need to apologise and take things from there.

The obstacle to doing this successfully was that Ellis was as intrigued by what he'd done as he was contrite. For a start, he asked himself, what made me think of my old history teacher when I was on acid? He seemed the dullest man but he was probably quite a good bloke in real life. Whatever real life is supposed to mean.

"Would the real real life please step forward?" he whispered to his drink.

He wanted to take a good look at those sketches. He was no artist and yet the glimpse that Chrissie had allowed him, admittedly brief, suggested there was some latent drawing ability there. If Chrissie could recognise the drawing of the two women as being of two women then the likeness can't have been bad, he reasoned.

Chrissie entered the pub and went to a table in the corner. Ellis followed obediently, reminding himself that the first words out of his mouth needed to be an apology, a really good one. Their knees touched momentarily as he sat down opposite her.

"I'm very sorry," he said.

She blanked him. He filled the silence, clumsily and blindly, just to get her talking again.

"Don't you think it's incredible that all those history dates were stored in my head without me knowing?"

She looked at him, incredulous. "Amazing," she muttered, shocked by the brevity of his remorse.

Misreading her response, he leant forward conspiratorially, pressing his knee against hers.

"Yeah, and to be able to draw just because you're off your head. Could I take another peep at those sketches?"

She stared at him, and realising that he was serious, she turned purple in the face.

"WHAT THE FUCK IS WRONG WITH YOU?"

The pub stopped to take a look. Ellis watched his sister march out. He stared at the open doorway, at the daylight hitting the buildings on Island Wall. Then he looked to the bar, where a line of drinkers were still watching him.

"Fuck off the lot of you,' he said, without projecting his voice.

"Keep it to yourself," Kitty snarled from behind the bar.

Dyke, Ellis thought.

He returned to his drink. The day had started so nicely, he reminded himself. But, then, watching pebbles defrost is a fairly safe way to start the day.

One of the problems, he couldn't help feeling, as he attempted some sort of analysis, both out of a sense of duty and just in case his sister stormed back into the pub and asked him what he had to say for himself, was that Ellis didn't "get" adult life, even though he had been flirting with it for nearly a year. He did not appreciate why Chrissie was so angry. He understood why but he didn't appreciate why. Why couldn't this episode be funny, something to be laughed off with a sense of knowing, even loving, despair? OK, he wasn't expecting to be offered the job after this, but why did it all have to matter so much? Why did it matter to Milek that his girlfriend's brother was an immature prat? Why did it matter to the agency that one of their photographers had suggested a guy who turned out to be a fool? And why couldn't Chrissie just find it hilarious? She, Milek, the agency, they were all on the same side; the side where you have a good job, clothes you buy but don't wear and a Sony Walkman cassette player. It was Ellis who was the loser in all this. Fair enough, Spandau Ballet-man is going to have been offended by the bullet hole in his spectacles. That drawing, admittedly, sent out a negative message. But why was it such a problem for the two women? Their sketch, from what Ellis could glimpse, had been pretty kind to each of them. In fact, he'd taken years off them both.

And here was the problem in a nutshell. Ellis couldn't take adult life seriously even in moments like this when he was thinking to himself, and the internal mechanics of that fact were preventing him from constructing a heartfelt apology for his sister. Unlike most eighteen year olds, Ellis was not finding life away from the confines of home, with all its freedoms and pleasures, amazingly satisfying. He was already getting a bit bored by it all and he'd hardly dipped his toe in. Some eighteen year olds would love to be living his life. Des Paine would swap places with him. Tim Wickham might, too. And, yes, Ellis loved living by the sea and he loved going to work rather than school. And he liked the feeling of being tired and stopping for a break and drinking a hot cup of tea and smoking a cigarette. But how many more times was he going to do that in his life and still find it wonderful? And that's why the job at the photographic agency would have been good, he reminded himself. Because it would have moved him on and been a new challenge and it would have opened up his life to new people and places. It would have been a step up, a marker of growing maturity. At that precise juncture in Ellis's life, not drawing a cartoon of his potential bosses shoving dildos into each other would have been the sensible course of action.

Jed saw Ellis up ahead on the beach, sitting against a breakwater. For Ellis, recovering from an hour of intense reflection in which he arrived at a degree of self-realisation was a radical departure from cohabiting with whatever random visual ideas entered his head, and the experience had left him mentally exhausted. In an effort to freshen himself up, he rolled over and attempted a headstand and made a pretty good fist of it.

"Good afternoon, my most peculiar friend," Jed said as he crunched his way across the pebbles.

"Hello there," Ellis replied, in a squashed upside-down voice.

"Weird but kind of impressive, that," Jed said, inspecting the headstand.

"Hurts my head," Ellis moaned, the words squeezed out of his brain as his face turned red. He collapsed on to the pebbles. "How was Ben?"

"Fine," Jed said. "Slaughtered him at snooker."

"Some would argue you should let your six-year-old brother beat you at snooker," Ellis said, brushing himself down.

"Maybe," Jed shrugged. "But we wouldn't want to knock about with them."

"I've decided to quit," Ellis said.

"Glad to hear it," Jed said. "Quit what?"

"Weed, for a start."

"Well, you're not exactly Keith Richards."

"And the drinking to oblivion and the drinking on weekday lunchtimes. My weeks are getting hazy."

"I'll stop too," Jed said.

"Serious?" Ellis asked.

"I've a lump in my pocket and that's all I've got. We'll smoke it now and then that's it. No more. Tomorrow's a new day. You're only saying what I've been thinking. It's all become a little boring."

"We could just chuck the lump in the sea and stop immediately."

"That's not going to happen, is it?"

They worked their way through the last of the stash and through Jed's hip flask of brandy. Ellis wondered if the two little pebbles would be freezing back into an embrace for the night. At one point Jed hugged Ellis and Ellis slapped Jed on the back.

"You're not very physical," Jed commented.

Ellis dismissed this as rubbish.

"No, it's true. You laugh a lot, you've got a Cheshire cat smile, you listen to your friends and you sleep with women, but you never embrace your friends or hold hands with the women you've brought home and slept with."

Jed reached into his jacket pocket and took out his wallet. With practised ease, he slid out a small photograph of his kid brother.

"He's my son," he said.

"I guessed," Ellis replied. "Is there a story?"

"Not an original one. His mother doesn't like me and I'd be lying if I said I wanted to be with her. That's it. I'm doing my best."

The first stars were appearing in a fathomless, dark blue sky. A line of fire laced the horizon to the west. The sea looked magnificent, a calm, tender, shimmering grey. The flask was empty and the weed was gone. They hauled themselves up unsteadily and walked on past the silhouettes of houses with names they would never forget: "Breakwater", "The Reef", "Bellbottoms", "Captain's House". Jed staggered up the embankment and stopped to admire his mobile home. Ellis remained on the beach, watching a London-bound train clatter past. His thoughts chased after the train and an idea came to him. He would catch a train right now and follow his sister up to London and make his peace with her.

"You coming?" Jed called out.

"No," Ellis said, and wandered away, deep in thought.

Jed picked up a couple of pebbles to lob at Ellis, but seeing that his friend had made one of his rapid trips into his own private world he let the pebbles fall out of his hand and watched Ellis disappear across the shadow line where the house lights of Joy Lane Beach ended.

As his train moved off, Ellis changed his mind, after a premonition in which Chrissie dismissed him as a fool for making the trip. He saw the estuary and Joy Lane Beach from the train, his hands cupped round his face at the window. An hour later, he watched the street-lit climbing frames, goalposts, potting sheds and glowing TV screens of suburbia from the same place and then the hospital where he was born. Something desperate reared up in his heart without revealing itself. The train pulled into the station and, unsurely, confusedly, Ellis found himself stepping down on to the platform. Crowds of returning commuters and shoppers brushed past him in the entrance to Orpington station. He stood deliberately amongst them, amongst each wave of them that came with each train, and waited patiently for someone to tap him on the shoulder and exclaim, "Why! You're the little boy who used to live here! Oh, I so liked your mother. I knew her well. I have the most vivid memories of her. I can tell you all about her, her voice, her expressions, her smell ..."

The house looked the same. Or a little smaller perhaps. The side alley was less overgrown than Ellis remembered it but the back garden looked exactly as it did in the slide. The low brick wall was still there and so was the garden gate his mum had beckoned him through. But, once inside the garden, breathless from climbing the fence, he felt immediately confused and kept glimpsing the mustard brown of the sweater he wore in the slide. Turning to catch sight of himself once too often, he became dizzy. He tried to reach the wall, knowing that his mother would have sat there many times, but his legs gave way beneath him and he slumped on to the grass.

He remembers the white room but nothing else. He has never dredged up a memory of what happened before the room. In the white room, there was only a table and chair and a phone. The receiver was lying to the side of the telephone when Ellis was escorted to it. He sat at the table and stared at the phone for some considerable length of time.

Denny had taken the call on the same evening that the nagging ache in his stomach first turned to stabbing pain.

The owners of the house had seen the man sitting on the grass in their back garden. They didn't risk approaching him, and as they watched him the stranger grew agitated. They could not see his face but his shoulders heaved up and down. Then they heard him sobbing and then wailing and they called the police. The police tried to talk to him but the stranger seemed unable to speak for grief. They took him away. The owners of the house saw him pull a bunch of grass stalks up from the lawn and put them in his pocket as he was hauled to his feet. The man didn't seem drunk or mad or angry. Just inconsolable.

Ellis was exhausted. A policeman led him to a cell where they allowed him to sleep on a bed. In his coat pocket they found a roll of masking tape and a diary. In the address book of the diary, under the letter U, they found a phone number against the entry "Us". When Ellis woke, he had no idea where he was. A policewoman led him into the white room with the table and the chair and the phone. He stared at the receiver but didn't think to pick it up. He looked at the blank walls and wondered if he'd died and, having wondered it, believed it. He had died and was being processed. He couldn't remember what age he had reached prior to dying. He heard a noise down the phone. It was his mum on the line. She was going to tell him where to go after he'd been admitted so they could meet. He hoped the rooms would get nicer than this one. He didn't want their reunion to take place in a room like this. He'd rather they met outside, in the fresh air. He picked up the receiver and listened. He could hear breathing but it wasn't as he'd imagined her breathing to be.

"Hello?" he ventured.

"Ellis?" came Denny's voice.

"Am I dead?"

"No, dear boy."

Ellis smiled at the sound of his dad's voice.

"Ellis?"

"Yes, Dad?"

"Was it the spiders?"

Ellis fell silent. Then he remembered splintered pieces of the evening.

"No. It was my mother."

There was silence again and it lasted a long time.

Then Denny said, "Why don't you come home for a while, to live?"

"OK," Ellis said.

16

The working men's club had been demolished and burnt. There was a bonfire scar where the skittles alley had been. Clouds of ink approached from the north-west and hard, steady rain reached the village. Mist rose from leaf mulch on the ground, lending the garden a primeval air. The weeping willow became a woolly mammoth in Ellis's mind's eye. Chrissie stood beside him at the open front door and watched the storm.

Summoned to the attic by the rain, Denny O'Rourke stopped on the stairs and watched his children lean against each other in the doorway. He smiled to himself and retreated silently back into the dining room, deciding that the buckets in the attic could move themselves tonight. He didn't care. His children were united under his roof and, tomorrow, his daughter was taking him on holiday. Nothing else mattered to him.

Ellis waved them off and as he returned inside he decided to decorate Mafi's bedroom, as a surprise for his dad. He worked to the rhythm of continuous rain, distracted occasionally by the thought that he should visit Tim Wickham.

Mafi's wardrobe was plain and worthless and too big for the room. Ellis took a crowbar to it, and as the wardrobe disintegrated the mighty black beam which ran through the middle of the bedroom wall reappeared. He had forgotten it was there. On the floor was a paper horseshoe, curled and yellowed by age. The wall around the far end of the beam was crumbling. He picked at it with a knife, dislodging as little masonry as possible so that a quick painting job didn't turn into a big plastering job. He filled the hole and delicately swept the paintbrush over it so as not to dislodge the spongy, patched-up surface.

There were never mornings like these on the coast. A freezing mist rose from the fields at Longspring. Ellis bent down to open the gate to the herdsman's cottage, and by the time he had closed it Tim Wickham was standing on the garden path and Chloe was in the doorway, her stony face half covered by her fingers, which played piano on her cheekbones. Ellis didn't know she had returned to Tim and now he didn't know what to say to him.

"I'm sorry ..." was what came out.

When Ellis stepped forward, Tim pushed out the palm of his hand in a "keep out" gesture.

"I said I'm sorry ..." Ellis reasoned.

"Your trouble," Tim said flatly, "is that you've never been in love."

"We're only eighteen ..." Ellis's reply was half-hearted. He hadn't come here to make a case for himself. He shrugged his shoulders, apologised one more time and walked away. Tim called after him.

"You know when we tried to take your dad's letters?"

Ellis turned and nodded.

"I could have unlocked that drawer. You know why I didn't? Because they're none of your fucking business, that's why. You think the world is your private playground because you've got no mummy. She's my wife! Not everything is here for your amusement. You were my mate and you just fucked off. You didn't even ask me to come with you."

"Are you bollocking me for leaving the village or for sleeping with your wife?" Ellis asked defiantly.

"For being you," Tim answered.

Treasure Island seemed barely large enough to perch on. Ellis hated being a giant in a place that use to fit him so well. He emerged from the woods on to the bridleway that led to the lane and stopped to admire the chimney tops and cat-slide roof of the cottage. A stick rattled across the frozen hoof marks and landed at his feet. He turned and saw Tim sitting on the stump of a tree, breathless from running. Tim walked towards Ellis and smiled. For a moment, it was the smile of the boy at the milk vat on a summer morning. Then, for the third time in his life, and the second with Tim, Ellis felt the sensation of his legs buckling, the sky flooding into his line of sight and a sharp pain stinging his skull. The ground was hard and cold. The ridges of the hoof marks dug into the back of his head. Tim stood over him, his right fist still clenched tight.

"That was original of you," Ellis muttered. "Do it a third time and you get to keep my nose."

"You didn't even ask me to come with you," Tim spat.

"You'd have said no," Ellis yelled. "You were in love!"

It might have been the ringing in his ears, but the cottage seemed lifeless. It was the half-hour after sunset, when a little daylight remained trapped in the rooms, light which illuminates but doesn't shine. Ellis walked from room to room and the air was leaden with Denny's absence. Without his dad there, the cottage had no meaning. In Mafi's bedroom, Ellis stared at the great beam. In comparison to his father's perfectionism, the faint-hearted repair Ellis had made to the crumbling wall was intolerable. He stared at the wall, seemingly unblemished but deeply flawed, and it stared back at him. He grabbed a chisel from the tool box and began to chip through his own paintwork into the crumbling masonry, which fell apart so readily it seemed that the rot had been supporting itself. An hour later, there was a hole in the wall four feet long and two feet high.

The beam was damp and rotten, in defiance of its enormous mass. Ellis poked his head in and looked along the beam into the guts of the building, where it was too dark to see. The muted sound of water sitting in pipes and the cold, still atmosphere told him that he was looking into an open space similar to the attics. Then came the sound of a single, faint, high-pitched drip.

He began to walk, mentally tracing the beam's path through the insides of the cottage, behind the walls of the stairwell, under the steps on the landing corridor and into his dad's bedroom where he pulled the bed away and found himself looking at the small black door to the spider well.

"Had to be ..." The words trickled out of him.

In a swift but controlled movement, he lunged forward, opened the door, flicked the light switch and retreated to the centre of the room. The light hadn't worked and he found himself staring at a square of blackness inside the well. He got the torch from downstairs. He lined himself up with the black doorway and attempted to step forward but merely flinched. He cursed himself, held his breath, crouched down and forced himself through the doorway. Inside, he remained on his haunches and stared at the darkness. His heartbeat quickened and his arms began to tremble.

"This is ridiculous, Ellis," he muttered.

He turned on the torch. Layers of triangular webs, worn like grey cloaks, adorned the well. In the centre of the well was an impressive crown post and the beam from Mafi's bedroom formed the horizontal section of it, jointed to a vertical post-beam as great and impressive as itself. Ellis shone the light on the mortised timber plate at the centre of the crown post. This was where the moisture was greatest, as if the pressure of the conjoining timbers was squeezing water from the wood, flakes of which came away easily in his hand.

Then came the same single, delicate, high-pitched drip he had heard earlier. Through the cobweb curtain, on the floor, he could make out what seemed to be a small piece of rusty metal. He directed the torch at the object but the torch-beam was smothered by the webs, and so was his path into the well. Many times since he had left home he had wanted to slow time down but now he wanted to reverse it. He wanted to go back to the start again, to the day they moved into the cottage, to the first time they opened this miniature black door. He wanted to step inside it and greet the spiders. He wanted to live happily with them.

Did I choose to be scared? he asked himself. Did I allow myself to be? Could I just as easily have chosen not to be afraid?

If he could go back in time now, he would not be scared. He would go to his dad when he was still young and ask all about the past and not allow the silence to build, layer upon layer, year after year.

Another drip. Ellis went down on to his knees and, for the first time in his life, willingly touched the webs. He let the revulsion sweep through him and it immediately seeped out of him and there was no fear or revulsion left. He parted the layers of silk with one hand and with the other he aimed the torch at where the sound had come from and saw the tin mouse Chrissie gave him on his ninth birthday, the grey tin mouse with red plastic wheels and a shiny black tail that he had let fall to the floor, like a spoilt little boy. He waited for another droplet of rainwater to fall and saw it bounce off the rusty mouse and make its brittle sliver of sound. He crawled through the silk curtain and the webs fell shut behind him. He picked the mouse up and held it.

All the while, you've been sitting here watching the rain come in, trying to tell us.

He was in the corner of the spider well now, tucked into the pit which, as a child, he had stared into from the attic above. Ellis put the tin mouse in his pocket and switched off the torch. Light from Mafi's bedroom seeped into the well through the hole that Ellis had chiselled. As it did so, the hulking black shape of the beam revealed itself again in the feeble light. Ellis watched it process in front of his eyes, a submarine in the depths, a shadow amongst shadows. Had his father perhaps pulled his bed away every night and opened the little black door and placed his sadness in this well? Was the indistinct shadow in front of him the tumour of set-aside grief that had gathered here?

Denny called Ellis his "hero". His act of heroism had been to discover the rotten beam and its minuscule, inexorable slipping movement that had created tears in the roof for years, silently and relentlessly. And, as if uncomfortable with keeping the truth from a hero, Denny decided to show his son a photograph. In it, Denny was young and wore a suit at an official dinner of some kind.

"You handsome devil," Ellis muttered, as he studied the other man in the photograph. Denny and the man were shaking hands. The man was extremely tall. Ellis had never seen a man tower over his dad. Around them, people were applauding and smiling. The tall man was old-fashioned and immaculate in appearance, with distinct, tight waves of greying hair. Ellis stared at the man for some time, even though he had recognised Hedley instantly.

"The frog-man ..." he whispered.

"I'm not proud of deceit, dear boy. I'm sorry."

Ellis handed the photo back. "I wouldn't sweat. There's deceit and there's deceit. I'm really touched."

And for a moment that was wonderful and unbearable to Denny O'Rourke, his son looked him in the eye.

"And very hungry," Ellis added, to break the spell.

He made a sandwich. And as he did so, his heart basked in the warmth of knowing that his dad had been watching over him all the time.

"Hedley was the senior partner before me. I took over from him when he retired," Denny said.

"When was that?"

"Fifteen years ago. Hedley retired to the coast. You happened to land on his doorstep."

"I thought he was after my gonads," Ellis said.

Standing at the kitchen door, Denny caught sight of a tawny owl and followed it out of the garden and into the woods, forgetting that he had a glass of Scotch in his hand. The moonlight was strong and blue and willing to share secrets. The owl was gone. Denny watched the silvern light skitter on the streams surrounding Treasure Island. He stepped across the water on to the island. He lit a cigarette and sat on the ground. All around him the water trickled and glistened. Medway, Rother, Panama and Mississippi. Children give names to places and then grow out of them, but all the different names remain, piled one on another like layers of paint on the walls of an old house that people have loved.

Denny sipped his Scotch. It tasted good against the outside air. It was time to set sail again. If he didn't, he would fade. He would grow old in an empty house, waiting for his children to fill the cottage with grandchildren, only to discover that they fill it merely a few times each year and leave it emptier in comparison. The notion that he might leave the cottage felt surprisingly real to him, possibly because an insurance company and a builder had, with apparent ease and relative speed, put an end to a problem that had agitated him for a decade. He would have found it difficult to leave with the roof still confounding him.

If he could bring himself to move on, there were great treasures awaiting him. He sensed this. He would buy a small house with a small cottage garden, and free up money for travel. He would revisit the places he saw as a young seaman and he would go to new countries too. And to many of these places, if life could be exactly as he wanted it to be, he would take his son.

When Denny went to view houses, Ellis stayed behind and took photographs of the village. With the onset of winter the quality of light at the beginning and end of the day grew more and more beautiful to him and he began to recognise its behaviour. From the woods on the hill, the four hundred acres of Longspring Farm looked small and vulnerable amidst the vast and ever-increasing acreage of Dale Farm and Westfield Farm. Ellis composed a photograph of the village cradled in the valley, carefully excluding the widening main road beneath him. He placed dead centre of picture the twin silos at Westfield that rose above the horizon. Then, he waited for the light to change. He had a smoke and daydreamed of being a photographer and wished he hadn't screwed things up with Milek. He looked through the viewfinder again and stepped away in confusion. He double-checked to make sure he wasn't hallucinating, but he wasn't. The silos at Westfield Farm had disappeared.

The concrete track to Haynes's farm at Westfield was a long, laborious walk. It felt like prairie land to Ellis and he didn't like it. He and Tim had watched enormous mounds of uprooted hedgerow being burnt all over Haynes's land when they were boys.

The silos lay dismantled in sections, in the shadow of a newly constructed grain store. The store was a massive portal-framed building, clad in reinforced steel with ventilation ducts like a shark's gills and docking bays for the huge tractors that would ship in the grain. Ellis stepped inside and tested the echo. He looked out through the colossal steel doors at the fallen silos and could hardly accept they were no longer a part of the sky.

The hamlet of Charcott was an hour's walk from Westfield across the land. Ellis had been there only a few times in his life. He wandered up there now and, with the trees bare, the village was laid out vividly from the small community on the hill and it pleased Ellis to find a fresh view of his homeland, even now. Charcott was no more than a single row of terraced cottages, a phone box and a furniture maker's workshop. In the middle of the terrace was a one-room pub called the Heron and lying star-shaped on the ground outside it was Des Payne, stupefied by a lunchtime drinking session. Unable to wake him, Ellis sat him up against the pub wall and watched over him. Theirs was the first generation of boys to grow up in the village with no work awaiting them when they became young men. They could either wander away, as Ellis had, or wander around, like Des. Tim Wickham had got the only job going.

Denny got in from work and sat down with a cup of tea and a pile of house particulars. The phone rang.

"Is Ellis there?"

"Hello, Jed. No, he's not."

Denny and Jed had never met but they spoke often and liked each other.

"Can I ask you something Jed?"

"Sure, Mr O. Fire away."

"Has my son had many girlfriends? Relationships, I mean. Good ones?"

Jed hesitated. "You've caught me off guard there."

"You'll tell me if it's none of my business."

"Well, he's definitely not gay, and there's a few females in this town who could testify to that, if you know what I'm saying."

"I think I can crack your code."

"But, relationship ... I don't know. Ellis seems happier not getting too involved."

"I fear I haven't offered my son much guidance on the subject of love."

"I shouldn't sweat," Jed said. "It's not like sons are really into accepting guidance from their dads anyhow. But, you know, if you're brought up by a single man you're not going to know much about men and women being together, are you?"

Denny wandered into the orchard for a smoke. He laughed at himself. There was nothing as frightening as a young person shooting from the hip. Change was trickling into his life whether he liked it or not. His wife's death had always felt to him the most recent event in his life but, lately, for the first time in fifteen years, it seemed a long way away. The years that had passed since she left were finally amounting to distance.

The phone rang again and Denny heard the pips of a call box and then his son's voice.

"If I invited you to come up to the Heron for a pint, would you consider it A, a genuine offer or B, an unsubtle attempt to get a lift home?"

"I'll have a Guinness. Unless this is C, an unsubtle effort to get me to come and buy you a drink because you're out of cash, in which case you'll have to wait for me."

"I've got cash."

"I'm on my way."

Denny found his drink waiting for him. "That," he said with measure, after his first sip, "is a decent pint of Guinness."

"Didn't know you drank the stuff," Ellis said, offering his dad a smoke.

"You should go to Ireland and try the real thing," Denny said.

"So should you," Ellis replied.

"I've been. A Guinness in Ireland is a pleasure indeed. Might take you there myself. I'll add it to my list."

"When did you go to Ireland?"

"In my youth, a number of times."

"First I've heard of it," Ellis said.

"You don't know the half of it," Denny said, and sipped again.

When their glasses were empty, they took Des Paine home.

Denny O'Rourke gazed at the snowdrops on the front lawn whilst the estate agent showed the cottage to a couple from Chiswick. The couple were in their early thirties, had two young children and hoped to have a third. They said the cottage was beautiful. They understood it must be a wrench to leave. Denny listened politely and smiled his handsome, disarming smile, oblivious of its qualities. He found himself picturing the wife from Chiswick naked. This was not something he usually did. But he was doing it now. They made love and she was sweet and warm. Embarrassed, he went into the dining room, under the pretext of having to record something on the radio.

"It's difficult for him," Ellis explained.

Ellis had made a point of never using the fact that he had no mother for his own advantage. But now, consumed by the urge to touch this lovely older woman, he bent the rule by leaning forward and touching her forearm, as he added, "His wife died, you see."

And by not saying "my mum died" he felt he hadn't cheated too blatantly. The woman's eyes shone pale blue in sympathy.

The estate agent called at two o'clock with an offer. Denny rejected it and said that if they offered the asking price the cottage was theirs. At three o'clock, the agent rang and said he'd never sold a house so easily. Denny suggested he reduced his fee to reflect the fact. The agent laughed nervously.

"You said it would take months!" Ellis protested.

"I thought it would."

They drank a little that evening.

"Strangest thing happened today," Denny admitted, when the bottle was empty, "with the woman buying the house ..."

"Yeah?"

"Came into the dining room and kissed me." Denny was as shocked now as he had been then. "Kissed me on the cheek, squeezed my hand and said, 'Do take care.'"

Ellis was appalled. "Lucky sod! I fancied her rotten. I was thinking all manner of unsavoury things about her."

This alarmed Denny. If he was going to start having fantasies about naked women in his retirement that was one thing, but he didn't expect to be fantasising about the same women as his son.

Gary Bird opened the door to Ellis, revealing that he had grown to twice Ellis's width and weight. His neck was as thick as his head. He looked at Ellis blankly.

Ellis gave in. "Hello, Gary."

Gary seemed not to be breathing.

"It's me, Ellis."

Gary raised his eyebrows in an unusual display of

animation. "I know it is."

"Oh. Right. Long time no talk." Ellis struggled on.

"Seven years," Gary mumbled.

"Quite a long time considering we live ..." Ellis faltered, gesturing weakly to the cottage opposite. "I was a bit of a git to you as a kid." This was not the conversation Ellis had planned. "You probably think I still am."

"I wouldn't know."

"Anyway! That's not the point."

"What is?" Gary asked.

"I don't know if you're in work right now but we need someone to help us pack and shift furniture all week."

"Right."

"You interested?"

"Yup." Gary remained lifeless.

"Oh, good."

"Two pound fifty an hour," Gary gushed.

"Fine. See you eight thirty."

"Nine," Gary muttered darkly.

"By the way, feel free to apologise for breaking my nose and smashing my brain into my arsehole seven years ago," Ellis said brightly, curious as to how Gary would react. He reacted by gently shutting the door.

Ellis woke to the sound of blackbirds fighting in the trees. After a week of working too relentlessly to think of time running out, and distracted by the bet he and Denny had made on whether or not Gary Bird would ever smile, the hollowness of his bedroom stripped bare reminded Ellis that today was the day.

"But we only just got here," he whispered.

The words floated upwards to the attic hatch and dislodged it. Soon after, he saw the first spider poke its head out.

"I thought you'd make an appearance." Ellis smiled.

The spider smiled back. It looked over its shoulder, nodded encouragingly, and another spider appeared.

"Hello," said the second spider.

Ellis smiled at this spider too. The spiders launched themselves down on to the blanket that Ellis lay under, the strands of silk catching in the orange glow of first light as they twisted.

"Are you feeling sad?" one of the spiders asked.

Ellis welled up. "A little." He shut his eyes and felt the bridge of his nose and the back of his eyes burn with a threat of tears. "I'll miss you," he whispered.

When he opened his eyes again, there was a sea of spiders at the hatch and a mist of them descending on drag lines to the floor. They gathered around Ellis, tens of thousands of them. Enough, it seemed, to lift Ellis up and carry him away.

"Ellis," said one of the spiders, "we've watched you grow up and we're very proud of you."

Ellis smiled. "Thank you. Please look after yourselves when the new people move in. It's going to be a dangerous time."

"Goodbye, Ellis," they called out.

Ellis shut his eyes and allowed them time to disappear so that when he moved he wouldn't harm any of them.

"Goodbye," he whispered.

He regretted his shyness with people when it came to taking photographs. He had photographed the village from every angle but he had not found the courage to approach people for their portraits. Tomorrow would be too late. Tomorrow, he would be an outsider. Year by year, with no photographs to sustain them, the people would fade from his mind's eye without putting up a fight.

The family from Chiswick pulled up in the lane two hours early. Ellis and Denny peered out from Mafi's bedroom window as if they were under attack. After watching his son march down the driveway and invite the family in, Denny O'Rourke bent down to check himself in the three-way mirror of Mafi's dressing table and found himself staring at a blank wall.

When the moment of leaving came, Ellis defied his own resolution and went into every room of the cottage and tried to recall and wrap up all the years in his heart. It proved a futile and panic-stricken measure. His dad was waiting for him at the foot of the stairs and saw the distress on his son's face. He held Ellis's shoulders rigidly and steadied him.

"Come on," he murmured, "let's not mess it up now."

He forced a smile and Ellis did the same. They marched out of the cottage into the courtyard, where the young couple were trying to keep out of the way.

"Time's not a problem," the woman said. "We'll leave you alone for a few minutes and wait down by the lane."

"Nonsense!" Denny O'Rourke laughed, more loudly than he'd meant to. "We're not like that."

He handed the keys to the husband. "It's all yours."

The woman moved forward to embrace Denny but he thrust out a hand to parry her move and they shook hands formally. Ellis stole a glimpse of the shape of the woman's body as she turned and watched Denny walk away to his car. He shook the husband's hand.

"I hope you're very happy here," he said, as sensibly as he could.

He turned his back on the husband and smiled his most endearing, most vulnerable, most motherless smile at the wife and, hijacking the sympathy she felt for his dad, embraced her.

"Look after your father," she whispered.

Ellis sighed in her ear, feigned the onset of tears, and rested one hand lightly across the top of her buttocks.

"I will," he whispered, and stroked her bottom once.

He marched away to the car. Denny was reversing down

the drive before Ellis had shut the door. They pulled out into the lane and paused for a moment. Denny took a deep breath and turned to his son.

"Ready?" he asked him.

Ellis nodded. "Ready for everything."

As they pulled away, Gary Bird emerged from his parents' house and headed up the lane, without acknowledging the O'Rourkes. Ellis leant out of the window and called across to him.

"If you had smiled at me just once in the last week I'd have won the sodding ten pounds and split it with you, you miserable git!"

He pulled his head back inside and grinned at his dad.

"Let's get out of here," he said.

"Let's," his dad agreed.

And they were gone.

They went to a place where the night sky was orange and there were no stars. But it was available, and cheap to rent, and it was only for a short time, until Denny found the perfect place. The rented house sat in a large, directionless sprawl of modern houses on the edge of the town, which had no edge to it. A line of old walnut trees ran along the bottom of the garden and in the middle of them was a wooden gate leading into the last remaining field, a handkerchief-sized relic of open country. Tunnel vision, selective hearing and an optimistic disposition could give the false impression of being back in the village. Beyond the field, the houses and roads began again. One relentless hour northwards, they became London.

Within a month the walnut trees were green and their large leathery leaves fluttered in the breeze and their percussive sound veiled the drone of the motorway. Denny and Ellis looked at the orange glow that hid the stars from them and, for the first time, Ellis saw doubt impoverish his dad's features.

"I think I might have made a mistake, dear boy."

"The moment you find a place you love, you'll feel differently."

"I'm sure you're right ..." Denny said unconvincingly.

Chrissie arrived with a parcel for her dad.

"They're not presents, they're homework," she told him.

Beneath the brown wrapping paper, Denny O'Rourke found *The Times Atlas of the World* and books entitled *The Art of Independent Travel*, *Great Train Journeys of the World*, *Fodor's Guide to New Zealand* and a Jiffy's Container Shipping brochure, in which were listed cargo ships that offered berths for civilians.

"How marvellous!" he said.

"Inspired idea," Ellis muttered to his sister.

She winked at him proudly.

Denny positioned a table and chair at the kitchen window, facing the walnut trees. He set the atlas and travel books out on it, along with a pencil and notebook. He opened the window to a refreshing breeze, played his music a little louder than the sound of the road, and began to read.

Ellis spent the spring preoccupied by the number of months that were amassing since he'd had sex. He could think of no one in his current routine who would want to sleep with him. The suburbs seemed to drain away the potential for romance or lust, and for anything else for that matter. He was bored. What he really wanted and needed was to work for Milek but that would mean asking for Chrissie's help and, right now, he didn't want to ask her for anything. Something had changed between the two of them. The tenderness had gone from her, unable to cohabit with her ambition. She was businesslike in all things and injected competitiveness into situations where none need exist. Ellis hoped it was a temporary change in her and that things would return to how they used to be, but in the meantime he was bewildered by her need to belittle him.

Denny had viewed four small houses in four different villages but none of them was right. The villages were too enclosed and the houses lightless. He missed the cottage. He missed the way in which his village had allowed the sky in, right up to the doorstep. He loathed the suburbs that surrounded him. He sat in the living room and the afternoon clouded over without his noticing. He rocked gently back and forth, his arms folded across his stomach. He took the phone up to his bedroom and shut the door before calling the doctor and making an appointment for the next day. He went to bed soon after eight o'clock. Ellis brought him in a glass of water and put it beside his bed.

"I've never done this before," Ellis said.

"What's that?"

"Looked after you when you're ill."

"I'm not ill, just a little off-colour." Denny smiled to back up his claim.

Ellis retreated to the door. "What sort of off-colour?"

"Just a tummy ache, that's all."

17

The week was slow and empty. Ellis noted with wry admiration his dad's ability to navigate clear of the word 'tumour' throughout it. When the time finally came, he drove Denny to the hospital. Chrissie couldn't. She had what she called "wall-to-wall meetings" all day.

Father and son were synchronised bravado. They wore identical smiles and the unruffled body language of the

Invincibles and they 'oohed' and 'aahed' at the same houses in *Country Life* magazine. But, in Denny's room, where hotel luxuries and medical equipment made a strange marriage, Ellis felt things change when Denny asked at what time the next day his son should collect him. The consultant looked amused, initially, then appalled.

"Are you aware of the scale of this procedure, Mr O'Rourke?"

Ellis watched the warm, confident smile evaporate from his father's face and realised that Denny had not begun to grasp the enormity of the impending assault on his body.

"This is surgery many people make a full recovery from but you are having a significant portion of your bowel removed this evening. It is major surgery. You are not going to be going home tomorrow. You are not going to be going home the morning after that, not for a couple of weeks."

"Why ever not?" Denny was stunned.

The consultant spelt it out. "Because you will be in a great deal of discomfort."

Ellis was shocked less by the seriousness of their outing than by the discovery that his dad didn't keep the unpalatable truths of life at arm's length just from his children but from himself also.

"Do you want me to take you through any other details?" the consultant asked.

"No thanks," Ellis said. "Send in someone funnier."

Chrissie seemed more indignant than upset that evening.

"All of a sudden we're talking about a tumour. You told me it was just a lump and they'd whip it out."

Denny placated her. "Well, it is a lump ... and, chances are, whipping it out will do the trick."

"Chances! I want to know for sure!"

"Yes, dear girl, me too."

"Think of it like this," Ellis began, making his sister

squirm at the prospect of taking his counsel. "It's great that the GP noticed this lump and it's great that Dad kept up his health insurance from work and it's great that Dad's in here so quickly and by tomorrow it will have been cut out. I mean, that's what happens, this is the reality of people finding out they've got stomach cancer and having it successfully removed."

"Don't say cancer, Ellis," Chrissie said.

"Thank God it's in my stomach," Denny said, "where there's loads to spare and they can just cut it all out. If this was on my lungs or liver ..."

"You'd be fucked!" Ellis said, trying to lighten things up.

Chrissie smiled, despite herself.

"OK," she retreated, "but don't use the word cancer."

They sat awkwardly and quietly, mulling this over.

"Isn't that going to be quite difficult?" Denny asked.

"What?" Chrissie said.

"Not using the word cancer."

"We've got to be able to talk about it," Ellis said.

"OK," Chrissie said, "but why don't we choose a different word for the c-a-n-c-e-r? We could say TB."

Denny was confused. "TB? As in tuberculosis?"

"Yes. It's quick, medical and easy to remember."

The room went quiet.

"I thought," Denny said diplomatically, "the idea would be to replace c-a-n-c-e-r with something a little lighter."

"Indeed," Ellis agreed.

"Oh," Chrissie said, confused. "OK, if you like. For me though, anything other than c-a-n-c-e-r is an improvement. That's why I went for something catchy but still relevant."

"How is TB relevant?" Ellis asked.

"'Cos you 'get it' and Dad's also 'got' something."

These days, Ellis and Denny found it difficult to know when Chrissie was being ironic and when she was being earnest.

"How about ..." Ellis said, gazing at the ceiling.

All three of them thought hard.

"The disease," Chrissie suggested.

"Again," her dad said, "a bit dark."

"You mind cancer but you don't mind 'disease'?" Ellis asked.

"Don't say cancer, Ellis. The 'thing'?"

"Too vague," Denny said. "We'll come a cropper the first time we are having a conversation about the c-a-n-c-e-r and also happen to mention a thing. All of a sudden, we'll have two 'things' in the conversation and we won't know what we're talking about."

"We just call it your condition," Ellis suggested.

"No, sounds like I've got a rash."

"We could name it ..." Chrissie said. "Geoff or Scottie or something."

"Girls have to name everything!" Ellis protested. "You give your cars names for God's sake!"

Denny climbed out of bed and took a seat in the high-backed armchair by the window.

"We'll call it my headache," he said. "Today, I've got a headache and tomorrow, my headache will be gone."

Denny was pleased with this and Chrissie seemed to like it, too. They settled into a comfortable quiet. But Ellis, seeing that there was still an hour to kill before surgery, decided he wasn't finished.

"But what if tomorrow you really do have a headache, which is quite possible considering what you'll have been through?"

"I think I'm getting one now," Denny sighed.

Chrissie despaired. "Oh, call it sodding cancer then, I don't care."

"Cancer it is!" Denny said.

"When all is said and done, cancer has that ring of

accuracy to it," Ellis said.

"I'm actually growing to like it," Chrissie agreed.

Denny sighed contentedly and looked out of the window.

"You're a pair of idiots," he muttered.

Ellis and his sister watched the steam rise off their plates of food until the steam had gone. Ellis scraped the food into the bin. The phone rang at ten minutes to nine. Chrissie darted to it ruthlessly. Ellis felt his heartbeat quicken and the blood and enzymes and chemicals pumping out of control. Chrissie slammed the phone down and grabbed Ellis into an embrace.

"It's gone very well," she told him.

It was late and the hospital was quiet, like a hotel on the moon, and the corridors seemed to smell of Fry's Peppermint Cream. Chrissie hurried ahead and was already at Denny's bedside when Ellis walked in. She felt her father's forehead and glanced up at her brother in the doorway.

"He's sleeping," she smiled, a tear rolling down her cheek.

Ellis smiled stiffly at her, resisted the urge to say "No shit" and ushered himself and his anger out of the room. He sat in the corridor on a soft chair, leaning over a coffee table. He stared at a column of magazines which were fanned out to reveal the titles. He rocked a little, back and forth, held his fingers across his lips and breathed heavily through his nose. All of these mannerisms belonged to his father, as if Denny had lent them to Ellis whilst he hadn't the energy to be himself in such detail. Ellis looked through the open door of his dad's room at the high-backed chair Denny had sat in earlier. He hummed to himself to contain the anger he felt at someone reducing his father to what he had just seen lying in the bed. Once, when he was thirteen, on a Saturday afternoon in winter, Ellis had taken a cup of a tea to his dad after they had been working in the garden. He found him sound asleep on his bed, his hands clasped together behind his head and his mouth open. He looked helpless. Lifeless. Ellis had wondered then if this was how his dad would look when he died. It was how he looked now.

He returned to the room, pulled a chair up to the bed and stroked his dad's left forearm. It was unchanged, still powerful and cobra-wide at its most muscular point. It was the rest of him that had been lessened. He could feel his dad's pulse and it dawned on him that he understood perfectly the task ahead. The body that he could feel functioning beneath the pressure of his fingers was the vessel his dad had been given to live in. They simply needed to protect, service, and correct this vessel and his dad would always be with them. It was uncomplicated. It was achievable. They had cut out the bad bit. They could always cut out other bad bits if necessary. It wasn't really his dad that was ill, it was just his body. And it was only his body that looked different for now. He was inside this lifeless shell, lying dormant whilst they repaired him. Tomorrow, he'd come back to them. Tomorrow, he'd be waiting for them when they arrived. Tomorrow, he'd come out to play. Ellis looked at his sister.

"You're right." He smiled, feeling great love for her. "He's just sleeping."

The phone rang at seven the next morning. Ellis heard it in his sleep, ignored it, then remembered everything and leapt out of bed. He threw himself downstairs in panic but Chrissie beat him to the phone.

"Who is it?" she demanded. Then her face softened. "Oh! Hi," she chirped. "You are thoughtful to call, Ree." She put her hand over the mouthpiece and assured Ellis it wasn't the hospital.

"For fuck's sake!" Ellis hissed. He stormed into the kitchen.

"I'm going to call you back, Ree." Chrissie hung up and found Ellis filling the kettle. She waited for him to be empty-handed, then wrapped her arms around him.

"I'm sorry, Ellie. That was a horrible start to the day for you."

He freed his arms and then wrapped them around her. He could no longer remember what it had been like to be smaller than her.

"Who the hell is Ree?" he murmured.

"Henry. He's a banker."

"Daft time of day to use the telephone."

"He's got a penthouse overlooking the Thames."

This sounded instantly ludicrous to both of them.

"Relevance?" Ellis asked.

Chrissie shook her head. "Don't know why I said it."

"Does Milek like Henry's penthouse?" he asked.

"They've not met."

"You don't say."

Denny O'Rourke stirred. His face creased up and his eyes flickered open.

"Pain ..." he groaned.

"I know," Chrissie whispered.

They watched the waves of agony cross their father's face. They held his hand, avoiding the tubes that ran into his nose, hand and stomach. Chrissie found a payphone in reception and settled down to make work calls. The day passed in silence and was beautiful. In the late afternoon, Denny's eyes opened again. He grimaced, looked at the ceiling and squeezed his son's hand. Ellis sat up. He blinked his eyes affectionately. Denny smiled back meekly and drifted back to sleep. He stirred again later as Ellis left the room.

"I'm just popping out for a cigarette, Dad," Ellis said. He

stood over Denny and grinned. "A lovely, smooth, satisfying smoke, outside in the sunshine. A lovely, lovely ciggie."

Ellis drew on an imaginary cigarette and exhaled ecstatically. In response, Denny muttered his first distinct words of the day: "You bastard ..."

They were days of sunlight and simplicity. Ellis needed no props, no magazines or books. There were no hours. There was only the sunlight that filled the room and his father, lying in bed, squeezing his hand, smiling bravely.

With the breeze playing percussively in the walnut trees and his son and daughter there to assist him, Denny washed the first of his chemo pills down with a bottle of wine. He said they were celebrating the removal of the headache and brushed aside talk of the shadow that had been detected on his lungs since the operation.

"These pills will take care of that as well, especially with a Chablis like this," he declared.

Ellis believed him and the belief took root fast and grew vigorously. Chrissie smiled at the men who were her family and knew that her dad would never get well again.

Denny spent the summer sitting in the garden and watched the evening primroses appear, the hedge become speckled white with flowering bindweed, and the walnut trees, whose leaves transformed from orange to green, stand out against light blue skies. He no longer heard the motorway and he ignored the surrounding houses, living within the open country of his mind's eye and noticing only that which enriched his days. The paleness departed from his complexion, his movements became less laboured and the soreness inside him abated, allowing him to laugh out loud again.

In midsummer, as if to take everybody's mind off the shadow on Denny's lungs, Chrissie dumped Milek for Henry the banker and moved into his penthouse overlooking the Thames. Ellis felt he could now ask Milek for work without turning to his sister for help.

"Look, Milek," he started, "I know that my sister dumping you, and me drawing a picture of your clients engaged in lesbian sex isn't a great platform, but I was wondering if you'd give me a job."

"Ellis, I presume."

"Yes. I really want to work for you and get into photography."

"OK. No problem."

And that was it. The job application and interview was over. He started the following week and Milek took him out for dinner and Ellis ate Japanese food for the first time and when Ellis saw the bill his heart skipped a beat and Milek threw a credit card into the wicker tray and slapped Ellis on the back.

"Come and meet my new girlfriend."

Milek seemed to be largely over Chrissie. Carla was Italian and worked as assistant to a costume designer called Richard. Ellis could not speak to Carla the first time he met her, such was the extent and exoticness of her beauty. Richard was the first gay man Ellis had ever met and Ellis told him so.

"I doubt that, somehow," Richard replied.

They took to Ellis immediately, the way rich women take to Pomeranians.

"She drinks pints!" Ellis muttered in admiration.

"That's the tip of the iceberg," Milek confided.

"I'll tell my sister she's a dog," Ellis said.

Ellis worked six days that week, two in a studio in Wandsworth, one in a forest in Buckinghamshire, a day at a lido in south London and the other two doing runs to the labs and stock shop. Milek corrected his invoice and adjusted it upwards.

"You don't calculate your overtime at the normal rate," he explained. "Welcome to the joys of time-and-a-half and double-bubble."

"I've earned six hundred quid," Ellis muttered in disbelief.

"Doing something you enjoy ... sick, isn't it!" Milek said.

That night, exuberantly happy and with an audience of strangers, Ellis announced that he was spending his first pay packet on taking his dad to Paris. It was an idea born of champagne and Japanese lager but as soon as he'd said it he knew he was going to do it. When most places were closed, Milek and his friends led Ellis to a basement bar with black leather sofas and neon floors and, here, Milek took Ellis aside.

"Ellis ... are you sober enough to listen and take heed?"

"Yes ..." and Ellis tried very hard to be.

"The following is non-negotiable, so listen well. You are working for me and when you are out enjoying yourself you are doing it on the money I pay you. You can party, you can drink, you can get high, you can enjoy. But no cocaine. Seven days a week, twenty-four hours a day, you are banned from cocaine and if you break that I'll kick you out. I've been in your father's house and I've been close to his daughter. I will not allow you to do that drug. No second chances."

"Are you banned, too?"

Milek nodded. "These days."

Ellis paid his dad the five hundred pounds he had borrowed since moving back home. He gave it to him in cash, placed within the pages of Fodor's guidebook to Paris.

In the September sunshine, they walked in the Jardin de Luxembourg, stopping every quarter of an hour for Denny to catch his breath, on a bench within the chestnut groves, or on the low wall around the fountains, beside the lake where

Denny stared at the toy sailboats. His hair had turned a little greyer in his illness and in the bright sunlight it was silvery and handsome.

"I've wanted to come to this city all my life," Denny sighed. "And now I'm here. Unbelievable, isn't it?"

"Easy, isn't it?" Ellis replied.

Every hour or so, Ellis would ask his dad how he was feeling or if he was tired. "I feel good," Denny would reply. Only on the second afternoon, when they had walked through the Marais after lunch, did he need to rest. He caught a taxi back to the tiny Hotel de Maison on rue Monge and fell asleep to daydreams of buying a garret in the Place des Vosges. As Denny slept, Ellis walked the halls of the Musée d'Orsay and bought a print of Redon's *Les Yeux Clos* because it made him think of his mother. He crossed from the museum to the river and reflected on the day.

It's similar, he told himself, to when you glance up at the sky and the clouds are the shape of a face or a mandolin. You look away and glance up again but either the shape has gone or it's there but without the magic of first seeing it. That's what it's like to walk into the Sainte Chapelle for the first time, if you've not been told what to expect. That's what it's like when the towering columns of thirteenth-century stained glass first flood into your vision, causing a sensory double-take at the volume of beauty in front of you as you arch backwards to take it all in. At least, that's what it was like when I took my dad there today.

"My God, Ellis," Denny whispered, putting his arm round his son. "We're in heaven. Thank you, dear boy, thank you."

My pleasure, Ellis whispered, to the fast-flowing river.

Denny telephoned Chrissie from a payphone on the street. When he stepped out of the booth, he wandered away thoughtfully and Ellis followed.

"Oh dear," Denny muttered, "I think your big sister is jealous of our trip."

They wandered towards the dome of the Panthéon and sat in the Place de la Contrescarpe. "I feel inspired to plan my travels when the evenings set in," Denny declared.

"And I feel inspired to rent myself a little pad in London," his son replied.

"I'm glad to hear it. Good for you. Good old Milek."

They talked about the countries they would visit together and they drank cognac and watched French women.

"Wonderful ..." Denny O'Rourke muttered.

They fell silent for an hour, lost in daydreams and a cool air that promised the autumn.

When he lost his dad, Ellis lost the one person who knew truly how to be silent. The silences they shared in Paris were their masterpieces, at the end of a lifetime's work. In that city, Ellis O'Rourke took care of Denny O'Rourke for the first time and it made him feel that he and his dad had known each other for ever and that they were each other's father and each other's son.

On a Thursday morning in mid-October, Denny O'Rourke rang his daughter and then his son and told them to come home that evening for dinner.

"The spot on my lungs has halved in size, more than halved in fact. We're looking good!"

"Let's get pissed!" Ellis said.

"You said it was only a shadow," Chrissie replied.

They got drunk on champagne and Denny went to bed undecided as to whether he should take his chemo pills after so much alcohol. Ellis and Chrissie settled down in their beds soon after midnight, as the long graceful sweeps of wind which had buffeted the evening became more forceful.

Panic-stricken, Chrissie woke Ellis at five in the morning.

"There's the most peculiar noise coming from Dad's bedroom!"

"Go back to bed!" Ellis grunted.

"How can you sleep! There's a hell of a racket in the garden. I don't know what it is."

Ellis sat bolt upright. "You don't know what it is?" He cupped his hands round his ears and listened theatrically. "It's wind, a natural occurrence. It won't bite."

"Come and sleep next to me, Ellie."

"No. Chrissie, you treat me like a right dork when it suits you. You can't have it both ways. Now let me sleep."

She returned at a quarter to six and this time she switched the light on and tore the blankets away.

"I'm not fucking around, Ellis! This house sounds like it's going to collapse! There is the most terrible noise coming from Dad's bedroom window and I cannot wake him."

Ellis didn't argue this time. He went to the window and looked out. "Fucking hell!"

In Denny's room, the window frame was groaning. The glass heaved as if it were trying to draw breath. The wind howled around the house and outside, silhouetted against an angry, early morning sky, were the walnut trees, bent by the gale.

"Never seen anything like it," Ellis muttered.

They pushed and prodded Denny but he didn't stir. Chrissie resorted to shouting in his ear.

"Dad! You've got to wake up!"

Denny opened his eyes, touched Chrissie's face and said, "By all means ask the captain but he won't be able to come about in snowfall. We're not even at Mauritius, you know." He turned over and went back to sleep.

"I'd stick my neck out and say Dad opted for taking his medication last night, on top of the booze," Ellis said.

At that moment, the bedroom wall let out a groan. The glass cracked and the entire window casement was sucked out of the wall and hurled across the garden. The storm poured in through the gaping hole. Ellis and Chrissie stared open-mouthed whilst their father slept on.

The shed had been picked up and deposited in a shattered heap on the other side of the garden. As Ellis dragged a section of it towards the house he was thrown backwards and sideways by the gusts.

"It's amazing out there! Amazing!" he spluttered exuberantly, as Chrissie held the front door open for him.

They had to fall against the door to close it. She helped him upstairs with the shed panel and they found their dad standing by the bed, looking as if he'd been electrocuted.

"There's a hole in the house," he said to them, with pupils the size of pinholes. "It's like going round the Cape. Fantastic! Let's go outside!"

"You're not going anywhere," Chrissie said.

Chrissie took Denny downstairs. Ellis slid the panel across the floor. As soon as he held it up, it was sucked out of his hands and flew at the wall, covering the hole where the window had been. The room fell silent.

"Like slaying a dragon ..." Ellis gasped.

When he'd caught his breath, he nailed the panel to the wall and then he went downstairs where his sister was making tea and his dad was buttering a piece of toast.

"Dad's got the munchies," Chrissie said knowingly.

"This toast couldn't taste any better if it was served up on Selina Scott's thighs!" Denny O'Rourke announced.

"You're off your tits, Dad," Ellis said.

"Ellis! You can't say that!" Chrissie protested.

Denny nodded his agreement with a mouth full of toast. "He's right, dear girl, I think I am."

Ellis had not slayed the dragon that night. No one had. The dragon slayed the town and the park. It slayed the wooded plateau leading to Ide Hill. It slayed millions. Oak, beech, yew, chestnut. Denny said that Jim Croucher up at Emmetts wept when he saw the devastation. On the television news, people in Jerusalem were praying for England's trees.

"At least it was natural," Denny said. "At least it wasn't us."

A month after the storm, the phone rang at midnight, waking Denny.

"Hello, Dad!" Ellis was in a call box.

"Are you all right?" Denny asked.

"Yup."

"Sober?"

"Just about. Wasn't earlier. But are you, more importantly?"

"Yes. Why do you ask?" A smile broke across Denny's face, one of the many that no one would ever see.

"'Cos I need picking up."

"Why so late and why the surprise visit, not that I mind either?"

"Well ... long story really, but it would be particularly nice to see you. That OK?"

"Course it's OK. You at the station?"

"Well ... I'm at a station."

"Which one?"

"Yeah, that would be my next question too. Battle station, near Hastings."

"That's an hour away!"

"This is true."

"Why are you there?"

"Because I met this girl in a bar and we went out and I said I'd see her home and first of all I presumed she lived in London and even when I found out she didn't I still thought she was going to invite me in for the night but when we got to her door she said 'Thanks, see you' and shut the door and by the time I'd walked back to the station the last train had gone."

"You saw her home from London to Battle?"

"Yes."

"Why?"

"I think you know why."

"And she didn't invite you in?"

"Like I said."

"And she shut the door on you?"

"Your hearing's not impaired by the chemo, then."

"She didn't even invite you in for a coffee?"

"Not even a Jimmy Riddle."

"You caught the train with her for an hour and a half and walked her home and she shut the door on you?"

"After saying goodnight, yes."

Denny roared with laughter and called his son an idiot. Driving through the darkness, he felt propelled forward by the happiness of being a father, and grateful to be included in his son's nonsense. Next morning, he cooked a fried breakfast and wanted to know more.

"So how does it work in this day and age, Ellis? Meeting a girl, getting to know her, courting her."

"It doesn't work," Ellis said.

Denny broke open his fried egg and spread the yolk across his toast. He dipped his mushrooms in a pool of melted butter and ate them one by one.

"Your mother's laugh reduced me to jelly. She made me feel wonderful. I know things are different today and there's no harm in ... whatever the correct term is ..."

"Putting it about a bit?" Ellis offered.

"Beautifully put. But I don't think the journey all the way to Battle is worth it unless it's for someone who makes you feel ..."

Denny shook his head, unable to find the words. He smiled at his son, with a look of openness and pleasure that Ellis was unfamiliar with.

"... someone who makes you feel like jelly inside. You'll meet someone special. And when you do, put her first in all things and love her unconditionally."

Denny set about his bacon. Ellis watched his father and wondered where the hint of exuberance had sprung from.

"It was fun last night," Ellis said.

Denny nodded. "Not the fun you were hoping for."

"Better," Ellis said.

They ate then in silence. Ellis cleared the plates away. Denny made fresh tea and set the pot down on the table.

"One can afford to just go with the flow a bit and not worry about everything," Ellis said, using the term "one" for the first and, he suspected, last time in his life.

"One can," Denny said, stirring the pot.

Then, Ellis said, "When I think of my mum ... when I think of being born ... there's just this empty space. I don't know how to be close to a woman. I don't mean physically close, I mean really close. I don't want some other woman to show me love until my mum has. But she isn't ever going to do that."

"But she did," Denny said.

Ellis continued. "At five o'clock on a winter's morning, in the darkness, Chloe Purcell feels the way I imagine good love feels."

Denny nodded his understanding. "You know," he whispered, tapping his son's hand with his finger, "you need to avoid sleeping with other men's wives in the future."

They both breathed a faint laugh and Ellis felt a familiar sense of bewilderment come upon him, a bewilderment particular to the memory of Chloe.

"Dad, I'm not trying to make excuses, but ..."

"What? It's all right, you can say it."

"She kind of ... seduced me."

Denny grinned. "You poor thing. How terrifying. How lovely."

And he loved the reluctance in his son to say anything that might sound ungallant.

"Ellis," Denny said. "Your mother loved you. She went away because she felt the world was happening without her."

"I can understand that feeling," Ellis said.

"I know you can and that's why I get scared by you."

Then there was silence and Ellis thought of the bundle of letters in his dad's locked drawer. This was the moment to ask if he could read them.

"Dad ...?" he ventured, but saw that Denny was far away.

"You know, Ellis ... allowing grief and fear to blight your heart is an awful waste. I've been guilty of it. You must never be. And you must never allow me to obstruct you. You must ignore me if I do. Life goes so fast."

He touched his son's hand again and left the table.

18

Ellis met her in the Warrington Arms, a large pub on a roundabout in West London. The pool table was winner-stays-on and Ellis was on a roll when Tammy came up against him. She was short and athletic and had freckly skin and long blond hair. After he had let her beat him and her friend Sinead had accused him of being a "patronising misogynist" for not trying properly, Tammy declined to play on and Ellis followed her to the bar. He asked her why she had such healthy-looking skin and she laughed and told him that she was brought up in Kenya and that lots of people raised in Africa had that look.

"I'll look like shit when I'm older, though," she said.

"I doubt it," Ellis said.

"I will. I'll wrinkle."

"You'll make wrinkles look good."

"Smooth."

"No, I wasn't trying to be. I'm not."

"I like your nose. Did you break it?"

"Twice so far."

She said she'd buy him a pint. She leant against the bar as she waited to be served, and Ellis took the opportunity to look at her breasts. They looked soft and large and they commanded his attention for a moment too long.

"They're bigger than they used to be," she said.

Ellis looked blank.

"My tits," she explained. "I've had a growth spurt."

"I'm sensing a domino effect," he said.

She looked him in the eye.

"I'm sorry I offended your friend. Is she a lesbian?"

"Not all women who use the word 'misogynist' are dykes. Ignore Sinead, she's in a shit mood. I think it's nice you let me beat you."

"I only did it because I'm old-fashioned and I'm crap with women."

She smiled curiously at him and he felt all at sea.

"Had I been trying, of course," he added, "I'd have whipped your arse. Best you understand that rather than get an unreasonably high opinion of your abilities."

She laughed under her breath again. "Anything else you want to get off your chest?"

"Plenty. I'd ask you for your number if it weren't for the fact that you're absolutely definitely bound to have a boyfriend already and your non-lesbian friend will probably have a go at me for hitting on you."

"You'll have to stand up to her then. I do have a boyfriend. 01 374 9804. He's in Dubai."

"Is he bigger than me?" Ellis asked, gesturing to the

barman for a pen.

She smiled and gave nothing else away. Ellis wrote the number down on his hand. She held his hand to check the number was right. Then she took the pen from him, unbuttoned his shirt and wrote her name across his heart.

They tended to meet twice a week, but in a haphazard way which didn't involve planning ahead. They didn't talk much and they rarely went out other than to the pub they had met in. They would play pool competitively and feign disgust at the other's tactics, accuse the other of gamesmanship and settle disputes with arm wrestles. They sat in Tammy's favourite corner and watched the behaviour of others. They lay on the sofa at Ellis's flat watching videos and MTV. They made love. They laughed a great deal. He took out-of-focus photographs of her at the window of the flat with views of the Westway beneath and dreams of becoming the next Anton Corbyn. They bathed together, staring at Ellis's map of the world on the bathroom wall. They didn't talk about the past or the future. He missed her when she was not there. He wished she was watching over him in certain moments. He scribbled down sums on bits of paper to work out how many hours or minutes it was before he would lie with her again.

London was a different city now Ellis had cash in his pocket. Jed and his new girlfriend, Emma, rented a flat in Dalston and Ellis saw them often, as well as Milek and Carla. He preferred to go out every evening. If no one was around he'd go to the cinema alone. Going to the cinema, he came to believe, was something that should absolutely, definitely, without doubt, be done alone. The exceptions were horror films and comedies, both of which could be group activities. He watched blockbusters on the big screen at the Odeon Marble Arch but his favourite cinema was the Curzon Mayfair, where he could take a cup of tea to his seat. The deep, soft, slanted seats of the Curzon cradled him through *Wings of Desire*, *The Big Blue*, *Midnight Run* – twice in one weekend – *Angel Heart* and *The Sacrifice*. And at Christmas, he wandered into a repertory cinema in West London and saw a film called *Days of Heaven* and left the cinema dazed by sadness and longing. He remained haunted by the film well into the New Year and bought a vintage poster of it from a shop in Soho and had it framed and gave it to Tammy.

"Promise me you'll watch this film the next time it's shown anywhere, whenever it is, whether or not your boyfriend is in town."

"I promise."

"If you see this film you'll know everything I think and feel about everything."

"If you told me then I'd know."

Once, when Ellis was at the off-licence, Tammy answered the phone in the flat and spoke to Denny. Ellis heard her laughter from the stairwell and the sound of her hanging up as he opened the door.

"You just missed your dad," she told him. "I told him I had you out doing my shopping."

"What did he say?"

"What's my secret. Then he told me I'd better not say."

"Did he ask who you were?"

"No. No questions. Like father, like son."

She sat on the bathroom floor and read her book as Ellis bathed and after a few pages she put her book down and said, "Why is your dad's breathing so heavy? Has he got emphysema or something?"

"No, no! Nothing like that. He just has to take these tablets at the moment and they make him a little weak so colds and things like that just hang around him a bit."

Ellis took a breath and submerged himself. She waited for him to resurface, then said, "A little weak? Sounded like he can't breathe."

"No. The big picture is good. A-OK. This is just a normal thing in the stage, like anyone else."

"Sometimes," she said, "I don't have a clue what you're talking about."

"That's why we don't talk much," Ellis said.

"Do you mind me asking?" she said.

"Not at all. But there's no problem. There's nothing to tell, that's why I'm not telling you much."

Their conversations were usually in whispers, with their heads almost touching. Lying together. Pillow, sofa, carpet, grass. They didn't use sentences, nor express their wishes or fears. They would, instead, gently push towards each other images of a love affair they dare not attach their own names to. Places two lovers might go. Things two lovers might do. Moments two lovers might share. But Ellis didn't risk asking for these things to really happen, he did not venture to lay claim to her love, for fear that her answer would be no or that she would simply disappear. He was naive enough, inexperienced enough, to believe that the affection and intensity that she showed for him could possibly be manifestations of a casual fling and that she could be repeating it all, or even usurping it, with her boyfriend. There was something perfect, almost sacred, to Ellis about the expectation of love, the hope for it during the long times they were apart, that outshone love itself. He thought sometimes of the Tudor ship that was lifted from the bottom of the sea. It was live on the television, one rainy morning when Ellis was young. As soon as the ship was out of the water, they had to keep hosing it down so that the air didn't kill it. He and Tammy belonged at the bottom of the sea together, where no one could see them and no one could stop them and the air couldn't harm them.

She's not a butterfly-lady, she's a mermaid.

The place still smelled of Fry's Peppermint Cream. He was

sure of it. In the waiting area, patients stole glances at each other and guessed what stage of the mock battle they had reached. Denny sat forward on his chair with his hands wedged beneath his legs. He breathed diligently. Beside him, Ellis slipped deep, deep into daydreaming of a small rented flat with Tammy. It had slanting ceilings and a narrow balcony high above the streets. Their bed was tucked into a corner and there were candles in a small recess in the wall above the pillows. Opposite the bed was a window that framed the sky and Tammy's sleeping body was drenched in sunlight. In one corner was a pile of books Tammy had read or was soon to read and in another were Ellis's photographs. Photographs of places they had been to together. Beautiful photographs, the work of master craftsman, Ellis O'Rourke.

Denny brushed against Ellis as he got up and walked towards the open door, in which stood the consultant, with a closely guarded smile for his two o'clock. Ellis watched the door close and turned his attention to a rack of pamphlets. He read eight of them in detail and by the time his dad reappeared he had a worrisome ache in his testicles and a large tumour pressing against the wall of his brain.

"I have to get a prescription," Denny said, heading off slowly down the corridor, grateful to be accompanied by a son who would not plague him immediately for information. He felt guilty thinking it but he knew things would not be the same if Chrissie were here. It would be more traumatic.

They sat on a bench at the entrance to the children's cancer ward and waited for the prescription. Hairless children appeared at the far end of the corridor, chasing in all directions like a swirl of leaves. Amid the shrieks of laughter, Denny and Ellis O'Rourke caught each other's eye.

"We should have no complaints," Denny said.

"No," Ellis agreed.

Denny took the chain from round his neck and handed it to his son.

"I want you to have this," he said. "It was your mother's."

Ellis ran his thumb across a worn-down St Christopher and put the chain round his neck. A nurse swept through the corridor, sending the children scattering, and suddenly they were all gone.

They went to the hospital café so that Denny could take his new pills with a cup of tea and something to eat. On a table nearby, two elderly ladies were selling Christmas cards in June.

"It's not very good news," Denny said calmly.

Ellis nodded and smiled weakly.

"I'll talk to you both together though."

Ellis nodded again. This is what it's like to feel empty, he told himself.

Chrissie had evolved into a person who was always late and always angry and surprised about being late, as if it was always the first time. As Ellis and Denny drove out of the car park, she drove in at speed, agitated.

Denny muttered, "I just want to get home."

Ellis went across to Chrissie's car. "Follow us home, OK?"

"What's happened?"

"He hasn't said a single thing, I promise."

She nodded and smiled.

"Drive slowly," Ellis told her, as she tended not to.

"Six months to a year," Denny O'Rourke said. "A year at the very most."

From his daughter and son came gentle nods of comprehension and faint, brave smiles.

"The consultant did say that if my breathing improved and I grew stronger, then there is a final option of intensive treatment. A last throw of the dice. It would change me radically and it would probably not work."

Ellis heard this with a degree of vindication. As he had suspected from the outset, all they had to do was to keep him breathing until an idea came along. They had a year to come up with something and that was time enough.

"I've already told him that I'm not going to have any more treatment," Denny said.

"But you could change your mind, if you do get stronger?" Ellis said.

"Ellis ..." his dad sighed. The sigh fell into a smile and he hadn't the willpower to say any more.

Chrissie experienced the same peaceful calm as her brother that morning. Life was simple for them. There were no dilemmas. There were no headlines or traffic jams, no financial worries or private life complications. There was no competitiveness. The world was quiet. There was just one inescapable truth. Life, at its worst moment, was less complicated than it had ever been.

"We'll have the summer together," Denny said. "Let's enjoy the summer and then we'll let it be."

Ellis stepped out of Charing Cross station and waited on the Strand for his bus. Some minutes later, a stranger brushed against him and he found himself walking past the National Gallery and following his dad's daily route to Jermyn Street, with no recollection of having decided to take a walk. He imagined the thoughts his dad would have carried with him along these streets over thirty years, then watched people come and go through the swing doors of Denny's office building. He felt all the while like an invisible man, at liberty to stand and watch without being noticed. He ordered some food in the café opposite the office and took a seat by the window. There was a blast of sunlight reflecting against a glass-fronted building. A middle-aged man with a brown leather briefcase walked by. Although he was walking briskly, the man seemed momentarily suspended in the sunlight as Ellis looked up, the same way the second hand on a clock seems not to move when you first glimpse it. The man was of a certain slim, old-fashioned build that reminded Ellis of his dad and Hedley and their colleagues. Men of a certain timeless appearance, reminiscent of an era when men in their twenties looked middle-aged. Men who have the sort of hair that needs to be brushed or combed, who wear suits that don't shine in the light, suits that accentuate height rather than breadth. Men who don't seem to rush or get flustered, who were born to Victorian parents but are growing old in an almost unshockable world. The man in his suit, hovering a few inches above the pavement in a heat haze and caught in the glare of sunlight, was one of these men. It struck Ellis as strange that of all the worlds Denny had inhabited, it would be this one, the one he valued the least, that would remain preserved for Ellis to visit at any time if he wished to. Jermyn Street had changed little in the decades Denny worked here and promised to carry on in the same vein, offering Ellis a living museum of a thousand faithfully recreated details, a perfect re-enactment of Denny O'Rourke's London save for the sight of Denny's own commanding frame and handsome face emerging on to the street at four o'clock in the afternoon with thoughts, hidden beneath his placid expression, of only his family and his home, and the irritating sense of never being able to get back to them quickly enough.

By the way he held on to her, Tammy knew that something was on Ellis's mind. When he buried his head against her chest, she stroked his hair. When she asked him if he were all right, she felt him nod. When she peppered his head with little kisses, he kissed her back and they made love unnecessarily, because she thought it was what he wanted to do and he didn't know how to say that it wasn't, without having to explain why.

The following Saturday, Ellis found his dad at the bottom of the garden, feeding papers on to a bonfire.

"You seem better today," Ellis ventured.

"Abusing the nebuliser with abandon," Denny said. "And clearing the decks. Making everything shipshape."

They watched the fire with the reverence that flames inspire and Ellis recalled the muted buzz of the football reports on a portable radio as his dad worked in the garden at the cottage on Saturday afternoons.

"What was that guy on LBC called?" he asked.

"Steve Tongue ... sounded like he was broadcasting from the moon."

"Adverts for the Houndsditch Warehouse and Dickie Dirts jeans ..."

"Chrissie forced me to drive her up to Camberwell to go to Dickie Dirts!"

A church clock chimed somewhere above the sprawl of rabbit hutch houses and Ellis sensed that his father would have liked an extra hour or two to himself this evening.

"I suppose we'll start going to church now," he said in a tone of voice which might have meant it and might not.

"I did, months ago. With Reardon," Denny said.

"Fat lot of good it's done you," Ellis said.

Denny flashed his son a smile. He welcomed that sort of chat. He wanted that rather than the other sort.

"I'm on a mission. Want to sort all this stuff out whilst I'm in the mood."

Denny marched back to the house. Ellis stayed and felt the warmth of the fire on his face and the cool evening air on the back of his neck. He watched the flames and his eyes were drawn to a familiar bundle of letters sitting on a book-shaped mattress of white ash. An image came to him, of the blue canvas-bound diary Denny had kept as a young merchant seaman. It seemed that the diary, which had for many years cradled the letters written by Ellis's mother, was now an ashen altar on which the letters were about to burn. The chevroned envelopes lay unchanged for a few moments more. Then an Indian stamp curled in the heat, the handwriting began to melt and a white flame licked around the bundle from underneath. The letters ignited. Ellis grabbed a pitchfork and dug them out of the fire, tossing them on to the grass. He picked them up and scurried across the garden, tossing the hot bundle from hand to hand –

"Fuckfuckfuck ..."

– and dropped them out of sight, behind the shed. He looked at his hands. They were red from the heat. A slow, incurable sting released itself across his palms, which he wedged under his armpits. At his feet, the bundle of letters reignited. Cursing himself, he took the pitchfork, speared the burning letters and returned them to the fire, pushing them into the centre of the glow. He shook the pitchfork free and a small shower of embers broke from the envelopes and floated into the air. One danced above his head and descended slowly, charmingly, towards him. Ellis cocked his head obligingly to one side so that the ember fell against his neck and burnt him there.

Ellis found his dad writing at the kitchen table.

"What's that on your neck?" Denny asked.

"A little burn."

"Looks nasty."

"I like it."

"Strange boy," Denny muttered, and smiled at his son.

"What you writing?"

"A letter."

"Who to?"

"No one."

"No one?"

"Pour me a drink, make yourself useful," Denny purred.

"No one writes to no one. Who's it to?"

"It's to you."

"Me?"

Denny put his pen down and feigned annoyance. "Yes, you. Now stop disturbing me."

"What's it about?"

Denny ignored him. Ellis laughed nervously.

"Why don't you just tell me? I'm right here."

"Don't want to."

"Just tell me!"

Denny snapped. "I don't want to tell you, Ellis!" He lowered his voice, without sweetening its tone. "I don't want to tell you. I want to write it and I don't want to give it to you now. It's not all about you, Ellis, you losing your father. I'm losing my life. I know you're scared of being without me but I'm terrified of going, so sometimes you've got to just bloody well leave me alone. I need to prepare and don't tell me I'm not going to die, Ellis, it's not appropriate any more!"

The room fell silent. Neither of them moved.

Then Ellis said, "You're right. I'm sorry."

"No, I'm sorry I shouted."

"You were right to shout ... you could have shouted more often."

Denny lifted a black metal box, the size of a shoebox, off the floor and placed it on his lap. He had kept bills and chequebooks and papers in there all his adult life but this evening, with the bonfire done, it was empty. He clicked his fingers, reminded of something, and started to rifle through the mess around him.

"Where the hell did I put that note?" he muttered.

"What note?"

"Note for you. She made me promise I'd write it down and put it by your bed."

"Who did?"

"Tammy."

"What's the message?"

"To call her."

"I think I can remember that without the note."

"Yes, but that doesn't mean you'll do it. She always sounds so lovely, that girl. Why don't you like her?"

"I like her too much."

"Well, you're an idiot then. Just call her."

"That's your expert advice, is it?"

"You can't like someone too much. More to the point, a young man as hideously unattractive and talentless as you is in no position to turn down a Tammy."

Ellis smiled. "Tell me then, smartarse, did she mention her long-term boyfriend?"

"Oh."

"Oh, indeed."

Denny gave up searching for the note and despaired. "That's ridiculous! I only wrote it ten minutes ago. I promised her I'd put it by your bed."

"Well, what exactly does the note say?"

"Call Tammy."

"Those two words?"

"Yes."

"Well, I've got that. Really."

Denny sat back on his chair and took a few deep breaths, none of which seemed to adequately fill his lungs.

"Do you want your nebuliser?"

"Yes please ... No, bugger it! Pour us both a little Scotch instead, dear boy, and pull up a chair whilst I fill this with junk."

When Ellis returned and placed a glass beside his father, Denny was filling the metal box with objects from the mess around him: his certificate of discharge from the merchant navy, a small bundle of old family photographs, a prayer card from his wife's funeral, an envelope with leaves from the garden of Gethsemane which his grandfather picked in the 1870s, a ticket stub from the 1950 FA Cup Final, a leather bookmark from Runnymede, his cufflinks, a pocket guide to butterflies.

Ellis watched the objects enter the box and felt he understood some sense of a criteria for their selection. They were all things he and Chrissie had played with and looked at as children or things they had been curious about.

Denny stopped. He looked hard at Ellis.

"I always knew I was going to have you," he said. "I knew it when I was as young as you are now. And the weight of that has made it impossible for someone as plain as me to ever say what I feel and I've probably never allowed you enough room to breathe for the same reason. And I apologise. But it's been impossible, always impossible, to put into words how deeply I love you, Ellis."

Ellis felt his mouth caving in. He stood as if he'd been shot. And when he did manage to move, it was not towards his father, as he intended, but out of the room. He sat upstairs in a daze and only stirred much later when the burn on his neck began to sting. He went to the bathroom and rubbed cream on to the burn and imagined it was Tammy rubbing the cream in. She talked in hushed tones to him, her lips close to his ear. She told him that everything was going to be all right.

He was still thinking about Tammy when the phone rang late into the evening. He was thinking about telling her that he wanted to be with her all the time and not to share her. He was thinking that he would ask her if she wanted that too, even though her answer might be that she didn't. He was thinking that he would like to tell her about his dad. He wrote down what he was going to tell her so that he could say it all as he meant to. He was putting the lid back on his pen and was about to lift himself off the bed and go to the phone and dial her number when the phone rang and his dad picked it up and, not long after that, Ellis was standing at the foot of a huge silver grain store in the plains of Iowa, watching the reflection of sunset in shimmering curves of steel and promising himself that as long as he remained in this alien, beautiful, wind-blown place, his dad would not be dying back home.

"That was Milek, in a hurry. If you're interested in a job in America you're to ring this number tonight."

Denny held a scrap of paper out to him and when Ellis hesitated he pressed the paper into Ellis's stomach.

"If you were to set back your career because of me, I'd be furious."

When Ellis came off the phone, Denny was waiting in the dining room, with the door to the garden open.

"Tell me," he said.

"It's a guy called Gerd. He's represented by the same agency as Milek. He takes photographs of small-town America. He's doing a book. He needs an assistant for a six-week trip. I'd have to fly to Boston day after tomorrow and meet him there."

"What a wonderful opportunity," Denny said.

They sat in uneasy silence. Ellis imagined the places he was on the brink of seeing. He savoured them and then he made balloons out of them and let them go.

"I'm not going to go," he said resolutely.

"It's only six weeks. We'll still have plenty of time before I pop my clogs."

"No," Ellis said. "No."

"Do all photographers have to have East European names?" Denny asked.

"It's standard," Ellis said.

They watched the line of walnut trees. Ellis confessed to himself how much he wanted to go. It would take little to persuade him.

"You're bloody well going, Ellis," his dad duly said.

After his son's departure, Denny O'Rourke packed the atlas and travel books away in a cupboard under the stairs. He went to bed and pictured his wife waiting for him. He anticipated their reunion with the same enthusiasm he had once had for moving his children into the run-down cottage in the Kentish Weald.

"He has a whole year in which to improve," Ellis reasoned. "He's already looking stronger and better this week. That's week one out of fifty-two. By the time I'm back he'll be strong enough for the nuking and we can actually sort this out once and for all."

"I can't believe you're going to Iowa," Jed repeated.

"Not just Iowa, that's just one of the places."

Jed shot him a glazed expression. "Not the point I was making, Ellis. What does Tammy think?"

"About what?"

Jed's face fell further. "About the chances of free elections in South Africa, what the fuck do you think I mean about?"

"I think you mean about either me going on this job or my dad's health," Ellis said.

"Or both?" Jed suggested.

Ellis took a long, exaggerated sip of his beer.

"Nice pint," he muttered.

"Don't tell me you haven't told her you're going away."

"No," Ellis said. "I won't tell you."

"Why haven't you?"

"Because she might not be that interested. She might turn round and say, 'You know, you don't have to let me know what you're doing, you're not my boyfriend.'"

"Does she ever speak to you like that? Ever?"

"No. Never."

"Well then." Jed slumped back, unimpressed.

"OK, before you start lecturing me," Ellis said, "a few things. Firstly, you've never met Tammy and that's because we're not going out together because, secondly, she is going out with someone else. Thirdly, no, yes, she doesn't know I'm going away but I've written her a postcard."

"A postcard! You dick! What on earth of?"

"What do you mean, what on earth of?"

"What's it a postcard of?"

"It's not of anything."

"It must be of something. Torbay, Beefeaters, painted tits."

"It's a blank postcard. Like you get from an office supplies shop."

Jed raised his hands in despair.

Ellis protested, "It leaves more room to write to the person. The address can be written where people like you would have some colour-enhanced photograph of sombrero-clad donkeys on Bournemouth beach! The blank postcard is the more communication-friendly choice compared with the picture postcard. And fourthly, she doesn't really know my dad is ill. Not really ill. She's not my girlfriend, she's with someone else."

"Nevertheless," Jed reminded him, "you and she are lovers. And you are incapable of holding a conversation which doesn't refer to her. So, are you not at worst curious and at best eager for her opinion and thoughts and guidance?"

"I'm eager for her to ditch her boyfriend and go out with me."

"So why don't you ask her to do just that?"

"Because I don't want her to say no."

"You'd rather not ask than hear her say no?"

"That's right."

Jed despaired. "I am going to say one more thing whether you like it or not. I think that you should say no to this job.

I think your dad is dying. I think that one good bonfire with him has persuaded you he'll get better. I hope I'm wrong but I don't think I am."

Ellis nodded obediently and smiled and looked away. When Jed returned from the bar, he had gone. He went to America the next day and took the postcard he had written to Tammy with him. He read it on the plane. It was the best set of words he had ever put together. He had told her he loved her. He had forsaken the coded imagery of their pillow-talk and written from his heart and laid himself bare. He had got every word right. But he had not posted it. He had got the words right because he knew he was never going to post it. Because the answer might be no. Because he might lose his grip and fall. Because he might drown.

19

Gerd was the only man Ellis had met who could eat pizza, smoke a cigarette, watch television and read a Graham Greene novel in his second language at the same time. He was waiting for Ellis at a coffee bar in Boston airport, an ashen-faced forty year old with potholed skin and a lost, thin-lipped smile. Ellis would learn that Gerd rarely laughed, although occasionally he smiled a narrow slit of a smile. Many things fascinated Gerd but few things amused him.

"The diner we were going to shoot in Famingham is off," Gerd said, shaking Ellis's hand, stubbing out his cigarette and standing up, all in one languid movement. He spoke with no expression, his chin raised and his eyes peering down his nose through a pair of non-existent half-glasses.

"Right." Ellis smiled eagerly.

"Let's go."

Gerd wandered away, carrying a silver metal suitcase in one hand and a carton of cigarettes in the other. Ellis followed on his heels.

"I'm Ellis," he said.

"OK," Gerd said.

Gerd placed his silver flight case in the trunk of the hire car, next to his camera case. He opened it to dig out a fresh cigarette lighter and Ellis saw that it contained a pair of jeans, a grey V-neck sweater and a white T-shirt, all identical to the ones Gerd was already wearing. There were two pairs of socks, no underwear, a toilet bag and a dozen cheap plastic lighters. Gerd had no coat, only the Mod-like charcoal jacket he wore every day.

They drove out of Boston on a series of looping highways.

"I have no interest in food, Ellis. Sometimes the thought of putting more matter into my mouth makes me temporarily depressed. So you are going to have to say when you want to stop and eat otherwise you could starve for being polite."

"Right." Ellis smiled. "Me, I love food."

"You're heading for small-town America so you might change your mind about that," Gerd said, lighting another cigarette. "They serve coffee in this country, so I'm happy."

You look happy, Ellis thought.

In Buffalo, Ellis had a motel room wedged between the sound of the elevator and the noise of the ice machines. He found a present from his dad tucked amongst his clothes. It was a brown leather travelling pouch and in it was Denny's fountain pen with a small tag tied to it on which Denny had written *Postcards please*. Into the pouch Ellis put his own camera, a notepad, the postcard he had written for Tammy and the photograph of him and his dad standing in the snow, taken by Mafi.

They went to a timber-clad bar beneath an ancient tulip

tree. The roots of the tree were breaking up the surface of the Lake Erie highway and the deep crevices in the bark hinted at a less modern, more robust America. Ellis met an elderly man named Moses Mahler who told him that he had lived at number 121 Lackawanna Street all his life, and still slept in the room he was born in. Ellis asked him about his life and Moses told him and Ellis bought Moses a drink and, later on, Moses bought Ellis a drink back.

"Don't you think that's amazing, Gerd, to live in the same house for seventy-five years? Why don't you do a book photographing people who have lived the same place all their lives?" Ellis suggested, as they drove back to the motel.

"Why don't you?" Gerd said.

"'Cos I'm the assistant, not the photographer."

Gerd emitted a despairing breath, an expression Ellis came to learn signalled mild amusement, mild reproach or both.

"Ellis, yesterday I spent three hours deciding not to photograph a barber's shop sign. Today, I spent eight hours photographing a juke box. I think you'll find time to fit in your own photographs here and there, don't you?"

Gerd photographed the neon lights of a bowling alley in Cleveland, a street lamp in Akron and a rusting 1940s petrol pump in Coshocton. The drive from Columbus to Cincinnati was dull but Gerd scrutinised the faceless Ohio road for something of interest. Ellis watched the road signs with naive fascination. He saw turnings for towns called London and Lebanon and Portsmouth, and was surprised by all of them. He took out his pen and paper with the intention of writing a list of what he saw but found himself putting them in a letter to Tammy instead. He was hungry and felt hot in the glass-sharpened sunlight. In the corner of his eye, he glimpsed Gerd leaning forward to light his cigarette and he saw his dad doing the same thing a thousand times before. He pictured

Denny's profile at the wheel. He remembered when his own feet didn't reach the floor. He heard Radio 3 playing on the car radio and the faint whistling sound his dad made when he was happy or thoughtful. He abandoned his letter to Tammy. There were too many things to write. He didn't know where to start.

In an effort to put thoughts of home behind him, Ellis decided to like Cincinnati the moment they arrived, to preoccupy himself with liking it. He liked the circular concrete of the Riverfront Stadium, home to the Cincinnati Reds. He liked the River Ohio cutting between the city and Kentucky, and he liked the steel bridges spanning the river like a jaded Meccano wonderland. He liked the rust-red roller shutters on the pawnbroker shops in the blazing sunshine. He liked the swagger of the people at the run-down end of Elizabeth Street, he liked the way the sunlight glistened on the downtown office blocks and the elevated walkways and he loved the warm breeze rising up off the river and sweeping through the streets.

They watched the Cincinnati Reds play the Florida Marlins and when the game halted at the seventh innings, Ellis climbed to the back of the stadium and surveyed the suburbs at dusk, the reflections of a pearl-pink sky embossed on every bridge and window. The city grew dark and became a sparkle of lights. Ellis watched the brooding, unlit goods trains drag themselves out of the metropolis. He saw car headlights appear and disappear amongst the forested hills. He imagined the lives going on beneath him. Millions of lives. People who had never seen England and never would. People whose every thought and action and influence was entirely unconnected to his own. He asked himself, What does it mean to travel? What am I meant to learn from this? How should the world change me? Could I change it? He shut his eyes and wondered if everything laid out before him would cease the moment he left the city and only resume if he returned. In a country this size, he reminded himself, towns and cities he had never heard of were in existence every day. In them were millions of people, each one as wrapped up in their own life as he was in his. When did we become so many? When did we build all this? How did it all ever get so big? He pressed his hands against his head and felt a surge of panic rear up in him. Before he could identify the panic, there was a tap on his shoulder. It was Gerd, wearing the expression of profound disinterest that only sport could bring to him. Behind him, thousands of people were leaving the stadium. They joined the exodus. Not until they were outside did Ellis realise that he had left the leather pouch under his seat. He ran against the crowd but the bag had gone.

There was a Hoover at one end of the motel corridor and it caught Gerd's eye as he and Ellis walked to breakfast. The corridor was bathed in meagre, deep green light which seemed to make the interminably long and narrow passageway darker not brighter. Carpet covered the floors and the lower half of the walls.

"Go on without me," Gerd muttered.

Ellis reported the stolen bag at the stadium office and to the Cincinnati PD.

"It's the photograph more than anything. I haven't kept the negative, I'm a bit disorganised. I don't care about the rest, just the photograph, you see?"

They didn't see.

He watched the steam boats on the Kentucky side of the river and listened to the rumble of cars on steel bridges. The vast maze of rail lines converging on the city made it all seem like a toy and he realised that he had to forget about the bag and its contents and make the decision not to care.

You can make that decision, Ellis, he told himself. You can choose to make it matter or let it be of no importance.

You can decide what sort of person you are going to be when it comes to dealing with these things.

He found Gerd motionless at his tripod in the motel corridor. The German was transfixed by the Hoover, as if it were about to perform a trick.

"You been here all day?" Ellis whispered.

Gerd laced a barely noticeable nod into his stillness. Ellis looked at the frame counter and then for evidence of how many films Gerd had been through.

"You've taken three frames in eight hours?"

Gerd nodded again.

"Three ..." Ellis repeated. "What have you been doing all day, earning its trust?"

Gerd put his eye to the viewfinder. "Get me a coffee."

"You're the Dian Fossey of the electrical appliance world."

"Coffee ..." Gerd muttered again, "or I'll kill you."

Across the river, on the quiet streets of Covington, Kentucky, jobless men and uninterested children slouched on benches kicking up the dust. Next to the German washhouse, where women sat on the steps, Gerd parked in the forecourt of the Anvil Bar and Grill. A red neon sign flashed OPEN 24 HOURS A DAY 7 DAYS A WEEK. Beneath it, on a white painted wall which glared harshly in the sun, were painted large blue letters, WE MAY DOZE BUT WE NEVER CLOSE.

Sitting at the horseshoe bar of the café was a thin, elderly woman who had lost most of her hair. Beneath her apron, her loose, sagging body was visible through the arms of a man's singlet. Her skin was the colour of ash. She was so lifeless, she made Gerd seem excitable.

A maze of small eating rooms led off from the bar. Each was clad in darkly veneered wood panelling and lit dimly by orange bulbs in wicker shades. It took time for Ellis's eyes to adjust to the gloom.

"This place I was told about," Gerd confided, examining a coffee-stained menu and turning to look for a waitress.

From the shadows in the corner of the room came a drawl. "It's order at the counter before noon."

The man who had spoken was sitting with two other men. All three of them looked to be in their seventies. They wore identical red and black checked shirts, the sleeves rolled up into a tight, thick, rope-like hem around their biceps. They had thinning hair, greased back. The man with his back to Ellis was a little slumped, as if he'd fallen asleep.

Ellis stepped back into the dazzling sunlight of the bar and wondered how, in a town where the sun beat down so hard, the people could look so pale. A television was on in the corner. The bald woman smoked a cigarette and read the paper. Two elderly men sat on bar stools looking at their coffee as if it were newly invented. A goods train crossed the steel bridge one block south, prompting a flock of pigeons to evacuate the bridge and land on the concrete forecourt of the Anvil Bar and Grill, projecting a dazzling waterfall of bird shadows on to the white wall as they landed.

"What'll it be?" the bald woman asked.

"Scrambled eggs, home fries and toast, please. And a pecan pie."

"You want cream or ice-cream with the pie?"

Ellis stepped back into the gloom. "Cream or ice-cream?"

"Is it fresh cream?" Gerd asked.

"Is it fresh cream?" Ellis repeated to the bar.

"Uh-huh."

"Uh-huh."

Gerd nodded.

Ellis returned to the bar. "Cream, please. Also, a coffee and a glass of milk."

"What about you?"

"What about me?"

"Not eating?"

"Yeah, I'm having the eggs."

"Then how about your friend?"

"Eh?"

"He not eating?"

"He's having the pie."

"Oh." The lady raised her eyebrows at the facts before her and shuffled into the kitchen. "He don't want eggs?" she called out.

"No, thank you," Ellis called back.

"And you don't want pie?" she called.

"No ... thank you."

"So, you're not having dessert and he's not having main?"

"Er ... yeah," Ellis called.

A man at the bar winked at Ellis and muttered, "She's on fire today."

As he sipped his milk, Ellis stole a glimpse of the three old men in the gloom. The man who had spoken stared back at him and didn't blink or look away. A waitress brought the food.

"Excuse me," Gerd said, the effort of trying to look pleasant neutralising his attempted smile, leaving only a grimace. "They said the cream would be fresh."

Ellis and the waitress peered at Gerd's bowl. Alongside the pie was an embankment of fluffy whipped cream, straight out of a spray can.

"That is," the waitress said, and walked away.

Gerd shrugged fatalistically.

"Pick a tune." The drawl came again from the man in the corner, who slid a nickel out in front of him and gestured Ellis to come over. Ellis obeyed. The man whose back was to Ellis was an identical twin to the man who had spoken, but his head was bowed and one side of his face was fallen. There were remnants of food and dribble on his shirt-front. Ellis looked at the nickel and yearned for the open road.

"Any tune," the man said, his southern accent hiding his tone from Ellis's untrained ear. He pointed to a small juke-box selector on his table.

"One on every table," he said.

"Oh," Ellis said, straightening up.

"The nickel goes straight through," the man said.

Ellis pulled a face at Gerd as he returned to the table and found the music selector hidden behind ketchups, napkins and the menu.

"What if he asks me to dance!" Ellis whispered.

"Choose carefully," Gerd advised.

There were seventy songs. Ellis didn't know any of them.

"Go E10," Gerd whispered.

Ellis peered at the machine. E10 was "Runaway Train" by Bo Fordford. He jabbed the buttons but nothing happened. The Anvil Bar and Grill remained musicless.

"Probably takes a while," Ellis muttered.

"I'll have that nickel back," the man in the shadows said.

The nickel had, as promised, gone into the slot and straight out again. When Ellis returned it, the man pointed to the bench alongside.

"Have a seat."

Ellis sat there, beside a Zimmer frame.

"Where you boys from?" the man asked.

"European, I'd say," the non-identical third man added.

"From London," Ellis nodded.

"Your friend sounded German to me," the man said.

"Yes, he is," Ellis conceded.

"Then he's not from London," the non-identical man stated.

"No."

Gerd came over. "Hello," he grimaced. "My name's Gerd. I'm a photographer. We're doing a road trip. Ellis here is my assistant." He shook hands with the two men facing him. When he held his hand out to the man with the bowed head, the talkative man raised his hand to block him.

"My twin, Dutch, is disabled by a stroke."

Dutch moved his head slowly round and smiled a lopsided smile at Gerd.

"We're both seventy-two years of age. This here is Warren, our younger brother by a year."

The men exchanged nods and smiles. The talkative man, the one whose name they didn't know, asked Gerd what sort of thing he took photographs of. Gerd told him. The men laughed.

"You make money doing that?" Warren asked, on cue.

"They make books of my photographs," Gerd said. "If the books sell, I make money."

The talkative one leant across to his twin.

"These boys here take photographs of vending machines for a living, Dutch!"

Dutch sneered with half of his mouth.

"You don't like to photograph people?"

"This man does," Gerd said, slapping Ellis on the back. "He's photographing people who have lived in the same place all their lives."

The talkative one took the bait. "You notice Walnut Street when you came into town?" he asked Ellis.

"No, sir," Ellis replied, scolding himself immediately for adopting *Little House on the Prairie* lingo.

"This here is Main Street we're on. Us three boys were born on Main Street. Now me and Dutch live on Walnut Street which is directly off Main Street and Warren lives on Main Street with his wife. I'd say we all live within two hundred yards of the house we were born in."

"Right," Ellis said, non-committally

Gerd stood up. "I'll leave you to it, Ellis." He wished the men a good day and went outside with his camera. Ellis cursed him for leaving and stared at the empty doorway a little longer than he should have.

Dutch raised his head slowly. He was dribbling. His younger brother leant across and wiped his mouth. Dutch fixed his eyes on Ellis.

"Hit the black button," he croaked.

"The black button," Warren repeated. "You haven't hit the black button."

Warren's eager eyes directed Ellis back to the table he and Gerd had eaten at. Ellis went to the juke-box selector, found the black button and pressed it. The music started and with it a high-pitched whine from above Ellis's head. Looking up, he saw, in a corner of the room, a small flower-patterned curtain sliding noisily along a rail to reveal a curved glass cabinet. Inside the cabinet, a miniature model jazz band played to the music. The band members were a foot tall. They were figurines of large-headed black musicians with white tuxedos, fulsome pink lips and oversized toothy smiles. One sat at a miniature drum kit, one held a saxophone to its mouth, another a trumpet. There were a dozen of them and they jigged about with their instruments as the music played. In one corner, a trombone moved back and forth on a rail and where the trombonist had once been there now sat a Barbie doll in a sequined blue evening dress. The handle of the trombone drilled repeatedly into Barbie's face, where a disheartening hole had been gouged out of her eye socket.

"What happened to the trombone player?" Ellis asked, with a forced smile.

"Someone hung him," the unnamed man said, patting the bench next to him.

Ellis sat.

"Barbie's been there many years," Warren added. "She wasn't there originally, as you've worked out for yourself."

"We didn't hang him," the man said. "There was some of that going on when we lived on Main Street in the fifties, but not us. Murder is wrong when you count to four and stop to think about it."

"Have you tried the pumpkin pie?" Warren asked.

"No, I haven't," Ellis said, feeling his enthusiasm for his first photography project wane.

"Can't beat Dolly's fresh pumpkin pie. Why don't you order some?"

Ellis presumed that Dolly had to be the bald lady at the bar. He wondered if Dolly was dying. He felt queasy about eating food prepared by a terminally ill person and was pretty sure that midsummer was not pumpkin season. The whole issue of what constituted fresh food at the Anvil Bar and Grill was not one he wanted to raise again.

"I'm full," he said, and patted his stomach appeasingly.

Dutch slid his bowl of half-eaten pie and dribble towards Ellis and nodded, inviting Ellis to finish it.

Ellis's heart sank. "That's kind of you, but I'm stuffed, really."

The unnamed one picked up the conversation. "When we lived on Main Street, we devoted a lot of our time to the battle to keep America as God intended it to be."

"Right ..." Ellis murmured.

"A battle we lost."

"Mmmm ..."

Warren leant forward and fixed Ellis in the eye. "Poor Dutch, here, he still enjoys a slice of pie. He ain't been robbed of that pleasure. He eats a bowl of pie with cream most days of the week. We come here every day. Dutch enjoys it. He's still the same brother we knew and loved."

"It's important to enjoy these things," Ellis agreed.

"We don't mind black people so we none of us didn't become militant," the unnamed one continued. "We remained affiliated but we never saw anyone go a certain way. Like I

say, I don't mind them ..." he paused for far too long for
Ellis's liking, "but I choose not to mix with them. We have
the right to choose, see. Don't see them rushing out to mix
with me, so no one's missing out."

"Anyhow," Warren added, "water under the bridge and
Barbie plays that trombone good enough."

Interstate 48 from Cincinnati to Indianapolis took them
across a razor-thin landscape beneath deep skies.

"Why didn't you go with those brothers and photograph
them?" Gerd asked, 175 miles west of Cincinnati.

"They weren't up for it," Ellis said.

Twenty miles of silence later, Gerd said, "You're lying,
Ellis. Look, you don't make a book of photographs called
Things I liked along the way. The book is *Things I encountered.*
Not everyone out there is sweet old Moses Mahler."

Ellis thought to himself that this was pretty rich coming
from a man who photographed Hoovers.

"I know what you're thinking," Gerd said, "but I'm
telling you, Ellis, you can't photograph from the outside
looking in. You can't do anything meaningful without getting
involved."

Ellis let this advice hang in the air for another twenty miles
of highway. Then he lit two cigarettes, passed one to Gerd,
and said, "You're right. But you're also a motherfucking
German whore for leaving me alone with them."

There was a moment's silence, then Gerd roared with
laughter. It took forty miles for the grin on his face to
subside, slowly and evenly, almost unnoticeably, until his face
had settled back to its preferred doom-laden setting.

If I achieve nothing else in life, Ellis told himself, I made
Gerd laugh.

On the Fourth of July 1988 at three in the afternoon, Ellis
was woken from a deep, sunburnt sleep by the realisation

that the car was not moving. He heard the lapping of water and felt a cool, drinkable wind blow through the open windows. He dragged himself out of the car and took in the view of a river so wide and strong that it made him gasp. To the north, two miles away, was a bridge bearing the interstate. Near to it, lining the great river on both sides, were low wood-clad dwellings which gave way to a community of houseboats. Gerd was at the water's edge where the riverbank was undeveloped and one could pretend that America had not grown up so fast.

"Unphotographable!" he said, with reverence. "Except from space. Do you know what you are looking at, Ellis?"

Ellis shook his head.

"The Mississippi river, Ellis. That's what you are looking at."

The river bank rose to a knoll. They sat there and watched the currents toy with the driftwood. Ellis settled on to his back and the blue sky laid itself across his line of sight. He told his dad that he was on the banks of the Mississippi. He pictured the day his dad was strong enough to travel with him. He brought him here, to the great river's edge, and they watched God flow past, wide and majestic. He felt sure that such a day would come, a day just like today, when his dad was well and life was infinite again. This time next year. When the days are hot but the river breeze is cool. This time next year.

By nightfall they had checked into the one remaining room at the Barron Motel, Barron, Iowa, a shaky L-shaped establishment alongside the railroad. At one-thirty in the morning, Gerd was woken by the clanging bells of the railroad crossing and the passing through of a goods train of great length and little speed. The walls began to vibrate.

"Ellis! Wake up," Gerd said, lighting a cigarette.

Ellis stirred. "What?"

"How can you sleep through this?"

Ellis turned over. When the train had passed, Gerd was left listening to the steady breathing of Ellis's sleep.

Barron was a town of one main thoroughfare, which was wide and quiet and ran from Church Street at the top of the hill to the railroad crossing at the foot of it. Three silver silos towered over the railroad tracks. They shimmered in the wind and sunshine.

There were few people to be seen in Barron during the day and none at night. Those that were there were at ease with the blistering heat which Gerd and Ellis sought shelter from in the cool rooms of the Barron Candy Kitchen. Michalis and Cynthia Eugenikos had run the soda jerk since 1930, when Michalis took it on from his father, a Greek immigrant. The chrome fittings and appliances were original and mint. It was the last of its kind and that was why Gerd had come. They arrived there late because Gerd had been distracted by a dead cockerel lying at the side of the road.

"For the record," Ellis said, "if, like last night, you find yourself watching me sleep through the train thing and wondering how I do it, it would be better to ask me how I do it the next day, after I have finished doing it, 'it' being sleeping through the train thing."

"Be quiet, Ellis," Gerd muttered, ushering him up the steps of the Candy Kitchen.

Cynthia Eugenikos threw herself at the Europeans as soon as they triggered the cow bell. She took a piece of paper from the pocket of her red and white striped apron and read a quick welcome speech. From the ceiling hung a banner: BARRON WELCOMES OUR FRIENDS FROM EUROPE, GERD AND ELI.

She led them to a table where two menus and a posy of flowers awaited them. "You'll sit here, on the Gregory Peck seat."

Cynthia placed a hand on Ellis's shoulder and he glanced at her bright red fingernails and wrinkled, liver-spotted skin.

"For as long as you're in town, everything here is on the house. The soda jerk is your home. I'll come take your order in just one moment when I've explained to my other customers who you are and exactly what your exciting photography assignment is all about."

"I'd be interested to know that myself," Ellis said with a smile.

Cynthia looked at him helplessly, pushed the menu closer to him and scuttled off to her other customers, none of whom was south of seventy.

"There's a place for sarcasm, Ellis," Gerd said strictly. "And it isn't Iowa."

There were thirty-four different malt milkshakes on the menu. Ellis went for a Malt Peck, formerly known as the Chocolate Truffle Malt until ordered by Gregory Peck on an impromptu stopover in May 1978. A silver plaque on the wall commemorated Peck's visit. Gerd toyed with the idea of a raspberry and pistachio milkshake as this was the other celebrity item on offer, having been ordered by Brooke Shields and her mother when they visited in 1984, the menu explained.

"I wonder why they didn't name the milkshake after her like they did with Peck?" Ellis whispered. "Maybe they only do that if you've won an Oscar."

"Maybe they just loved *Moby Dick*?" Gerd said. "Either way, I'm not having one. I'll have a Butterscotch Malt."

"They aren't going to have named a milkshake after Gregory Peck on account of *Moby Dick*. It would have been *To Kill A Mockingbird*. Surely?"

"I agree with you one hundred per cent," Gerd said.

"You agree as in you agree? Or you agree as in shut up Ellis?"

"The shut-up-Ellis one."

"It was probably that shot of her having her first period in the Blue Lagoon," Ellis said. "Put them off naming a milkshake after her."

Gerd shot him a certain look.

"Brooke Shields," Ellis explained unnecessarily. "Especially a raspberry milkshake."

The German grimaced and lit a cigarette. "You're a strange man, Ellis O'Rourke."

Ellis lit one too. "But you're not. Everyone spends two hours photographing a dead chicken."

The Candy Kitchen was an orgy of original Light-Up Soda Fountains, Palm-Press Syrup Dispensers, Royal Crown Coolers, Rippled 12oz Soda Glasses, Classic Double Ring Bar Stools and more, at every turn and glance. Gerd was in chrome heaven. Ellis observed his choice of lenses, the use of long exposures in preference to flash and the painstakingly slow deliberation over composition. The stillness of the soda jerk during its many quiet hours was finally focusing Ellis's young mind on the opportunity that watching Gerd offered him. The key to successfully assisting Gerd was recognising when to leave him alone. In such moments – which lasted for hours – Ellis stepped outside, or if Cynthia were loitering he'd divert her to the far end of the counter, sit on a high stool and let her talk. The more he listened to Cynthia Eugenikos the more she spoke and the more she spoke the closer Ellis grew to understanding what it meant to travel.

"Just listen," Gerd had advised him, after his failure to stick it out in the Anvil Bar and Grill. "And when you've listened, listen some more and then you can photograph ... maybe."

Cynthia seemed set on calling Ellis "Eli". He decided to let it go. A comfortable opportunity to correct her hadn't materialised and suddenly it was too late. She got distracted by a ninetieth birthday party and Ellis escaped outside where the air tasted crystal clear. Ellis sucked it in and thought of the meadow above Innsbruck where he had slept in the long grass. He found Michalis Eugenikos sitting on the railroad track reading a paper.

"Don't get run over," Ellis said.

"One train a day," Michalis replied, "and that comes at night."

"Every night?"

"Every night."

"Gerd will be pleased."

Michalis folded up his paper and slapped it down on the dust track.

"I don't want to disturb your paper," Ellis said.

"You're not." Michalis stood up and wedged his hands into his pockets. He was barely five feet tall, a foot shorter than his wife. He wore a bow tie and his shirt-sleeves were rolled to below his elbows. He had thin straight hair, more of it than he might have had at eighty-four years of age. It was combed back and he occasionally ran the palm of his hand over it.

"I'm not really a newspapers man," Michalis sighed. "Just like to get out of earshot of my wife now and then."

Ellis watched fast-moving clouds reflected on the silver silos. Michalis yawned. The railroad tracks stretched infinitely into the flat open plain.

"How long you been on the road?"

"A month."

"I'll tell you something for free," Michalis said. "Where you are standing is just about as far as it's possible to be in this great country from the ocean shore."

"How far are we talking?" Ellis asked.

Michalis pointed due east along the tracks, then due west. "Either way you go, more than a thousand miles."

Ellis grimaced at the thought. "But what about going to

the seaside?"

Michalis shrugged. "I've raised three children, seven grandchildren, two great-grandchildren so far. Love my wife, though by Christ she can talk. Love my home town, though by Christ that can talk too. But I've never seen the ocean."

"Never?" Ellis was incredulous.

The old man looked at him inquisitively. "So, what's bugging you?" Michalis asked.

"Me?" Ellis was taken aback. "Nothing. I'm fine."

Michalis dismissed Ellis's answer, swatting it away with one hand.

"Something's on your mind," he said, wandering away, back towards the Candy Kitchen. "I still drive at my age," he called out. "If you ever need a ride."

Ellis looked west, where the clouds marched towards the horizon, slipping through an invisible slit between the domed sky and the land. The sky hummed a monotone drone, as if the clouds were scraping against it as they hurried through. He shut his eyes. For all the open space around him, Ellis felt he could scarcely find enough air to fill his lungs. A panic swept through him, a fear that he would not breathe in again after he next exhaled. When he opened his eyes, the strength of the sunlight made him blink and in the highest part of the sky, where the clouds were still, he saw the shape of his dad's face amongst the white wisps.

"Found me," he whispered.

Ellis couldn't sleep. He felt a thousand miles of America press against each wall of the motel room. Then he heard the train. He watched Gerd begin to stir. The rumble strengthened, the railroad crossing bells sounded and, on cue, Gerd's eyes opened. The German stared at the ceiling, his body motionless, then rolled his eyes to the side and saw Ellis watching him. Ellis winked at him and whispered, "Tray-ayyyy-n!"

Gerd sat up and squeezed the bridge of his nose. "I'm gonna count the bastards!" he said, lighting a cigarette.

The train was 134 carriages long. Gerd was wide awake and wore the haunted look of the sleep-deprived. He switched on his bedside light, dragged himself into the bathroom and, without bothering to shut the door, took a pee. As the toilet flushed, he screamed and locked himself inside the bathroom.

"What the hell's wrong?" Ellis asked.

"Fuck me!" Gerd said, trying to be calm.

Ellis went to the door. "What is it?"

"Spider ... the size of a train!" Gerd shouted.

The spider was on the bedroom floor, tucked against the wall by the bathroom door. It was huge. Ellis gazed at it as if it were the first familiar face he'd seen in America.

"Hello, old friend," he whispered.

Gerd shuffled nervously on the other side of the door.

"Ellis ...?" he said. His voice was meek and it made Ellis laugh. "What are you laughing about?"

"Nothing."

"You little shit!"

Ellis knelt by the spider and placed his index finger near to it. It flinched and withdrew its legs fractionally, lifting its body. Ellis stared at the spider and felt a calm overcome him. The calm went deep and filled him with a sensation of understanding, although there was no detail to the understanding quite yet.

"Has it gone?" Gerd whispered, through the keyhole.

"Not yet. We're still discussing it."

"Ellis!" Gerd hissed. "Get on with it!"

"It's a lynx spider," Ellis said affectionately. "Don't get them in England."

He cupped his hand and placed it over the spider. He slid his other hand underneath until he felt the faint tickle of its legs on his palm. He felt a wave of love sweep through him.

Love for the spider. Love for its weight resting on his skin. Love for its impending safety. He opened his hands a touch and peered in. The spider looked back at him.

"Are you going to kill me?" the spider asked, in an American accent. It sounded more pissed off than scared.

"Uh-uh." Ellis shook his head. "Put you outside."

"What you say?" Gerd asked.

"Nothing," Ellis said.

"Can I come out now?"

"Not just yet. He's a tricky bugger."

The spider winked at Ellis.

"Just stamp on it!" Gerd pleaded.

Ellis winked back reassuringly. He went to the door and let the spider out and sat on the doorstep. He checked that the calm was still in him. It was. A mighty calm. A momentous, all-embracing peace with a hint of enlightenment and a sense of direction.

"Safe!" Ellis called out.

Gerd opened the door tentatively. "Definitely gone?"

"Promise," Ellis assured him.

"OK, thanks," Gerd said, and joined Ellis on the doorstep.

Ellis drew in a lungful of air, then let it go with a sigh. He wandered out on to the moonlit forecourt, leant backwards and gazed up at the stars. Gerd wondered if aliens might beam his assistant away. The night had that sort of feel to it.

"The old man told me that they don't have autumn out here," Gerd said. "He said that in October one day it's hot, like today was, and then the winter comes across the plains overnight and the next day the temperature has dropped twenty degrees. That's it. Summer's over. Winter's here. Nothing in between."

"Gerd ... I'm going home."

Gerd waited for Ellis to say more.

"Tomorrow."

"Tell me why," Gerd said.

"My dad's dying. Sorry."

"No, I'm sorry."

They had breakfast in the Candy Kitchen. They ate well and they didn't talk and they felt good. Michalis Eugenikos arrived with the newspapers.

"Michalis?" Ellis said. "Could you drive me to Chicago?"

"Sure. When?"

"This morning."

"Sure thing. I'll go tell Cynthia."

Michalis entered the kitchen with a spring in his step.

"That's a three-hour drive," Gerd said, in protest. "I'll take you."

Ellis shrugged. "He wants to take me."

They joined the highway at Rock Island and when they saw Chicago signposted Ellis panicked, momentarily, that he would never leave America, that he and Michalis Eugenikos would drive on the interstate for eternity. Amongst the cornfields of Lockport county, he thought of Fanny Robin running from All Souls to All Saints. It had taken him five months to read *Far From The Madding Crowd* when he was thirteen and Mr Pulman had said to Ellis's dad that "the boy may be slow in some way, perhaps dyslexic". In response to this, Denny O'Rourke had asked his son if he was enjoying reading his current book.

"I love it. I'd like to live there if I could."

"Where?"

"1874."

"You've been reading that book a long while."

"It's a long book."

"But you're enjoying it?"

"Oh, yes. I like it so much I read passages of it again and again until I can taste the words. I read descriptions of Fanny and Bathsheba until I know them off by heart and I whisper their names aloud at night until I feel one of them in the room with me, lying next to me, stroking me."

Denny and Mafi had looked at each other, taken aback, whilst Ellis returned happily to his food, adding, "I'm not the runt my teachers think I am ... so don't sweat."

Ellis delved into the grocery bag Cynthia had packed him for the journey. It was not small.

"What in Christ's name has she given you?" Michalis sighed.

"Let's see ... extra large Chocolate Malt, two spare straws, chocolate brownies, one ... two ... four of them, two iced doughnuts, packet of cookies, packet of marshmallows, two packets of Reese's peanut butter cups and an apple."

"Good Lord," Michalis said, "where the hell did she find an apple from?"

20

Ellis stood at the doorway to Denny's bedroom, with his body aching from aeroplane sleep, his gums tingling from the sugar of Cynthia's goody-bag and his eyes deceiving him, surely, as to the extent of his father's deterioration.

"Tell me about America." The voice was too weak to belong to Denny.

"No, Dad. I shouldn't have been there. Pretend I never went."

When Chrissie found Ellis, he was staring into space.

"He looks awful," he muttered.

"Yes!" she said, impatiently, as if it were Ellis's fault. "I had to take him back for more tests."

"What did they say."

"We were in there all day!" This also appeared to be Ellis's fault.

"What did the tests say?"

"We go back tomorrow to get the results. Hopefully you'll start sharing the duties."

Ellis walked away. She pursued him into the kitchen.

"We were having a conversation, Ellis!"

"It didn't feel like it."

"Well, we were," she corrected him.

"Look," Ellis said, "it's not that I haven't and won't do all those things. It's just that I'd never describe them as duties."

She grabbed the kettle and filled it. Ellis saw that she was close to breaking down.

"He can't be this bad," he said helplessly. "The whole year can't be like this."

She turned on him. "Ellis! There is not going to be a year!"

Ellis stripped to the waist and felt the sun on his back. Occasionally, he stopped working and stood beneath the walnut trees, close enough to the rippling leaves for them to eclipse the sound of the motorway. At dusk he went inside and loitered in the kitchen.

"That smells nice."

"Thank you. I think you'll like it."

"I always love your cooking."

"Yeah, well it won't be ready for a bit so get yourself a beer and go and sit with Dad."

"Isn't he asleep?"

"It doesn't matter if he is."

"I'll lay the table first."

Chrissie took hold of her brother's hand.

"Ellis," she said, being firm but not unkind, "you know

full well we're not going to eat at the table. We'll do exactly what we always do if it's just us, which is sit on our arses in front of the TV. There is no table to lay. You've cut the grass and you've weeded the beds that don't belong to us, you've washed Dad's car even though it isn't going anywhere, you've unpacked the shopping for me, you've filled that horrible enamel tea-bag tin with tea bags. There is nothing left to do but go upstairs and take a good look at him. Ellis, I can just about live with the fact that you are so much closer to him than I am, but not if you're going to screw it up at the last."

Denny was sitting on the side of the bed taking deep breaths in preparation for the effort of coming downstairs. Ellis sat beside his father and their shoulders touched. For the first time in his life, Ellis was larger than his dad. They embraced and buried their heads against each other.

"We'll have a few trips out ..." Denny whispered.

When he had composed himself, he looked out across the houses. "If you'd move me into the spare room I'd be able to look at those walnut trees. You can use this room when you stay."

Ellis smiled sympathetically. "Sod off. Your view's rubbish."

His dad laughed and it hurt him. His face grew rosy. They settled into silence. Denny abandoned his attempt to come downstairs and got back into bed. Ellis sat beside him.

"I want you to make sure you have a strong image of us together, one that won't fade."

"A photograph?" Ellis asked.

"Not a photograph. A memory ... a moment ... it's important. They say that you can find yourself forgetting someone's face or voice after they've gone ..."

"That will not happen," Ellis said firmly. "I've got hundreds of memories. Not all bad."

Denny laughed again. "You want to be able to tell your

children what a handsome devil I was."

"I'd rather you told them."

It was night-time and Ellis thought his dad was asleep but Denny's feeble voice broke the silence.

"I'm sorry I hit you."

"You're sorry you what?"

"That birthday."

"Oh, that ..." Ellis shrugged it away.

"I'd redo that night if I could. I'd admit I was worried about Mafi. I'd give you a hug and tuck you in."

Ellis said, "I'd watch you leave my room and then the door would open again and you'd creep back in and sit on the side of the bed and say to me, 'Whilst we're talking about things, Ellis, it's also that at times like this I really miss your mum.' You'd tell me all about her and I'd know that even though she went away she did love me."

Denny reached out to his son and Ellis took his hand.

"She loved you so much," Denny said.

Ellis woke in the far reaches of night-time, with the morning close by and the world still quiet. He straightened up in the chair, rubbed his aching neck and realised that his dad was watching him.

"I'm an idiot for not telling you. I was missing her and I was angry at her but that's no excuse."

"Yes, it is," Ellis said. He drew closer. "Dad, I know what my image is. The New Year's Day you and I went to the top of Catt's Hill, to watch the sun come up over the Marsh on the first day of the year."

Denny shut his eyes and joined his son on the hill.

"We sat on the field gate on the upper lane. The pasture was crunchy with frost and there was just enough light to see. There was a single bright star left in the sky and it hovered above Fairfield. You commented on it. As the sun rose, the wind stirred. Slowly, the fields became green and the sky was purple-grey and fast. We heard the sound of a shepherd whistling to his dog, coming from somewhere on Becket's Farm. In the silence that followed it, we both listened at the same moment to the same single faint sound, as if the whole landscape had just heaved a sigh of contentment. A breath that had nowhere to have come from. The morning seemed like the past even as it was happening. It was as if we were walking through someone else's memory."

Ellis fell silent at his own words.

"As if," he realised, "this was my lasting image already, even before I knew it, before I got there. It was waiting for me."

Denny whispered, "Life is just a dream, soon we shall awaken."

"Where's that from?"

"Can't remember. Find out and put it on my headstone."

Denny changed bedrooms and had a view of the walnut trees. Ellis carried the tape deck, amp and speakers up to Denny's room. Denny asked Ellis to put on the *Four Last Songs* and muttered unintelligibly along to the last of them. When the music ended Ellis asked him what he had been saying.

"*Dass wir uns nicht verirren in dieser Einsamkeit,*" Denny replied.

"What does that mean?"

"We must not go astray in this loneliness."

"Is it German?"

"Yes."

"You speak German?"

"My father urged me to learn, after the war. So that ... his hope was that if people understood each other better, it would never happen again."

Ellis didn't try to hide his surprise. "I can't believe you

speak German! You never mentioned it."

"It never came up."

Denny smiled and beckoned. "Come closer, I'll tell you what the song says."

Ellis edged nearer. His dad's voice was weak and he spoke slowly, drawing a new, hard-earned breath at the end of each line.

"'Through troubles and joys
We have gone hand in hand;
Now we both rest from our wanderings
High over the still countryside.

The valleys descend round about us;
The skies are already growing dark.
Only two larks, remembering a dream,
Are rising into the haze.

Come, let them fly –
Soon it is time to sleep.
We must not go astray
In this loneliness.

O wide still peace!
So deep in the sunset glow,
How weary we are with wandering –
Can this be death?'"

It was not a procession of visitors – they came a few hours apart – but it gave the impression of one. First, the GP, who told Ellis that his father was becoming more ill faster than he'd expected. Then, whilst Denny slept, and to Ellis's surprise, Bridget appeared, closing the village shop on a weekday for the first time in thirty years.

It had never occurred to Ellis that the village would miss

the O'Rourkes, only that they would miss the village. But not only was the village fearing for Denny and his children now, they always had been. As Bridget spoke, it became clear to Ellis that Denny had always been perceived as a widower and a lone parent, and Chrissie and Ellis as motherless children, whereas Ellis, however much he thought of his mum and dreamt of meeting her, did not define himself in terms of being without her. The yearning he felt for her was deep but not constant. As a child, it could usually be diluted by his dad's affection or play-acting. Ellis liked being the son of a single father. It was distinctive and to be able to give all his love to one parent made that love so potent that he didn't always wish that things had been different.

"I miss your father so much," Bridget said.

Ellis made a note to himself: I must get out of the habit of presuming that women with enormous bosoms don't have deep feelings.

He led her upstairs. She stood in the doorway and gazed at Denny O'Rourke as he slept, then nodded to herself, as if concluding what she had come to say.

After Bridget came Reardon. He sat at Denny's bedside and read him short stories by Ronald Blythe. The sight of the Land Rover parked outside nudged Ellis with a nostalgia for the rides in the back he and Tim had taken and, suddenly, the prospect of photo shoots with pampered models and neurotic stylists and others perched on fold-up chairs in various poses of self-appreciation left him with a sickly taste.

Reardon's face burned with sincerity. "Is there anything you want or need, Ellis?"

"Do you know what I did to Tim?"

"Yes, Ellis. I know."

"Do you hate me?"

Reardon grabbed hold of him. It wasn't an embrace, his fingers dug in too deeply for that.

"Oh, Ellis! Ellis!" His eyes were kind and fierce. "You were just a child! You still are! You come to me for anything, you hear? Anything at all. For as long as I'm alive, you turn to me. Do you hear me, Ellis O'Rourke?"

The district nurse installed oxygen cylinders at the bedside. She washed Denny and his face settled with contentment. Ellis wondered how often since his mother's death his father had been held or caressed. Maybe never. Certainly not often enough. Denny needed the oxygen more and more. And he suffered fevers in which he was curled up in pain. The nurse left morphine tablets. The morphine made Denny talkative. He spoke of his father and characters in Ilford when he was a boy. He also sang, very softly. "I Dream of Jeannie" was his favourite. It made Ellis laugh. One morning, after a bad night, Denny sang "For Those In Peril On The Sea" again and again and became distressed. His temperature rose to 39 degrees and as Ellis struggled to cool him with iced drinking water and cool towels, it occurred to Ellis that there was now probably a number on the conversations remaining for them. Not a stellar number but an everyday one. Thirty-eight more conversations perhaps, or maybe only fifteen. Sixty at the most. Whatever the number, it was trickling away into a stream of morphine.

"Sweetie ..." Denny muttered, as he strayed into unconsciousness. Then his eyes shot open and he smiled at Ellis. "No ... you're not sweetie, you're my dear boy. Chrissie is sweetie and your mother is the love of my life."

Ellis rang Chrissie and told her that their dad had said she was his sweetie and that he loved her dearly.

"Thank you for telling me. That's lovely." She was tired and had just arrived home from the airport.

"Where have you been?" Ellis asked.

"Frankfurt. Thank you for calling, Ellis, you are thoughtful."

"Chrissie, I think it's time for you to be here all the time."

"I don't need to be told that by you, Ellis. I already know that."

"Then why aren't you here?" he asked, quite innocently.

She told him that it was called "real life".

Ellis felt low. He wondered if he and his sister would grow closer or drift apart after the end. He told himself he loved her but knew how little he enjoyed being with her now. He concluded, with regret, that, without Denny there, they would drift apart.

He watched a little TV that evening. Soon he was staring at the screen but watching nothing. A fear came to him, the idea that after his dad died Ellis would remain where he was, sitting in front of this television, in a house full of other people's furniture, unable to switch off the set and leave. He unplugged the TV, pulled the aerial out of the socket and ripped the power cable out of the back of the set. He sat down again. Later, he heard Denny's voice from the doorway. "Good night, dear boy. I'm going up now." He knew before he turned to look that his dad wasn't there, but he looked anyway and saw the old beamed stairwell of the cottage and heard the creak of the cottage floorboards as his dad went up to bed. He stared at the blacked-out television screen and began to cry. He said Tammy's name and immediately hid his face in embarrassment. He went outside and crouched down beneath one of the walnut trees in a half-hearted attempt at kneeling. And he was tentative, because he had never prayed.

"God ... cure him. Make him completely well again. You can do this if you choose to. Make my dad completely well again now. I believe you can do this. I know I'm lucky and have a lot but I am only twenty years old and I do not want to live without him. That's what I'm asking for. Please."

Denny spoke to his wife a great deal the next day. He told her about Chrissie and Ellis in outpourings of soft, breathy pride. Occasionally, he'd stop and catch sight of Ellis as if his son had only just appeared in the room.

"Your mother was the butterfly-lady ..." he'd say, and drift away again.

In the late afternoon, the delirium had passed and Denny was lucid and it was hard to believe he was so unwell.

"When I was your age, I was fearless. Your mum stole that from me when she disappeared. I don't want to have taken it from you. Be fearless ..."

"OK, I'll try."

"She was always awake when I woke in the morning ... her green eyes looking at me. 'What's the capital of such and such a country?' she'd ask. If I knew the answer she made the tea. If I didn't know, I had to get out of bed and make the tea. If she really wanted to stay in bed, she made up a country that didn't exist ..."

Ellis listened and before him appeared a boy who played in Valentine's Park in Ilford, an adolescent who went to war, a young man who saw a woman in a field of butterflies and loved her. From time to time, Denny's eyes met his son's and they looked at each other without embarrassment. Once, after morphine, Denny squeezed Ellis's hand tight and said, "I've known you since I was your age."

A parcel arrived from Gerd. In it, Ellis found a cheque for his full pay, a batch of film stock and a photograph of the Hoover in the Days Inn in Cincinnati. The Hoover stood at the end of the claustrophobic green corridor like a schoolchild outside a headmaster's office. Ellis tried to reconcile the banality of what he had seen there with the haunting image Gerd had produced, in which every lonely, lost soul inside every motel room in America had been evoked. He pinned the beautiful photograph to his wall.

Ellis put Chrissie's suitcase in his room, changed the sheets and made up the sofa bed downstairs for himself. He offered to cook supper but Chrissie said she wanted to. Whilst she sat with her father, Ellis drank half a bottle of wine beneath the wide, low spread of the walnut trees. He imagined living by the sea with Tammy in their tiny attic flat, with lots of nooks and crannies. Later, he sat with his dad whilst Chrissie cooked. Denny turned his wedding ring on his finger and said, "You'll wear this, won't you?" Ellis nodded, then he lay on the bed beside his father.

"She loved you," Denny whispered. "She thought you were perfect."

Ellis stroked his dad's arm. "Don't let on, when you see her."

Then Denny cupped his hands round Ellis's face and Ellis did the same to Denny in response, as if they were peering through a window at each other.

"You're perfect to me, Ellie-boy ..."

"You're perfect, Daddy."

Chrissie and Ellis watched from the doorway as the nurse hooked up a morphine drip that would be operated by Denny's hand squeezing it when he felt pain. Feeling a directionless but urgent anger, Ellis marched away and rang Jed.

"Unlike vets, doctors in this country aren't allowed to put their patients to sleep so they've devised a way for the dying person to do it themselves. Maybe it's for the best because I'd probably kill the doctor who put my dad to sleep, although that's really what they're doing anyway ..."

Jed listened and didn't try to make Ellis feel better, and for that Ellis was grateful.

Chrissie dabbed glycerine water on to Denny's lips with a cotton bud. Sometimes, she and Ellis stopped breathing because they were listening so intently to their father's life.

Outwardly peaceful, Ellis's mind raged, even now. Why can't we just keep him alive, prop him up and piece him together so that he stays here with us? Why can we not do that? I could take care of him.

Chrissie fell asleep in a chair in the corner of the bedroom and Ellis saw the soft edges return to her face.

"You need to go to bed," he said as he woke her.

She looked nervously at her dad.

Ellis said, "We've got to accept that it doesn't matter, it mustn't matter, if he goes when one of us isn't in here."

"I agree," she said.

Ellis watched his sister kiss her father goodnight and decided that if his dad were to die with him there and Chrissie absent then he would lie and pretend he had been out of the room or asleep. In the few moments in which she lay on her bed before sleep engulfed her, Chrissie resolved to do the same.

Denny opened his eyes. A child's eyes, curious, trusting, a little frightened. He squeezed Ellis's hand and his eyes closed again, very slowly. Ellis held Denny, gently, to camouflage the truth that he was trying to cling on to his father's life, the same way he held on to special objects and stray dogs in his dreams in the hope of bringing them back with him to the other side of sleep.

"When old or sickly spiders leave home," Ellis whispered, "they draw a strand of silk out and wait for the silk to catch on the wind. When it catches, the spider is lifted into the air like a balloon on a gossamer line and set free. Charles Darwin found spiders caught in the sails of HMS *Beagle* hundreds of miles from land where the waves are huge and silent. It is your ship now rising out of the deep swell and you can see land ahead where none is charted. You are gliding gracefully towards the land and when you step ashore you know that Mum will be waiting for you and you will never feel pain or loneliness ever again."

Eyes closed for ever, his breathing almost done, Denny smiled.

Chrissie woke Ellis at five o'clock and for a few moments he listened for the dawn chorus in the village and yearned for the air that rose from the fields there and moved through the cottage. He pulled on his clothes, washed his face and went to his father's bedside. Chrissie had made a pot of tea with Mafi's rarely used china and that way, she felt, invited her great-aunt to join them.

There was no talking but as they drank their tea they found themselves sipping and swallowing in harmony. They allowed this to continue for a little while and laughed gently at it.

At seven o'clock, Chrissie said some prayers. Ellis bowed his head and hid his face. Chrissie lay alongside her father a while on the bed. Later, Ellis found himself kneeling beside the bed. Chrissie did the same, opposite him. Ellis rubbed his father's lips with the glycerine water. Denny gently pushed his tongue forward three or four times and Ellis painted the water gently on to his tongue. Denny's eyes were closed all the time. His breathing became slower and very calm. Ellis rubbed the water on to his lips again. He put the buds down and he and his sister stroked the soft skin on Denny's forearms. Then, Denny's eyes moved beneath his eyelids and he gently expelled the air from his lungs. A serenity fell upon him and the ashenness lifted from his complexion and disappeared, and a breeze swept through the walnut trees.

21

On a flight back from Lisbon with Milek, Mafi appeared to Ellis. She was a stewardess. She touched him gently on the arm and said, "Any day you see the sea is a good day."

Ellis hired a car at the airport and drove to the Marsh. On the shingle peninsula, near to the lighthouse, there was a small house to let. It was timber-framed, with a flat roof, and a part of it had once been a meat wagon. He viewed the house as a blizzard consumed the beach. From the dining room window he looked through a veil of snow flurries at the container ships heading south-west on the Channel.

He drove to Fairfield to think things over. He crossed the pasture to the church and hid from the winter wind at the spot where he and Denny had often stood.

"Good place for a bench," he heard his dad say.

When he had fixed things with the agent he rang the vicar of the Marsh churches and offered to purchase a bench to be situated on the sheltered side of Fairfield church.

"There's no sheltered side at Fairfield," the vicar said.

"That's true," Ellis agreed. "It was just tradition to say there was. I want to put a dedication on the bench, to my father."

He drove off the Marsh towards the Downs to the cemetery on the hill. He carried a bottle of champagne and stood over his father's grave.

"I'm moving to the beach, Dad, like I said I would. Come and find me there, because I can't find you anywhere."

A voice called out, "I wondered if we'd bump into each other here."

Katie Morton was kneeling at a freshly dug grave nearby. He went to her.

"Your mother or father?" he asked, immediately fearing

it could be her brother.

"My mother."

The sand and earth on Mrs Morton's grave was still piled high in a comically human shape, an observation Ellis kept to himself. He raised the bottle a fraction.

"To your mum ..."

He swigged and handed the bottle to her.

"To your dad ..." she said, and drank.

He held her when she cried. "You're freezing cold," he told her.

He wrapped his coat around her. She told him that Denny had visited her parents' house the day after she and Ellis were caught together.

"Did you know that he came round?"

"No ... I had already gone away."

Katie had watched from the top of the stairs.

"My parents shrank in comparison to him. They often did that with people."

"What did my dad say?" Ellis asked.

"Yesterday is the last time you ever humiliate my son. No matter what you think he might have done wrong, you need to feel ashamed."

Ellis said nothing. How many other moments had he never seen? What other things had he not credited his dad with being capable of?

As he watched Katie Morton walk away from the graveside that afternoon it occurred to Ellis how her body, the first he ever truly saw, would venture out across the earth now, covering maybe a few miles of it, or perhaps many thousands. She will forget him, or she will go years and years between remembering him. She will grow up and grow old. They might each become unrecognisable as the people they were. But she will still be there. That person who bared herself, those eyes that smiled and laughed at him, that very young woman who invited him to touch her.

And the aching he felt, he could not be sure whether it was urging him to smile or to sob. We don't love each other, but we knew each other. We knew each other for a moment. And one day, one of us will take their last breath and the other won't know of it. Those days of innocent exploration, when life is abundant with potential, will be distant but Ellis O'Rourke, he promised himself, will remember it all. And unlike the jewellery on Mafi's dresser, which it was impossible to believe had ever been brand new, the Katie Morton who led me by the hand and slept tight against me will always be there. However the shell around her ages, even when it is worn out and dies, she will always be there. And I will never behave as if none of these things happened. I will never hide from my children all that I have ever been.

He stood up and stretched and looked at the sky. In it, he saw Mrs Morton, with wings and a harp, looking very pissed off indeed as she glared from a film-set heaven at him, that wretched boy, standing on her own grave, with a bottle of champagne.

Lovely! Ellis thought to himself, grinning back at her and resisting the urge to dance. You deserve this, you mean old cow.

On the window sill of the kitchen, the champagne bottle stands with a candle in it, Ellis washes his face at the kitchen sink. He feels tired out by a glut of memories. It is early afternoon. He returns to the dining table and draws the metal box to him. A small piece of blue peeks at him from the very bottom of the box. Ellis clears the way to it and sees his father's diary emerge. He runs his hand across the blue canvas book he thought had burnt in Denny's final bonfire. As a young boy, Ellis pestered his dad to read episodes from the diary. Mostly, he wanted to hear about entering Auckland Harbour on VE day, crossing the Western approaches and seeing the German wolfpacks attack the North Atlantic convoys. He has never read the diary for himself. It's possible he's never even held it before now. On the cover is a faint ink thumbprint, left years ago.

The diary falls open towards the back, where a photograph and an envelope are wedged between the pages. The photograph is of Ellis and his father standing knee-deep together in snow. On the envelope, in his father's writing, is Ellis's name. He breaks the seal and pulls out a single piece of folded paper. In the letter, Denny describes a walk he frequently made when he was a boy, growing up in Ilford in the 1930s. It was along a footpath, through a field, in the nearest open country to his home. There were two big old trees in the field. At a certain point on the path, the sun would be hidden behind the first tree, and as young Denny walked it would appear from behind it and then, a few paces later, disappear behind the second tree.

I would imagine that I was watching the sun rise and set, a whole day come and gone in a few moments. My dear boy, when your time is up, it seems to have been just a moment. So don't waste any of it. There's a lot for you to cram in.

If Ellis thinks of Denny being born in 1926, if he thinks of the number, 1926, then his father's life doesn't appear short because 1926 seems a long time ago. The rising sense of panic Ellis is feeling today is not caused by the brevity of his father's life but by the relentlessness of all life. He summons up the scant few details he can remember from history lessons and maps out his father's era. When the Empire State Building was built, my dad was five years old. When war broke out, he was thirteen and he dreamed of going to sea like his father. He was a teenager on the Panama Canal when the *Enola Gay* flew over Japan. He was twenty-eight when Bannister broke the four-minute mile – he would have read about that in the papers with admiration – and he was thirty-four at the time of Sharpeville and by then he was married to Mum. And then Chrissie was born and then there was Aberfan and soon after that there was me and Neil Armstrong and Chrissie's desperate, heartbreaking crush on Ryan O'Neal that she insisted she would never get over. And then Dad was alone with *us* and he found the cottage and he had that and he had us and he was happy and we were together and then there was our great storm in England and there were floods in Bangladesh and an earthquake in Armenia and a bomb over Lockerbie and cheats at the Olympics and my dad died and I want to halt the earth and ask when does all this stop for a single moment's breath and when do we get the chance to be still and stop moving forward so quickly through time?

The deception of childhood is the impression it gives of never ending. The risk of growing up in a place you love so much is to be haunted by it. Perhaps, if they had never left the cottage, his dad would not have died. The cottage was the glue holding everything together. But then again, nothing ever is held together like that. The elements of any life are constantly shifting. From time to time they gather into a constellation that works well and feels good. And we dare to imagine that those constellations we are happy with might gain permanence.

As he looks at the beach, itself a peninsula of ever-shifting land with no pretensions to permanence, it occurs to Ellis that no one ever does have it all sorted out. A few might think they do, but what sort of people are they? Denny never did have everything in order. The cottage was never completed, his income never secure, his children never safe and sound and guaranteed to remain that way. And certain of his scars were for life, bearable but not the sort that heal.

It is the same for all the men and women walking so purposefully along Jermyn Street, it is the same for the fishermen on the beach. It is the same for Joseph Reardon, who doesn't even own the farm that has consumed him. A wonderful life of chaos and hope and disarray awaits all those prepared to risk it.

As Ellis folds his father's letter and slides it back into the envelope, he sees a Post-it note clinging to the back of the envelope like a stowaway. On it, in Denny's handwriting, are the words *Call Tammy*.

He listens to the gulls and to the shore break. He watches the woman sketching on the beach. A few hours ago he imagined her entering his house and making love to him. He added her to a long list of nameless, non-existent women who had loved him in this way. It was only a few hours ago but he is already embarrassed by what he used to be.

He goes to his bedroom. In a drawer, underneath his vests, is his address book. He goes to the kitchen and makes a call. He does it all swiftly so that he doesn't leave time to talk himself out of it. A woman answers and says "Hello" and Ellis speaks tentatively.

"Does Tammy still live there?"

The phone goes quiet but he can hear her breathing.

"Is that you, Ellis?" Tammy asks.

"Yes."

She laughs under her breath. He asks her how she is. She asks him where he is calling from and he tells her that he has moved to the coast. She says, "Nice." He asks her if she's OK again. Her breathing is as if she's lying beside him.

"I don't want to do lots of talking about everything under the sun, like people seem to want to do. But I'd really like to see you," he says.

"See me but not really talk? Didn't we do that before?"

"I suppose ... have you got a boyfriend?"

"Ellis, I don't want to be unkind, but after more than a year I'm not sure that's any of your business."

"No. That's true. But have you?"

"I'm not very good at being on my own. I get lonely."

"I am good at being alone. But I get lonely too."

"Then maybe you're not as good at it as you think."

He thinks to himself and nods, neither of which helps the

340

conversation.

"I just like my own space," he says.

"Why?" she asks. "What's so fascinating about it?"

Ellis covers the receiver with his hand and swallows hard. That was, he can't help feeling, a very good question, to which he definitely does not have a good answer.

"Sorry," he mumbles, and hangs up the phone.

He lies on his bed. He stares at the photograph of himself and Denny in the snow and he cries. The tears clog his throat and place pools of liquid in front of his eyes. He shuts his eyes and the tears are squeezed out and stream across his face.

When he wakes, the world is so silent that it must be the dead of night. There are no lights on in the house. The pilot buoy and the shipping lanes twinkle brightly above a black sea. Ellis walks through the house. He remembers the excitement as a child of being awake when the world was asleep. He recalls the night the police came to the house and supported his dad by the arm. That was a special night too. They were awake when the world wasn't. It was exciting in its own strange way.

He returns the photograph to the page of the diary where he found it. Low down, amongst the tightly packed lines of Denny O'Rourke's faded blue handwriting, are the words *Ilford, 10 February 1946.*

Ellis reads his father's words.

I am in the bar of the General Havelock hotel in Ilford. I wanted somewhere less busy than the pub, to write my final entry in this diary. Today was my last day at sea. We put in at Tilbury at 6 p.m. at the end of a six-month voyage that has taken us from Liverpool to Panama to Auckland, round the Horn and to Spain. My one and only peace-time commission, and my fourth voyage in all with the New Zealand Shipping Company. I have spent

4 years at sea. I had hoped it would be 44. After missing a daylight buoy signal on a four-hour watch off Hobart I have been diagnosed with glaucoma. So, my career as a merchant seaman is over. I don't know if the upset I feel about it has affected me but today has been a strange day. As we made our way through the English Channel, I came out on deck to have a smoke and watch the sunrise. We were passing the lighthouse at Shingle Point and I was looking at a small vessel that has run aground on the sandbanks there, when I saw a young man standing on the shore. He was watching the ship. Immediately, I thought he reminded me of someone but I couldn't think who. He was watching me. And then the idea came upon me that he was my son. I wasn't sleepwalking and I hadn't been drinking, but it was as if he was my son and it made perfect sense that he was. Of course he wasn't, isn't, couldn't have been. He was about my age for a start. But despite all those things, I felt that it was my son there, that that is who I was looking at. I even thought of waving. He was watching me all the while. Well, that's how it felt. He was more likely just watching the ship, of course, if he was there at all. Now, I am sitting here and I don't know what to do with the rest of my life. I half expect the young man to walk in through the door and sit with me. Maybe he could advise me. I will have a few drinks, go home as late as possible and tomorrow morning I will tell my parents the news. Father had always hoped I would join him at the P&O one day and will be distraught that I am no longer at sea, although he will not show it.

Ellis sits motionless at the table. Hours later, the stirring of sunrise distracts him. He opens the back door and goes to the shed. He takes out the shrimping frame and buckets and his shrimping belt and loads them into the car. He runs a bath. Steam fills the tiny bathroom. He opens the window and the steam snakes towards the cool air outside. He pours blue bath foam into the water. The label has been peeled off and in its place, in black marker pen, are the words *Spider Blood!* He wrote that when he was drunk. He lies in the bath and the water is too hot. He feels his body temperature rise and he reads the Spider Blood label over and over again. He decides that it is time to call a truce with himself. A truce with his yearning. A truce with the mute world of accepted forfeiture he has made his domain. He considers the lengths his father went to to avoid being hurt again, and it occurs to him that he does not want to emulate his father; that he does not want to be like him in every way. He toys with this idea as if it were blasphemy. He allows it to settle. It does so without kicking up a fuss.

I do not want to wait until the end to say what I am feeling.

He makes the phone call, again.

"Hello?" Tammy's voice is dense with sleep.

"Hello," Ellis whispers, as if not wanting to wake her.

"Is that you, Ellis?"

"Yes."

She isn't annoyed but she tells him it's five-thirty in the morning.

"Sorry,"

She breathes heavily and it is almost a laugh. He knows she is smiling right now. Smiling at him.

"Did I tell you that my dad died?"

"No."

"Well, he did. And I'd like to tell you about him, so I was wrong when I said about not talking much because I could end up talking for a week."

There is a long pause before she says, "I'll listen for a week."

"What if you break my heart?"

"Or you mine."

"No, I wouldn't do that."

"You don't know that. Ellis, given how young we are, there is a good chance we won't last for ever and that one day one of us will hurt the other. But that might not happen. Even if we stay in love for ever, we are going to get hurt from time to time. You do realise that?"

"That's one of the few things I do know."

"But are you up for that? There's no place to hide, you know?"

"I enjoyed being with you more than I enjoyed anything."

"You never told me that."

"I know. I'm telling you now."

He hears her smile to herself. "Yeah ... you are," she mutters, then adds, "You're an orphan, Ellie."

"No ... not really."

"Well, you are."

"I'm too old to be an orphan. I just lost my mum and dad, that's all."

"Sounds awfully like being an orphan to me."

They fall silent, as if their foreheads are touching.

"Ellie ..."

"Yeah ..."

"I want to be loved to bits."

"OK."

"I'm glad you rang."

"Me too."

"Don't go yet. Tell me something, Ellie ... any old thing, just talk a while."

There is silence. Ellis looks at the very first traces of colour bleed into the sky from the east. Then he says, "There's a ticklish spot on the hind legs of a tarantula and if you can get your little finger in there to caress it, then that hairy old tarantula is putty in your hands and if you're very quiet you can hear it chuckle. My dad told me that and he never lied when it came to spiders."

He walks to the lighthouse, thinking all the while how he loves her calling him Ellie. At the foot of the lighthouse, with his back pressed against the concrete, he looks up and watches the sway of the tower. It is always moving, even in this stillness before dawn.

The tide pulls on the shingle. Relentless. Unstoppable. Each shore break could be a passing soul. Denny once said that Ellis was both infinite and minuscule in the same breath. It is the same with deaths, each one unique yet commonplace, shocking and predictable.

Ellis asks of the morning: Do I have what I came for? Have I captured it, retrieved what I needed? And so, if I have, can I go now please? May I leave the table? Because I've been here at the water's edge long enough.

Time is finite and Ellis intends to waste no more of it debating the likelihood or absurdity of a life beyond. The soul may be a fanciful luxury. The afterlife mere solace. Faith, a spiller of blood. Church, a house of fear. But something has passed and even if the true dimensions of eternal life are no more than the volume of Ellis's imagination, something resides there. Even imaginary, it is real. To doubt it is to glimpse it.

The morning stirs and the wind picks up across the beach. A series of clouds are draped across a world which, becoming lighter, reveals a familiar crimson sky. Until now, his mother has always appeared at dusk, but today she is in the sunrise, first to arrive. The strengthening wind sweeps across the peninsula like a shadow and Ellis finds himself crossing the shingle as if pursuing it. At the water's edge he sees the waves being stirred by the wind, each one lifted a little higher than the last and becoming the colour of storm. He takes deep breaths and realises, with surprise but without doubt, what it is he is on the brink of doing. It is no longer a challenge in words, it is no longer a fear that crushes him, it is an image, an image of cold blue, an image that makes perfect sense to his mind's eye, an image he can lose himself in. He is already stripped to his pants and, for a fraction of time, airborne above the water. And he is swimming and immediately he feels the brutal strength of the currents. He remembers to swim towards the steeple on the Marsh and yes! the currents are taking him to the *Bessie Swan* and oh! it feels wonderful and Christ! the water is so cold, it's so extraordinarily cold that only panic and exhilaration prevent his blood from freezing as he is yanked towards the silt ridge by the will of the sea and deposited there on his knees, left with the strength only to hold on to the world as if it were a passing raft.

Out by the wreck, the wind is even stronger. Sucked through the bottleneck of the Channel, it rages at Ellis. He gets to his feet and digs his heels in, to anchor himself. Inside the furious gale comes Denny, roaring across the face of the earth. He is as forceful and pure as a child again. Instantly, Ellis sees that his father has better things to do now than remain with his son. The wind howls around him and rocks his body. His father circles him once, twice, then soars into the sky and heads across the water towards Ellis's mother in crimson. Ellis watches Denny's final moments as a lost soul and sees him reach his mother. They are reunited on the horizon at the vanishing point and then they disappear out of sight.

Ellis's body shivers to the point of spasm. His heart is at the brink of transparent joy. He could not have dreamt that it would feel so good to let go. He would not have imagined that the words he uttered a thousand times through his school days, which tormented him and riled his teachers, would be waiting for him here to offer him such peace, such self-knowledge.

"I don't know …"

"I don't know ..."

"I'm sorry, I don't know the answer ..."

I don't know the answer, God.

I know you don't, comes his reply. And that's fine. Neither did I, my dear boy. Neither did I.

The sky is left dishevelled, like bed sheets in the morning. The wind has calmed and the world seems quiet. Ellis is alone with the *Bessie Swan* and he sees her for what she is, a vessel abandoned, having done the best she could. Now comes the sound of an outboard motor and the sight of Towzer Temple's small clinker-built boat cutting through the water. Instead of sitting, as he normally would, Towzer is standing, his body contorted so as to reach down to the tiller whilst straining upwards to look across the water at the sodden figure standing out by the wreck. Towzer grabs the black woolly hat off his head and throws it down at his feet.

"You mad bugger!" he yells, and begins to laugh and cough and splutter. "You mad fucking bugger!"

And the sight of this hysterical man, held together by whisky and weather-bitten skin, makes Ellis laugh as he shivers. He waves his arms exuberantly and shouts back, "I did it! I did it! Now I've done it too!"

Towzer leaps up and down, unable to contain himself, and the boat rolls from side to side.

"Too! Too! You're the fucking first, you mad bugger!"

And he falls into his boat and screams with laughter. The boat shoots off at an angle until Towzer regains control of himself and the tiller. He comes alongside the silt ridge. Ellis clambers aboard. Towzer removes his coat and throws it to Ellis. The coat smells of cigarettes, of drinking and of fish. Ellis puts it on. They head back to the shore, to the lighthouse shore. To the beautiful, bleak, spent shore. Ellis looks across the surface of the water to the lights of the café next to the lifeboat station, as they flicker on. The café is the sort of place where being lonely felt warm and familiar and solid to him in yesterday's world, when lonely was something he thought he was meant to be. But, this morning, he has no desire to go to the café or do anything else familiar. And there's no need to keep watch here any longer. His father will not be returning. It will take him only a few minutes to pack his belongings and lock up the house and put the keys in an envelope for the agent, but even that will seem too slow because, for the first time in a long time, he cannot wait to get going.

A F T E R W O R D :

ABOUT TOM CONNOLLY :

Where were you born and where did you grow up?
I was born in Farnborough, where South London and Kent merge, and I grew up in a village in the Weald of Kent.

Were you encouraged to read widely as a child?
If I was I probably turned a deaf ear as sport was all I was interested in. Hugh Pullen, an influential English teacher, made us read *The Catcher in the Rye* at exactly the right moment in my, at the time, dubious academic life (when I was fourteen), and that was the start.

What was your favourite subject at school?
Football, basketball, cricket. When I finally and belatedly began to study, I grew to love English literature.

What did you want to be when you grew up?
Married to the girl next door. Then she moved to Belgium, when we were both seven. That was a kick in the teeth. Belgium … you don't bounce back from that in a hurry.

Did you write compulsively as a child?
I started writing when I was fifteen. I have written ever since.

What book did you love as a child and why?
I can't remember any as a young child, but early on at "big school" Hemingway's *Indian Camp* was the first story I loved and found thought-provoking. I was a very childish seventeen year old, if that counts, when a girlfriend gave me Alain-Fournier's *Le Grand Meaulnes*. It was the first time I read and re-read a novel. I loved that book, still do.

Did writing the book change you?
No.

What do you do when you are not writing?
Earn a living. Coppice woodland. Windsurf badly. Swim. Walk for miles in East Sussex and Kent. Watch Arsenal and moan about us leaving Highbury.

What would you be if you weren't a writer?
When I was a boy I wanted to be a shepherd on Romney Marsh. So, maybe that. I don't know. I'd be a completely different person, so who knows?

What is the best job you have had?
I once got paid to spend two months making mini-documentary films about football for a beer company. That was a pretty good combination.

Which authors do you most admire?
William Maxwell, Gabriel García Márquez, Richard Ford, Marilynne Robinson, Harper Lee, Ernest Hemingway. And Raymond Carver for his poems. I've just started reading Bukowski and that is a fantastic experience. Then there's individual books that I have admired greatly, like *Middlesex* by Jeffrey Eugenides, *Never Let Me Go* by Kazuo Ishiguro, *If Nobody Speaks of Remarkable Things* by Jon McGregor, *Paradise* by Abdulrazak Gurnah, *A Box of Matches* by Nicholson Baker. Where do you start? Where do you end? I should say, to try to boil it down, that William Maxwell's work is incredibly important to me.

Which book do you wish you had written?
Gilead is the most perfectly written book I know about, or *Middlesex* for its invention. Or Barbara Cartland, for the dosh.

Do you have a favourite book?
So Long, See You Tomorrow... by William Maxwell.

What do you look for in a novel?
I don't look for anything. It either works for the reader or it doesn't.

Do you have a favourite literary character?
There is something acutely beguiling and hypnotic about Frank Bascombe (Richard Ford's novelist–sportswriter realtor) which means that I find myself identifying closely with someone whose life is, on the surface, so foreign to mine. I feel bereft at the end of a Frank Bascombe novel, at the prospect of being parted from him. An awe-inspiring writer, Ford.

What is your idea of perfect happiness?
As Ellis would say, not being asked questions like that. But if I were

forced at gunpoint to answer, it would involve regular contact with the people I love – but not too regular.

What is the trait you most deplore in yourself?
I give myself a very hard time when it comes to my work. Some would say, with good reason.

Which words or phrases do you most overuse?
"By definition." And I swear, which I hate.

What is your greatest extravagance?
I don't have any. Oh, yeah, going on trips abroad when I am broke – I remember now. When being hassled by utility companies and the council tax people for payment, I tend to sit down with a calculator and put my serious head on, with the intention of working out a budget and a master-plan for cutting costs and surviving a few more months, and ten minutes later I find that I have gone online and booked a fortnight's windsurfing somewhere hot and real nice, trusting that things will have sorted themselves out by the time I'm back.

What would your superpower be?
A moderate command of English grammar.

What is your view on spiders?
They are good for old houses so I have a vested interest. The more I learned about them, the more awe-inspiring they became. Often, at sunrise and sunset in my garden and in the fields around, I see thousands of silk threads caught in the low light and it reminds me that they are everywhere, creating these extraordinary feats of engineering called webs. I'm a fan.

How did you start the book?

At a certain point in my life, I had a period of having very vivid recollections of the village I grew up in and of particular incidents. These were not dramatic or unusual but they were "mine" and I felt the need to record them. Somewhere in that time, what I was writing down changed from recording memories to creating wholly fictional stories and characters and setting them in various places I have lived. By 2003 I had decided these notes would be a novel, my first novel. Very few of those early notes and real memories survived the cull from a 700-page first draft to a 300-page book. In all, it took five years to write.

What encouraged you along the way?

My brother Pip, my best mate, Jim. And the fact that I was very focused on doing this, whatever the outcome and however long it took.

Did you visit the locations you were writing about?

I set the book in three places I have lived. Everything else about the process of writing a novel was foreign to me, including the story itself, so I decided that the locations would be the elements that I really knew and was expert on. My memory of these places is profoundly vivid and detailed, so I did not return to them for the purposes of the writing, and, in the case of my village, the changes that have occurred naturally over time would have hindered me. It is also the case that in writing the book I have manipulated the layout and reality of those settings to suit my story.

Did you know how the novel would end when you began it?

I knew, but it had other ideas. It won. My ending was terrible.

How did you want the reader to feel on finishing the book?

It would be immensely pleasing for me if the reader loved and cared for the characters, would miss them a little, and had their own vivid picture of the landscapes. But I'd settle for them not demanding their money back.

Are any of the characters based on people you have known?

No. There are real people who I have in mind and who inspire small physical or psychological elements of a fictional character, but I do not take real people and put them in a story - where's the fun in that when you can play inventor and create characters just as you want them? The best example I can give is Reardon. In the village I grew up in there was a farmer who I found daunting and impressive when I was a child, and who I grew up to admire and love. He was a one-off, and, to me, an inspiration. He was incredibly encouraging of my work and we shared an appreciation of similar landscapes and art. I was by no means amongst his closest circle of friends, but he meant a great deal to me. I had a desire to write a character of a farmer who meant a great deal to Ellis, but the Reardon of the story and the Reardon-Ellis relationship are entirely fictitious. So, none of the characters are based on real people, but the essence of a real person (or maybe just a very detailed characteristic) is sometimes a starting point for what becomes a fictitious character.

Did any image or piece of music inspire you?
Strauss's *Four Last Songs* and the paintings of Andrew Wyeth.

How important was research to the writing of the book?
I referred to the *Collins Field Guide: Spiders of Britain and Northern Europe* by Michael J. Roberts, and to the excellent *Spiders* by Michael Chinery.

How important is the temporal setting of the novel?
Perhaps, a bit like the settings I used, it was comfortable for me to set the story in the same years that I was Ellis's age. I loved my childhood so, by association, I have vivid and positive images of rural and coastal life in the 70s and 80s.

How did you decide on the novel's title?
What was important to me about Denny's idea for the truces was that it went against the grain for him. He used his heart and his strength to bring his children up, but he did not use his imagination. The truces were the first time he did use his imagination, and risk embarrassing himself too. I love Denny for doing that.

ABOUT WRITING :

When do you write?
Very early in the morning is the best time of all.

Where do you write?
My study. My kitchen. Under the oak tree in my garden. Pond Wood. Pett Beach. The Breakfast Club in Soho. On the train. I wrote a lot of this book in the New Piccadilly Café in Denman Street, London W1, the closure of which leaves an empty space in my experience of London.

Why do you write?
You either do or you don't. If you do, there's no "why".

Who or what inspires you?
Absolutely everything and nothing much in particular.

What do you read if you need a prompt?
I don't. I go out and do something. Usually a walk or a swim.

Do you listen to music as you write? If so, do you have a favourite piece to write to?
Not when I am writing from blank page. But sometimes I do when I am editing or adding dialogue. Arvo Pärt. Vaughan Williams. The *Concerto for Two Violins* by the undervalued contemporary British composer George Newson. Some film soundtracks. Sigur Rós. Amiina. Elliott Smith. Crosby, Stills and Nash. Folk compilations.

Do you use visual prompts?
Not really, not at the writing stage. But I do trawl through my scrapbooks and postcards and art books when first collating ideas.

Do you revise and edit your work as you go?
Yes, a huge amount, endlessly.

What tips would you give aspiring writers?
"Love the art in yourself, not yourself in the art." Stanislavsky.

What single thing would improve your writing life?
More talent.

What distracts you from writing?
The kettle. The weather. Birds on the feeders. Horses on the lane. The fields. The beach. Women. Football. The pub. The kettle. The weather.

How do you balance writing with other commitments?
Writing takes up a disproportionate and unreasonable amount of my time.

How does your background in film inform your writing?
It informs my re-writing. The process of editing film has two significant qualities; firstly, one is ruthless in cutting out material that does not earn its place in the story (I learned that from not being ruthless and making some poor work). Secondly, once a structure is working well in the cutting room, one puts it aside and tries something radically different (when allowed the time). Both these are a part of my re-writing and editing process with a book. As for whether or not being a film-maker makes my prose writing "visual" I think that's an over-egged idea. I can't think of any great prose that isn't profoundly visual, at least in my experience of reading it.

Are you working on a new novel?
Yes. *Men Like Air*, about four men in New York City in April 2006. And there's also a lot of preparatory work done on a third book, *See You Next Friday...* Set in the small town of Blackbrook, it's about a drunk, his son and the waitress who serves them every Friday.

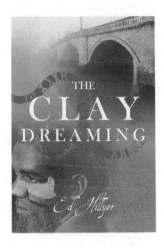

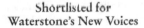

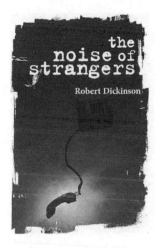

**Shortlisted for
Waterstone's New Voices**

Set during the first Australian
cricket tour of England in 1868,
this magnificent novel explores an
extraordinary friendship between
one of the Aboriginal players
and a young woman whose quiet
routine takes on a new aspect
when the cricketer enlists her
help to uncover his ancestry.

From Lord's cricket ground
to the banks of the Thames at
Shadwell, they follow the trail of
Joseph Druce, a convicted felon
transported to New South Wales
eighty years earlier.

Taking its lead from true
historical events, Ed Hillyer has
created an epic brimming with
memorable characters, historical
intrigue and documentary detail.

An Orwellian dystopia in the
guise of a fast-paced thriller, this
is a coolly satirical novel laced
with humour, suspense and
intrigue.

After years of civil conflict,
gated communities separate
government workers from the
Scoomers cruising the streets
in their battered Fiats. But
when Jack and Denise witness
a fatal car crash one night, this
precarious security is ruptured.

Through conversations between
characters, leaked tapes of official
meetings, transcribed phone
calls, fly posters for prayer
meetings, and provocative articles
in an illegal newspaper, this
haunting vision of corruption
and surveillance is at once deeply
unsettling and frighteningly
familiar.

ISBN: 978-0-9562515-0-3

ISBN: 978-0-9562515-1-0

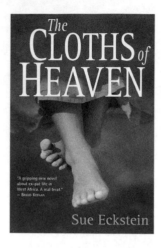

"One of those brilliant books that offers an easy, entertaining read in the first instance, only to worm its way deeper into your mind. A modern Graham Greene – fabulous...fictional gold."
Argus

"Graham Greenish with a bit of Alexander McCall Smith thrown in, very readable, a charming first novel...very humorous."
Radio 5 Live Up All Night

"Entertaining and rewarding... an excellent début. If you like Armistead Maupin, Graham Greene or Barbara Trapido, you will love this."
bookgroup.info

"Populated by a cast of miscreants and misfits this is a darkly comic delight."
Choice

ISBN: 978-0-9549309-8-1

"Skilfully evokes the era and the slow-moving quality of childhood summers, suggesting the menace lurking just beyond the vision of her young protagonists. A study of memory and guilt with several twists."
Guardian

"This emotionally charged thriller grips from the first paragraph, and a nail-biting level of suspense is maintained throughout. A great second novel."
She

"Such is the vividness of the descriptions of the location in this well structured and well written novel that I want to get the next train down. On the edge of my seat? No way – I was cowering under it."
shotsmag.co.uk

ISBN: 978-0-9549309-4-3

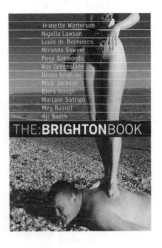

"An exquisitely crafted début novel set in a post-apocalyptic landscape. I'm rationing myself to five pages per day in order to make it last."
Guardian Unlimited

"An all-too-convincing picture of life...in the middle of this century – cold and stormy, with most modern conveniences long-since gone, and with small, mainly self-sufficient, communities struggling to maintain a degree of social order. It is very atmospheric...leaves an indelible imprint on the psyche."
BBC Radio 4 Open Book

"A decidedly original tale. Psychologically sophisticated, it demands our attention. Ignore it, O Philistines, at your peril."
bookgroup.info

ISBN: 978-0-9549309-2-9

"*The Brighton Book* is a fantastic idea and I loved writing a piece with crazy wonderful Brighton as the theme. Everybody should buy the book because it's such a great mix of energy and ideas."
Jeanette Winterson

"Packed with unique perspectives on the city...*The Brighton Book* has hedonism at its heart. Give a man a fish and you'll feed him for a day. Give him *The Brighton Book* and you will feed him for a lifetime."
Argus

A celebration of Brighton and Brightonians – resident, itinerant and visiting – in words and pictures, with original contributions from Piers Gough, Lenny Kaye, Nigella Lawson, Woodrow Phoenix, Meg Rosoff, Jeanette Winterson and others.

ISBN: 978-0-9549309-0-5

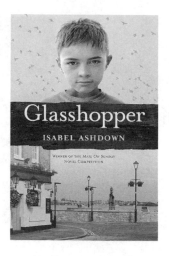

"Tender and subtle, it explores difficult issues in deceptively easy prose...Across the decades, Ashdown tiptoes carefully through explosive family secrets. This is a wonderful debut – intelligent, understated and sensitive."
Observer

"An intelligent, beautifully observed coming-of-age story, packed with vivid characters and inch-perfect dialogue. Isabel Ashdown's storytelling skills are formidable; her human insights highly perceptive."
Mail on Sunday

"Isabel Ashdown's first novel is a disturbing, thought-provoking tale of family dysfunction, spanning the second half of the 20th century, that guarantees laughter at the uncomfortable familiarity of it all."
'Best Books of the Year', *London Evening Standard*

"An immaculately written novel with plenty of dark family secrets and gentle wit within. Recommended for book groups."
Waterstone's Books Quarterly

ISBN: 978-0-9549309-7-4